M000199299

SISTER NADEEN'S WAYS

SISTER NADEEN'S WAYS

FELICIA BROOKINS

Tandem Light Press

Tandem Light Press
950 Herrington Rd.
Suite C128
Lawrenceville, GA 30044

Tandem Light Press paperback edition March 2017

ISBN: 9780997679724
Library of Congress Control Number: 2016947461

PRINTED IN THE UNITED STATES OF AMERICA

I would like to dedicate this book to Mr. and Mrs. Vercell Vance who connected me with an outstanding author, Dr. Anthony Harris, who believed this book would be published and introduced me to Tandem Light Press publisher Dr. Pamela Larde and editor Caroline Donahue.

I also dedicate it to God who allowed me to be able to write it and have great success. If he had not heard my prayers in his Son, Jesus Christ name, this book would not exist. I thank him for bringing me to and bringing me through.

ACKNOWLEDGMENTS

This book would not be in your hands if it had not been for the support of Mr. and Mrs. Jerry McWilliams, my uncle and aunt; my mother, Sarah Kelly-Wilcox, who I hope I have always made proud. My aunt, Lanie Bolden, who is my second mom and cheerleader; my dear friend, Thelma Cousin who has cheered and prayed along this journey to bring this book forth; my unforgettable friend, Kia Stokes, the person who gave me the courage to have faith and speak life into anything I wanted to do—everyone should have someone like her in their life and in their corner; Prophetess Bernice Grant encouraging me and reminding me that I have done more than I know in the lives of others; Twyla Russell, My sparring partner who would not have allowed me to stop trying to get this book published. Momma Debra Brewer, who always has a smile and a hug for me. My awesome cousin, Mashonda Ruffin, who took on a public restaurant to pass out my flyers for my writers conference in her city. I will never forget your act of love, support, and kindness.

My husband, Jason Brookins is a gift truly from God above. When I labored he labored right beside me. I would like to thank my son, Phillip Brookins, for being such a wonderful son who believed in his mother's ability to see the publication of this book through. Dr. and Mrs. Cooley you took a chance on me and I will always be grateful. Vanessa Cosby-Collins, Brandi Butler-Chambers, Aunt Carol Williams, Aunt Sarah Smith, Laura Jones, Tameka Williams, Lisa Brookins (my talented sister-in-law), Mr. Bobby Pamplin, Geilia Turner, Valesha Williams, Mary Clark, Amber and Andre, My twins, Genilla Windham my "no matter the distance" friend, Tenyeka Pringle, my "Patti," Anquette Bridges (college mom) and Dana Dockery whose excitement about this book debuting kept me smiling inside. You all never stopped waiting for the big book release and you supported my dream.

My Aunts Lorene Ormond and Jessie McDonald, my little chef, Alex C.F. Clark, who I love just like my own. To all of my brothers and sisters who I know support me. I hope you enjoy the book, there is more to come.

To my Pastor and First Lady, Darryl and Rhonda Garrett, for just *knowing* that this was going to happen and congratulating me before I even held it in my hand. Thank you for praying for me and asking God to remember me. For my God Children, Sharefea Hornsby, Christine M. Baker, Zion Williams, Brooklyn Edmond, Harmony Williams, Ariel Baker, Adon Williams, Jamie McGruder—regardless of distance or time; my newest darling, India.

To my father-in-law, Mr. Howard Brookins, thanks for everything you have done. To the most dynamic and fierce mentor any protégé' could have, Dr. Johnnetta McSwain, who asked me if I wanted to be great. To Terrell Dinkins-Jackson, I appreciate you for being that ear and for reminding me to get my financial dreams going again.

To all of my beautiful nieces and nephews. I would never complete this page without acknowledging other individuals who have been there to make me laugh, smile and keep going. Taronta and Trinitee Stokes. To the family members who always remind me of my daddy, Mr. Ulysses Kelly, who is at rest now in eternity and who I know reflects in the memories of my Aunts and Uncles of The Lee Family. The Hill Family. To Mrs. Irene-Hornsby who will always hold a very dear place in my heart for taking me into her family and making me feel a part of you all. I will never forget your kindness. It is one of the reasons I am here today. I am also grateful to Melissa and Devitta Kelly.

Finally, I dedicate this book to family members who poured into my future even though they would not be here to see this moment, Elizabeth McWilliams, Ulysses Kelly, Robert Sterdivant, Jamie McWilliams, Helen McDonald, Rebecca Brookins, Earline Hunter, Dorothy Evans, Lessie Mae Johnson.

There are so many others I want to say "Thank you" to but I don't have a book large enough to do it. Just know that I appreciate everyone's love, prayers, and support.

1

"When you looked into my eyes in that crib you had my heart," her father Kenny said. "Nadeen asked me what we were doing. I told her I was just trying to get that wet diaper off your butt." That story always made Patsy smile when her dad told it. Her heart swelled with love for him every time he told it. She looked directly into his hazel brown eyes that looked like dark espresso and saw that same love for her.

Patsy could smell the alcohol on his breath, but she didn't mind. When he came through the door he gave her a look like he'd been caught sticking his hand in the cookie jar. She loved him regardless of what was on his breath.

"I'm gonna lay down and watch a little television bring me some water and a plate of food, okay?" Kenny asked.

"Yes, sir," Patsy said respectfully. She didn't mind taking care of him. The less he walked around in the house, the less chance he would break something or wake up Nadeen. Kenny was trying to walk straight, but Patsy could tell he was flying instead of walking. Patsy never asked, she just worked on getting him somewhere that he could sit down and sleep it off.

As he started down the hall to the upstairs bedroom, Patsy prayed under her breath. "Please, Lord, don't let him bump into that wall." Her ears were keenly listening for any sounds of him knocking over anything. If she heard that, she knew the next sound she was going to hear would be her mother, Nadeen, cursing as she came tearing out of her bedroom door towards the noise.

By the grace of God, Kenny made it up the stairs to the guest bedroom and she made it to the kitchen. She began preparing his dinner. Patsy knew the routine. He would eat and go right to sleep until later that night. She filled his plate with the dinner she cooked. She was the oldest and was responsible for keeping the house and her younger sisters in order. Lately, her mother had been working fourteen-hour shifts between the church office and the nursing home, so everyone in the house walked on tiptoes as much as possible.

Nadeen was not to be crossed. She was dealing with the stress of not being sure if she was going to be permanently hired as the night supervisor at the Gardens of Peace Nursing Home. She'd been Interim Supervisor for about six months and hadn't been told of any further action by the nursing home's hiring board. One of her church members, Brother Ryan, had told her about the job. She was fasting and praying every other week so she could "hear an answer from the Lord about it," she'd said.

Patsy walked slowly down the hall past her mom's bedroom door with Kenny's plate and carefully walked up the steps. Kenny hadn't made it to the bedroom after all. Patsy found him sitting on the bottom stairs, slumped over. Patsy touched him on his shoulder and gently shook him.

"Kenny? Kenny wake up. I got your plate."

He opened his eyes and looked up at her. "Thank you, baby. It looks good." She tried to help him up with one hand and steady the plate with the other. He smiled up at her, "I thank God for you little girl."

She kept her hand under his arm as they made it to the top of the stairs. Once he made it to the couch, he slumped down on it. Patsy handed him the plate. He picked up the fork and began to eat, trying not to waste it all over himself, but he didn't manage too well. As soon as he finished she would take the plate and clean the food from the floor and the couch. There would be no evidence of the mess he made. She would make sure she got it done before Nadeen got up.

A few minutes later he rested back on the couch and handed her the plate.

"That was good, Patsy. You getting better, girl." He said as he rose up from the couch to go to the spare bedroom.

She held her breath as he got up and walked. In her mind she was praying, *Lord please let him make it to the bed.* Just as she finished her prayer, he staggered towards the small table where Nadeen kept her crystal picture frame. Patsy held her breath and felt the fear rising slowly up inside of her; Kenny quickly put his hand on the door casing and steadied himself. He opened the bedroom door and fell straight on the bed. As soon as he hit the mattress, she could feel a weight release from within her lungs. She had been holding her breath as long and as hard as she could thinking it would somehow help him make it to the bedroom, she bent down on the floor and began to clean up the small mess he'd made.

"Patsy what you doin?" It was the soft voice of her middle sister Ann; she'd come in the room while Patsy was picking up the food off the floor.

"Trying to clean up this mess before your momma gets up and comes through here raising hell about her carpet and how hard she works just to have nothing to show for it."

"I know, right? You taking care of her usher uniforms for Sunday? We got communion and you know she likes to be on point Communion Sunday."

Patsy came up off the floor with the mess in her hand and looked Ann directly in her eyes. "Ann you better be on point getting that done. It's your turn. I did it last week. I had to starch both of those dresses twice before she was happy with them. She cut up in here over a small little wrinkle on the bottom of that dress. You got duty with the *Communion Cussin'* Usher tonight." Patsy chuckled humorlessly.

"How much time I got?"

Patsy looked up at the clock on the wall. It was a black cat with silver buttons running down the middle. The tail had been broken during a prayer meeting in which Nadeen got caught up in the spirit she said and knocked it off the wall.

"Not enough. You better get busy putting a crease in that dress sharp enough to draw blood. Didn't she tell you to soak her white gloves too?"

"Yeah. You could do that for me, Patsy? Gosh," Ann said. "I mean, she don't need them gloves until Sunday. Why we always gotta soak 'em in woolite, iron them on low heat, and hang them up five days before Sunday?"

"It takes that long for her to transform into Super Saint. You know that white is Holy. It has the power to make her an Archangel when she puts it on," Patsy said.

They both laughed softly trying not to let Nadeen hear them.

"Did you see the way she held up that communion wine last Sunday when that lady was talking in the line? Girl, Nadeen cut her a look and made that lady stand there until she apologized for talking while they were giving it out," Ann said.

"Yeah, and Reverend Craig asked her about it and she told him she runs her communion line upon line and precept upon precept—nobody gets the communion unless they know how to act in the presence of God and she has directed her Ushers to make sure," Patsy nodded, scowled, and shook her finger at Ann in imitation of Nadeen.

"Reverend Craig said she needed to talk to him about that first and Nadeen told him when the Lord tell her to do something can't no man make her change her mind. Then she turned and walked off from him. I almost spit my wine out," Patsy chuckled softly at the memory. "Come on Ann, and bring that glass with you to the kitchen. Be quiet coming down this hall. Where's Josie?"

Josie was the baby. Nadeen told Kenny Josie was a revelation baby cause after she got pregnant with her the Lord opened up her eyes to see the demons she had really been allowing in her bed. From that point, she had refused to allow him to touch her while she was pregnant. She said she didn't want his bad seed transferring into her baby.

"She probably in our room pulling things out of dressers and writing on the walls." Ann knew when Josie got really quiet they needed to find her fast.

Josie was only two years old and she loved to play in Patsy and Ann's room even though she had her own room beautifully decorated in buttercup yellow. Josie also liked to sleep in their bed. If she couldn't sleep with them she would scream in her own bed for hours. It was like she was challenging Nadeen and she was determined to win. After hours of crying, fussing, spankings, and cussing, Nadeen would demand Kenny go get Josie out of her own bed and put her in their bed before she flung her across the room. She told Kenny Josie was struggling with those demon seeds inside of her from him when he started putting that junk in his veins and depositing it inside of her womb without her knowledge. Kenny would try to tell her he wasn't putting anything in his veins then or now, but Nadeen said the devil was a liar and so was he.

Once Kenny knocked on their door and handed Josie to them the crying would stop and she would put her head on Patsy's shoulder and instantly go to sleep. She was worn out from the fight. Even then, Patsy knew Josie was a stubborn little girl, spoiled rotten, and she would be the one to one day go to battle with Nadeen. Patsy hoped to be far away from home when that time came. Kenny would always say, "Josie just like her momma. Nadeen can't win fighting with her own self."

Far as Patsy was concerned, Ann caught it worse with Nadeen. She always seemed to beat her harder. It was like she hated her more than she did Patsy. What it really was though, was the fact that Nadeen hated Kenny so much that every time she could release her anger towards him she did it. Everyone said that Ann looked just like Kenny's sister, Ernestine, who had tried to stop Kenny from marrying Nadeen. She always told Kenny something didn't sit right in her spirit about Nadeen and her momma. They seemed wicked even when they smiled. She and Nadeen mixed like oil and water. Kenny loved them both so he was caught in the middle. He saw the way Nadeen treated Ann and he knew it was because of him. He'd tried talking to her about the way she used the Word to run the house like a prison warden, but Nadeen always told him to go talk to Jesus about his problems 'cause she wasn't hearing it. She was going to raise her girls the same way her momma raised her: God's Word, her way, and a heavy hand.

If Ann did anything, she had to face the penalty of a beating with the longest, thickest branches Nadeen could find or send Ann to find. She would wrap them up and make

Ann strip down to her panties. She would beat her so bad Patsy would cry. Nadeen always told Ann when she beat her that "Jesus was beaten with many stripes and he did nothing wrong, so how much more do you deserve?" Patsy always wanted to rescue Ann, but she knew she couldn't without risking serious harm to herself. *One day Lord. One day. You gonna set us free from this,* Patsy thought as she headed to the bathroom to soak Nadeen's already spotless gloves.

Ann asked Patsy again about taking care of Nadeen's uniform for Communion Sunday. Patsy loved her middle Sister and would do anything for her. She told Ann she was gonna make sure they were crisp and clean like Sunday's Best.

Patsy worked quickly to have everything ready. By the time she heard Nadeen's voice come down the hall she'd gotten everything in order. The next sound she heard was Nadeen swinging her verbal whip down the hall.

"Patsy and Ann come here and don't be slow about it!"

Patsy could almost hear the knots tying themselves in hers and Ann's stomachs.

2

A s they entered Nadeen's bedroom, she went into her bathroom and commanded, "Bring me my Bible and dinner. Is Kenny home yet?"

"Yes, ma'am," they both said in unison.

"He asleep," Patsy volunteered.

"Probably back there so high he floating over the flames of hell," Nadeen said as though she was spitting out vinegar. Neither one of the girls answered. They just stood in the bedroom waiting for the next command. Their mother had an exotic look. She was most definitely beautiful on the outside. She had skin the color of golden honey with a beautiful pair of cognac brown eyes to match. Her hair was a long black river down her back and she prided herself on keeping it curled full of body. She was built like a Coca-Cola bottle, Kenny always said. He told them she was tall, slim and filled out in all the right places.

"Why isn't my garbage can clean?" Ann didn't I tell you to empty this garbage can and clean it?" Her voice rose in anger with each word. Her eyes seemed to get tighter as she spoke.

Ann answered, submissive and tense, "Yes, ma'am, but you were asleep and I didn't want to wake you up."

"That's no excuse. You get in here and get it right now! I'm gonna beat your Aunt Ernestine's lazy spirit out of you yet, girl. I won't have that passed down in my girls!" Ann walked into the bathroom and right into Nadeen's left hand. It made quick contact with her face twice with force. Patsy saw the spit come from Ann's mouth and go across the room. She wanted to cry, but she knew not to make a sound. "You just as sorry as your daddy!" Nadeen yelled. "The only thing you contribute are excuses for not getting things done. I work too hard for you not to do what I tell you when I tell you! Do you hear me?"

Ann answered with tears in her voice, "Yes, ma'am."

She knew that was all she better say or it was going to get worse. She'd seen Nadeen get upset with Patsy over a lot less. She remembered the day Nadeen asked Patsy about an incident involving a little girl at the church. Patsy tried to explain to Nadeen that things didn't happen the way the lady at the church said it did, but Nadeen kept yelling at her that she didn't want to hear it. Patsy had gotten upset and whispered under her breath, "You never do."

The next thing Ann remembered was Nadeen grabbing Patsy by her shirt and ripping it as she yanked her to the floor. Nadeen forced Patsy's face on the down and put her foot on the back of her neck. Ann watched in complete shock and disbelief. She listened to Nadeen call her oldest daughter every four-letter word she could remember—only one of them came close to having anything to do with God. She beat Patsy so bad that Ann thought she was going to die with Nadeen's footprint on the back of her neck.

Once Ann's face stopped burning, she picked up the bathroom garbage can and walked out the bedroom past Patsy with tears in her eyes. Patsy could see the imprint of

Nadeen's hand on the side of Ann's face. The same hand she raised unto heaven and shouted "Glory to God!" with every Sunday.

Patsy wished she could've stopped Nadeen, but she knew better. Nadeen had the love of Jesus for everybody in the church on Sunday and the fire of hell for them on Monday. Kenny said running to Greater Trials church every time Reverend Craig needed something was the reason she was so cranky all the time. She would work different shifts at the nursing home then get off and go into the church office. Reverend Craig had asked her before if it was too much for her to handle, but she told him no. Nadeen said she was the only one who really knew the way her Pastor liked his church run and she was going to make sure he and First Lady Craig were happy.

Kenny told her over and over again that she could stop working at the nursing home any time and let him take care of them. But she wouldn't quit. She said she'd put her wellbeing in his hands once before and he had proven he wasn't man enough to take care of her. She'd walked out on her last job at a Hospice Center because she said she didn't like the tone that her male supervisor used when he talked to her. Kenny told her she picked a bad time since he needed her help to make sure the bills were met on time. She told him he needed to learn to "look to the hills from which cometh his help," and she sat at home for two years volunteering every day at the church as a secretary.

A few bills got behind during that time and Nadeen told Kenny he wasn't doing a good job making her feel secure about the roof over her head. She sat at home until one of her church members, Brother Ryan, told her about the position at Gardens of Peace Nursing Home. He had been working there for many years before he even joined their church. Nadeen promised Reverend Craig that once she started this new job she would still come in and work in the church office. Somehow, she had been able to do just that along with keeping her position as Head Usher at Greater Trials MB Church and President of the Ladies Prayer Circle.

Nadeen's voice knocked Patsy out of her daydream, "This house would go to hell in a picnic basket if I didn't keep it in order. I gotta be the man and the woman around here. Can I, at least, get a meal," she yelled from the bathroom.

Patsy hurried out the bedroom towards the kitchen. She didn't want to tick her off and be next in line for punishment. Ann had gone outside and Patsy knew she would be out there a moment, crying and talking to herself about how much she didn't want to be there. How she wished she lived somewhere else. Patsy needed to talk to her before she went all the way in and started doing that *evil thing* to herself.

Patsy brought Nadeen's dinner in the bedroom. She had just finished reading a scripture when Patsy came in "Lord help me to raise these girls according to your Word and not according to the World." She prayed out loud. She picked up her black eyeliner pencil and began to apply her makeup; she never even looked Patsy's way.

"Turn the radio on. Ann done vexed my spirit with her laziness and I need some comfort right now."

Patsy turned the bathroom radio on and heard the soft words of a song saying, "Jesus will work it out." Nadeen began to sing. Patsy wondered how she could sit there and sing having just slapped Ann with enough force to make Satan run. *If Jesus was gonna work it out he needed to do it soon*, Patsy thought, *'cause there was a volcano brewing in this house and with the pressure Nadeen put them under, someone, someday, was going to explode.*

The sound of the phone ringing made Patsy jump.

"Who is that, Patsy?"

Patsy walked over to the phone and looked at the number, "I don't know."

"Bring me the phone."

Patsy took it to her. She hated to take Nadeen anything while she was in the bathroom. It was a tight spot and there was nowhere to try to dodge a blow from her.

Nadeen answered the phone in a sweet voice, "Hello? Well hello, Sister Esther. How are you doing, sweetie?"

Ann came back into the room while Nadeen was on the phone. She had a little bit of relief on her face. The brief reprieve gave her the chance to place the trash can back in its proper place and walk out without getting a backlash from Nadeen about how long it had taken her to bring it back. She wouldn't show that side of herself to a member of her prayer circle.

"Sister Esther, yes ma'am," Nadeen said respectfully, "Tell pastor I'll be glad to stop by in the morning and bring you some groceries. Anything you need. You just keep on praying, Sister Esther. God is going to heal you. I'm gonna pray for you too. I'll be there as soon as I can in the morning. All right, sweetie. God Bless you," Nadeen said sincerely.

As soon as she hung up the phone, she began to complain. "I don't know why she calls me whenever she need something. I have no problem doing the work of the Lord, but I ain't gonna let nobody make a fool out of me either. I got a very demanding job—I can't sacrifice my time to go and see about her needs. I'm not over the Sick and Shut-in Ministry. Why can't her son go to the store for her? I have to work every day and then take her groceries too? She gets in that car and goes to the boat when she want to. Why don't she stop by the store on her way to the boat? I bet pastor don't know that. I'm not going to let this be a habit," Nadeen said to no one in particular.

Poor Sister Esther, Patsy thought to herself. *She thinks Nadeen is the sweetest angel. She has no idea. She would have a heart attack in her rocking chair if she could really hear the things that come from her mouth. Them words have nothing to do with being Holy or giving Thanks and Praise. Out of her fountain comes bitter and sweet!*

"Patsy? I saw your friend, Sandra playing around in them halls Sunday. I meant to tell you that. She was grinning in Ms. Bessie Mae son's face. That boy going to college. She ain't got no business up in his face and she ain't got no respect for the House of the Lord." Nadeen said.

"You wonder why I keep you and your sisters in my eyesight? Well, it's to keep y'all from getting a reputation like hers around the church. The sisters of the Prayer Circle been talking about her. She a little on the wild side it seems." Patsy never responded. She and Ann both knew that their role was to be quiet and listen to Nadeen's tirades. Ann had retreated to the hallway bathroom after bringing the trashcan back and only Patsy was left to stand and pretend to care.

"Her momma, Sister Gladys, backslid and she can't seem to find her way back. She out there running the streets and church hopping while her daughter running the Sunday school hallways. How sad." Despite how Nadeen felt about her, Sandra was Patsy's best friend. She knew all about her and what she did. Her mom was dealing with her own demons and couldn't raise Sandra the way she needed her to. Sandra pretty much ruled herself. She came and went when she wanted to. Some weekends she didn't even come home. Nadeen said she wasn't gonna have the entire church whispering behind her back about how scandalous her daughters were the way they were doing about Sandra.

She wouldn't have her daughters associating with that kind of girl. *She* was raising God-fearing ladies, not club girls who would end up in online videos twerking. *She* was trying to be a good example of decency, hard work, and living for Jesus. She always told them the same sermon week after week. It was taking its toll on Patsy and Ann.

Patsy's only other connection with the outside world was going to school each day and seeing her boyfriend, Dustin, whom she was not supposed to have. If Nadeen ever found out about him or that Kenny was letting him come over, it would be a terrible scene and Patsy knew it. She probably wouldn't survive the beating that Nadeen would bring down on her and everyone else in the house for violating her rules, which seemed more like commandments.

"Bring me my watch!" Nadeen yelled from the bathroom. Patsy jumped.

She passed the hall bathroom on her way up front to look for the watch and whispered through the door to Ann, "Girl, come out of that bathroom."

"No!" Ann said softly in a firm voice, "I'm not coming out until that nut leaves. You go in there and let her talk stupid to you."

Patsy dreaded it, but she knew Ann wasn't coming out until Nadeen left. Patsy located the watch and admired how beautiful it was. Nadeen said a friend of hers at work gave it to her for taking on some extra days for her so she could go on vacation. It was black quartz with a metallic dial and diamond shaped numbers on it. Patsy thought this "friend" must have needed that vacation pretty bad to buy Nadeen an expensive watch like that. When Kenny asked her about the watch, she told him she deserved to have nice things because she was a Child of God. Kenny decided to choose his battles concerning the watch from that point on.

Patsy stepped halfway through the bathroom door and handed it to Nadeen.

"Tell Kenny I need him to leave me some money so I can buy some things for my Prayer Circle meeting. That's the least he could do since he spends all his money everywhere but in the House of the Lord."

"He still sleep." Nadeen gave Patsy a look that said she was gonna slap her in just a minute if she didn't get out of her face and do what she said.

"You better get to movin' girl!" Nadeen said with her teeth clenched.

Patsy quickly stepped backward out the door and went to get Kenny. She went halfway up the stairs and called out to him.

"Yeah," he answered groggily.

"Kenny. Nadeen wants you to give her some money to buy some stuff for her meeting at church." Her internal anxiety escaped in the trembling of her voice.

Kenny groaned and got up out of the bed. He looked like a match had been lit in his eyes, but he was sober.

"I wished she gave me as much as she gives that Usher Board and Reverend Craig," he said as he headed down the stairs.

Patsy stepped back to let him pass. She went halfway down the stairs to listen in case an argument broke out. Patsy felt her heart beating faster. That spirit of fear was rising up in her; it kept her on edge and affected every area of her miserable life. It was with her all the time even when she tried to smile and hide it. Kenny went into Nadeen's bedroom and placed twenty-five dollars on her dresser.

"You about ready in there, girl? You pretty enough you don't need that stuff on your face."

"Just cause you don't care how you look don't mean everybody else is like that," Nadeen snapped back at him. Kenny just laughed and walked out the door. She came out a few minutes later with the money in her hand and headed up front.

"It's a shame this the only way he gives his money to the Lord," Kenny laughed at her comment as she walked past him out the door like he wasn't even there. He bent towards her to kiss her jaw. She jumped back.

"Move!" she yelled at him as she pushed him away.

"That's that Christian love I'm looking for," he said as he headed back upstairs.

As he passed the bathroom, Ann opened the door and stepped out. She went straight to her room and shut the door. Patsy went to check on her—after what happened with Nadeen, Patsy didn't trust her being alone.

"Ann, you okay?"

Ann spoke in a soft voice, "Don't worry Patsy. I'm fine. I'm not doing anything but wishing I was anywhere else but here."

Patsy sat down on the bed next to her.

"But then you wouldn't have me and Josie. It's gonna be okay. Just hang on and don't do anything crazy."

"Crazy? Crazy just walked out the door."

Patsy had to laugh at that. She knew Ann wasn't gonna try anything. She must be feeling better with a joke like that. Just then the telephone rang and Kenny answered it.

"Hey, Dustin. How you doing? She's right here hold on. Patsy! It's your sweetie on the phone!" Kenny yelled down the hall.

Patsy smiled and went to get the phone. She sometimes wondered if seeing Dustin behind Nadeen's back was being deceitful. She hoped in her heart it wasn't. Nadeen always said she didn't like sneaky people, yet to Patsy, she always seemed to be doing something sneaky when Kenny wasn't around. She would whisper on the phone a lot and sometimes when Patsy or Ann would pick up the phone, they would hear a man's voice on the other line. Patsy also thought it was strange how she would tell Grandma Ruth she was off on certain days but then turn around that same evening and tell Kenny she had to leave out early for work. Patsy knew better than to ask about it, though.

Nadeen always told them a child should stay in a child's place, and that was not in an adult's business. Sometimes Nadeen would talk on the phone until she heard Kenny come through the door then she would hang the phone up, turn on her television or roll over in her bed and pretend to be asleep. *Was that being deceitful or sneaky?*

Patsy recalled Pastor Mack, Kenny's preacher at Deliverance Rock Church, give a sermon to his congregation one Sunday when Nadeen did attend with Kenny about deceit and the so-called Christian. As a matter of fact, as far as Patsy could recall, Nadeen hadn't been back to Deliverance Rock with Kenny since Pastor Mack gave that sermon. She told Kenny his Pastor needed to take care of his own business instead of judging the personal business of his members. Kenny tried to explain to her that he was just preaching the truth he wasn't getting into any one's business; he was trying to save souls.

Kenny's explanation fell on deaf ears and Nadeen went on back to her church where Reverend Craig preached what sounded good to his congregation and the choir gave them a show every Sunday.

"Hey, babe, what's up?" Dustin asked her in a deep, sensual tone of voice that caused a warmth to radiate all through her body. She loved the feeling yet it scared her because she knew in the back of her mind that she wanted to lay down in it and let it wrap itself all around her.

"Not a whole lot here. Just the usual night of drama and excitement." Patsy tried talking to him while she scooped up her little sister, Josie, who was in her and Ann's room just as Ann predicted, pulling out socks from their drawer. She giggled as Patsy picked her up and took her upstairs to Kenny. He could watch her until Patsy got off the phone with Dustin.

"You been on my mind all day long. Do I have to come to Greater Trials to see you? Because if I do I will."

"You show up at my momma's church trying to flirt with me and you will be rolled out on a stretcher," Patsy laughed and said.

"Patsy, your little sister seems to have made a mess in her diaper!" Kenny yelled down the stairs to her. Patsy knew what this meant.

"Dustin, I'll give you a call back in a few minutes. It seems Josie has decided to make a mess and, of course, I gotta clean it up."

"That's cool. I'll be home. Just give me a call back. I love you."

Patsy smiled. She knew she was a lucky girl to have his heart.

"I love you more." Patsy reluctantly hung up the phone and headed up the stairs to get Josie.

3

Morning came too soon.

"Rise and shine girls!" Kenny yelled through their bedroom door.

"I got breakfast on the stove." Ann and Patsy could smell the grits, toast, and sausage. Kenny made the best homemade biscuits they'd ever tasted other than their Grandma Ruth, Nadeen's mother, when Patsy opened the bedroom door, Kenny was standing in front of her putting on his work jacket.

"I'm leaving girls. You all get out that bed and get dressed before Nadeen gets here. I don't wanna hear about it this afternoon when I get home. I'm gone to work." He walked out the door and started that old loud work truck of his.

Patsy just knew he woke up the whole neighborhood when he left.

"Get up, Ann. We got to eat and clean up before Nadeen comes in." She walked slowly to the bathroom and left Ann struggling to get out of the bed without hitting Josie.

When Patsy went in the bathroom, she sat on top of the toilet cover. She just needed about fifteen more minutes. When she woke up, it was to the sound of Nadeen's voice singing. *Oh. No,* she thought frantically. *Where is Ann? We overslept. Oh, Lord! Where are my clothes?*

She ran out of the bathroom and shot in their room. Ann was on the end of the bed. She shook her quickly with an urgency.

"Get up, Ann! Get up! We overslept and Nadeen's home!"

Ann's eyes widened. She knew this wasn't good. Ann grabbed her clothes and ran to the bathroom. Patsy grabbed her blue jeans and shirt and threw them on. She took off her scarf and brushed her hair into place it was a good thing she kept it wrapped. It fell perfectly into place and rested on the top of her shoulders.

Ann came hurriedly out of the bathroom. Patsy ran in behind her to brush her teeth. Just as she closed the door to the bathroom, she heard Nadeen yell down the hall.

"You all up in here?"

"Yes, ma'am," they both yelled at the same time. Patsy spit the warm water out of her mouth, wiped the toothpaste from her lips and walked out.

"Why is there breakfast on the stove yet it looks like nobody has eaten? Don't tell me you all just getting out of that bed when I came through that door! I know better than that! Somebody better start talking or somebody is going to regret it!"

It was bright and early in the morning, but a dark cloud had formed in that kitchen like a bad storm coming in the distance. Ann just looked at Patsy. Patsy had to think of something quick! She headed up front to face Nadeen.

"We were coming up front to eat, but the toilet got clogged up and started to overflow. We had to get some towels and wipe up the water. Ann had the plunger and she unstopped it. We put the towels in the washing machine and the dryer, then folded them when they got dry so that made us a late but we been up since Kenny left." Patsy lied.

She felt like crap as soon as she had finished spitting that lie out, but it was just too early for storms and rain. Nadeen gave her a look that said: *you know you lying!*

"I better not find out that you all were in that bed sleep when you should have been up getting ready," she said in a threatening tone that they knew held a promise.

"Why are these dishes in my sink? Patsy you better not leave these dishes and I want the beds made before you all leave for school. You hear me?"

"Yes, ma'am," Patsy quickly replied.

While trying to figure out how she was going to wash the dishes from breakfast, make up their bed and make it to the bus stop on time, Patsy started to feel disgusted because she knew already that it wasn't gonna happen. Nadeen enjoyed putting them in situations that were impossible by asking them to make things happen that any rational person knew couldn't.

Nadeen walked past Patsy and went to her bedroom. Ann tiptoed up front, "Patsy what you gonna do? You want me to stay and help you?"

Patsy noticed she was scratching her wrist. Patsy wanted to keep her calm so she didn't show her own frustration. She smiled a little.

"No, Ann. There's no need. I got this. You go ahead and I'll just stay and do what I can."

Ann looked at her with sadness in her eyes. She didn't want to leave her, but she also didn't want to miss the bus. School was the only time Ann could have some peace of mind. She picked up her backpack and walked to the door. She looked back at Patsy.

"I hope you make it to the bus stop. I don't want to leave you to take this."

Patsy looked at her and managed to smile bigger, "That's what big sisters do, Ann. They take the heat so you don't have to. Go on. I'll see you this afternoon," Patsy said trying to be brave. She could see Ann was torn.

"Tell Sandra I'll catch her at school and to let Dustin know not to look for me."

Ann picked up her backpack and walked out the door dragging her feet with her head down. Patsy went to the sink and began to run the water to wash the dishes. They had a dishwasher, but Nadeen never wanted to use it. That would mean things would be easier for her and Ann and it seemed to Patsy Nadeen didn't want anybody's life in that house to be easy. Patsy believed she wanted them to be as miserable as possible.

As Patsy ran the water, she heard Nadeen coming back up the hall.

"You better not miss that bus! You should've done this already. If you miss that bus I'm going to beat you all the way to that school. I promise you that!"

Patsy was screaming at her in her head, *If you weren't so mean and full of the devil I wouldn't have to miss the bus! You come in here asking me to do something you know isn't possible then you want to beat me for missing the bus because of you! You're here all day please tell me why you can't wash the dishes or just let them stay here until we get out of school! No, wait. I know why, that would make too much sense and everyone in this house knows your crazy!*

Patsy stood at the sink and began washing the dishes. She glanced at the clock above the cabinet occasionally watching it tick closer to the time the bus would arrive. At least Ann wouldn't miss the bus. Patsy knew it was useless to try to make it. The bus would be there in a few more minutes and she still hadn't made their bed. When she finished washing the dishes and making the kitchen sparkle, she walked down the hall to their bedroom. Josie was asleep so she picked her up and set her on a blue blanket laying on the floor. She made the bed and gently put Josie back on top of it. She turned to go back out the door and saw Nadeen standing in the bedroom doorway like a Doberman pincher just waiting for her to move so she could strike.

"I told you not to miss that bus didn't I?" Nadeen's voice was a low growl and her eyes seemed to spread around her face in front of Patsy.

Patsy didn't answer. She was so tired of being treated like crap she couldn't really feel anymore. She realized years ago her mother had no consideration for the feelings of anyone but herself and Reverend Craig. She always wanted to make sure he was happy.

She waited for Nadeen to step back before she walked out to get her backpack. She went back down that same hallway where she always seem to be going or coming into a pit of misery and picked her backpack up out of the kitchen chair.

Patsy headed out to the car for a ride she dreaded to take. Nadeen came out behind her with two long branches wrapped and put them on the front seat of the car. Patsy was so empty she didn't care. She felt helpless and tired.

Didn't the Bible say something about not pushing your children to wrath? Patsy thought. She was sure that she'd heard Pastor Mack preach on that one of the Sunday's they'd gone to church with Kenny.

Guess Nadeen hadn't read that far yet. She was the reason Ann was doing evil things to herself. Things Patsy didn't know how to tell anyone about.

As Nadeen was putting Josie in her car seat, Patsy went to get in the back of the car. Nadeen looked over at her and yelled out, "You ain't riding in my car! You better start walking! You gonna have your Damascus Road experience today sister! You been playing games for weeks well, I'm gonna teach you the rules for playing with Nadeen Simmons today!"

Just briefly, Patsy thought, *I know she's kidding. right? She is not about to make me walk five or six miles to school while she drives.* But just as soon as she thought it a voice came to her and said, *You forgot who you dealin' with? You surprised?*

Patsy closed the car door, turned and began to walk out of the garage. Nadeen backed the car out behind her and drove slowly. Patsy wanted to just lay down on the ground and let her run the tires over her body. It would be a relief. Everyone was gone from the bus stop. *Thank you for that, Jesus,* Patsy thought among the clouds of sadness rolling slowly in her mind. That was one less embarrassing scene she would have to suffer. She walked all the way to school with Nadeen driving behind her. She'd been taught in church that to take your life was wrong, but when the spirit of misery overcame her, she just couldn't seem to shake it off. She kept trying to focus on that scripture that talked about God knowing the plans he had for your future.

Mentally she didn't know how much longer she could hold on. She often prayed, *Lord if you can just get me through the next two years I'm going to walk out of those doors and never ever come back!*

Patsy was exhausted when she made it to school. She was relieved to see that there were no buses and class had started. As she stepped up on the sidewalk to go to the principal's office for her excuse, she heard Nadeen's voice behind her.

"You wait right there!" Nadeen got out of the car with the braided branches in her hand. Patsy just stood there waiting, with her head down, wondering how could a mother who acted like she was full of the Holy Spirit on Sunday be so full of hell on Monday?

As Patsy stood there, she felt the first blow of the branches come down across her back. She felt the sting of them come across her face. She began to cry not because of the familiar pain coming down across her back, arms, and face, but because she was so tired of feeling like she wanted to die. Where was God and why was he allowing her mother to treat her this way? When the branch struck her in the eye, she screamed and put her hand over it.

That's when Nadeen stopped.

"Now, you miss that bus again! That kitchen better be spic and span when I get home!"

Nadeen walked away and got in the car not even asking Patsy if she was okay.

"What kind of wife you gonna be one day? Won't even get off your behind and clean your own home?" Nadeen lectured as she threw the remaining of the branches onto the front seat of the car. Josie had slept through the whole thing. Patsy was glad for that.

Nadeen drove off leaving Patsy on the sidewalk crying, full of hate and wondering where was that *on time God* they always singing about at church? Where was he now when she was in front of her school being degraded?

Her eye was stinging and so was her soul. She walked into the school hallway and stopped at the bathroom to clean up her face then she noticed the red welt that ran across her eye. Her face looked just like she felt inside—all tore up. She washed her face, put on her jacket to cover up the scars on her arms and wondered how she was going to explain the welt across her face. She tucked away the hopelessness inside of her heart, but she couldn't seem to hide the hate. Pastor Mack always said that it was wrong to hate, but Patsy couldn't help it. Nadeen had put it there. Whatever was growing inside of her was from her mother and only God could clean it out. Right now she had to pretend she was happy. She had to put a smile on her face for her classmates and teachers. She had become good at pretending a long time ago. She pulled up the strength from somewhere deep within her soul and stepped out of the bathroom headed to the principal's office to get her pass to go to class.

When she walked in the office, Miss Parson, the secretary looked up at her with a shocked look on her face.

"Patsy, what happened to your face?" She got up from her desk and came over to Patsy cupping her face gently in her hands. "You been in a fight this morning? Your face is all scratched up and looks like you been crying."

Patsy laughed that she had guessed this morning's events so easily.

"No. I have food allergies. Certain things I eat cause my face to break out really bad in welts. I'm not quite sure what it is. Probably something my dad cooked with this morning. My momma gonna take care of it when I get home."

Miss Parson gave her a look that said she didn't really believe this story, but there was nothing she could do about it.

"You want to see the school nurse? That's a pretty big welt across your face. I've never known a food allergy to do that. You need to have someone look at it."

"No. Miss Parson I'm fine. I just need a pass to get to class." She smiled with all the effort she had inside of her. The harder she smiled the easier it was to hold back the tears at the edge of her eyelashes.

"Okay. If you say so. Here's your pass. You come back and see the school nurse if those allergies give you any problems, okay?"

"Yes, ma'am. I will," she said as she walked out of the principal's office. She spent the rest of the school day telling that same lie to anyone that asked.

She knew lying was a sin and she was going to have to repent for it, but right now it was a lifesaver. She was sure God didn't see it that way. She hoped though that he understood why she had to do it and have mercy on her. She hoped that mercy included teenagers as well as adults, though it seemed to Patsy that all of it was probably being used up on Nadeen.

4

Friday. Time for the weekend. As Patsy got out of bed to get ready for school, she thought about the fact that in a few months she would be sixteen. She hoped Nadeen would give her a little more growing room. It was the year of a girl's passage into freedom.

Nadeen said she was going to the beauty shop after work this morning; she'd been going more frequently over the last few months, so they would have a smooth stress free morning. She and Ann would drop Josie off at Mrs. Wilson's house next door on their way to school. Nadeen liked Mrs. Wilson because she pretty much kept to herself.

"Pat. You and Ann out that bed yet? You might as well turn that sack a loose!" Kenny yelled through the bedroom door.

"We up! Ann's getting ready!"

"All right. I'm leaving now."

Patsy heard his truck trying to start and went back to get dressed, taking special care to show off the necklace Dustin had given to her as a surprise last year. She only wore it at school. She would be the envy of all her enemies today, especially that evil mouthed Daphne Porter who was just itching to get her hands on Dustin.

Everyone at school knew about Dustin and Patsy's relationship. Ann was her confidant too. They kept each other's secrets. The doorbell rang and Patsy went to see who it was. Sandra stood smiling on the stoop.

"Hey, Pat. You want to walk to the bus stop together?" Sandra leaned her head over to the side and gave Patsy a mischievous grin. Sandra liked to come over and walk to the bus stop with them sometimes. She would share with Patsy all the exciting details of her weekend escapades. "Come on in. I have to get Josie ready to take to Mrs. Wilson's, Wash up the dishes, make the bed, and comb my hair then Ann and I'll be ready to go."

"Girl, you gonna be too worn out to go to school by the time you do all that."

"You right. But if I don't do it you know what'll happen." Patsy said in a matter of fact tone of voice.

"Do I need to ask what happened to your face? I been out sick the last few days so I hadn't seen Dustin or else I would already know." Patsy turned away from Sandra.

"Just drop it, please. I really don't want to talk about it. I'll live. I always do."

Sandra decided to let it go. She had been Patsy's friend long enough to know how she got the scar on her face. Things like that made Sandra think maybe it wasn't so bad having a momma who didn't care what the church or anybody else had to say.

Thirty minutes later. Patsy and Ann gathered up Josie along with her baby bag and their book bags and headed out to drop her off at Mrs. Wilson's house. Mrs. Wilson was looking out the window at them come across the street when they walked up to the door so she opened it right as Patsy was about to ring the doorbell.

"Good morning, Patsy, Ann, and Sandra how are you?"

"We're doing fine Mrs. Wilson," Patsy answered as she handed Josie over to her. Josie was getting too heavy to carry. It was about time to put her down and let her walk.

"I saw a strange car in this neighborhood the other night it was parked a few feet from your house. You all be careful over there at night. Especially on those nights when Kenny comes in late long after your momma's gone."

"We will," Patsy said as she turned to walk away so Mrs. Wilson wouldn't see the fear in her eyes. She looked over at Sandra and Ann. They both knew whose car it was "Lord. Please don't let Mrs. Wilson see Dustin getting out that car." Nadeen would kill them both for sure. Patsy knew Nadeen kept a gun under her pillow that Aunt Eva had given her to hold and she was pretty sure she would use it if she found Dustin in her house. She always told them she believed in God's Angels of Protection called Smith and Wesson.

"Oooh. Girl, I know who that car belong to. You better tell Dustin to tighten up his game. Your momma will break your back in half like a communion wafer if she finds out."

"I know, Sandra. I'll tell him when I talk to him at school today. Mrs. Wilson just being nosy."

They made it to the bus stop just as it pulled up. Patsy sat down on the back of the bus ready for it to take her into a different world if only for a few hours. Ann was dropped off first. They said goodbye to each other. Patsy watched her walk off the bus and go over to her friend, Mia, who was standing in a circle of giggling girls. Ann stepped right in. They were good at that, able to put on a good face immediately to hide all the pain inside. The bus pulled off and Sandra slid in the seat next to her. "Look. I want to see Lavon tonight so I'm gonna ride the bus home with you." Sandra whispered to her.

Patsy looked at her with a crazy look on her face. "How you gonna get home?"

"Lavon is gonna take me home. He told me if I can just make it over there he'll make sure I get home."

"You on your own with that, Sandra. You know his parents not gonna be there right? They left yesterday going to Milwaukee for a church conference. So, you might end up in a situation you don't want to be in...or maybe you do want to be in it."

"Lavon is my brown sugar baby. I can handle him. Anyway, my momma doesn't care too much about when I get home. Half the time she ain't there when I get there."

The bus stopped in front of the school and they both got up to try to beat the crowd that was about to form at the door. As Patsy stepped off the bus, she looked out of the window and saw Dustin; he was looking way too good with those beautiful green eyes and soft luscious pink lips. He looked at her and winked. Patsy stepped off the bus and walked over to him leaving Sandra behind. "Good morning," She said as she looked into his beautiful eyes. He kissed her and put his arm around her neck.

"Good morning, baby. How was your morning?" His eyebrows drew close together in a look of concern as he softly touched the scar on her face. She could see the hurt in his eyes.

"It went pretty good," she was glad he was concerned. It was nice to have someone be.

"I see you're wearing my necklace."

Patsy looked up at him and smiled.

"I think I'm wearing my necklace, you just happened to pay for it." They both laughed at that. Patsy loved his beautiful smile. She knew the girls were always in his face. He was very attractive and had quite a reputation before they met. She could hardly believe it when he approached her for the first time. He told her he had been watching her but he never saw her out after school or on the weekends. When they officially became a couple he told her he liked the fact that she wasn't out all the time like the other girls. He knew she was a good Christian girl. He told her he liked that the most. He was tired of the girls that were easy and willing to do anything to get his attention.

"Hey. I might get out for a little while and drive by the dance. I'll come over to see you after that."

Patsy remembered how Mrs. Wilson mentioned the strange car that morning. She needed to keep it to phone conversations for a few days.

"You probably shouldn't."

"What? Why not?"

"My neighbor across the street saw your car. She doesn't know it was your car, but she mentioned seeing it this morning so she may be watching for the next few days. It would be best if we didn't see each other for a little while. Okay?" She looked into his face hoping to see understanding.

"I understand. I don't want any trouble for you. I'll give you a call, later on, tonight. We can talk until we both fall asleep."

"Sounds good." Patsy kissed him on the jaw before heading off to her Geometry class. The day went by fast and way too soon it was time to go home. Patsy dreaded it. She took her time walking to the parked buses.

"Patsy, wait up," she heard a familiar voice yell. It was Sandra running to catch up with her. "You forgot I'm supposed to be hanging out with Lavon tonight?"

"That's on you, Sandra. I told you that earlier," Patsy said firmly.

"Don't worry, girl, it's no big deal. I'm only gonna hang out with Lavon for a little while anyway."

When they made it to their stop, Patsy and Ann got off the bus. Lavon was waiting for Sandra.

"See y'all later." Sandra had a huge smile on her face as she walked off holding hands with Lavon.

Poor Sandra, Patsy thought. *Lavon is gonna use her up and then he's gonna move on. I've heard so many stories about how he just gets the panties and then he's a "ghost." She won't even know what happened until he walks past her at school and won't even speak to her.*

"Where's Sandra going?" Ann asked. "She going to get herself used up?"

"That's her business and I'm gonna let her handle it. We got enough drama in our own little world to worry about anybody else's. That is Sister Gladys's problem not ours," Patsy shrugged.

They walked the rest of the way talking about what was gonna come on television and wondering what Kenny was going to bring home for dinner. They unlocked the door and walked in to hear Nadeen on the phone.

"Sister Polly. I don't know what's wrong with her girl. I hate to see a woman be so foolish. Let a man walk all over her like that. I wouldn't stand for it you hear me. I would boil some hot water and show him I meant business. He'd be standing before the Throne of Judgement before he could dry off." She laughed. Patsy felt a little sick in her stomach when Nadeen said that. "Well I better go I got to go in early again this weekend and I need to get some sleep. I'll make sure that announcement is in the bulletin on Sunday."

She hung up the phone and turned to them, "Why do people call you when you are in the middle of something? She calls me every day at the same time pretending she wants to pray for the sisters in the praying circle! Just because she doesn't have to work doesn't mean I have time to gossip with her. We might need to put her name on the list for prayer cause she needs deliverance from gossiping."

But she had to have somebody to do it with, Patsy thought. Ann noticed Josie in the middle of the kitchen floor playing with what looked like a new toy. She was having a good time entertaining herself. When Josie saw Patsy she reached her arms up towards her. Patsy picked her up and they all went to their bedroom to change clothes. Patsy was headed up front when Kenny walked in with dinner. His eyes were big and he staggered a little bit. Patsy caught the box before he dropped it.

He mumbled at her and half smiled, "Thanks, baby."

Patsy took the box and put it on the table then she went to the cabinet to get out the plates and glasses to set the table. She was holding her breath. *Please don't let her come up here right now. Lord, please.* Well, God must have been busy somewhere else at that moment cause the next thing Patsy knew Nadeen was coming up the hall with her Bible in her hand.

Patsy's heart began to beat fast. She could feel the knots twisting in her stomach, the fear in her belly rising up to her throat, which was suddenly very dry. She knew this could get real ugly real fast.

Nadeen looked straight at Kenny with disgust on her face. "I hate the very sight of you!"

The words came out of her mother's mouth with such venom Patsy almost passed out from the fierceness of the unholy spirit that spoke them. Nadeen looked at Kenny sitting there ignoring her as he tried to eat. "I hate you so much I could take a knife and run it right through you! You need Jesus in a real way, Kenny!"

Kenny put his fork down and slightly smirked at Nadeen, "I need you to show him cause from what I know in the Bible I read, the way you talk to me ain't him."

Patsy almost passed out when she heard Kenny. Ann spit her water out on the table and hurried to clean it off.

"You'll know him when you looking up from hell at me standing in the pearly gates looking down at you laughing at your pathetic soul," Nadeen shot back.

Patsy couldn't taste her food for the fear in her mouth. She knew the taste; it was dry yet sharp like the blade of a knife. Patsy sat in disbelief. Did she really just hear the President of the Ladies Praying Circle and the Head Usher of Greater Trials MB Church, open her mouth and speak death, not life, over her own husband? Whom, by the way, she never prayed for. The words paralyzed Patsy's insides.

She couldn't even lift her head, but she could hear Ann whimpering. The spirit of fear that was wrapped around Patsy was spreading out wrapping itself around Ann like a python. This kind of stress was what drove Ann do to what Patsy called the "evil thing." Kenny heard what Nadeen said, but he wasn't sober enough for it to really register. He just kept eating and mumbled something under his breath.

Patsy wondered how such a self-proclaimed *Saint* could sit in front of her children and say such a horrible things? How could the same hands that held the communion plate and the cute little cups that symbolized the body and blood of Jesus that was shed for them all be talking about shedding someone else's?

Minutes seemed like hours before Nadeen went back to her room. Patsy got up immediately after she left the kitchen and took Kenny by the arm.

"Come on, Daddy. Go upstairs and lay down okay?" She pleaded in a soft voice, near the verge of tears herself as the fear slowly ebbed from her stomach, down her legs and out through her toes. He looked up at her. Ann came over and helped Patsy lead him down the hall and up the staircase, making sure to keep a firm grip on him. They made it to the couch and let him drop. Kenny hit the couch hard.

Once he was situated upstairs, the spirit of fear went back and waited, hibernating until another moment or day that it was called forth. It left a residue in Patsy's soul to remind her to stay prayerful and watch because at any moment it would be back. The next few hours were tense for her and Ann, but they managed to stand on guard and keep Kenny out of Nadeen's way until she left to work the early shift at the nursing home. A few hours later while Ann and Patsy were playing a video game, the doorbell rang, *Who could that be?* Patsy wondered. She had already told Dustin not to come over for a few nights. Patsy went to the door and asked who it was.

"It's me, Sandra. Open the door."

Sandra? She should have been at home a long time ago. She opened the door and Sandra walked in with Lavon.

"Girl, I need somewhere to stay the night. Lavon car won't start and he couldn't get a ride to take me home. It's too dark to walk home and I can't call my momma because our phone off. Can I sleep here?"

Patsy stood there with her mind racing. *What was she supposed to do?* She closed the door behind her. Ann came up the hall and looked at Sandra kind of strange.

"Sandra if my momma catches you here she'll kill me. You can't stay here."

"Take her home," Ann said. Patsy looked upside Ann's head like she'd sprouted a unicorn horn.

"What? How am I suppose to do that?"

"Take her in Kenny truck. He so out of it he'll never know. Just sneak upstairs and get the keys. You can make it. Lavon can go with you." It sounded crazy enough to work. Sandra stood there grinning.

"Ann, you got a little gangsta in you don't you? Stealing cars."

"Look, Patsy, if you get the keys I'll drive the truck. You can ride, too. We'll take her home and come right back."

After several minutes of the voices of persuasion in her ear, Patsy agreed to do it. She eased upstairs and took Kenny's keys off of his work belt. She left Ann home with Josie. Lavon coasted the truck out of the driveway and they hit the highway. Lavon and Sandra started laughing. Patsy just sat in amazement that she had actually done something like this and that Ann had thought of it. When she finally settled down, she had to laugh herself.

"Sandra, I gotta stop fooling with you. You gonna get me put out my house."

"Well. You been wanting to leave anyway. Tonight is as good a night as any." They all had to laugh at that. When they pulled up to Sandra's house the lights were on and the music was playing.

"Momma having a party." She kissed Lavon good night and jumped out the truck. They watched her to make sure she made it in the house okay.

"Now, you gotta get my daddy's truck back in one piece."

Lavon drove back like he was being chased by hellhounds. Finally, they eased the truck back in the driveway and Patsy ran in the house. She didn't even think about dropping off Lavon. He could walk, after all, this was his fault getting Sandra strung out over him. Ann met her at the door.

"I'm glad you made it back. I was sweating bullets. Kenny still sleep."

Patsy eased up the stairs and put Kenny's keys back on his belt. She hurried to the room and put on her pajamas. Her heart beat fast all night. She couldn't believe what she'd just done. She did have to admit though, it felt good to be bad.

5

few hours later, Kenny came down the stairs. He
was looking like he had been ridden long and
hard. He had on his work clothes and his keys
were jingling on his belt. "Good morning, Patsy. What
you doing up so early?"

"I just had to go to the bathroom." She lied. She'd
really been too nervous to sleep after stealing Kenny's
truck. "Well, I need to get an early start and finish up
some work this morning. My deadline is Monday and I
have a few more touches I need to make on this condo
Stan and I working on. *Stan?* Patsy thought. *He's a bad
influence.* He would have Kenny out all night knowing
Nadeen was going to accuse him of sleeping with every
trick in town. He was divorced so he could go and come
like he wanted to. He knew how crazy Nadeen was yet he
didn't seem to care Patsy felt Stan was an "undercover
hater" trying to destroy the good things in Kenny's life.
Patsy believed he loved to hear about the fights going on
in the house. To her, he was an enemy disguised as a
friend.

"Okay. I'll fix you some hot coffee and put it in your
thermos."

When Kenny came into the kitchen, she had his
thermos ready.

"Thanks, baby girl. I'll be back by noon today."

As he walked out the door, Patsy hoped he really would but part of her knew that if he was hanging around Stan he wouldn't be. His spirit was willing, but his flesh was weak. It had no strength against the battle inside of him. It was a fight he seemed daily to be losing yet he kept getting back up in the midst of the near deathblows. A few hours later, Nadeen came through the door.

"Get up and start cleaning up this house! I've had a long night surrounded by smelly old devils. I gotta go take a shower and wash them dirty spirits off of me."

After she got out of the shower, she told them to keep quiet while she dialed into the morning prayer line that First Lady Craig recently set up. As Patsy and Ann walked around the house cleaning they could hear her praying. They could tell when the call ended because Nadeen's phone started ringing. The members of the church were calling her telling her how anointed her prayer was and how she really blessed their souls. The last call though was a bit different, it was from a member of her Usher Board who wanted to call and complain about the newest usher board member, Sister Anita, she'd been on the board for two weeks and was still being trained on the way Nadeen wanted things done. Patsy could hear Nadeen discussing the new usher with her church member who had also just been on the prayer call with her.

"Well, we gotta pray for her too. I know Sister Anita come up in there in them dingy white uniforms looking like she got them from a garage sale in the district. Last Sunday she was smelling like moth balls I almost threw up at the door. Lord have Mercy! She had black marks on her shoes. I still don't know why Reverend Craig felt the need to put that girl on the usher board. She needs to be put in a bathtub. You know cleanliness is next to

Godliness. I'll make sure I have a talk with her. Sister, as a matter of fact, to be decent and in order, you should be there when I talk to her.

Don't the Bible say if you got a problem with your brother you need to take somebody else with you to straighten it out?" Patsy heard her laugh then she said, "I got a problem with her coming in that church working on my Usher Board smelling like an old muscadine." *How she gonna talk about Sister Anita like that and then embarrass her in front of somebody else.* Patsy thought to herself. Ann came into the living room with a hand full of clothes.

"Nobody else has to get up this early on a Saturday," She said grouchily. "Why do we?" As Patsy started up the vacuum cleaner, she leaned over in Ann's ear and whispered,

"Cause nobody else's momma is the Head Usher at Greater Trials MB Church." She said and walked off laughing softly.

While they were busy cleaning, Patsy thought about Sandra. *Ms. Gladys really need to get herself together cause if she don't, Sandra gonna fall apart. She letting Lavon use her for the attention she should be getting at home.* But Patsy wished she had some of the freedom Sandra had just to know what it was like to live on the wild side. With all of the chores done, Ann, Patsy and Josie sat down to watch television for a while. They ate cereal and enjoyed the quiet. Hours later, Nadeen came in the room

"Who swept that kitchen floor this morning?" The way she said it let them know that whoever admitted to sweeping the floor was about to have to hear an earful or even worse.

"I did," Patsy said.

"Well, you best to get back up there and look at those rugs again!" Nadeen yelled at her pointing towards the front with her Bible in her hand.

"They're not in the right place. Get up there and put them where they belong!"

Patsy got up and went up front. The floor was clean, the rugs were clean and they looked fine. She didn't see the problem. As hard as she tried to think about how the rugs were placed on the floor, she couldn't for the life of her create in her mind how or why they were out of place.

"You don't seem to be able to figure it out!" Nadeen shouted behind her. "You got from the time I finish reading my daily devotional to have these rugs in the right place or I'm gonna help you remember how they go!"

Nadeen turned and headed to the back. Fear once again began to creep over Patsy. Ann came up in the kitchen when Nadeen walked out.

"I'll help you. Do you remember how they went?" Ann began to move the rugs around. The both of them just kept moving the rugs not remembering how they were supposed to be. They could hear Nadeen in the back room shouting "Hallelujah" and "Thank you, Jesus!" They turned around when they heard her say: "Look at this confusion on my floor!"

They knew she had neatly wrapped up her robe of religion and put on her garment of hell. She looked at the two of them and turned to head out the back door.

"You still can't figure it out, huh? Well, I'm gonna help you!" Ann and Patsy already knew that was not a good sign. When she walked back in, she had two long branches wrapped together.

Patsy braced herself for what she knew was coming next.

"You about to get an eye opener this morning!"

Nadeen yelled at her as she began releasing what felt like electric currents across Patsy's back. Ann jumped out of the way and ran back down the hall. Patsy had on a thin T-shirt so the branches came down across her back like a quick wave of fire. They stung her like a million wasps on her skin.

As Nadeen hit Patsy, she kept yelling, "Fix them! Fix them back the way you found them!"

As hard as she tried Patsy couldn't remember how they were supposed to be. She just kept moving them around, each time she moved them Nadeen would come down across her back with the branches of fire.

Is this how Jesus felt when they whipped him all night long?

Her face was still healing from the beating in the school parking lot a few weeks earlier. Maybe this was her punishment for taking Kenny's truck last night.

Patsy felt the tears coming down her face. Not so much for the pain from the branches but the pain coming from her heart. *Why was God allowing this to happen? Didn't he know it was wrong? Didn't he care?*

Finally, Nadeen stopped. She must have gotten tired.

"Get this mess off of my floor! I'm gonna put these rugs in place one more time and the next time you sweep my floor they better be where I put them! You paying attention?"

Patsy bent down to pick up the pieces of the twisted branches off of the floor and out of the rug. She tried to watch Nadeen put the rugs in place from behind eyes full tears. What really made Patsy boil inside was the fact that Nadeen only moved one rug. One rug was not centered in the middle of the floor just right. One rug had caused all of this! Patsy went to her room, put her face in her pillow and wished for death! In between her tears, she kept asking the Lord, *Why? Why am I having to go through this? I'm so tired.*

She was so busy crying she didn't hear the door open. Josie had crept in and pulled herself up on the bed. She put her little head on Patsy's arm. Patsy looked up at her and weakly smiled. She loved Josie. She was her heart. She felt sorry for Josie though, because in a few more years if there was no change she would go through this same trial. Patsy wouldn't be around to help her through it. She was determined that she and Dustin would be leaving from home the day after her high school graduation.

Patsy wondered where Ann was while she was snuggled with Josie. Probably hiding in the bathroom— her favorite hiding place. Patsy hoped she hadn't been pushed to the brink of doing something terrible to herself. She wanted so bad to tell Aunt Eva or Grandma Ruth what Ann was doing but she didn't have the courage to do it yet.

After what seemed like hours, Ann walked in the room and sat on the edge of the bed.

"You okay?" Ann didn't look right at her big sister; she put her head down and scratched profusely at her arm. Patsy knew that meant she was near a breaking point.

"I'm okay, Ann. You know I'm tough as leather. Don't let this stress you out." Patsy moved closer to her and gave her a hug. Josie hugged the both of them.

"Let's take a nap. We need it." They all laid down on the bed and drifted off into a semi-sleep state. The other half of Ann and Patsy's senses were tuned in to the bedroom door listening in case Nadeen burst in.

When darkness fell, they wondered where Kenny was. He should've been home by now. He must be out somewhere with Stan getting busted.

A few hours later, the house phone rang. The next thing they heard was, "Patsy? Get your sisters together we got to go to the hospital. Kenny's been in a bad accident. His truck has been hit by a train!"

Patsy's mind couldn't come together. The words were jumbled in her head. She was moving, but she wasn't aware of what she was doing. *Who was in the hospital? Not Kenny. Not her daddy.* Anxiety slithered through her body. *Was he dead? Was he alive? Was he crippled?*

They all piled into the backseat of the car and went to the hospital. Nadeen left them in the ER waiting room and went to talk to the doctor. It seemed like hours before she came back. Ann was crying and Patsy was rocking Josie. She was in a daze but she was the big sister and she had to be strong for them. Patsy looked down the hall and saw the doctor coming towards them with Nadeen. Her heart began to beat fast. *Please, Jesus! Please let him be alive.*

"Hello, young ladies." The doctor said with a smile. "I've been talking to your mother about your father's condition. That train hit the front of his truck pretty good. I hear it knocked the truck fifty feet from the track, yet your father is alive to tell about it. He must have Angels of Protection working real hard in the heavens. He is truly blessed to be alive. He shattered his knee pretty good. The police said the impact of the train should have sent him through his windshield, but they found him, seatbelt on and looking dazed.

"A little more force from that hit and you'd be at the morgue right now having a different conversation. But God apparently has something else for Mr. Simmons to do and that's a good thing." Nadeen smiled back at the doctor.

"Yes. God is a protector. Kenny is strong. He'll come out of this just fine. I'm going to take good care of him when he gets back home."

"That's what I wanted to hear. You girls got a praying momma. Those prayers must be what kept him in the land of the living. We're going to move him to a room after he wakes up from surgery. Then you can come up and see him."

So the Lord does hear prayers. Patsy thought.

She was glad to hear Kenny wasn't dead or crippled for life. She wished she could see him. He was hurting she was sure and needed someone there to make him feel better. Kenny was placed in a room after hours of surgery. The tubes in his nose and in his arm scared Patsy. She reached over to touch his arm and called his name softly, "Kenny? Kenny wake up it's me, Patsy. Ann and Josie here with me too." He didn't respond right away and she began to fear that he wasn't going to wake up.

The doctor came in and looked at him.

"He's pretty well sedated. It might be a few more hours before he comes around. Give him a little time."

Nadeen went over to the small plastic basin and wrung out a cool white towel. She wiped Kenny's face and straightened out his sheets. She ran her fingers through his hair.

"He's gonna be all right. I asked the good Lord to see him through and God has never failed me yet. I'm his servant and I know he hears me," Nadeen looked down at him as though she loved him.

Patsy was watching this scene like it was a scary movie. *Who was this? Where was Nadeen? What was really gonna happen once the doctor walked out of this room?* The phone by Kenny's bed rang so the doctor left. Nadeen picked it up. Patsy could tell that it was Nadeen's Pastor, Reverend Craig by the conversation.

"Yes, Pastor I know. I'm believing that he'll be up and walking again real soon. I'm just gonna keep waiting on the Lord!" She shouted as she threw her hand in the air. "Amen! Tell First Lady Craig I hope she feels better soon." She hung up the phone, turned around and started looking for her purse.

"What I really believe is that it's time for me to go. I can't be up here much longer. Nobody told him to blank out drunk on a train track. Old fool. I bet he doesn't even have a halfway decent insurance policy to even take care of us. As good of a wife as I've been to him!"

Now here was the Nadeen Patsy knew. This was the person Patsy could relate to. That other one who was the caring, loving wife and church usher board president, she couldn't relate to. That person only popped out on special occasions, like church or prayer circle meetings. She never stayed long either. Just long enough to play the required role and when the good ole church folks and Reverend Craig turned the corner, she was gone. Sister Nadeen packed them angel wings in a Ziploc bag and took out her whip!

Kenny began to move in the bed. Ann went over to him and looked down into his face. When he opened his eyes she was looking at him with relief. He couldn't really talk well, but he put his hand on top of hers. Ann smiled with relief.

He looked around the room and then closed his eyes back. Nadeen walked up to his bed "Kenny I come up to this hospital twice a week with the church already. I ain't gonna be making extra trips to come and see about you cause you choose to live outside of God's will. I won't be wasting my prayers on a hopeless sinner like you." Kenny kept his eyes close and didn't say a word. Patsy got all their things together and before walking out of the door she kissed Kenny on his forehead. He opened his eyes and winked at her.

6

Kenny stayed in the hospital for four weeks for rehab on his knee. Nadeen was there reluctantly every day doting over him in front of the doctor. She'd found out the doctor's mother attended Greater Trials. The doctor told her that his mother always talked about how much of a Woman of God she thought Nadeen was so Nadeen couldn't put her church reputation in jeopardy. Kenny seemed to be loving the attention despite the pain he was in and the shakes he was having. Maybe he was scared of this new wife by his bedside every day. A few weeks before Patsy was suppose to get out of school for summer break he came home. She was glad to go to the hospital for the last time to pick him up. When they walked in the room he was trying to shave but his hand was shaking so bad he couldn't do it without cutting his face.

Patsy knew this was from his withdrawal. "Pat, baby, come over here and help your daddy out,"

"Okay." Patsy took her time and shaved his beard. Then she took a warm towel and put it on his face. He had this look on his face like he was floating in a warm relaxing bath. When she finished she gently put some aftershave on his face. Nadeen just sat on the couch and watched. She was ready to go as soon as she got there.

"Patsy, you need to hurry that up. I don't know why he just didn't wait until he got home to do that. I got to get back to church this afternoon for an usher board meeting and I don't want to be late."

"You ain't the only one likes to look good girl," Kenny said jokingly. "I like to dress up and step out right too. Ann, hand me that shirt y'all got me last Father's Day. It'll go real good with these slacks and cowboy boots."

Ann brought the slacks over. He grabbed her and rubbed his face against her cheek. "It ain't scratchy now is it?"

Ann put her head down and laughed. She always tried to pull away from him when he grabbed her and tried to give her a kiss on the jaw. She said his face was scratchy yet she seem to be holding on and laughing while he did it. Nadeen got up and started packing his bag. The nurse came in and said Kenny was released. He looked like he was ready to go home though Patsy couldn't figure out why. They loaded up the bags, the nurse made Kenny get in a wheelchair and they walked out the hospital room like one great big happy family.

When they made it home, Patsy sat his bags in the den and rolled him in front of the television. Nadeen didn't stay five minutes.

"I gotta go. There's some food in the kitchen the neighbors brought by. The kids can make you something to eat." She picked up her keys and walked out, nothing more being said. Patsy sniffed her perfume which lingered in the air. Her mother was so beautiful on the outside, why couldn't she be the same on the inside?

"I'm ready for some home cooking. Bring me some grub." Patsy walked out to go and fix Kenny something to eat. There was so much food to choose from. She decided on the ox tails and potatoes. He loved that. Ernestine, his sister, sent it over last night by one of her church members. She and Nadeen couldn't be in the same room long without insults starting to fly around so she didn't come around much. Ann made Kenny a big glass of sweet tea with a lemon and they headed to the back. Patsy handed him the plate but noticed his hands were shaking so bad the plate was jumping up and down. *Poor daddy. He's having some serious withdrawals.*

She wanted to save face for him so she pretended she just wanted to be of help to him.

"Kenny, let me get you that food tray we got for Christmas last year. Now's a good time to use it so you won't get that shirt all dirty trying to suck up them oxtails."

"Thanks, baby. That's right. Look out for your daddy."

Patsy went to get the tray and sent Ann to get a towel to put under it. Josie crawled up next to Kenny once he got situated and opened her mouth. She loved to eat out of his plate and he loved to sneak and feed her. "Don't tell your momma. If she finds out, we'll all be living outside on the curb."

Josie smiled as she sucked on the potato in her mouth. They must have all fallen asleep cause they woke up to Nadeen standing over them fussing.

"You all been eating in my chair, I see. Got crumbs all on the cushions and Josie got what looks like pot liquor all down her dress."

Everyone moved into action immediately. Patsy grabbed Kenny's plate and glass and took it back up front; she would come back for Josie. Ann got a towel and the vacuum cleaner. Kenny sat up in the chair trying to clean it out.

He had somehow fallen asleep and let the plate fall on the floor leaving the juice from the oxtails running down his slacks.

"Kenny Simmons you look worse than your daughter! Come on in here and let me get them nasty pants off of you. You need to be ashamed of yourself making such a mess all over my carpet!"

She pushed him into the spare bedroom to help him change clothes. Patsy got a little nervous when Nadeen closed the bedroom door. She just never knew what might happen to piss her off. She could snap on him and Patsy couldn't stop it from behind a locked door. She was tense until the door opened and she could see Kenny. He was putting on his lip chap and Nadeen looked calm. Then Patsy's heart started beating at a normal rhythm. Later that night Ann and Patsy had an interesting conversation.

"Patsy, you think Kenny was trying to kill his self on that railroad track?" Ann looked carefully into her sister's eyes and asked. The question jolted Patsy. She looked at Ann like she had two heads.

"What made you ask me a crazy question like that? Girl, you know Kenny ain't trying to kill hisself. He got us to live for."

"I guess. But he falls asleep at the wheel half way across a train track?"

"It was an accident. He probably got his tire stuck or something," Patsy said with certainty.

"Sometimes love isn't enough to make you want to stay in this life." Ann began rubbing on her thigh. Patsy wasn't sure what to say after that and Ann was sure she didn't want to say anything else.

When they got up for school the next morning, they talked about the fact that this was the last day of school. They wouldn't see their friends again for three months. They both dreaded the thought of being locked away for three whole months. The kids on the bus were already talking about where their parents were sending them for the summer. Patsy and Ann already knew they were going to have to work at the church for the summer crusade camp. Nadeen volunteered them every year. Ann pushed Patsy in her back and she turned around.

"What the crap?"

"You standing there looking like you day dreaming. We got to go catch the bus." Patsy knew she had to walk out that door, but she was concerned about leaving Nadeen and Kenny alone in the house together. Before she left, she prayed that she would come home and find things "different" in a good way.

When the bus pulled up, Ann sat behind Patsy with Ralph, a boy from her school that Patsy had heard was stuck on Ann. Patsy leaned back in her seat and listened to them laugh with each other while Ann's question kept playing across her mind like a CD on repeat. When Ann got off the bus, Daphne Porter came and sat in the seat behind Patsy. Daphne was the kind of girl Patsy avoided as much as possible. She was loud, violent and promiscuous. She also let it be known that she wanted Dustin. She leaned over the seat where Patsy was and asked her in a curious sounding voice, "Hey, Patsy. You know this man at your church by the name of Brother Ryan?"

Patsy turned and looked at her.

"Why you asking me about him?"

"I just wanted to know. Maybe I know him."

"Yeah. I know him his kids are in Ann's Sunday School Class, why?"

"He use to work at the office where my Sister Champagne works now. I heard her mention him a few times and that he goes to your church, you attend Greater Trials Missionary Baptist Church right?"

"Yeah, that's right,"

"Well, he invited my sister to come to that church a few times. She seem to like it." Patsy didn't care if her sister did or didn't and she didn't care to be talking to Daphne. "I hear your momma is the Head Usher at the church. She run everything I heard."

Patsy rolled her eyes at Daphne. "You need to check your source, Daphne. They got their facts mixed up."

"You think so huh Lil Ms. Junior Usher?" Patsy had just decided to ignore her when the bus came to a stop in front of the high school.

"Anyway, y'all hold it down over there. Take care of your First Lady. I heard she got one high heel in the grave and the other on your Pastor's neck." Daphne laughed as she got up to walk off of the bus. Patsy could smell a strange odor coming from Daphne as she walked by. It smelled like something that had been burnt. *She probably just got through sitting down to eat a piece of toast with the devil himself.* Patsy thought. This made her laugh a little bit as she pictured that in her head. Daphne kept Patsy at the altar every Sunday repenting. It was something nasty inside of Daphne and it seemed to always stir up a familiar feeling of hate when Patsy saw her. It also didn't help that she literally lusted after Dustin. Patsy stood up and tried to get off the bus as fast as possible when she looked out the window and saw Dustin. He was standing near the library steps looking like some butter pecan ice cream in a honey-flavored waffle cone. He smiled as their eyes made contact.

She walked up to him and kissed him on the jaw. He leaned down and kissed her on the lips.

"Hey. I heard your dad was back home. How's he doing?"

"He's much better. He's going to have to continue rehab on that knee, though."

"Good. I like your dad."

Dustin let go of her hand and headed into his Spanish Class. "Maybe I can catch you during lunch?"

"That would be nice." Patsy wished all of their classes had been together this year but then again, she probably wouldn't have passed a single test for looking across the room at such a delicious distraction.

Patsy didn't see Dustin before she loaded the bus for the last day of her Junior Year but that was okay. She'd enjoyed having lunch with him earlier. A few stops later Ann got on the bus with Ralph following behind her. They even sat together. Patsy hoped Ann was taking notes on this boyfriend thing it was crucial she didn't slip up and let Nadeen find out. As she and Ann walked into the house from school they came into the kitchen area where Kenny was sitting at the table reading the newspaper, at least trying to read it, the paper was shaking so bad Patsy didn't see how he could read the next line.

"Hey. Kenny" Her and Ann both said as they put their backpacks down. Kenny looked up from the newspaper.

"Hey, girls. Y'all finished another year, huh?"

"Pretty much. I got exempt from my exams and Ann did too. So we're done," Patsy shrugged. Kenny grinned real wide.

"That's my girls. My sister, Ernestine, was smart like that. Guess I was too busy looking down the hall for your momma to focus on my lesson."

Patsy and Ann both laughed at that. "Patsy you got a birthday coming soon don't you?" "Yes, sir, I do and I can't wait."

"What you gonna do for your sweet sixteen?" Kenny asked raising his eyebrow.

"It would be a real good birthday if I could go out on a date." Just as the words came out of her mouth, Nadeen came into the kitchen.

"What did you say?" Patsy's throat began to close up. She wanted the floor to open up and swallow her whole before she had to say it again

"Turning sixteen doesn't change anything honey! There won't be no dating. Dating causes due dates and I won't be having that around here."

Patsy looked down to the floor." Can I invite some friends from my school to the house for my party?" She asked in a meek voice. Nadeen put her hand on her well rounded hips and let out a laugh.

"Friends? Baby, there is no such animal on God's green earth and as far as other folks in my house. Touching my stuff, being nosy trying to steal things out of my house! No, ma'am. Every spirit ain't the Holy Spirit and that's the only one I want in my house,"

"But it's gonna be my sixteenth birthday," Patsy was near tears.

"What did you say? You better shut up before you don't' make it to sixteen! Don't start acting brand new up in here. You know me real well and you know that in just a few minutes you gonna be picking your teeth up off my floor if you don't watch that mouth of yours."

Patsy felt her throat tighten up and the knots in her stomach get bigger and bigger. She was use to this feeling. It was the feeling of disappointment and hate all swirled together.

Kenny never said a word in her defense, but she knew he was hurt inside too. Nadeen wore the pants, the belt, and the drawers in this house and everybody knew it. Kenny somehow at some point let her put them on and she wasn't gonna give them back.

That was just the way it was and there was no end in sight of it ever going to change. As the pastor would say on Sunday morning, "If you leave the door open, Satan will step right on in and he doesn't know when nor how to leave."

7

Nadeen had Ann and Patsy up early getting ready to go volunteer at the Church Summer Crusade camp. As they were busy getting ready, the phone rang. They could hear Nadeen talking in a sweet tone of voice.

"Well, yes, sir, Reverend Craig. I understand. My girls can find something else to do for the summer." When she hung up the phone her voice transformed. "Since when does Johnnie Mae Trotter run anything at Greater Trials?. My daughters have been camp leaders for the last three summers. Who is she to decide we need to give other folks children more opportunities? They own momma's too lazy to even pick up her feet in the sanctuary and give God praise, and she telling Pastor her children need more opportunities!

"I'm gonna get an opportunity, an opportunity to see her and when I get through telling her about putting her nose in my church business she gonna wish she'd missed the opportunity to mess with me and my children. Patsy? Ann? You girls can stop getting dressed for camp. Pastor just called me and told me they gonna use some of Johnnie Mae Trotter's children this summer. She got ten of the little bastards they can all do parking lot patrol as far as I'm concerned. She want some opportunities for them. I got one. Take the opportunity to tell your momma about birth control and they won't end up with another brother or sister."

Patsy and Ann both bust out laughing. Obviously, Sister Johnnie Mae hadn't been told who really ran Greater Trials. They were surprised Reverend Craig let it go down like that. Guess he wasn't thinking since First Lady Craig hadn't been feeling too good lately. However, it happened Sister Johnnie Mae Trotter unknowingly had an appointment with the Devil's daughter set to take place the next following Sunday. When Kenny asked her what was wrong, Nadeen filled his ear with what Sister Johnnie Mae Trotter had pulled. Kenny was very careful with his answer.

"Baby, I know that caught you by surprise. The girls have always been Summer Camp leaders. Maybe Reverend Craig decided you been working so hard that you needed to take a little rest. It takes a lot out of you to work at the nursing home, create the church bulletins, and run the Usher Board."

Nadeen told Kenny the Lord was her strength and he decided when she was tired not Reverend Craig or Johnnie Mae Trotter.

Kenny didn't say a word he just let her release until she was tired then he went to do the exercises for his knee that his doctor had prescribed.

"Sister Johnnie Mae Trotter has no idea what opportunity she's really created," Kenny whispered under his breath.

Nadeen couldn't even focus at work she wanted to get to Johnnie Mae Trotter so bad. She practiced every word she would say and devised what she considered to be the perfect lesson for her. The week couldn't past fast enough.

Nadeen was up before the sun on that following Sunday. She drank a large cup of black coffee and told

Kenny the girls could stay with him 'cause she didn't have time this morning to wait on them. She was eager to get to the church and get the bulletins out. She wanted to be the very first face Sister Johnnie Mae Trotter saw that morning. When she pulled up, she saw Reverend Craig's car in the parking lot. Next to it was a crème colored Lexus.

It stood out to Nadeen because it was parked in First Lady Craig's parking spot. Nadeen thought this must be an out of town guest 'cause everybody at Greater Trials knew not to park in First Lady Craig's parking space. She would make sure she let Reverend Craig know that his guest needed to move their car before service started. Nadeen set up the church vestibule with the bulletins and the sashes for the greeters. She positioned herself at the front door of the sanctuary for the first early morning service and to make sure she didn't miss Sister Trotter. Nadeen didn't have to wait too long. She saw Johnnie Mae Trotter coming with a train of children ranging from Pre-K to Junior High looking like ten little bad Indians. She was laughing and talking with the other sisters of the Praying Circle as they started into the Sanctuary to pray before the Sermon. Johnnie Mae stepped up to Nadeen with a big smile on her face.

"Good morning, Sister Nadeen. What a wonderful day to be in the house of the Lord, isn't it?"

Nadeen forced the smile to her lips. "It sure is. There is no other place I'd rather be this morning."

"By the way, Sister Nadeen, I really appreciate you being so understanding about letting the other children have an opportunity to work at the church summer camp. I didn't mean any harm by making the suggestion to Pastor. I just want to make sure all of our kids get to experience God in a whole new way. You know we have to be careful not to covet our positions in the House of the Lord." Sister Johnnie Mae smiled piously.

"No, this sloppy mouth catfish didn't just try to tell me my children are coveting positions in the church?" Nadeen mumbled to herself. She had to be careful of how she responded to Sister Johnnie Mae because the other members of the congregation were standing behind her.

Nadeen handed her a bulletin and looked her straight in the eye.

"You absolutely right about being careful in the church, Sister Johnnie. There are so many foul spirits trying to be in control around here. We gotta always be looking out for them. You know sometimes I can smell 'em? They smell like hot trash." She made sure to say "hot trash" slow and deliberate.

Sister Johnnie Mae got the message. She rolled up her church bulletin and entered the sanctuary, shocked that the Head Usher would say such ugly things to her. What she didn't know was that this battle of words was just the beginning. Before she left the sanctuary that day, she was going to know two things about Greater Trials—one: you don't play with Sister Nadeen Simmons, and two: you don't cross Sister Nadeen Simmons and her children.

Sister Johnnie Mae Trotter messed around and got caught up in the Spirit. Before she knew it she was in need of an Usher. Just so happened Sister Nadeen was standing by the pew she had danced out of. The sweat was pouring down her face. Nadeen reached out and gave her a crisp white towel to wipe her face. She cleared the sweat from her eyes and all of a sudden she felt her legs start to wobble. Her head started spinning and her eyes began to burn. The next thing the congregation knew, Sister Johnnie Mae Trotter fainted in front of the whole congregation face first, dress up and a hot pink thong with a pair of dimpled butt cheeks hanging out for the entire congregation to see. Usually the Usher Board put the white sheets on the front row to be able to grab them quickly but this Sunday they weren't there.

They looked everywhere and no one could find them. One of the male members of the congregation got up with a blushing face and gave Nadeen his suit jacket to cover up Sister Johnnie Mae's loud pink thong and the huge dimples in her butt.

When Sister Johnnie Mae finally came to and got up off the floor. The men were grinning at her and the women hung their heads down in shame. She was so embarrassed about falling out and exposing her thong in front of the entire church that she moved her membership to a church way across town but the story of her hot pink thong even followed her there. Sister Nadeen had taken advantage of the perfect opportunity.

When they made it home, the phone was on fire! Everyone was calling asking Nadeen what happened with Sister Trotter. Nadeen said she guessed Sister Trotter just forgot she was coming to church instead of going to the club and she got up in church trying to shake off all that sin from the night before and fell out. Nadeen said she must have forgotten to put the sheets out since she had been so busy with Kenny lately that it just slipped her mind. She spent the rest of that Sunday evening laughing about pink thongs and butt cheeks. She also made a mental note to make sure she spoke to the newest usher board member, Sister Anita next Sunday about her attire. She had come in with what looked like blood on the collar of her dress this Sunday. This was not acceptable for someone on Nadeen's Usher Board.

A few days later Patsy's sixteenth birthday arrived. She waited for the phone to start ringing with calls from Aunt Eva and her Grandma Ruth. They always called her on her birthday. "Patsy!" yelled Nadeen. "Come get this

phone. It's Eva!" Aunt Eva was her favorite relative.
They could talk about anything from boys to sex to gossip
Aunt Eva heard while out in the clubs or at church. Patsy
found her Aunt's life to be so exciting. Patsy heard her
Aunt had gotten into some trouble while living in Arizona
about three years ago so she had to come back home,
that's when she gave Nadeen a gun to "hold" for her.
What Patsy heard was that she shot her boyfriend in the
face while he was sitting in his car with another woman.
There was no other witness but the other woman and she
was so scared she wouldn't identify Eva as the person
who shot him. She told the police the person that shot him
took her driver's license and promised to return them to
her with a bullet if she opened her mouth.

Patsy heard Eva tell the story a few times when she
got to drinking Johnny Walker. "Happy Birthday, Patsy,
baby!" Eva yelled into the phone. "You sixteen today!
What you gonna do for your birthday? You going out and
celebrate or let that cute little boy you talk about all the
time take you out to the movies?"

"I'm not doing anything. Momma said I couldn't go
out and you know Dustin can't come to the house."

"Patsy you lying! She's not going to let you celebrate
your sixteenth birthday?"

"No, ma'am."

"Patsy, I'm so sorry to hear that. Look I'll come and
get you later. You can come over and hang out with me
and David. He my new man girl! He is loaded. Don't tell
your momma, but I let him move in so he can help pay
these bills. We gonna get married sometime next year.
We still testing the waters to make sure we can make it.
I'll get some money from him and go pick up some stuff
for your birthday party. You can invite some of your
friends over. You can even invite Dustin. How does that
sound?"

"That sounds great Aunt Eva. I'll see you then. Don't forget."

"I won't sweetie. Talk to you later. I got choir rehearsal tonight. We got to learn this new song that is really gonna make them folks at Greater Trials do a split in the aisle next Sunday." Patsy could hear her aunt laughing at the thought of that as she hung up the phone.

Well at least I'll have a chance to go somewhere for my birthday, Patsy thought. She went to the room to try and find a really cute outfit for her secret birthday party. Ann came in the room as Patsy was putting her clothes on the bed.

"What are you doing? Running away on your birthday?"

"I wish. Aunt Eva said she was going to come by later and get us so I can have a birthday party at her house. She's gonna ask Nadeen when she comes back. I don't know where she went." Ann had excitement in her voice, "Oooooh. That's gonna be fun. I can't wait. "By the way, I think she went to the store to pick up your birthday cake. She should be back in about twenty minutes."

"I'd rather have a piece of freedom than a piece of cake."

"You better not let her hear you say that or you might not get either one."

Nadeen came back about three hours later with cake and ice cream. Patsy and Josie were sitting on the front porch bench when she pulled up.

She must have picked them up last because the ice cream was hard as a rock. Patsy wondered where she had been all this time if she only came back with these few things and was suppose to have been back hours ago. Her face looked a little flushed to Patsy but she guessed it was the heat. Kenny was sitting out on the porch listening to the radio. He looked like he wanted to ask her what took her so long but he didn't want to get a Sunday School Lesson in vulgarity.

"Come open this door, Patsy. You see this stuff in my hand." Patsy went to help her and sat the cake and ice cream in the refrigerator. The phone rang as she was closing the refrigerator door. Nadeen hurried to answer it.

"Who is this?" Patsy stopped in her tracks as though if she moved her ears wouldn't work and she would miss something being said. "Dustin? Who are you and why are you calling here for my daughter? I usually don't allow little boys to call my home for my daughters but I guess since you were so polite I'll let you wish her a happy birthday. Don't keep my phone tied up too long you hear me? Patsy come get this phone." She gave Patsy a look like you know I don't play this. Patsy's throat was so dry at that moment she thought if she opened her mouth the dust along with the butterflies in her stomach would come out. She knew better than to walk away like she had something to hide or say in private.

"Hello," she said as though she wasn't sure why he would be calling her.

"Hey, babe. I hope I don't get you in any trouble. I just wanted to wish you happy birthday. I wish I could spend it with you."

"Well, Thanks for calling." She wasn't gonna get killed on her birthday about Dustin. She hung the phone up hastily.

Kenny came in with Josie on his lap. She was grinning with a chocolate stain running down her white dress. He'd been feeding her chocolate.

"Patsy just had some boy to call her to wish her a happy birthday. She better let him know it don't need to be no habit!" Nadeen told Kenny.

Kenny looked over at Patsy real quick but didn't say a word. They both were walking a thin line when it came to that situation so he said less as possible while he played with Josie.

"She got friends at school Nadeen. She's a popular girl. It's a special birthday for her today. You only turn sixteen one time. Where's the pizza I'm hungry?"

Just as he said that the doorbell rang and it was the pizza delivery guy. Ann had ordered the pizza and Kenny paid for it.

"It doesn't matter what day it is. He better not call here again. I don't like sneaky people. You hear me, Patsy? I catch you sitting up talking to that boy on my phone again it's gonna be bad for you. That sneaky spirit brings in a lying spirit and I won't have a lying spirit floating around here in my girls. Your daddy's demon is enough to battle." She rolled her eyes at Kenny. Kenny smirked at her.

Nadeen headed down the hall and Kenny had to raise his voice after her. "Nadeen, there's no need to criticize anybody. It was just a phone call."

"I said what I meant and I meant what I said." Nadeen's comment was muffled, but everyone heard it. They tried to ignore it by opening the pizza.

"Come on y'all let's eat this pizza before it gets cold," Kenny suggested.

Nadeen came back up a few minutes later. "You need to go ahead and cut that cake so you can get out of my kitchen. I got work to do."

Patsy got up to go get the cake out of the refrigerator along with the ice cream. "I need to start on this casserole for Sister Ida. She's sick and the usher board decided we each would take a day and make her a meal."

"You don't want no cake, Nadeen?"

"Not now. Maybe later." Josie, Ann, Kenny and Patsy all sat down and enjoyed Patsy's cake. Josie sung happy birthday and clapped when Patsy blew out all sixteen candles.

A few hours later Eva called and talked to Nadeen. She told her she wanted to spend some time with her nieces since it was Patsy's birthday. Nadeen said it was fine with her but only one night. She told Eva she could pick them up the next day but she was going to pick them up early the following day. Nadeen didn't like her children being in other folks houses even if it was family.

Patsy couldn't sleep all night. When the sun came up the next morning she was up before everybody. Her bags had been packed the night before. She didn't want to waste any time getting to Aunt Eva's house. When Eva pulled up Patsy heard the car horn blow. Eva was waving out of the car window. She was driving a beautiful platinum colored Mercedes-Benz. Patsy started unlocking the security door to take the bags out to the car quick as possible. *This new guy must really be loaded,* Patsy thought.

"Momma!" Patsy yelled down the hall. "Aunt Eva is outside waiting for us." Ann was coming up the hall as Patsy headed outside.

"Hurry up!We need to get out of here before your momma changes her mind." Nadeen came to the door and talked to Eva.

"Nadeen I know all that. Everybody that deals with your kids know all your rules. You ain't got to run' em down to me. It's one night. My goodness! How much can the girl get into in one night sitting at my house? You need to release and relax!" Nadeen stepped aside from the doorway to let Ann out. She put her hands on her hips and looked at Aunt Eva with a threatening look on her face.

"You let something happen to my girls and I 'm gonna release all right and it won't be nice." She said firmly between her teeth. Eva looked her in her eyes.

"You might scare Kenny Simmons but you don't scare me, Nadeen! I can go toe to toe with you any day but trust me that ain't what you want!" Eva closed the door as she turned and walked to the car. Patsy hurried behind her before Nadeen got mad and told them to turn right around and come back.

Eva's new boyfriend, David, was in the front seat. He got out to help put the bags in the trunk. "Hello there birthday girl, How are you?"

"I'm doing good. Excited about my birthday party." She noticed his funny gray eyes and the way he licked his bottom lip when he looked at her.

Creepy, Patsy thought and shivered.

"Make sure you got Josie in that car seat good." Eva warned them. "I would have to run my little sister over with this car if something happened to her baby girl." Ann put Josie securely in the seat and they headed to the Party Center Superstore to get the decorations and food for the party. When they finally arrived at her Aunt's house, Patsy pulled out her blue address book and starting call her friends. Dustin was the last person she called. When she told him about the party, he was surprised then cautious.

"You sure your mom doesn't know about this party? She might show up and cause a real scene if she knew you were having a party at your Aunt's house without her permission and I was going to be there."

"She doesn't know and anyway this is my Aunt's house she can do whatever she wants in her own house."

"Well it's a wrap. I'll be there. See you then" She was so excited she hung up the phone and went to pick out her clothes for the party. Eva and her boyfriend David did all the work. They cooked the food and put up the decorations. They had a special area in the backyard for Josie to play while the party was going on. Patsy put on her favorite pair of shorts, a halter-top and some of her Aunt Eva's heels. She looked beautiful if she had to say so herself. She asked Eva about that pretty pomegranate lip-gloss she always wore. Eva gladly applied it to her lips, put some blush on her cheeks, curled her hair, and let it hang down her back. Patsy looked at herself in the mirror and liked what she saw. She was slim, sexy and a beautiful shade of honey. Just like her mother.

She smiled and turned to give her aunt a hug and a kiss.

"You look so pretty!"

Eva put her hands on either side of Patsy's face and kissed her forehead. "You remind me of my sister when she was your age. Your momma was beautiful like you when she was younger. The boys were always on our porch once momma said she could take company. They let her start taking company at sixteen. Your granddaddy use to sit in the living room by the open window and Nadeen would sit out on the front porch on the swing with whatever boy came a courting that day."

If Nadeen was allowed to start having boys over at sixteen why was she being so hard on her? Patsy thought.

Just then she heard the doorbell rang. David answered the door and a familiar voice that made her stomach flutter said, "Hello. I'm Dustin." Eva looked at Patsy and smiled.

"Sounds like your sweetheart is here. Let me go take a look at this boy that's got my niece's nose wide open." She kissed Patsy on the jaw and walked out the bedroom door. Patsy's heart was beating fast. She gave herself one last look in the mirror before she went to meet him. Eva went into her living room where Dustin was sitting talking to David.

"Well, well. Look at this fine specimen right here. Bring your handsome self over here so I can get a closer look. I've heard a lot about you. No wonder my sister is keeping Patsy on lock down."

Dustin stepped toward Eva and smiled sheepishly.

"Honey, you look so good it's dangerous. Make a young girl fall from grace." Eva gestured at Patsy as she walked into the room, blushing. Dustin was still smiling with his head down.

"Hey, Dustin." He looked up at her and stared. She was breath taking. He'd never seen her look so sexy. She stirred up something inside of him he'd been trying for months to keep down. He'd never pressed her about taking their relationship to the next level but looking at her standing there with her skin all out and her hair falling down on her shoulders made him weak. He tried to pull his self together to speak to her.

"Hey, Birthday Girl. You look amazing." He said feeling a shameful heat run through him.

"I think this is where David and I exit the room. Your other guests will be coming soon."

As they headed out, David walked past Patsy with a smirk on his face and licked his lips. His smoky gray eyes moved up and down her like a hungry wolf. Patsy felt a little bit uneasy but quickly turned her focus to Dustin. He came up to her and kissed her. She felt the warmth of his body. She loved him and having him at her party was all she needed. She didn't care if the other kids came or not. Just as he kissed her on her neck the doorbell rang. She didn't want to let him go. She didn't want him to stop.

They were both breathing heavy and needed a minute to get it together.

"Patsy! Your guests are here. You and Dustin come on out of there!" Eva yelled. Dustin looked her in her eyes and she knew it was a good thing they weren't alone. The party was wonderful, all of her friends came over and she felt normal for the first time. She was being admired for her hair, her clothes, her makeup, and her birthday party. It was fabulous. Dustin stayed close to her all night. He was holding her hand and hugging her. It couldn't get any better than this.

The party lasted until one a.m. Ann and Josie gave out about eleven when they said good night full of punch and cake. Dustin stayed to help clean up so he could spend a few more moments with Patsy. When they finally finished, she walked him to the front door and kissed him good night. It was a deep and meaningful kiss. She could hear her heart beating fast against his chest. She was scared because she liked this way too much. Dustin had to pull back from her. His face was flushed.

"Patsy, I better leave. I can't take this. I can't take you looking like this. It's messing me up. I respect you and I don't want to lose you 'cause I can't keep it together. I enjoyed being with you on your birthday."

She wanted to stay near to him. His cologne was all over her. She would sleep with that scent on her all night. "I'll call you when I get home. If that's okay?"

"It's okay. Aunt Eva won't mind. She'll probably still be up." Patsy released his hand. She knew he had to go. She kissed him softly once more on the lips and walked back in the house.

Her body was feeling funny. She couldn't release the feeling. Finally, she must have drifted off to sleep after talking to Dustin on the phone for about an hour once he got home. She fell asleep thinking about all the fun she'd had at her birthday party and what a great aunt she had.

Sometime during the wee hours of the morning, Patsy must have rolled over on her back. She was in a deep sleep but thought she felt a hand pushing up her gown. She kind of moved her hand downward thinking it was a dream, but she touched what felt like a large hand and the veins in that hand were pumping really fast. The hand was so hot that it had to be real.

Her heart started beating louder than usual it seemed. She began to pray in her mind. *Please Lord. Don't let anybody be in this room!* She was so scared she didn't want to open her eyes. She decided to play sleep and roll over on her side. As she grunted and rolled over she slightly opened her eyes she could see the figure of a man sitting in a chair next to her bed. Ann and Josie were behind her. She hoped he hadn't touched them. She peeped under her eyelashes and saw David! He was in a white robe. When she moved to turn over, he slid his hand back. She could see him sitting there looking at her with those wolf gray eyes like he was waiting to see what she would do or say. She chose not to say anything even though she was screaming for her Aunt Eva in her head.

"David? Where you at honey?" Patsy heard Aunt Eva yell and slam the screen door as she came in. She must have been sitting out on the back porch and fell asleep out there. Sometimes she would do that. He jumped up immediately, softly opened Patsy's door and walked out. Patsy started crying.

He had been touching her! Oh my God. He had put his hands on her in a place no one was suppose to touch her. She didn't know what to say or do. She got up to go to the bathroom and as she walked across the hallway, she heard her Aunt talking to him.

"Did I see you coming out of that bedroom?"

"Eva, no! Are you high? I done told you to leave that weed and Johnny Walker alone. It makes you stupid."

"I can get stupid! If I even thought I saw you coming out of my niece's bedroom. I don't play that freaky mess." Her tone sounded like Nadeen's when she was in her dangerous zone.

"Get out of my face, woman, before I slap you to the floor talking like that to me!"

The next thing Patsy heard was the loud sound of someone hitting up against the wall, she went halfway up the hall and saw that it was David, Aunt Eva had pushed him up against the wall and grabbed the large butcher knife off of the table at the same time.

He was frozen against the wall. Eva was up in his face. She grabbed his hair and exposed his neck. She put the knife to his neck. "You must not know who you dealing with? The Lord has done many a thing in me but I ain't all the way delivered yet! I will slit you open on this floor, roll your body out of my front door and set it on fire in front of your momma's house before I let you put a hand on me or my nieces do you hear me!" She said between clenched teeth. "You could be in a church asking for repentance and I will come in there and blast you all over the Hail Mary!"

Patsy froze. She felt a familiar sick feeling inside of her stomach. Was this Aunt Eva or was this Nadeen? She couldn't really tell they seemed to have merged together all of a sudden. David didn't say a word at first he just stood still. Then in a calm voice he spoke to her.

"Baby, look. Calm down. I'm sorry I said those things to you. You know I would never hurt you or your nieces. Put the knife down okay. Let's just go to bed. You been drinking and smoking that weed. It's got you hearing things differently." He never moved an inch from the wall. Eva held him there for a moment just looking into his face then she released his hair and put the knife down to her side.

She looked at him for a few minutes then turned to walk away. Patsy tip toed as fast as she could to the bedroom and closed the door. Eva opened the bedroom door to their room a little later and peeped in. Patsy kept her eyes closed shut and pretended to be asleep. She heard her Aunt lock the door to the bedroom as she closed it back. Patsy knew if she told Eva what happened, David would be going out of those doors in a hospital stretcher or a body bag.

Maybe Aunt Eva wasn't as different from Nadeen as I thought. Patsy wondered where all that anger came from. David was wrong for what he'd done, but Patsy didn't want to see his throat slit open, especially not in front of her. It seemed she was always surrounded by the spirit of fear. She tried not to let it overtake her, but it always did. Maybe she needed to pray harder.

8

Patsy woke up hoping she'd just been having another nightmare but as Ann got up to take Josie to the bathroom she couldn't open the door. Patsy knew then that she hadn't been dreaming. Ann turned the lock and opened the door. As she left Patsy got up to start packing their things. This was the first time she hoped Nadeen would come extra early to pick them up so she wouldn't have to see David. She was embarrassed and didn't want to face him.

While Ann was in the bathroom, Eva came in and sat down on her bed.

"Did you sleep well, honey?"

"Yes. I was so tired after the party. Thanks again, Aunt Eva. It was the best party I ever had. Well, it's the only party like that I have ever had."

"Good. I'll take it to my grave. Patsy? David didn't happen to come into your room last night, did he baby?"

Patsy looked up into her aunt's eyes and she could see danger behind the concern. As much as she hated what he tried to do, she didn't want her aunt to go to prison for killing him.

"No Aunt Eva, not that I know of. Why you ask me that?" Patsy tried to sound convincing.

"Just asking. He sometimes sleep walks and there's no telling where he might end up."

Eva looked at Patsy for a little longer then got up and walked towards the door.

"Your mom called this morning said she would be by in about an hour and a half to pick you all up so I better go ahead and get breakfast ready."

Breakfast was great, but Patsy didn't have much of an appetite. Ann and Josie ate up everything! Patsy just told her Aunt that she was having some cramps and felt a little nauseated so she couldn't eat. Really she was too nervous to eat. When Nadeen came, Patsy hurriedly got the bags and put them in the car. She was surprisingly relieved to be going home. She couldn't even tell her what happened because she knew that somehow Nadeen would blame her and then she would come back over to Aunt Eva's house and have to "lay her religion down" as she would say just before she cussed everyone in the house out. So just like Aunt Eva, Patsy would take this crime to the grave and if David ever touched her again he'd be going with it.

Kenny was watching a televangelist on TV when they came in the door. He seemed to be really enjoying the message, yet he managed to get out a hello to them as they walked by.

"Daddy you ought to go to church instead of watching church when your knee heals."

"I plan on doing just that."

Nadeen let out a *hmph*. "He would need a GPS to find his way back to Deliverance Rock Church." Kenny ignored her and focused on them.

"You all have fun at your aunt's house?"

Patsy wanted to tell him that David put his hands on a part of her body where it didn't belong and she wanted him to go over there and whip him like a dog in her aunt's house. But she knew the penalty for exposing David was more drama than she wanted to be involved in so she just lied.

"Yep. It was great. I will never forget it. I have the best Aunt ever." Nadeen interjected then,

"You ain't got time for all that talking. Go back there and put on some clothes for church. We got just a few minutes before it's time to go. I need a few minutes to talk to Sister Anita this morning about her appearance. Some of the sisters called me again last night and said they shame to even stand at the door with her she be looking so bad. I don't know what's going on with her, but we got to put a stop to it today." They hurried to the back and threw on some clothes.

A few minutes after they got Josie dressed, Nadeen knocked on the door, "Let's go."

They hugged Kenny goodbye, ran out the door, and piled in the car.

The ride to church was quiet except for the radio. Nadeen was listening to a local preacher talk she was so caught up in the Hallelujahs and Amens that she almost ran a stop sign. Of course, she blamed the devil for trying to make her have an accident. Everything was always somebody else's fault but hers.

When they made it to the church people were standing around talking and some were crying. "What happened?" Nadeen asked out loud. "Lord I hope Pastor and First Lady Craig okay."

She stepped out of the car and went up to one of the members, "Sister Brandi what's wrong with everybody?" Sister Brandi could barely get the words out.

"It's Sister Anita. Sister Kia went by to pick her up for church in the van this morning and the ambulance was at her house. It seems her husband beat her into a coma. She was trying to leave him and he picked up a pipe and beat her almost to death." Sister Brandi wiped the tears from her face. "There was blood all over the porch. They say he's been abusing her for years. He didn't even want her coming to church. She was sneaking out just to come. That's why she was looking the way she was on Sundays. He'd burned a few of her usher uniforms so she had to hide the only one she had left which meant sometimes she couldn't wash it cause if he found it he would burn it too."

Nadeen put her arms around Sister Brandi and held her. "It's gonna be all right. Some people don't know how to treat their mates. God got it. Come on now. We got a service to attend. Let God do his work and we'll do ours." She slowly walked Sister Brandi into the church.

Later on, as they were driving home from church, Nadeen told them. "Won't God fix it? I didn't really want to have to tell Sister Anita about herself and now I don't have to."

Patsy was trying to figure out how Sister Anita getting her brains busted on her own front porch was better than having to tell her she needed to make her usher whites whiter?

The ushers had taken up an offering that Sunday also and bought Sister Anita three new usher uniforms and two pair of new white shoes. They took them up to the hospital later on that week along with a fruit basket. She told them she'd never had any sisters and she was so grateful for them especially Nadeen, who had come up earlier and given her a nice warm bath. She even combed her hair and dressed her. She said she would never forget their loving kindness.

"Sister Anita you are more than welcome. Our job as Christians is to minister to each other's needs. We look forward to you coming back to the church in your nice new uniform. You know our image represents the Pastor and he represents God so we have to always look our best." Sister Anita shook her head in agreement.

"Sister Nadeen, I sho' appreciate you taking me under your wings and teaching me how to be a good servant in the Kingdom of God."

Nadeen smiled and rubbed her hand. "Sister Anita, God just put it in me to help other people. I do it all to the Glory of God. The sisters and I are glad to have you. Right now you just work on healing. We can work on making sure you have the appropriate look for church when you get out." Nadeen pulled the ushers together and they prayed for Sister Anita then they left telling her they'd be back next Sunday not knowing that the following Saturday they'd be burying Sister Anita in her pretty new usher uniform.

Sister Anita was coming out of the shower in her hospital room when she walked out to see her husband and his mother. She'd bailed him out of jail and brought him up to the hospital so he could talk Anita into dropping the charges and coming back to him. She'd told Anita that God made Woman for the Man out of his side so she needed to stand by his side and work things out just him, her, and God. Sister Anita had refused to accept this and told them both that she was not dropping the charges nor going back into the hell she came from. His mother told Sister Anita she was out of God's Will for their marriage and offered to pray for them. As she reached over to take Sister Anita's hand, her son pulled out a gun and shot her daughter-in-law point blank in her face. As he pulled the trigger he said to her, "I'll see you at the Judgment Seat."

When the police arrived to arrest him, his mother told them Anita didn't want to come home with him so he sent her home with her God.

When Nadeen got the call, her only comment was "Lord, have mercy! Now I gotta try to find somebody to replace her and we just bought those uniforms."

The funeral was held at Greater Trials with a small gathering of family and friends. Reverend Craig gave a stirring eulogy. Nadeen assigned each member of the Usher board a role in the service. As they stepped out from the office to perform their own burial rite for their fallen sister, Nadeen told them to take a good look at Sister Anita in that casket because if they didn't get control of their own households they would end up just like her.

After the service, First Lady Craig came up to Nadeen and told her what a wonderful job they did with the home going service. She thanked Nadeen for always being there for her and Pastor Craig. Nadeen tried not to grin too hard.

"First Lady everything I do, I do for the Kingdom of God. I love his people I can't help it. I'm just a servant trying to do my part."

First Lady Craig patted her pristine white gloves. "You're an Angel Nadeen Simmons. Your family is blessed to have you."

Nadeen noticed that First Lady was looking a little pale in her face. She had dark rings under her eyes.

"Thank you, First Lady. You doing okay? You need anything?"

First Lady Craig managed to give her a weak smile, "I'm fine, Sister. I'm in God's care. Between him and my husband, I'm doing real good. I know I been missing every now and then but you know sometimes we gotta rest these old bodies."

Nadeen reminded her again that if there was anything she needed at any time to just give her a call and she would be right there. Reverend Craig came up and touched his wife gently on the arm.

"Come on, darling. It's time for you to get some rest. Today has been traumatic for all of us. Such a sad situation. We have to get back to putting God's Word first in our marriages. Isn't that right Sister Nadeen?"

Nadeen straightened her gloves and answered, "That's right, Pastor."

He gave her a nod of approval and walked First Lady Craig to the car. Nadeen thought she noticed First Lady leaning a little bit.

Later on in bed that night, Ann and Patsy talked about the funeral. "I can't get Ms. Anita out of my head. She looked so happy laying in that casket but she was dead." Patsy had been seeing that same picture in her head. She kept seeing the indention in her forehead where they had tried to cover up the bullet hole but didn't do a very good job.

"It's sad that her husband killed her. He hated her going to church so much he killed her. She reminds me of Kenny not standing up for his self. I just pray he doesn't end up just like her." Ann started scratching her arm.

"Me too."

Patsy noticed she was scratching and knew that wasn't a good sign so she decided to change the subject. "I miss Dustin,"

She could see Ann starting to slow down her scratching. "He been working this summer at the pool huh?"

"Yeah so I haven't seen him much but I heard Daphne Porter been seeing him. She at the pool every day. If I could get to her I'd pull her to the bottom of that pool and choke her out." Ann laughed. "You sound like your momma now,"

"Well you know her blood run through me. I try to keep it in check but sometimes the Holy Ghost have to put handcuffs on me to keep me still." They both giggled with their hands over their mouths to stop Nadeen from hearing them. After talking about Daphne Porter for an hour they finally drifted off to sleep.

The next morning Nadeen had them up and ready to go to Church Summer Camp. Since Sister Johnnie Mae Trotter had been shamed out of the church she'd stop bringing her children to the camp so Reverend Craig had to call and ask Nadeen to please let the girls come help out. Nadeen told him she would do anything to help. As they were getting ready Kenny came through the door he'd gone outside to talk with Stan. Nadeen had told him the last time Stan was there that she didn't want him back in her house so Kenny had passed the message along. Kenny said Stan just laughed when he told him and said. "Man them Christian sisters is something else." Kenny walked in with a wild, glassy look in his eyes. He was talking more than usual, seemed to be hype and was just walking up and down the hall a lot. Something was different about him but Patsy just couldn't put her hand on it. He told them he was gonna run out for a minute and he'd be back before they came home from camp. When they got back that evening he hadn't been home. Nadeen got up later on that night and looked upstairs for him, he wasn't there. "You girls seen your daddy? I guess he's in the street somewhere with that Stanley. He thinks that's his friend but he's not. He's a snake in the grass. I told him these streets gonna catch up with him one day.

"That pastor of his, Reverend Mack at Deliverance Rock, ain't worth a grain of salt. When the last time he been here or called about his church member? If that was Reverend Craig, he would have been come by and checked on me but not Reverend Mack; he too busy building on to his church to check on his member who's falling faster and faster into the pit of hell."

Patsy and Ann went to bed late that night trying to wait on Kenny to come home but he never did.

When they got up the next morning, the dread filled Patsy stomach. Josie was irritated and crying constantly. Ann was rubbing on her legs and Nadeen was slamming doors. Patsy could smell the storm coming. She decided to take Josie outside for a little fresh air before they went to camp in hopes that she would calm down.

When they came back in, she walked into the bedroom to see Ann with a shiny, silver razorblade cutting herself under the bottom of her thigh. Blood was dripping onto the white sheets and Ann was sliding the razorblade across her thigh without even blinking. Patsy closed the door and quickly sat Josie down. She ran over the bed and grabbed the razor blade from Ann.

"Ann! Ann stop!" Her tone was firm but hushed tone so she wouldn't get Nadeen's attention. "Ann, please stop it."

She grabbed Ann and held her. She tried to put the sheet up to her thigh to stop the blood. She had been trying to prevent Ann from doing this for weeks. This was the evil thing she had to look out for when Ann got nervous or upset.

Ann started crying on her shoulder. "I want my daddy. Where is my daddy? Patsy where is he?" Patsy held her close and rubbed her hair.

"I don't know Ann, but I know if you keep cutting yourself like this you won't live to find out. If you don't stop I'm gonna have to tell Nadeen." Ann pulled at her shirt and looked up at her.

"Tell her! She don't care. As much blood as she shed around her it won't matter."

"Ann I gotta get you cleaned up if she comes in here and see's this blood she is gonna lose her mind."

Patsy went to the bathroom and got a warm towel, some alcohol, and Band-Aids to cover up the cuts on Ann's thighs. She helped her get dress and Nadeen called them out the room to go to camp. Ann was limping slightly but Nadeen never noticed. As they drove to the camp, Nadeen was cussin Kenny out for all he was worth. *Wherever he was right now,* thought Patsy, *was better than here.* She dreaded coming back home from summer camp today.

When they made it to Greater Trials MB Church, Brother Ryan was standing at the outside of the door like he was waiting on someone. Nadeen pulled up to the parking lot and they all got out.

"Good morning, Sister Nadeen, and how are you girls, especially the birthday girl?" Patsy wondered how he knew about her birthday. She didn't talk to him like that.

"Fine, Brother Ryan." He opened the door for Nadeen and then walked in behind them. Patsy wondered, where was his wife? As a matter of fact, she hadn't seen Mrs. Ryan at church in about a month. Maybe she was sick. Brother Ryan followed Nadeen into the church office where they stayed until the end of the day. When camp was over, He carried Josie to the car for them and asked if he could take them out to dinner for some fellowship. Just as Nadeen was about to answer, Reverend Craig came up to them.

"Hello Sister Nadeen and Brother Ryan, how are you?"

"Doing just fine, Pastor," Brother Ryan smiled.

"Nadeen, how's your husband? Nadeen smiled at Reverend Craig

"He's much better, Pastor. Thank you for asking and for praying for him. You know he been goin over to Deliverance Rock, his sister and mother's church home."

"Well, tell him to come back and see us. He needs to join. It ain't good for a family not to pray together. It helps them to stay together." He turned to Brother Ryan, "Brother Ryan, I need to talk to you about a personal matter before you leave." Brother Ryan looked down at his shoes.

"Yes, Pastor," then he looked back at Nadeen.

"Brother Ryan, we thank you for the offer but we better get on home and you better get to Pastor's office. See you at work tomorrow."

Nadeen took Josie from him and put her in the car seat. She reached out and shook his hand, Patsy noticed he put his hand on hers for what seemed like longer than a minute. Brother Ryan dragged his feet against the rocks in the church parking lot and headed towards the Pastor's study. Patsy was thinking about Kenny. She was stuck between wanting him to be home and not wanting him to be when they got there. As they turned the corner to go to their house, she saw his truck, it was parked a little crooked which was a bad sign. She felt that familiar sick feeling twisting inside her belly. She looked at Ann who was looking at her like she knew something was about to happen. Josie was the only one in the car that didn't have a care in the world right then. Nadeen got out of the car first, they followed slowly behind.

When she opened the door, Kenny was in the kitchen fixing himself a sandwich. Stanley was sitting at the kitchen table drinking a beer. He had to have been drunk to even speak to Nadeen and even more so to be sitting in her kitchen when he and Kenny both knew she didn't want him around.

"Hey, Nadeen. How was camp?"

"Get out of my house right now before I call the police!"

Stanley gave a nervous laugh.

"Call the police? Call the police for what, speaking to you?" Everybody stood still waiting for the next move.

"No. For making me bust your head wide open for even being in my presence. Get out! I don't like you and I don't want you in my home! I thought Kenny had relayed that message to you!" He looked confused but he rose up from the table with his hands in the air.

"Hey. I don't know what kind of Sermon Reverend Craig teaching y'all down there at that church but I'm not your enemy. Kenny, look man. I'll catch you later on. Don't worry, I can get a ride back home with my ex-brother-in-law. He works right up the street. Talk to you later man."

Stanley got up and walked backwards towards the door holding his beer can in his hand and watching Nadeen.

She started in on Kenny immediately.

"How dare you disrespect my house like this and come in here whenever you want to!" Kenny looked up at her with a tired look on his face, "Nadeen, my truck stopped on me. I ran out of gas and I couldn't get anyone to answer the phone to come and get me so I could get some gas. It was late and I thought you were at work so who was I gonna call? I slept in the truck till about nine-thirty and then I called my boy Edmond and he took me to get some gas.

"Stanley just happen to stop by on his way to see his ex-brother in law. You didn't have to attack the man like that. Anyway, I need to talk to you. I got some things God been dealin' with me about and I need to tell you."

Nadeen slapped Kenny so hard his face barely missed the door of the kitchen cabinet. He didn't move. He just stood there.

"God?! What you know about hearing the voice of God? You been dancing with the devil for years now. You can't hear God! You think you can just walk in here when you want to you sorry excuse for a man and try to tell me about God! I'm not like Stanley's stupid ex-wife. You got me mixed up! I don't want to hear anything coming out of your mouth! It's all Satan talking and I don't listen to him! Get out of my face with those lies before I do something against the Will of God! Do you hear me?"

He just stood there looking at her like she was some strange creature. Patsy and Ann were embarrassed and felt sorry for him. *Why wouldn't he stand up to her sometimes?* Patsy just didn't understand why a man would let a woman treat him like that. Nadeen took her other hand and pushed Kenny with her Bible against the oven as hard as she could.

"Go back to where you stayed last night!" She glared at him through her fiery brown eyes then she turned and walked down the hall still holding onto her Bible with her other hand.

Patsy and Ann both looked at Kenny as he went back to making his sandwich.

"Nadeen is crazy. I don't know why she thinks I was out doing something shady. I love her. No matter how crazy she is, I love her.I really need to talk to her. Why does she have to make it so hard?" Before she could think about what she was gonna say, Patsy turned to him.

"Why don't you hit her back, Kenny? You never defend yourself. You always let her hurt you. I'm scared she's gonna hurt you bad one day." Tears filled up in her eyes.

"I ain't studyin what she talking about. Patsy, a man should never hit a woman. God made woman for the man. We are supposed to protect and love her."

Patsy thought in her mind, *You better knock her out and protect yourself before she buries you.* Later on that night, Patsy would find out where Kenny had been before his truck ran out of gas. Nadeen was in her room whispering on the phone. Ann was taking a nap with Josie and Patsy was working on a crossword puzzle. The doorbell at the back door rang around nine p.m. Patsy wondered who could possibly be ringing their doorbell this time of night. She went to the door and peeped out of the stained glass window.

She saw the face of an old classmate of hers that had dropped out of school, his name was Cole, he was in the eighth grade with her, but dropped out because he said he just couldn't do it anymore. *Why was he at their door? How did he know where they lived?* She slowly opened the door and he looked at her.

"Hey, Patsy Simmons. What's up?" He was slightly smiling and looking around nervously as though he was making sure no one saw him.

"Uh, nothing much. What brings you out this way to my house?"

She stepped outside and closed the door behind her. He glanced at her, embarrassed.

"I need to talk to your dad."

"About what? A job? He ain't hiring right now."

"No. It's not about a job."

She looked him right in the eye and he looked at her. Her mind started to go down a list of reasons he would be asking for Kenny if it wasn't about a job. He better not be here to ask about taking her out because she told him before she wasn't interested in him. He always seemed to have a crush on her though so she tried to stay out of his way when they were in school. Why was he at her house?

"Pat. Look. I've always liked you so I don't want to lie to you. We go too far back for that. I got some business with your daddy."

Business? You ain't got no business with my daddy. The only thing you do now, from what I heard, is sell crack. As soon as the thought went from her mind into the air she froze. She locked eyes with him and opened her mouth. She heard the words come out but wasn't ready for his answer.

"Cole, is my daddy on crack?"

She was so hurt when she asked she couldn't stop the tears she felt welling up in her eyes. He looked at her as though he felt so sorry for her.

"Yes."

She thought she was going to faint if she didn't hold on to the screen door handle.

"He is, Pat, and he owes me for some product."

Patsy had heard about some of the bad things that happen to people who owe the dope boys but don't pay up. She was afraid for Kenny and for her family because if Cole knew where they lived he could do something to them.

"I'll pay it, Cole."

"No. I don't want you to do that Pat. Me and your dad can take care of this. He usually takes care of his business with me. I don't want to take that from you. He was supposed to handle it last night, but I guess he got sidetracked. One of my boys said he passed his truck out by Transition Road."

Patsy turned to go back in and get the money from her birthday savings, but she had to ask one more question, "Cole? How long he been doing this?"

"He been hittin' the rock since before his accident when he totaled his truck with that train." He sounded as though he felt sorry for her.

"He says he needs something to get the weight off his back. He said he tried prayer, but the weight just keep getting heavier. I really hate it for him man, I mean, I got some heavy things inside of me so I know how the man feels." He paused and thought for a minute. "Hey, can't your mom help him? Ain't she some big wheel in y'all church?"

Patsy couldn't answer him.

She felt so devastated, she just shook her head. She went inside, got out the purse with her birthday money in it, and took it to him. She gave him the money and asked him not to ever come back to their house again, please. Just as he was about to answer, Kenny came to the door, he saw Cole and he rushed out the door.

"Go in the house, Patsy!" She put her head down and went inside she could hear him outside telling Cole to never come to his house again and don't speak to his daughter. What he did in the street stayed in the street. He was going to settle up with him tonight for what he got from him last night. Cole told him no need it was settled.

Patsy heard Cole's car drive off and Kenny came back in the house. She also heard Nadeen. "Kenny! Tell me you were not just out there talking to Sister Ruby's son. I know what he's out there doin' and there is only one reason he would come here! You put me and my daughters in danger for a rock?"

"Nadeen, that boy did some work for me while I was out with my knee. We were talking about settling up that's all."

"You lyin' Kenny. I know you lyin'!" She went back to her room and slammed the door. Kenny knocked on the bedroom door.

"Nadeen. Baby, I need to talk to you for real. I gotta tell you what God been telling me. Come on Nadeen." He stood at the door for a few minutes, but Nadeen never answered. He finally gave up and went upstairs. Patsy went to bed after telling Ann about what happen with Cole. Surprisingly, Ann told her that one of her friends told her that she thought she saw him in the crack neighborhood a few weeks before his accident but Ann told her friend that couldn't have been her daddy. He wouldn't do anything like that.

She got mad with the girl and stopped speaking to her. Patsy stayed awake all night thinking about what Cole told her. Kenny couldn't be doin' that. He just couldn't. Patsy knew then that the enemy wasn't only trying to destroy Kenny's life, he was also trying to take it.

9

Summer took it's time coming to an end. Patsy was glad when the new school year finally started. It was her senior year. Her prelude to Freedom Year.

The first person she saw when she got off of the bus for the new school year was Dustin, The lifeguard job had given him a beautiful tan and his green eyes brought out his beautiful caramel colored skin tone. She missed him. She ran up to him and gave him a great big kiss. He held her so tight she never wanted to let go.

"Man, I missed you."

"I missed you too, Dustin. You look great!"

"Too bad we can't just skip school and go hang out at my place."

Patsy thought he might be serious just a little bit but she would never risk her life like that. A violation like that would get her put out of the house forever and labeled as a Babylonian whore by Nadeen.

"Well. We can't. So let's just go to class."

This year they had two classes together, Biology and Biology lab. *This was gonna be a great school year.* As she walked down the hall holding Dustin's hand, they passed by Daphne Porter. Patsy hadn't seen her since last year but was in no hurry to talk to her. She was a gossip and she liked to be in the middle of some mess all the time. She was standing in a circle of girls and she leaned over and said something to one of them. They all started laughing and one of them said "Well Amen Sistah!" whatever that meant. *One thing for sure, it better not be a reference to Dustin,* Patsy thought. Daphne Porter was bad news.

"Hey, Lifeguard Dustin." Daphne smiled and said. Her girls giggled and looked at Patsy. Dustin held Patsy's hand tight.

"Hey, Daphne. You ready for the new school year?"

Daphne smiled real big. "I'm ready for a lot of things."

Patsy pulled away from Dustin but he gripped her hand tighter.

"We'll talk to you later I gotta get to class." Dustin had to drag Patsy along. He felt her pulling away towards Daphne. This wasn't the way he wanted to kick off their senior year together.

"Dustin, you better talk to your friend. I told you before she keeps trying to push my buttons. She wants you and she wants me and the whole school to know it."

Dustin stopped at her classroom door, bent down and kissed her on the jaw.

"But who's got me?" His question made Patsy blush.

"I do."

"That's right and don't you ever doubt that. I'll see you in Biology." Dustin looked into her beautiful brown eyes and knew he had managed to assure her of his love so her turned and headed off towards his classroom.

The rest of the day went well. Patsy settled into the new school year prepared to deal with Daphne's subtle harassment and life at home. Nadeen had started leaving earlier and earlier for work at the Gardens of Peace Nursing Home. She said she had to make sure she was doing her part to get promoted to permanent supervisor because she knew God was going to do his. In the meantime, Kenny was coming in later and later. This always put Nadeen in a foul mood by the time she made it home the next morning.

One of these mornings, Ann was cleaning the bathtub before leaving for school and she hadn't rinsed the inside of the tub good. Nadeen walked into the bathroom to inspect it and saw the residue. She called Ann back into the bathroom and started beating her across the head with the can of powdered cleaner. Ann had to change clothes and Patsy had to try and clean the powder out of her hair before they left for school.

Ann had started cutting herself more and more. She would cut the side of her thigh until the pain felt good. Each time she cut a slit into her thigh she hoped it was the one that would hit just the right vein to put her to sleep for eternity. She dreaded getting up every morning. A rebellious spirit was growing within her and even though she knew the cost would be great, she just didn't care.

Before she starting cutting herself Ann was so upset once, that she took a match and lit it on a white leather couch. She put it out right quick but there was a mark on the couch from the burn. Nadeen saw it and asked who did it. Ann said she did, Nadeen made her strip down to nothing. She forced Ann to the floor, put her foot on the back of Ann's neck and beat her with a thick leather belt all the while declaring she would not have such a destructive spirit in her home. Ann screamed until she lost her voice. The pain was Ann's way of releasing her own hopelessness and anger. She could scream it all out while taking in more.

Patsy asked her later that night what would make her do such a crazy thing like that. Ann told her she didn't know for sure. She'd been having crazy thoughts for months and that day the impulse to do something just got too strong to ignore.

She told Patsy when she burnt the couch it felt really good to her. Patsy didn't know what to say to that. One thing she knew though was that feeling crazy wasn't a good enough reason to get beat until you almost passed out.

Patsy recalled an incident two years ago where Nadeen hit Ann so hard in the eye that she had to stay out of school for about a week. Ann told Patsy that while she was home, Brother Ryan started coming by the house. He came by almost every day it seems to supposedly discuss the upcoming Sunday School Bible Trivia Contest with Nadeen or to talk about work. They always went into the living room and closed the door. Ann thought that was odd. It didn't make sense. He could talk to her at church or at work. Why was he coming over every day while Kenny was at work? Maybe he was upset about his recent divorce. Ann had heard thru the grapevine at school that he and Sister Ryan had gotten a divorce. She moved her kids back home with her mother in another state. Maybe he just needed someone to talk to? Nadeen was always there for her church family, but she was "ghost" when it came to her own. If only Ann had known that before the week was out she would have an answer to her questions.

After Patsy helped clean Ann up they decided to get out of the house as fast as possible. Patsy didn't really know what to say to Ann about what happened so she just kept quiet. After a few minutes, Ann opened up.

"Patsy I just want to kill myself. I'm so miserable living in that house. If I kill myself, I can get away. I can be happy." Patsy blanched and turned to Ann.

"Ann, please don't talk like that. You have to be stronger than that. You have to stick around. We love you. Just block out those crazy thoughts."

"They might be crazy to you but they make sense to me cause I'm tired. I have nobody to talk to about it but God and he must be on vacation or something cause he never comes to our house to see about us."

Patsy was about to answer her when she heard Sandra yelling her name.

"Patsy! You and Ann come on! We gonna miss our bus!"

Sandra caught up with them so Patsy decided she'd pick up this conversation with Ann later. Sandra did most of the talking the rest of the way to the bus stop. She had gotten herself pregnant over the summer slipping around with Lavon and she was all excited about having the baby. Patsy just wondered how she was going to raise a baby when she was still a child herself mentally. Her mother, Sister Gladys, wasn't around to raise her so how was she gonna help raise a grandbaby?

When Patsy got on the bus the only seats remaining were the ones in the back. She saw Daphne Porter sitting back there with her group of geese- face friends and really didn't want to have to sit near them. She and Ann sat together and Sandra went further to the back with Daphne's crew. She noticed Daphne was staring at her longer than usual this morning. She could even feel it on her back. Ann got off at her school and the bus pulled off slow enough for Patsy to look back and give her a wave.

This brought a small smile to her face. When they got to the school Patsy remained sitting while everyone from the back of the bus got off. Daphne walked by and bumped her leg. Patsy felt a heat rising up in her and she was just about to stand up and go off when God sent a ram in the bush. She turned to the window and saw Dustin. Dustin's face caused a rush to come over her and the feeling of anger left her immediately. She got off the bus and took his hand. They walked to class together.

Patsy had to stop at her locker before going in to class so she told Dustin she would meet him in front of the library. She was headed toward her locker when she felt a hand pop her on her butt real hard, she turned and saw Eddie Porter, Daphne's cousin, laughing at her along with several other boys. She filled with anger.

"Excuse me? Don't put your hands on me! You don't know me like that!" She could see a crowd starting to form.

"Oh, excuse me, church girl. I must have you mixed up with your momma!" Eddie spoke with a stupid grin on his face. "Oh, that's right. I hear she like to get that butt spankin' not you! I bet she don't act so holy with Brother Ryan." Patsy couldn't believe what she'd just heard.

She stepped up to his face and before she knew it she slammed him into the lockers and put her teeth right into his chest. She was biting him so hard she could feel his flesh tear thru the thin t-shirt he had on. She could hear him screaming and pushing at her face trying to get her to release him but she was gonna draw blood from this disrespectful dog! She could taste the blood in her mouth when she felt Dustin pulling on her and yelling

"Patsy! Patsy, baby, let him go!" She was so angry she wouldn't let go. The rush of anger flowing through her veins felt so good she wanted to hold on until the feeling subsided. Dustin and Sandra both had to pull her back. As they manage to get some space between her and Eddie, Patsy grabbed his shirt and stretched it until it hung down to the middle of his chest. He was in a lot of pain by the look on his face.

"Now talk stupid to me again punk! I ought to kick you in your face so hard I knock your teeth down your throat! You don't talk that street trash to me! You and your ignorant cousin got me twisted!"

As Dustin and Sandra released her, Daphne came up and saw her Cousin Eddie bleeding from his chest and grimacing in pain.

"Eddie! Eddie what happened to you?" She asked in a panic.

"Your Junior Usher friend over there bit me cause I called her momma out!"

Daphne turned towards Patsy. Patsy stepped towards her and was just about to go at her face when Dustin grabbed her. Sandra stepped in between to stop them from making contact. She was trying to restrain Daphne while Dustin restrained Patsy.

"Come on, baby! Let that go. Come on. I'll deal with him myself. Come on now!" Dustin begged.

As he dragged Patsy down the hall she heard Daphne say,"Ain't no use in getting mad at my cousin church girl cause your momma fellowshipping with Brother Ryan, Monday thru Friday then acting like she Usher of the Month on Sunday!"

"You're a bald headed liar!"

Dustin took her outside to calm her.

"Baby, you gotta calm down. You can't let a jerk like Eddie Porter get to you. You know he's stupid. Man. I have never seen you go off like that. Where did that come from?" Sandra came out the door a few minutes later.

"Pat! You went way out. You snapped! I think you bit his nipple off. He's bleeding thru his shirt pretty bad. Daphne took him to the school nurse. I never seen you explode like that. You are your mother's child honey! You say what you want about Nadeen Simmons, but you just like her!"

Patsy shot her a nasty look. "I'm not like her! Don't you say that to me. Don't you ever say that to me again, you hear me?"

Patsy snapped at Sandra. Sandra looked a little scared. "Sorry. I'm just saying. You've never acted like that. I didn't know you had a temper like that and to jump on that boy who is every bit of six foot six. Girl that was something! Everybody is talking about how you jumped on him like a Doberman pincher."

"Come on, Pat. Let's go back in. We already late for class."

Dustin and Sandra walked with her to her first-period class. She went in and sat down in the back hoping everyone would stop looking at her. In her head, she kept hearing Sandra say that she was just like her mother. She couldn't be like Nadeen. She just couldn't be carrying that curse within her. The principal's voice came over the intercom. "Patsy Simmons. Please report to the office immediately!" She knew what this was about and she knew she wouldn't be coming back to class. She got up and walked out with her head up. She wanted it to be clear, she was not to be played with and was not going to be disrespected by anyone especially a male, *now try it if you want to and see if your momma won't have to pay a doctor bill!* She was startled by her own thoughts; she felt like something or someone had taken over her body.

When she walked into the principal's office, the secretary just pointed to the office and told her to go on in. Mr. Rogers, the assistant principal, was sitting there looking over his glasses.

"Sit down, Patsy. Now what is this incident I heard about this morning between you and Eddie Porter? He had to go to the school nurse and get several stitches. You almost completely detached his nipple. He's going to have that bite mark for life."

Patsy just looked at him. She wasn't going to tell him that what he said about her mother was what really ticked her off!

"Mr. Rogers, he popped me on my behind. That was disrespectful and he was out of line. I don't allow any one's son to treat me that way."

"I do understand that but you could have just reported it to a teacher. Fighting is not the answer. I'm afraid I'm going to have to suspend you for five days. I've called your mother and explained to her that you were fighting at school and would be suspended. She's on her way to pick you up."

Oh, Lord, thought Patsy. *She is gonna come up here and embarrass me in front of everyone in the office. Please don't let Dustin be out in the hall.* Patsy sat in Mr. Rogers's office for what seemed like hours. Finally, Nadeen came through the door.

"Hello, Mr. Rogers. I came to pick up my daughter." Mr. Rogers looked at her and said in a regretful tone.

"I'm sorry Mrs. Simmons, but we are going to have to suspend her for attacking this boy. He was hurt pretty bad. He required stitches. I'm also going to call him in once they finish with him at the nurses station."

"I understand. But he should have kept his hands to himself. My daughter is not a prostitute and she better not have let him treat her like one. She did what she needed to do. I wouldn't have expected any less. Come on, Patsy. Let's go home." She turned and walked out. As Patsy got up to walk out she saw the shock on Mr. Roger's face and laughed inside of herself. She walked behind Nadeen a little bit as they went down the hall she was glad it was empty. She wasn't sure how to read Nadeen right now. Was she waiting until they got outside to slap her or cuss her out? She got in the back seat of the car.

Nadeen spoke to Pasty through the rearview mirror. "You should have took a combination lock and bust him in his filthy mouth! Just because you a Christian don't mean you got to let people walk all over you! You have to let these men know who wears the pants and that they can't run over us. I'm glad you handled him."

Nadeen's reaction scared Patsy. She played the scene back over in her head and realized she had reacted just like her mother, with violence, Mr. Rogers was right she should have just went to the principal or even told Dustin. He would have handled it at the right time in the right place.

"Lord, please don't let me become like my mother. How could I have flipped so quickly?" She whispered to herself. Nadeen sang "Amazing Grace" all the way home.

The other side of this outburst was the real reason she attacked Eddie, He had publicly accused Nadeen of sleeping around with not only her co-worker but a member of her church! This just couldn't be true, but she thought back to what Ann said about Brother Ryan visiting when Kenny wasn't home, the walks with them into the sanctuary and the walks back to the car.

How could you go to church and praise the Lord with a man you're having an affair with? Surely the Lord would give you both heart attacks and kill you on the spot the moment you both entered the sanctuary. Patsy wondered, *how many people at her church and now at school knew about this and how long it had been going on? She couldn't even look at Nadeen now. This was a whole other level of low to her. How could she sit up in the bed she was sleeping with another man in and read the Bible? Did she think only certain parts applied to her?*

Patsy was glad she had been expelled maybe the kids at school would let it die down over the weekend and she could have time to try and process the horrible news she found out in front of half of the school!

When Ann got home she came immediately to their bedroom.

"Patsy. I heard you got into a fight with Eddie Porter today. People saying you messed him up pretty bad! You look okay. Nadeen didn't beat the taste out of your mouth about getting suspended?"

"No. She said she was glad I did it. Gotta show these men who wear the pants around here." "I heard he put momma on blast, said she was sleeping around with Brother Ryan," Ann whispered.

"Yeah, he did. That's really why I tore into him. He had no right touching me but he sure had no right to spread such a vile lie!"

"I don't think it's a lie, Patsy. You know his kids went to my school and was in the same Sunday School Class with me. They started treating me real cold a few weeks before they changed schools. The rumor at school was that someone heard their mom on the phone talking to Brother Ryan's wife and she told their mom she found the phone number of some woman in his pocket. She called the number and the voice on the other end sounded familiar to her. She told the lady that women at Greater Trials Church call themselves Christians and are the biggest and sneakiest Jezebels in the world. Not long after that the kids were enrolled in another school and Sister Ryan moved out the house."

"I wonder if Kenny heard about that. Would he say something to her or whimper down and act like it wasn't happening?"

"This is one time I think Kenny would say something, Patsy. I mean we're talking about something real scandalous here."

"I just can't believe Nadeen would do something like that though. She's always going off on Kenny accusing him of doing it and what she's gonna do if she catches him. If it was anybody that knew for sure if she was messing around with Brother Ryan, it would be Aunt Eva. She tells her everything. I need to ask her."

"You think she would tell you that Pat?"

"She might."

"Patsy! You need to go up front and cook. Josie is hungry. She's in here eating up my grapes. "You gonna clean out that refrigerator too since you gone be out for a few days. You need to be in school. I like to have my quiet and privacy during the day."

I bet you do, thought Patsy. She started up front to the kitchen. As she prepared the skillet, Kenny came in. He was edgy but sober.

"Hey, Patsy. What's for dinner?"

"I think I'll do meatloaf and homemade mashed potatoes."

"That sounds good. I'm gonna go and take a shower before dinner. You let me know when it's ready."

"Okay."

It was nice to see him come home sober for a change. It seemed that the more Nadeen berated him the more he drank and the worse he got. About an hour later, Patsy had everything ready, she called everyone up front. She fixed Josie's plate first. She filled it with mashed potatoes since that was one of her favorite foods. Josie smiled and clapped her hands. Somebody had to be happy in this house. Nadeen and Ann came up next to fix their plates. As Nadeen was going down the hall Kenny was coming up front.

"Where do you think you going?" Patsy's stomach flipped. "Go eat at your momma's house. That's where all your money went last week. I got the voicemail, she come calling here talking about she appreciate her son getting her air conditioner fixed yet I asked for a mink coat and was told you couldn't get it right then. After all the crap I put up with from you? Since you love her so much go park your feet under her table and beg her for some lovin'."

"Nadeen, my momma and sister needed that air fixed. It was steaming in that house. I can get your mink coat for you at another time. It's not a necessity."

"See, that's why I do things the way I do with you. Until you get in line with the Word about how to treat me I'm going to treat you like you obviously want to be treated."

Kenny spoke calmly to Nadeen. He wasn't up to this fight.

"Baby, look. Her and my sister were burning up in that house. They had half of the money they just needed me to help them with the other half. I tried to sit down with you and tell you but you always at the church office when I come home for lunch or try to reach you."

"You haven't tried to reach me. You think I'm kidding with you about this food...I am not. Don't you touch it! I don't care if your tongue rolls out of your mouth and touches the dirt."

"Come on now, Nadeen. I been out working hard all day. Stop acting like that. I pay the bills in this house. I take care of you all. That coat is a want it's not a need. It can wait."

Nadeen stopped in front of him.

"Yeah and you can wait too. You can wait until hell freezes over about a whole lot of things in this house, Kenny Simmons, and this dinner is one of them!"

"Nadeen there is an entire pantry full of food I just saw it earlier this week." Nadeen swung around and gave him a nasty look.

"That food is for the people at the homeless shelter. You gonna try to eat the food that the church has collected for hungry women and children now, Kenny? Has it come to that?"

"I'm trying to sit down with my children and enjoy a hot meal I helped bring in this house."

"They don't want to sit down with you. My children deserve better than you."

If those words didn't hurt Kenny, they hurt Ann. She put her fork down and looked at Patsy. Patsy had already lost her appetite so she put her plate down. Kenny whispered something under his breath, turned and walked out the front door. Nadeen went into her bedroom. Shut the door and turned her radio up loud on her favorite gospel station. About an hour later, Kenny came back inside. He didn't say a word he just went upstairs. Patsy decided to make him a plate of food and take it to him. She took it upstairs where he would sometimes be sleeping in his big lounge chair next to the window. Many times he would come up here and just stare out the window. She knocked on the bedroom door softly but he didn't answer. It was cracked a little bit so she looked in.

Kenny was down on his knees praying. He was asking God to please help him. Patsy stood still. She knew Kenny had a good heart. He was just being attacked and it seemed Nadeen didn't care. She would pray for other people but she never prayed for her own husband. She had a need in her own home and she was too blind to see it. When he finished Patsy knocked hard on the door as though she had just come up. He was just getting up off of the floor.

"Kenny. It's me. I brought you something to eat."

"I was just having a talk with the Lord. I know who he is and he knows me." He leaned over and kissed Patsy on the jaw. "Thank You baby. I appreciate you looking after your daddy."

Patsy smiled. "I'll be back in a little while to get your plate."

"Okay, baby," Patsy knew one thing about Kenny Simmons, he loved all of them—even Nadeen.

10

After a few days of suspension Patsy got over being mad at Eddie Porter. She began to think about how she'd let anger control her. She reacted too quickly and it would probably cost her graduation with honors. It was going to be hard to pull up all those zeroes. She would never let anyone control her like that again and cost her so much. Nadeen was gone to the church office most of the day to help Reverend Craig so she said. She missed seeing Dustin every day, Sandra said he was missing her too. He was always asking about her. She managed to sometimes talk to him when he got out of school if Nadeen was napping. She would go outside with Josie and talk to him on the phone about what was going on at school. One day while she was outside, she saw Brother Ryan drive by the house in his Range Rover. He drove by slowly, stuck his arm out and waved. Patsy thought to herself, *Yeah pull up in this driveway and see won't I tell my daddy.* He just kept driving looking back in his rearview mirror.

Sometimes she would walk down to the bus stop with Josie to meet Ann. She knew she missed her walking with her to and from the bus stop. The week seem to move by slowly but finally it was time to go back to school. Patsy was ready and she hoped that the fight with her and Eddie had been forgotten. The morning she was to return to school was on a Friday. She and Ann rode to school with Nadeen because the principal wasn't going to let her back in school without talking with her mother first. He gave them the speech about how important it is to act like a young lady in school and how disappointed he was in her for letting someone like Eddie Porter cause her to mess up her grades. Patsy just agreed with what he said. Finally he let her go. Nadeen got up and walked out the door first. The school secretary attended Greater Trials too so she spoke to her as she walked by her desk.

"Good morning, Sister Simmons. How are you?"

Nadeen ignored her and walked out the door, when she got in the hall she released an arsenal of venom towards her.

"That's a sneaky, backstabber right there! She tells everything she knows. She is the worse gossip in Greater Trials and I can't stand the sight of her!" Patsy thought she saw Nadeen's eyes turn from light brown to jet-black. It scared her so bad she froze in place.

"She is always nice to me when I come in the office."

"That office is your problem. Stay out of there and you might stay out of trouble. Bad spirits jump on you when you hang around bad people. Just remember that. Now get in that classroom."

"Yes, ma'am."

Patsy didn't say another word to Nadeen she just headed down the hall to Biology Class. She wanted to see Dustin so bad. When she opened the door there he was in the front row looking good enough to sop up like syrup with a hot butter biscuit! Looking that good, He made it hard for her to keep herself. She recalled the kiss on the night of her Birthday party. It was intense and full of heat. She was glad they weren't alone. She wasn't sure right then if she would stop him if he started. They both tried to do the right thing. So far they had managed to stay in the Will of God despite their strong attraction. They had been dating for about three years and all of her friends had gone to the next level. Her and Dustin were holding on and praying. She hoped deep down inside her belly that they would make it to their wedding day despite her flesh being curious.

They both looked at each other and smiled. Patsy found a seat in the back of the class and looked at him the entire class. His biology was the only type that had her attention. It took forever it seemed for the bell to ring. As soon as it did Patsy ran up to Dustin's desk.

"Hey, handsome"

"Hey, beautiful. I missed you."

"Good. I hope I stayed on your mind the whole week I was gone."

"Baby, you are always on my mind. So much so I think I got an addiction." Patsy laughed at that statement.

"Come on let's go. I can't be late for my next class on my first day back." Dustin pushed his books in his backpack and followed Patsy out into the hall. On the way to their next class they passed Eddie Porter. He gave Patsy a look like he wanted to do something real bad to her but he was afraid to. Dustin was with her and she knew he wouldn't dare say anything to her with him around.

"Don't let him shake you, Patsy."

"I won't babe. He has learned his lesson well. Anyway I don't think he wants to have to deal with my big strong man if he gets back in my face."

"You got that right. Look I'll get with you later I need to look over my notes for this test."

He kissed her and they went their separate ways.

On the way home from school, Ann and Patsy took their time walking up the hill to their house. They weren't in any hurry to get home.

As they came around the corner they saw Brother Ryan's Range Rover parked in front of their house and behind it was Kenny's truck. *This couldn't be good,* Patsy thought.

"Ann. Why is Kenny home early and why is Brother Ryan's truck at our house?" They both ran towards the house. They could hear Kenny before they got to the front door. He rarely ever raised his voice but now he was raising his voice and cussin'.

"What you mean bringing your tired behind to my house when I'm not home! You trying to get with my wife Brother? Answer me when I talk to you cause in a minute I'm liable to whip you in the street!"

"Brother Simmons, I swear. It's not what you think. I just stopped by to talk with Sister Nadeen about First Lady Craig. She hasn't been feeling well lately and I didn't know if she knew about it. I just thought the Sisters of the Praying Circle would want to know. I didn't mean no harm. I swear I didn't!" You could hear the fear in his voice. When they walked through the front door, to their shock, Nadeen was hiding behind the broom closet door. Kenny was holding Brother Ryan by his shirt. Kenny had his other hand balled up in a fist and it looked like a pair of brass knuckles on his fingers. Nadeen didn't say a word—she looked like she had been crying.

"Kenny! What are you doing with that? Please stop before someone gets hurt."

Kenny spun around and looked at Patsy with a wild look in his eyes.

"I'm gonna hurt somebody! This so called deacon of the church wants to make house calls to my wife in the middle of the day while I'm out busting my butt to make a living for my family!"

"Brother Simmons. I swear it was just a short friendly visit to tell her to check in on our First Lady." Brother Ryan was sweating. Ann said later she thought she saw pee coming down his right leg.

"You lost your wife and your children and now you want to come over here and take mine? Well if you think that's gonna happen you been pulling on a crack pipe! I been hearing some things about you and about my wife but I figured Nadeen had more in her than to bring a man into my own house!" He looked over at her. Nadeen put her head down.

"The only reason I won't whip you right now is because my children are present. If it weren't for my children, I would beat the devil out of you right now! Get out of my house before I stick my work boot so far up your butt you'll have my toes for teeth! I better not ever catch you in this neighborhood or near my house again and you better not be in my wife's face at church!"

Brother Ryan almost flew on angel's wings out the front door and ran to his Range Rover breathing hard. Some neighbors had gathered by that time and were laughing at him as he ran to his car. Ann and Patsy looked at Kenny with amazement. *He had a "pair" after all, and some pants to put over them,* Patsy thought. *What about that?*

Nadeen didn't move. She just looked pitifully at him and softly spoke.

"Kenny. There was nothing going on, I promise you, there wasn't."

"You lying to me, Nadeen! I know you lying! You think I didn't hear about the real reason Patsy got suspended? Well I did. I heard about it 'cause kids talk and so do their parents. I had one of my boys to come up to me and tell me I need to be going down to Greater Trials and keep an eye on you and Brother Ryan."

"They just gossiping and lying, Kenny. You know how people talk."

Kenny looked at her funny and in a sarcastic tone said, "Mighty funny that when they call and tell you a bunch of lies about me and some woman I'm supposed to be spending time with you don't say they just gossiping and lying! I come through the door and you raisin hell with me!" He slipped the brass knuckles off his hand and into his pocket. "Now, you need to get out of my face!"

Nadeen eased by him and put her head down she didn't even look at them. Patsy looked at Kenny in amazement. She had never seen this man before. She felt a whole new sense of pride to call him her daddy. Maybe things were about to change around the Simmons's household.

Kenny stayed home from work for a week after that incident. Nadeen was quiet around the house not demanding and controlling as she was usually. She didn't even go into work early. She didn't even go to the church office and work on the bulletin. She created it at home and printed it out for the upcoming Sunday. Patsy thought maybe this was a turn for the better. *Had it really only taken one time for him to stand up to Nadeen and show her that he wore pants?* That's the way it seemed, but as Patsy would later learn, sometimes things are not as they seem. They are only disguised for a little while.

About a month after the run in with Brother Ryan, Kenny shocked everyone and said he was turning over a new leaf and going back to church. He asked Patsy and

Ann if they wanted to go. They both said yes. Kenny decided he was never even going back to visit at Greater Trials, because the whole place needed a revival from the pulpit to the parking lot. He said the only real Christian in the whole place was the Pastor's Wife, First Lady Craig. He chose to go his childhood Church, Deliverance Rock AME Zion Church.

Deliverance Rock was a small church but the Pastor was anointed. He was serious about the Word and he didn't hold back. When his members were in trouble he would pray with them right during service. Kenny had only brought them here a few times but he hadn't been in several months. When they stepped through the doors of Deliverance Rock, the Pastor, Grady Mack, was on fire! He sounded like he couldn't catch his breath and was trying to get a mouth full in between words. First Lady, Mack, had danced out of her hat and was kicking off her first shoe when they came in. The congregation was giving up the praise and worship. The men and women were running, speaking in tongues and jumping up and down, even the children were running!

Kenny began clapping as they walked to the pew seats. Patsy listened to her father as he called on the name of the Lord, It was something powerful and mighty about the sound of his voice. It sounded like it could shake the throne of Grace itself. To hear a man give God praise, there was something chain-breaking about that.

As the people lifted up the praise, Pastor Mack begin to walk the aisles, he was calling on those that needed to be delivered. He was calling on those who were drowning in a sea of sin. Those that wanted to be free but didn't have the strength to resist temptation. He was asking them to not care about the people in the church but to care about their soul's salvation. He was asking them to come down to the altar and give it to Jesus. They'd carried the burden too long and only Jesus could take it and set them free. He was looking up and down the aisles stretching out his hand.

All of a sudden he stopped, right in front of their pew. He looked at Kenny. Kenny took his hand and stepped over Ann and Patsy to get into the aisle. "Brother. You know Jesus. I know you do. You got a burden on you that's wearing you down. When are you going to give it to Jesus? You ought to be tired by now."

Kenny shook his head yes. He began to cry as he walked towards the altar holding Pastor Mack's hand. The church swelled with "Hallelujah's" and "Thank you Jesus!"

First Lady Mack and Pastor stood behind him. Pastor Mack put his hand on his back and he prayed out loud for Kenny to be empowered to resist the enemy and his tricks. He also prayed for his deliverance. Ann and Patsy just stood and cried, Patsy under her breath was saying "Thank you, Jesus!" Over and over again.

They didn't see Josie crawl out of the pew. The next thing they knew she was at the altar hugging Kenny with her little hands. He just held on to her. After service Pastor Mack encouraged Kenny to come back and to keep in touch with him. He gave him his card and said to call him any time he wanted to talk or to pray.

11

Kenny talked the entire ride home from church. He seemed to be so full of Joy and relief. "Girls. Your daddy got to get it together. The enemy don't want me and your momma to be happy but I'm not gonna let him destroy our family. I love that woman! She can act plumb nutty sometimes but I still love her."

He smiled when he said it as though he was remembering better times with them.

"I know I ain't always right but I'm trying. When I'm upstairs in my room all alone I pray. You didn't know that did you? I pray. I been asking God to take this off of me for a long time. I know one day he's gonna do it. Today just may be that day."

When they got home, Kenny changed clothes and announced he was cooking Sunday dinner. Patsy and Ann said yummy at the same time. Kenny was a good cook. He went to the back, changed into his cookin shirt that had holes in it and old stains from past cooking adventures. He put everyone out of the kitchen until he was finished. Nadeen was in her room when they came home. She didn't even know they were there until she opened her door and smelled the aroma coming from the kitchen. She walked up front to see who was cooking and saw it was Kenny. He looked at her and kept chopping.

"You can come up here if you want to, you might learn some tips from the master." Nadeen just sighed and sat down at the kitchen table. Neither one of them really knew how to break the silence but Kenny as usual was going to try and break it. "Went to Deliverance Rock today, the spirit was so high I swear the lights were blinking on and off to the beat of the drums."

"I see it got you in a good mood. It had to be the power of the anointing to make you come in and cook." Nadeen said jokingly.

"If the anointing can shut a lion's mouth, it can surely open yours so I can get some good cooking in it." They both laughed. The next sound Patsy heard was constant conversation, laughing and slamming of cabinets as Kenny prepared Sunday dinner. Nadeen even set the table for him. They were acting like a happily married couple. This rarely happened. *The anointing really was powerful,* thought Patsy.

Patsy wanted so much to believe that from this day forward things would be different. Kenny would be different, Nadeen would be different, as she was in the process of thinking and listening to so much happiness around her, she heard a voice cheerfully say,

"Come on up front and eat girls. It looks so good! Kenny put his toenails in this pot roast!" Things were going to be good just a little while longer it seemed, at least for today. Eight weeks later Kenny hadn't taken a drink. He'd been really trying and he was proud of himself for doing so well. He was attending church more often and had even become a Deacon. Patsy and Ann were so proud of him. Kenny was even thinking about taking Nadeen to the church ball. One Friday evening as darkness took over and everyone seemed to be cuddling in for the night, the phone rang. Patsy answered it.

"Hey, Patsy. It's Stanley. Your daddy at home?"

Patsy thought he was away in Rehab somewhere out of town. Kenny told them back in the summer he'd been court ordered to go into a Rehab program or face years in prison for getting high and breaking into his ex-wife's house. Patsy wanted to lie and tell him Kenny wasn't home. She wanted to tell him the Kenny he was looking for moved out months ago. No one at this house by that name, but instead she reluctantly told him.

"Yes. He's home."

"Let me talk to him. My baby brother Jerome is in town and he wants to see him. Tell him we gonna watch the game and talk about old times."

"Hold on a minute." Patsy walked as slow as she could down the hall to where Kenny was relaxing drinking homemade soup in a cup. "Kenny. Mr. Stanley is on the phone. He said he wants to talk to you. His baby brother is home and wants to see you."

Kenny looked at her for a minute.

"Tell him I'm not available right now. I'll give him a call later when I have time." Patsy was glad to take that message back. Maybe Kenny finally realized Stanley was bad news. He needed to be dumped in an ocean of the blood of Jesus. He needed to go all the way under the baptismal pool waters and stay for a while as far as Patsy was concerned. Patsy went back to the phone, "Mr. Stanley, my daddy can't come to the phone right now. He'll call you back later."

"All right. I'm gonna wait on him to call. Jerome is gonna be here until the end of the month and I want us to get together. Talk to you later. Be good."

Be good? You be good! Patsy thought. When she hung up the phone she went to the back. She was always able to talk to Kenny and she wanted to tell him how she felt about Stanley. "Kenny, I need to talk to you."

"About what, baby?"

"About Mr. Stanley. I don't like him. He's bad news to me. He always seems to be around when something bad happens. It's like he's in the background just watching and waiting. He's not your friend to me."

"Baby me and Stanley been friends since high school. We been in a lot of devilment together. He use to be kinda sweet on your Aunt Ernestine. He all right. He just has some issues but so do I. Stanley and I both are gonna be just fine."

A few hours later, Nadeen got up to get ready for her shift at Gardens of Peace. Kenny made sure she had lunch ready. Josie kissed her goodnight and she was off. As soon as she'd gone out of the door, the phone rang, Patsy thought it was Dustin. She picked up the phone.

"Hey, girl. Where your daddy at? He was suppose to call hours ago."

"Who is this?"

"This his boy Jerome, Stanley's brother. I'm in town and I want to see him. I got a deck of cards waiting on him. Go get him for me and tell him his boy on the phone."

"I think he sleep," Patsy knew she was lying but she didn't feel good about Jerome calling either.

"Girl, your daddy ain't never went to sleep this early. Now go get him! I know your momma gone. He up probably looking for something to do!"

Patsy put down the phone and went into the kitchen where Kenny was reading his Sunday School book.

"Kenny, Mr. Jerome on the phone for you."

"Jerome? I haven't talked to him in some time. Guess it wouldn't hurt. Bring me the phone." Patsy brought him the phone but she took her time doing it. When she gave it to him, she went to her bedroom with Ann and Josie. She just waited to hear the outcome of the conversation. She was starting to feel dread deep inside the navel of her belly.

A few minutes later, Kenny came down the hall and knocked on their door.

"Girls, I'm gonna go out with Jerome for a little while and play some cards. When Nadeen calls, tell her I went out and I'll give her a call when I get back. Don't want her to worry." Not long after that, the front door bell rang and Kenny walked out.

Patsy and Ann had been worried about Kenny when he didn't come back before Nadeen came back home. Patsy didn't have a good feeling about this and even Josie seem to be fussy. She was walking through the house calling for him. She just kept crying and looking in his room but he wasn't there. Nadeen didn't say a word about it but her actions said plenty. She was snapping at Ann for every little thing and slamming doors. It would be three days before they saw him again and the man they saw was not the man that had left.

When the doorbell rang, Patsy knew, she just knew, it was him. Nadeen went to the door. Ann and Patsy went behind her. When she opened the door there was a police officer and Kenny was with him. His name was Mr. Butler. Mr. Butler lived in their neighborhood. He was a nice guy, married with twins, a girl and a boy. Patsy sometimes saw them outside playing in the yard.

When Nadeen opened the security door, he tipped his hat and said, "Mrs. Simmons. I decided to bring your husband home instead of lock him up. I found him inside a warehouse downtown. Looks like some others had been there with him. He was pretty strung out. I found his wallet, empty of course, but it had his ID in it. I thought I recognized him so I decided to give him a break this time. He asked me to take him to his Pastor but I thought it best he sleep this off before going to see him."

"Thank you officer Butler. I appreciate it so much. Me and the girls were so worried about him." She said sweetly.

"Mr. Simmons you got yourself a real sweet, Christian wife here. You need to get off that stuff and leave those dead beat friends of yours alone."

"Sweet as pie officer. Sweet as pie. Kenny said, as he walked past the officer and Nadeen. "Hey babies." He said to Patsy, Ann and Josie as he walked by. "I messed up. I know. I never should have went with Jerome. I'm sorry girls. I let him convince me to take one drink with him and the next thing you know I'm looking up at a police officer. He must have put something in that beer. I only had two. I think."

Kenny stumbled past them towards the back. Nadeen smiled at the officer as she closed the front door then she walked past them.

Instantly, a familiar sick feeling formed in the pit of Patsy's stomach. The spirit of fear paralyzed Patsy so bad she couldn't move. She felt tears coming up in her eyes. She wanted to run but her feet wouldn't move. She wanted to run out the door and get officer Butler. She wanted to beg him to please come back. Come back and help her daddy 'cause he wasn't going to help himself. Come back and protect them because Nadeen wasn't the angel she seemed, but she couldn't move.

Ann looked at her and said she was going to go sit on the back porch. She took Josie with her. A few minutes later Patsy heard Nadeen come out of her room. She heard her cussing at Kenny as she headed up the stairs where he was. *God. Please let Kenny have that door locked.* She heard the door hit the wall and then slam. The next thing she heard was a lot of knocking around and bumping against walls. Nadeen was cussing and she could hear the sound of slapping against flesh. She heard Kenny telling

Nadeen to stop. Patsy was afraid. She ran up the stairs. She didn't care about the price she would have to pay. She burst in the room and he was in a corner.

Nadeen was standing over him with a large lamp over her head, "I'm gonna bust your head wide open! I hate you. I hate you so much!"

Just as she was about to bring the lamp crashing down on his head, Patsy grabbed it. She screamed as tears ran down her face.

"Stop! Leave my daddy alone. He didn't do anything to you!"

Nadeen spun around as Patsy grabbed the lamp from her grasp.

"Girl, you better get out of here before I stomp a mud hole in you big enough to plant potatoes in! This sorry excuse of a man has the nerve to come into my house after three days of being out doing God knows what with God knows who. Bringing those demonic spirits in here! He gonna keep on and I'm gonna kill him! I promise you that! You hear me Kenny Simmons? I'm gonna kill you one day and send you straight to the hell you in such a hurry to get to! She yelled as the veins popped out of both sides of her temple.

Kenny just sat there on the floor with blood running down his head from where she'd hit him with something earlier in the struggle. *Why did he never fight back? If he never fights back she'll kill him.* Nadeen turned to Patsy and started out the door, she grabbed Patsy by her shirt.

"And you bring your smart mouth on to me! You don't get in my business! You hear me? Go get me those branches and wrap'em! I'm gonna teach you a lesson today!"

Patsy—just like Kenny—didn't say a word. She just went. She knew what was coming. It wouldn't be the first time she'd take a beating for Kenny. It was the price she had to pay. Ann peeped out the door with a sad look on her face as Patsy went by. She apparently eased back in the house while Patsy was upstairs trying to stop Nadeen from putting Kenny in a coma or a pine box.

Patsy went and got the branches. They were braided tight. She knew it would draw blood and scar up her skin. As she headed back to Nadeen's room, she heard her yell down the hall "Bring your grown behind to me! Move! You ran up there to help that piece of trash then you need to run in here! I'm gonna give you some business to get in and I bet you remember next time to stay out of mine!" Patsy stepped into the room and handed her the twisted branches, "Strip!" Patsy took off everything except her underwear. "Panties too! You will learn today!" As soon as the last word came out of her mouth Nadeen let the branches come down across her back. Patsy screamed. It felt like hot tongs. The branches hit her right between her legs. It felt like a hot poker slid across her most delicate, precious piece of fruit. Patsy crumbled to the floor. She was trying to cover this part of her body. She couldn't protect any other.

She felt Nadeen push her in her back with her foot. She was yelling at her but Patsy couldn't hear above the pain between her legs. She was crying so loud she couldn't hear anything but she felt pain everywhere. As she beat Patsy Nadeen kept yelling, "I won't have this spirit in my house! I won't have it! I will beat it out of you or die trying."

Nadeen probably would have beat her all night if it hadn't been for Eva. She had come by to see if they wanted to go to the movies with her and David. Ann must have opened the door, Eva heard Patsy screaming for her life. Patsy heard the door slam open and thought maybe Kenny had come to help her, then she heard the voice from heaven.

"Nadeen! What is wrong with you beating that girl like that?" Eva grabbed the branches from Nadeen. "Have you lost your mind? I'm sure she didn't do anything to deserve this!" She pushed Nadeen to the bed then came over to Patsy and put her arms on her shoulders. "Patsy. Baby. Come on. Get up."

She helped Patsy to her feet. Patsy was in a lot of pain.

"Put on your clothes if you can, baby, and go to your room. I'll be there in a minute to see about you."

Patsy didn't even look in Nadeen's direction. She knew this wasn't finished. Aunt Eva had just interrupted it. It would be just a matter of time, a small infraction and it would be picked up where it was left off.

Patsy closed the door behind her and went to her bedroom. Ann was sitting on the bed with Josie digging in her leg. While holding Josie. They both had been crying.

"Nadeen. You didn't have to beat that girl like that! She's a good child. I know she hasn't done anything to warrant all those whips on her body. You act like you done forgot how bad momma use to beat us with that mule whip butt naked on a cold dirt floor for nothing!" Eva yelled at Nadeen.

"Most of the time she was just mad at Daddy, but she took it out on us! She even burned me one time on my back. I still got the mark on me to this day! Said I moved too slow when she told me to go hang out some clothes on the line. I was eleven years old! Now here you go beating your children the same way momma beat us and from what I been told you knockin' Kenny around too! One day he is gonna stand up and knock you out! I won't care if he does. Because you deserve it! You are mean and hateful just like your momma!"

"Get out of my house, Eva! How you gonna come in my house and tell me about myself and you ain't no better! The only reason you came back home was because you know the law looking for you in Arizona! You done got mad at that man for seeing another woman and shot him in his face! You killed him! How are you any better than me?"

"Don't go spitting out something in anger you might regret. Nadeen! Shut up before I make you shut up! Better yet, it's been enough blood shed around here today so I'm gonna leave. Don't make me come back over here for you actin a fool like your momma!" Eva yelled back at Nadeen as she turned to leave the bedroom.

She threw the branches down at Nadeen's feet. As Eva walked out the door she said, "I ain't playing with the Lord Nadeen. God knows who I am and everyone that knows me know who I am. I ain't perfect and don't pretend to be. I have to go to the altar every Sunday about something. I repent daily! But you, you are deceitful and they got a special place in hell for folks like you Sister Simmons!" Eva slammed the bedroom door and walked down the hall.

"Patsy you call me if you need me sweetie and Kenny Simmons I be glad when you get set free, put your pants back on and take control of your woman and this house!"

Patsy heard Nadeen in her bedroom. "I like her nerves! coming into my house and telling me what to do with my daughter! I ain't nothing like momma! I ain't nothing like that crazy woman! She almost made me and Eva lose our minds in that house. How can Eva forget that? If it were not for the grace of God, I would be in a mental hospital right now. I'm gonna raise my kids right and I ain't gonna have a husband that won't respect the God in me!" She yelled as she slammed her bedroom door.

Ann tried to help Patsy take care of the cuts on her back. Patsy was balled up with her hands between her legs. The pain was so bad she couldn't speak. She just laid there softly crying.

As Ann applied a warm towel to Patsy's cuts she just kept wishing God would take Nadeen away. *Why wouldn't God take her away? Surely he saw the things she did?* Ann thought to herself. She felt the urge to cut. She wanted to cut her nervousness and sadness out of her. She wanted a razor to cut away what had just happened to her sister. While it inflicted pain, it felt good in a weird way. Patsy prayed to make it through but Ann cut. She cut because she couldn't scream loud enough to get the pain out of her body. She cut because prayer wasn't working for her. God wasn't listening to her cries in prayer so maybe he would hear them in pain.

Ann recalled that Pastor Mack always said God sat high and looked low so surely he could see into the Simmons's House. When was he gonna wash away all their tears? When was he gonna take away their pain? When was he gonna set Kenny free and let him be the daddy they needed? Why was Patsy moaning on the bed and burning so bad between her legs if God was so merciful and good? Mercy and Goodness was supposed to follow you all the days of your life according to the Bible, but right now Ann was thinking they must have got side tracked because they couldn't have been behind her big sister or her daddy after what just took place in that house.

12

Getting dressed for school the next day was hard for Patsy. Kenny knocked on the door to wake them up. He'd come in and talked to Patsy for a few minutes. He told her he was so sorry about what Nadeen did to her. It was uncalled for.

"I don't know what they teaching her at that church but it ain't Jesus! She leave home cussing and she come back home cussin'! I know I messed up, baby. I never should have gone with Stanley. I think they put something in my beer. I really do. I just had two and the next thing I know, I was in a warehouse dazed and confused without my wallet. I'm done with that part of my life, Patsy. I promise you that. I didn't mean for this to happen to you. I'm so sorry. You don't have to fight my battles, baby. God does that."

"I just wanted her to stop. She uses those same hands to pass out communion at church. How can she be so mean if she supposed to be a Saint?"

"We all got demons, Patsy. Some of us look them straight in the eye and deal with them and some of us turn our backs and refuse to admit they behind us pulling our strings. If I had listened to God that night when he told me in that still soft voice to stay home I wouldn't be in this mess and you wouldn't be hurting this morning. I had to convince myself that I was strong enough alone to hang out with them but I wasn't and the Holy Spirit warned me but I didn't listen. I chose to lean to my own understanding of my strength and found out just how weak I really was. I regret it now. Seeing you hurting makes me regret it."

He reached to hug her but she jumped back. Her entire back and arms were covered in whips she couldn't bear to be touched. He put his hands down and hung his head sadly.

Ann tried to help Patsy put on a long sleeve shirt for school that morning to hide the whips. She had a large whip between her legs and across the inside of her thighs it burned really bad. Patsy tried soaking in a tub of warm water last night to ease the pain but it stung so bad she had to get out. She wouldn't be dressing out in gym class for several days. As a matter of fact, she would probably volunteer to work in the office for the next two weeks. The secretary liked her, she would let her work there as many days as she liked.

"It's okay. I knew she was mad and I knew it was going to be a bad day when the police officer brought you home." Kenny leaned over and kissed her on the only spot that didn't hurt, the top of her head.

"Keep praying for me baby. God is going to take care of me and he's going to change your momma. He's gonna do it for his Glory. I been knowing the Lord a long time. He save my life once before so I know he got something else for me." He pinched Patsy's jaw as he left.

Ann finished helping Patsy get dressed. Patsy noticed Ann limping a little bit. "Ann what's wrong with you? Why you walking like that? One of us bruises is enough around here." Ann tried to pull her gown down past her mid-thigh.

"Nothing. I just slept too hard on one side I guess." She said without looking her sister in the eye. A voice in Patsy's head told her otherwise. She looked closer at Ann's thigh.

"Ann you been cutting yourself again? Ann you gotta stop that. You gonna hurt yourself real bad one day. Please stop." Patsy asked in a pleading tone of voice. Ann just ignored her and buttoned up her shirt for her. When she finished she went into the bathroom. She didn't want to talk to Patsy about this shameful, evil thing she couldn't stop.

When Patsy made it to school, she took her time walking off the bus, As her foot landed on the last stair, she saw Dustin. When he met her at the door of the bus, he looked into her eyes and knew something was wrong.

"What's wrong Patsy? Something happen at home?" She tried to find the words to tell him but they wouldn't come out. He touched her arm and she jumped, "Ouch!"

"Your mother beat you again, Patsy?" She nodded slowly. Dustin took her by the arm and led her to his car. "Come on with me. Get in."

"I can't, Dustin. If I leave school and my mother finds out she'll hurt me worse and then she'll hurt you!"

"Patsy. Get in the car." He opened the door. She stood by the door.

"I can't!"

"Yes you can. Get in the car. I'm gonna go to the office and talk to your counselor. I'll be right back."

Patsy gently eased onto the car seat. Dustin walked off towards the principal's office. He was gone for about twenty minutes. When he came back he said, "I spoke to Mrs. Morgan. It's fine with her. She talked to the principal. I told them I was gonna take you home and let my mom take a look at you so she could put something on those whips then we would come right back to school.

She called my mom to make sure she was home and explained the situation to her. My mom said to bring you over immediately."

Patsy got in the car and closed the door. When they pulled up at Dustin's mother's house, she was standing on the front porch in a thick royal blue sweater. She had beautiful soft jet black hair that hung down her back. She walked down the stairs toward them as they got out the car. She had the most beautiful hazel colored eyes Patsy had ever seen. She went over to Patsy and took her hand.

"Come on sweetie. Momma Jessie is gonna take good care of you now. She's gonna make it all better for you." Patsy walked slowly up the stairs. She was still burning between her legs where Nadeen hit her. The jeans were a little tight so they rubbed her. She wanted to cry even then. She went with Dustin's mother into her bedroom.

"Patsy you gonna have to take your clothes off for me so I can rub you down with this salve. okay?"

"Yes, ma'am," Patsy replied respectfully. Ms. Jessie stuck her head out of her bedroom door, "Dustin. Bring me a cloth, a bowl of warm water and some antiseptic. " Dustin knocked on the door. Jessie cracked it a little and took the items she'd asked Dustin for. She covered Patsy with warm towels she'd soaked in vinegar. She put a smelly brown salve on the open wounds on her back and arms. It felt so good. So healing. She continued this until she had done almost all parts of Patsy's body

"Your momma she hit you down there? I saw the way you walked up those stairs."

"Yes, ma'am." Patsy was ashamed to tell anyone. She hadn't even told Dustin that.

"It's okay, sweetie. We both females in here. I hope she didn't do any other damage to you. You haven't been with my son in that way have you? You know what I'm talking about?"

"No, I haven't Ms. Jessie. Me and Dustin been trying to keep ourselves. I promise"

"I'm just asking honey cause that is a delicate flower you have and it could easily be ruptured. I'm gonna have to put this warm towel down there with some antiseptic and a warm paste to help the scars heal. You gotta be strong cause it's gonna sting like a bee hive. "

Patsy thought she'd braced herself but when Ms. Jessie placed the antiseptic soaked towel on her she wanted to scream and jump off that bed. It seemed like it took forever for the stinging to stop. Patsy bit her lip. When Ms. Jessie removed the towel, she told her she could get up and get dressed. While Patsy was getting dressed, Ms. Jessie went across the room and came back with a bottle of oil.

"Do you believe in Jesus?"

"Yes, ma'am, I do."

"You believe he can heal you and your momma from whatever hurt and pain you have inside of you?"

Patsy couldn't answer because she wasn't sure about Nadeen. Ms. Jessie smiled at her, "Do you mind if I pray over you and anoint you?"

Patsy shook her head. "No. I don't mind."

Ms. Jessie touched her forehead—her hand was warm and the oil was soothing. She began to pray. Patsy released years of anguish in those few moments. Dustin's mother put the bottle of oil down and held Patsy in her arms. She whispered something in Patsy's ear that Patsy would remember years later.

When she released Patsy she kissed her and told her "It's done. You just believe it and walk in it. My son got him a cute little girlfriend. You so nice and respectful. I'm glad I got to finally meet you, I just hate it was under these circumstances."

She walked them back to the door, "Patsy. Pray for your momma. She got something bad down on the inside of her and it ain't personal against you. Sometimes children see things when their growing up. They experience things that they can't shake off when they become adults. It's like a curse. It just keeps growing inside of them and it passes on to the next generation. Pray for her. God will deliver."

She kissed Dustin on the jaw and went back inside. Dustin blushed, and got in the car. Your mom is nice. I hate I had to meet her like this."

"She reminds me of you. She's my sunshine."

When they made it back, Patsy went straight to class and tried her best to sit down. When it came time for gym class she went to the office to get an excuse and before she could even ask, the secretary said, "I left some papers for you to type up for me. Might take you about a week to finish all of it."

Her counselor, Mrs. Morgan, walked by and very gently touched her on her back. "Take your time and finish that Patsy. I've already told your gym teacher you're gonna be out." She winked and said.

Dustin must have told them what happened, Patsy thought, but it was okay. She knew he was just looking out for her and she appreciated it.

When Patsy got home, Kenny asked her if she wanted to go to Bible Study with him. Even though she really wanted to lay down she told him she would go. Ann and Josie went too. Patsy wanted so bad to tell Kenny what Ann was doing to herself but she couldn't. On the way to the church, Kenny talked to Patsy.

"Baby, I just want to tell you again how sorry I am about what your momma did to you the other day. She was angry with me for slipping up. I was angry at myself, but you know I can't hit your momma. That's not right."

"I know. You tell us that all the time. You won't hit her but you let her almost kill you. Why do you stay?" Patsy asked, about to cry.

"Husbands and wives have their problems, Patsy. One day you'll see. She had a rough childhood. I guess she hasn't healed from all that. She got a temper like your grandma Ruth."

"Grandma? Grandma Ruth ain't got no bad temper. She don't even raise her voice at us." Kenny laughed.

"Your Grandma Ruth has plenty temper. You all just don't get to see it. The teeth in that ole lion has softened over the years but she still keep' em sharp! Once when I was dating Nadeen, I was over at the house and Ms. Ruth was making a cake. She asked Nadeen to bring her something from the cupboard, a measuring cup or a bowl or something. Well Nadeen took her time getting up from that chair and the next thing I know, when she got up on your grandma, Ms. Ruth hit her so hard with a pan that it drew blood from Nadeen's nose. I just sat there in shock. She looked at Nadeen and told her, "When I tell you to get up and get me something you get up right then, you hear me? You don't drag about it! I'll knock you into that front yard!" Kenny said it with his teeth ground together. It scared Patsy a little bit.

"What did momma do?" Ann asked.

"She didn't do anything and your granddaddy didn't either. He just stood there looking at her about to cry. You could see it hurt him but he never said a word. Nadeen just wiped the blood from her nose. That's why she has that small scar on the side of her nose to this day. Ms. Ruth looked at me like I better not have anything to say about it or she would do the same thing to me." They all laughed at that. "Ms. Ruth had even your granddaddy at her beck and call. If she said she wanted something he got it."

"Granddaddy was always so quiet." Ann said. "He liked to be outside. One time before he died I saw him outside planting in the garden and he took his shirt off. He had this real big circle on his chest it was real dark like a burn or something."

"That was courtesy of your Grandma too. One day not long after Nadeen and I'd gotten married we'd gone over to their house to eat dinner. Your grandmother was setting the table and the house phone rang, well your grandmother went to answer it and the person on the other end asked to speak to your Granddaddy. Ms. Ruth called him to the phone. He was looking a little nervous when he got on it.

He mumbled a few words and hung up. He didn't even look at Ms. Ruth, but Ms. Ruth was looking at him. She was frying some grease in a skillet to make some cornbread, as he walked by her to go out on the back porch, she slung that hot grease straight on his chest. As he tore out the door she screamed behind him, "You run and tell your church tramp that! Tell her she don't know me. I don't play that! I will not be disrespected in my own house!" Nadeen was crying and running behind her daddy. She helped him get the shirt off even though the skin was coming off with it. We had to take him to the doctor.

When the doctor asked what happened He told him that he bumped into a hot skillet. The doctor looked at him for a minute then put some old funny smelling crème on him and told him to stay out of the way of skillets for a while. When he got back home Ms. Ruth was on the front porch shelling peas, drinking ice tea and listening to the ole time gospel hour radio show. Your grandpa just went in the house and laid down. Few days later, we went by to check on him and she was fixing his plate for him and getting his newspaper like nothing ever happened. He say the day Ms. Ruth burnt him, he knew it was gonna be ugly after that woman called. She was an old girlfriend of his from when he was about seventeen years old.

"She was a widow at their church now and would call him sometimes to act like she needed some help around the house. She did it just to get at Ms. Ruth 'cause she knew she didn't like her. Ms. Ruth would roll her eyes at the woman while they was in the church. Your grandpa tried to tell her the woman was just a friend in need and it had been over thirty years since he courted the woman.

"But when Grandpa died a few years ago, Nadeen had to hold her to keep her from jumping into the grave with him. She was screaming and calling his name. Begging him to get up."

"Well, Ann, I guess she did love him in her own sick way. They never left each other. He told me once that Ms. Ruth just got a hot temper 'cause her momma was so rough. Her momma would beat them with an extension cord while they were wet from the bathtub and quote scripture while doing it. Her daddy left them when Ms. Ruth was real young. He ran off to Miami with a young girl. She beat Ms. Ruth up until your granddaddy married her at twenty years old.

They'd talked so much that they got to Deliverance Rock in no time at all. Pastor and First Lady Mack were calling everyone up for the prayer circle.

When they got to the circle, Pastor Mack asked Kenny to pray. He opened his mouth and everyone bowed their heads. He put a word of prayer at the foot of the Lord that was so powerful First Lady almost shook Patsy's arm out of socket. She was trying not to brake that prayer circle and run. When he finished everyone let out a loud Amen! When Bible study was over, First Lady Mack called Kenny back up to the altar. She anointed his head right over the scar from where Nadeen had hit him. Then she held his hand.

She began to pray for him. While she was praying, God began to speak to Patsy. She just knew it was him. He opened her eyes right there in that sanctuary. She looked upon her daddy and saw what seemed like smoky gray old clothes upon him, then the Lord spoke to her, *Look at him. Look at him and see death. Satan is trying to take his soul. He wants him. You must pray for him.*

"I will." Patsy said in a whispered voice. She couldn't wait to get home. She needed to go into her prayer closet.

13

When they arrived home it was dark in the house. Nadeen was asleep. They'd stopped by Denise's Diner and ate till they were about to bust. Kenny brought Nadeen her favorite, turkey necks and rice with a roll. Patsy took Josie to the back to watch television with Ann. She told them she needed a few minutes of privacy. There was a strange feeling inside of her belly and her mind just kept telling her she needed to go and pray. It was so strong she couldn't ignore it. She went to the bedroom she shared with her sisters and locked the door. She opened the closet and unfolded her prayer blanket.

She laid out on the blanket, prostate before the Lord. Patsy prayed for Kenny and Ann both. She refused to let the enemy take them. She must have gotten pretty loud in there because after a while she heard Nadeen yelling across the hall. "Patsy. You need to stop all that loud talking. Who you talking to in there?"

Patsy finished her petition before the Lord and got up. She felt like she'd been fighting. She didn't mind. She'd also prayed for Nadeen. God was the only one that could change her. Anyway, Kenny would have told her that it was the right thing to do. Kenny had his own burdens that were trying to take him out, but he kept reaching for Jesus in the midst of the mud!

When Patsy came out of the room, Kenny was talking to Nadeen. "Are you going to slow down long enough to talk about us?"

Nadeen didn't acknowledge his question; she just walked out the door. Kenny decided he'd call Nadeen at work on her lunch break and try to talk to her. He wanted so bad for them to be a normal happy family. He tried over and over again to get free from what was trying to take away everything he'd worked so hard for. He wanted to tell her that he'd cut off his friendship with Stanley because he realized he'd left him in a bad place. He was trying to beat this thing if she would just be the Woman of God to him that she was to everyone else. When he called for her, the night manager said she wasn't there. Kenny said she needed to check one of the other sections of the nursing home because she'd left for work a few hours ago and should be there by now. The supervisor said she would check and if she located her would have her to call him. Kenny sat by the phone all night, when he opened his eyes again it was morning.

The phone hadn't rang. A few minutes later, Nadeen came through the door telling Ann and Patsy to get the house cleaned before leaving for school. Kenny came into the kitchen on his way to work. He put his jacket on the table. He turned and looked at her sadly.

"I called your job last night. I wanted to talk to you about something very important. For some reason the night manager said she couldn't find you. She said she was going to locate you and have you call home. What happened?"

Nadeen began moving around nervously straightening out the napkins on the table.

"By the time she found me. I was in another dorm and we had to do inventory. It took all night. I was too busy to call you. You know I'm trying to get that permanent supervisor position at work. I can't slip up."

"Well. I really need to talk to you. If you're awake when I come home tonight we need to have a serious discussion." He turned to Ann and Patsy.

"Come on, girls. Put that stuff down and get in the truck. You can do that when you get home. Nadeen, you really need to stop making such demands on these kids. If you stop running every time your Pastor calls, you can take care of things at home. That man got a woman and it ain't you. Did you know that?" Kenny narrowed his eyes at Nadeen as they headed out the door. The only thing Patsy heard after that was Nadeen yelling.

"Who do you think you are to tell me what to do for God?" Kenny slammed the door on his way out. Patsy and Ann grabbed their book bags and ran out behind him.

"Thanks, Daddy. We were going to get it this morning. Cause there was no way we were gonna get all that done without missing the bus."

"People live in houses. They're supposed to be dirty sometimes. It's all right. Go to school and make me proud. Come on. I'll take you both this morning."

They jumped in the front seat with Kenny. Ann put the radio on the reggae station and they rocked that truck all the way to school. It was the best school morning of their lives.

When Patsy and Ann got home that afternoon, Grandma Ruth was there. They ran over to her car and got in.

"Hey, grandbabies. You looking just like me and your momma more every day. She called me this morning and asked me to watch you all today. She said she got called in at the last minute for an emergency so she had to go in early. We going to have a good time today girls. I'm gonna bake you a homemade cake, some biscuits, steak, rice and gravy! I know that's your favorite."

It had been a few months since they'd been over to spend time with Grandma Ruth. She was usually busy with her church organizations and the casino so she wasn't at home a lot. She liked to go to the casino. Sometimes she would take her bill money and go. When she didn't win she would come back home and say "The Lord giveth and the Lord taketh away." Somehow, to Patsy, that never added up. Why would you gamble and take a chance on losing your money? Pastor Mack always said it was more important to pay your tithes and trust in God; Give him his blessings and he would give you yours. Nadeen always paid her tithes and her offerings. She always made sure they had offering money too. When they got to Grandma Ruth's house, they noticed she had gotten it painted and even built on a sunroom. Grandpa made sure she was taken care of when he left this world.

"Grandma," Ann said, "Your house is so pretty. I see you got a new room added on. It looks so big."

Grandma Ruth turned off the ignition and sat in the car a few minutes looking at her home.

"Your Grandpa did that for me baby. He took good care of me. He always did. I loved that man. Sometimes I acted up a little bit with him but I know the Lord understand."

"Maybe what Kenny told us was true about grandma after all," Ann whispered to Patsy.

"Get Josie, girls, and get out the car. Let me show you the new room. I painted it blue. It's got cute little kittens on the border."

Patsy couldn't wait to see the room. It was filled with pictures of Grandma Ruth's past. The picture of her mother was intriguing to Patsy. She was Patsy's great-grandmother but she looked just like Nadeen. Her eyes seemed to hold a secret. Her hair was neatly wrapped in a bun. Her smile even looked like Nadeen's. It held a dangerous nature behind it. Patsy knew it well. It was the door into a place you would never want to go with Nadeen so it was best not to turn it into a frown.

"Patsy come up here and help me in this kitchen. You can look at those pictures later. That room is full of all the saints in our family that has come before us."

Patsy decided they would sleep in this room the next time they stayed over. She wanted to get to know her mother's family tree maybe she could better understand her.

"Coming, Grandma Ruth!" They helped Grandma Ruth in the kitchen and sat down to a good home cooked meal. Grandma sure could cook. They helped her clean up and was just about to sweep up the floor when they heard Nadeen come through the door.

"Hey, Momma," she never hugged Grandma like they did when they came over.

"Hey, Nadeen. You get your business taken care of?"

"Yes, ma'am, I did. Thanks for watching the girls." Her voice sounded a little different, kind of like a little girl being real careful what she said.

"They good girls, I don't mind. I never have any problems out of them. If I did though you know I can put them back in line real quick don't you?" She said as she winked at Nadeen. Nadeen didn't reply back to her she just began to get their things together. "Come give Grandma a hug. Come back and see me. I'm so lonely since your Grandpa went to heaven. I miss that man so much. I'll never find another man like that to put up with my funny ways."

Nadeen just looked at her. "Come on, girls. Let's go. I gotta get to the house and get some rest."

As she walked past them, Patsy smelled a funny odor like a man's cologne. She guessed Nadeen must have had to get up close and personal with a patient again because she'd smelled that odor before. When they got home Kenny was already there. He was cooking dinner and seemed to be in deep thought. "Hey daddy." Josie said. She was the first in the house.

"Hey daddy's baby girl. Where you been?"

"We went to grandma's" Ann said.

"Oh, okay. By the way, Nadeen, I came home early today so we could talk instead of waiting till this evening and you weren't here. I drove by the church office too and didn't see your car in the parking lot. I thought you went to the church during the day?"

"I went shopping with Jean. She called about a sale on some towels and stuff and I went to window shop with her. Why you questioning me anyway? I don't question you when you stay gone all night." She snapped at him.

"No need to get defensive girl. I was just wondering. I told you we got something important to talk about."

"I don't want to talk. I don't feel like it. I'm tired. I'm going to take a nap." Nadeen walked out the room. Patsy wondered why Grandma just didn't say Nadeen had gone shopping if that was where she was? She said she had to go to work early due to an emergency. Something didn't sound quite right.

A week before Thanksgiving holidays, this story would come back to haunt Patsy and she would see things a little bit clearer. Nadeen had gone to work early again, said she had a patient emergency and her manager needed her immediately. Kenny was home watching television with them. Thirty minutes after she left, Kenny got up and got his keys. He told them he would be back in a few hours.

Patsy looked up at him with worry in her face, "Where you going?"

She was scared he was about to get into something bad.

"Don't worry, baby. I just gotta go check out something for myself. I'll be back real soon."

Patsy started praying right then. She didn't know Kenny had already spoken with Nadeen's manager.

14

A n hour later, Kenny came back home. He came in the house slamming things around. Patsy was too scared to look out the door so she just put her ear to the door.

"I can't believe she would do this! I just can't believe she would do this! After I warned her what I would do if I found out she had been fooling around with him!"

Oh, God, thought Patsy. *Nadeen got been busted. Please don't let it be Brother Ryan. That would be so shameful!*

A few minutes later Nadeen came in behind him. She was firecracker hot! *She was the one that had been caught so why was she mad? She ought to be glad Kenny didn't go over the deep end.* Patsy thought.

"How dare you call yourself sneaking around following me! You went looking for it and you found it! When you're out all times of the night I don't go looking for you!"

"You supposed to be such a God-fearing woman and you out laying around with a member of your own church Nadeen? That's a shame before God. This the same man that stood before the church and said the Lord done called him to preach the gospel!" Kenny yelled at her.

"He's just a man, Kenny! Just a good church friend...a...prayer partner. Besides, I stopped loving you a long time ago. I was just waiting till I had some other things in order before I asked you for a divorce!"

Patsy's heart began to beat fast *A divorce? That would mean they would be all alone with her.* Patsy thought.

"You being tricked, Nadeen, and you don't even know it! You're gonna regret having an affair!"

"I don't have to regret anything! I'm not having an affair. I just know God wants me to be happy!"

"You blind, Nadeen!"

"Well I might be. But I hope you can see I don't want you anymore! Can you see that?" She ran down the hall to her bedroom and locked the door. Kenny beat on the door hard as he could

"You open this door or I'll bust it down!"

"If you bust it down you will regret it. I promise you that!" Nadeen shouted through her door. Patsy knew that tone of voice. It fertilized the fruit of fear that always starting growing inside her belly. She stepped out of her room and grabbed him by the arm.

"Stop, Daddy!" Patsy begged. She was scared for him.

"You better tell him, Patsy. If you want to see your daddy in the morning. You better tell him to get away from my door!"

Patsy knew something bad would happen. She used every bit of strength she had in her body but couldn't push him. She grabbed onto his pants leg and slid down his body until she hit the floor.

"Please, Kenny. Please move away from the door. If she hurts you I just can't live any longer. Ann was standing in the door scratching at the old scars in the bend of her arm from where she had first started cutting herself.

Kenny looked down at Patsy.

"I'm gonna go, baby girl. I'm gonna go and not bother the Head usher of Greater Trials MB Church anymore."

He walked away and went upstairs to the spare bedroom. Patsy walked to the door and could hear him crying. Patsy didn't sleep that night. She just listened. She listened for every little sound. She heard Kenny moving back and forth in the hall. He would stop in front of their door then go back up the hall. The last time she heard him he seemed to be looking for something in the bathroom cabinets.

The next thing she remembered hearing was Josie's screams. She was screaming and crying so loud it woke everyone up. Nadeen tore open her door, then the door to their room.

"Where is Josie?"

Patsy jumped up, she felt over Ann to the edge of the bed. *No Josie! Where was Josie? Was that her screaming?* Patsy jumped up pulled her mind together and went towards the screams. Kenny was on the floor hitting Josie in the back. She was foaming at the mouth.

"Call 911! Call 911 right now! She's dying! She's dying!" His voice cracked and sounded tired when he cried out to Patsy.

Patsy called 911 and sent Ann next door to wake up Mrs. Wilson. Mrs. Wilson was a retired pediatrician. She would know what to do.

"Oh, Lord. What's wrong with my baby?" Nadeen screamed. She pushed Kenny back and grabbed Josie out of Kenny's hands. She started shaking Josie and crying. She put her finger in her mouth.

"What's in your mouth, Josie? What did you swallow? What did you take?" Josie couldn't answer. She was too busy throwing up and screaming herself. Mrs.

Wilson made it and took Josie from Nadeen. She put her nose towards Josie's mouth and sniffed.

"It smells like Drano or something," she said frantically. "Move back let me rinse out her mouth."

She rushed Josie to the bathroom sink and began rinsing her mouth out with warm water. "Bring me some cold milk with ice chips. That may help. We have to get this out and coat her stomach."

Kenny got up from the floor with a look of fear in his eyes and ran to get the milk from the kitchen along with a cold towel to wipe Josie's face. The ambulance made it a few minutes later. They found the cap of Drano on the floor turned over.

"She's ingested poison. We got to get her to the hospital now," they said.

"Oh Lord! Please save my baby!" Nadeen was screaming.

Kenny ran to get his keys and without hesitation, everyone got in the truck and followed the ambulance to the hospital. The ride seemed to take forever. The lights were flashing and sirens were loud. When they got to the hospital, the paramedics took Josie immediately to a back room. Nadeen and Kenny went with them but Patsy and Ann stayed in the waiting room. Mrs. Wilson came a few minutes later in her car. She still had rollers in her hair. One was hanging on by a thin piece of hair.

In any other situation, Patsy would have laughed about it, but right now it resembled Josie's chance of living. It was thin. She was so little and so fragile. *What was she doin' playing around with Drano in a cup? How did she get it to put it in a cup?* Patsy had questions. Mrs. Wilson came up to Ann and touched her shoulder.

"Don't worry girls. Your baby sister is gonna make it. I been asking the Lord to work a miracle on my way driving here." He loves the children. He's going to give those doctors and nurses all the wisdom they need to get that mess out of her."

Neither Patsy nor Ann responded. They just listened. They sat in that waiting room for what seemed like hours, finally the doctor came. Nadeen was still crying and Kenny had his arms around her trying to comfort her.

"Good morning. My name is Dr. Chambers." He stood, uncomfortable in the doorway. "I just wanted to let you all know your little sister is going to make it. She has some bad burns around her mouth, inside her mouth and down her neck from where she threw up the Drano. It burned her pretty bad. I know you said it was an accident Mr. and Mrs. Simmons but I had to report this to the Children's Services Department, so they may give you a call later just to clear up some details."

I expected as much Dr. Chambers. We don't have anything to hide. It was just an accident. She must have gotten it out of the bathroom cabinet somehow." Dr. Chambers slightly nodded his head and told her he would check on Josie the next morning.

"Kenny. Take the children home. Patsy I need you to pack me some pajamas and some comfortable clothes."

"Nadeen. I'll be glad to cook the girls a good breakfast this morning if you like and make sure they get on the bus." Mrs. Wilson said.

"No, thank you. Kenny got it. He usually takes care of them in the morning."

"All right, sweetie. I guess I'll go on home then. If you all need me give me a call or come on over and ring the doorbell."

Mrs. Wilson gave everyone a hug and walked out singing *What an Awesome God*.

"Now, what make her think I'm going to let some other woman come into my house and do anything in my kitchen or with my children? What kind of fool do I look like? She get up in my house and the next thing you know she sleeping in my bed, with my husband! He liable to be too out of it to even know."

"Nadeen!" Kenny scolded. "She was just trying to be helpful. She's a member of the hospitality committee at the church, they help families all the time in need and she's a good God-fearing woman. She would never do anything disrespectful. You ought to be ashamed of yourself."

Nadeen cut him a look like she could care less about what he was saying.

"Just take my children home, please. I know women much better than you do."

"Come on, girls. Let's go home so you can get some rest. I'll bring you back later this afternoon."

Ann and Patsy got up and left with Kenny. They were tired but couldn't go to sleep. They were worried about Josie. When they got in the car, Kenny turned on the radio. Patsy noticed he was deep in thought. After a few minutes of riding in the car she fell asleep.

When she woke up Kenny was stopping the truck in the driveway. They all got out and went inside of the house. Patsy wondered if anyone else felt a strange breeze like sensation pass through as they stepped inside the doorway. It was cold and it made the hair stand up on her arms. "Cold in here a little bit." Kenny said. He'd felt it.

Hope it was the evil spirits in this house running out the door, Patsy thought to herself.

15

Ms. Ava, The social worker at the hospital, stopped by the next day to check on Josie and get a better understanding of what happened. Nadeen was sitting near Josie's bed reading her daily devotional when she came in. Ms. Ava was wearing a navy blue jacket with Children's Services on the front so Nadeen knew immediately who she was. "Good morning, Mrs. Simmons. How are you and your baby this morning?"

Nadeen made sure to smile at her. "We are truly blessed to be here." She replied. Ms. Ava went over to Josie's bedside and looked closely at her mouth. Nadeen watched her facial expressions to try and read what she was thinking.

"I just wanted to make sure I had all the details straight about what happened to your daughter before they released her from the hospital back into your care."

"I understand. Like I told Dr. Chambers. We had all gone to bed. Josie must have tried to go to the potty by herself. We been working on potty training her you see. So she must have opened the bathroom bottom cabinet and gotten that Drano out. Guess whoever used it last didn't put the top on it tightly. She just thought it was juice or something because it was blue."

She picked Josie up and patted her back. "It really was just a freak accident. My husband already went home and put all the cleaners in our washroom on the top shelf so this has no chance of happening again."

Ms. Ava was busy writing down every word Nadeen was saying. When she finished she looked Nadeen in the eye.

"Mrs. Simmons. I hope this doesn't happen again because if it does you may have your child removed from your home if she lives. Accidents like these put families on the front row of the church and it's a seat you don't want when your baby is in a coffin because of neglect."

Nadeen bit her tongue. She felt the venom rise up mid-way to her throat.

"Ms. Ava there is no neglect in our home only nourishment. I pour the Word into my babies and I take good care of them. Do you have any more questions of me? If not, I would like to get the discharge nurse in here so I can take my baby home and take care of her myself." Nadeen was suppressing the urge to talk to her like she really needed to be talked to accusing her of abusing Josie.

Ms. Ava could hear in Nadeen's voice that she was straining to keep it together.

"No, Mrs. Simmons I don't have any other questions at this time. I'll let you go get ready to take Josie home. Make sure you look after your baby."

Nadeen assured her she would and walked her to the door. She pushed the button for the nurse at the desk to let her know they were ready to go.

At home, Grandma Ruth was sitting in the kitchen peeling potatoes for a casserole she was going to cook later that evening. Patsy sat down to help by handing them to her. Grandma Ruth had her head down as though she was concentrating on what she was doing. As she slowly scrapped the potatoes, she asked, "Patsy, baby, I never did get a clear understanding on how my grandbaby got ahold of that Drano?"

Patsy looked at her. "I guess someone must have left it out and it wasn't closed good. She thought it was juice or something. I don't know."

"How that little girl get her hands around the top of that Drano bottle to open it and pour it out?"

"I told you, the top must not have been on there good. Somehow it was left within her reach." *What was grandma trying to get at?* Grandma Ruth looked up from the bowl and stilled her hand. She looked Patsy in the eye.

"Watch that tone, girl! That's my grandbaby in that hospital and I got a right to know how she got there. Nadeen been a momma two times before and I just can't see her being that careless. Something must be going on up in here. Got everybody out of place and distracted. It better not happen again or Kenny and Nadeen both gonna have to answer to me! I don't care how grown they think they are!"

Just as the words came out of her mouth Kenny came through the door with Pastor Mack behind him.

"Good afternoon, ladies." Pastor Mack said.

"Good afternoon, Pastor." Grandma Ruth said as she got up and wiped off the mess from the potatoes. She went over to the oven to start preparing her casserole. Kenny went over to her and kissed her on the jaw.

"Hey, Momma Ruth. How has your day been?"

"It's been good. How about you?"

"It's goin. Gonna spend a few moments talking with Pastor Mack. We gonna be in the living room."

Kenny walked into the living room with Pastor Mack. Patsy finished helping Grandma Ruth in the kitchen and they both went to the back to watch Grandma Ruth's favorite tele-Evangelist, Bishop Willie. Even though it was all over the news about him foolin around with members of his church, Grandma Ruth thought he really knew how to bring that Word and she didn't allow no talking when he was on.

A little while later, Ann came to the back. She asked Patsy to come to the room for a minute. When Patsy came through the door Ann looked down the hall to make sure nobody was coming. She pulled her away from the door and whispered. "I heard Kenny talking to Pastor Mack a few minutes ago. He's the one left that Drano out. He said he was so upset about catching Nadeen at Brother Ryan's house and the way she acted about it that he just wanted to kill his self."

Patsy looked at her like she was growing a horn out of the top of her forehead.

"Ann you got something twisted. Kenny wouldn't set out Drano for Josie to drink." Ann stared her older sister straight in the eyes to make sure she knew she hadn't heard anything wrong.

"He poured it in the cap and sat it on the arm of the couch Patsy. He went in his room to think about what to put in his farewell letter and said he started crying asking God to help him.

The next thing he knew, he woke up on the floor to Josie screaming and crying. Soon as he opened the door and saw her with the cap on the floor he knew what had happened."

Patsy looked at Ann for a few minutes because she wasn't understanding the words coming out of her mouth.

"What are you saying, Ann? You heard Kenny tell the pastor he tried to kill his self? He was gonna drink that Drano?"

"Yes. That's exactly what I heard and exactly what I'm saying to you." Patsy had to sit down on the bed. She put her head in her hands. She didn't know how to feel. She was confused.

"I wonder if he's gonna tell Nadeen that's what happened?" Ann asked. "She might really snap."

"She probably wishes that he'd done it, then she could be with that crooked church member of hers God is gonna get the both of them. They're the reason all of this happened anyway!" Poor Kenny. Poor Josie. They were both caught in a bad place. They'd both been hurt badly and would carry scars forever. Kenny would wear them emotionally and spiritually and Josie, well hers would be there for the whole world to see. They would know she'd been through something terrible and survived but Kenny, no one would know about him, unless he told.

There was a big celebration courtesy of Aunt Eva when Josie finally came back home. She said the house needed some laughter and joy in it and what better time to fill it up than Josie coming back home. Everyone was glad to see her. Pastor Mack and Reverend Craig came over along with their wives and some other members of both churches. First Lady Craig anointed Josie's scars and prayed for her.

"Sister Simmons, God will take care of all of you. I know him to be a keeper." She said. Nadeen thanked her and told her she would see her on next Sunday. First Lady on her way out of the door turned back to them, smiled and said, "If it be God's will. Everything is at the will of God."

A few days later Nadeen got a phone call from one of her sisters in the prayer circle, She called to tell her First Lady Craig was dead. She died at home with Reverend Craig by her side. He barely made it on time, it seems he had gone out to minister to one of his members who he said was having some marital problems. First Lady Craig had gotten up that morning and walked around. She said she felt much better and might want to try to make it to service later that night. Reverend Craig told her to lay down and get her some rest. He told her he'd be back right after church service to see about her. The home nurse that was there said First Lady started to take a turn for the worse about six o' clock that evening. She wondered where the Reverend was since service had been over for several hours. First Lady was asking for her to hurry up and find him because she wanted to tell him something. She said she didn't think she had much time.

The nurse started calling all over town and couldn't locate him. Finally about two hours after she had started calling he pulled up in the yard. She went outside to tell him to come quick cause it looked like First Lady done took a turn for the worse. The nurse said he smelled like perfume and had his tie off. He rushed in the room and she was calling his name. He made it to her bedside and held her hand just as she was about to take her last breath. The nurse said she whispered, "I forgive you," in the Pastor's ear.

The service was held at Greater Trials. It was a full house. Everyone had nothing but nice things to say. When it came time for the viewing of the body everyone stepped up to say their final goodbye's. Patsy was sitting on the edge of a pew and she saw a lady with long black hair and high heeled red shoes walk up to the coffin. She smiled, put her hand on First Lady's hand and tapped it. Patsy thought that was odd.

16

Nadeen took First Lady Craig's death pretty hard. She was worried about who was going to take care of Pastor Craig. She called to check on him every day and asked him if he needed anything. He always told her no and thanked her for calling. He told her to focus on taking care of her baby and getting her back healthy and strong. Nadeen seem to be torn between taking care of him and taking care of Josie. Kenny noticed how she was always on the phone directing members of the church in ways they could help Reverend Craig during his time of bereavement. She seemed to make Josie's needs a second thought.

Kenny and Nadeen barely spoke to each other but that was okay with Patsy and Ann. The less said the less drama. Kenny was trying to do better about coming home on time. He said he was going to keep it real with people and just be himself. It was no use in trying to pretend. God was the one you needed to be concerned about he would say, cause people can't put your soul in heaven or hell only God can so he didn't care what people had to say about him.

He was still going to church every Sunday and to Bible study trying to get it right. One morning when they went to church with Kenny, Pastor Mack stopped him on his way to the Men's class

"Brother Simmons, I would like for you to teach the Sunday School lesson for today."

"Me? I'm the least one to teach someone. You sure, Pastor?"

"Yes. I'm sure. You're the perfect one. I know you're gonna go in there and be honest with those brothers. That's what they need. They need to know someone else is going through and they need advice on how to do it."

Patsy felt real proud of her daddy at that moment. She wished she could be in that class for just a few minutes. The men came out of Sunday school telling Kenny how much he blessed them with his testimony and how they enjoyed just being honest with each other. Pastor Mack told Kenny he wanted him to consider being a permanent teacher for the Men's Class. Kenny told him he would think about it. When they got out of service, Kenny stopped by Nadeen's favorite place, Denise's Diner and got everyone dinner.

They also stopped by and visited with Kenny's sister, Ernestine and his mother, Grandma Simmons. She seemed so happy to see them. Everyone said how good it was to see Kenny back in church and taking the girls with him. Grandma Simmons asked about Nadeen. Kenny told them she was doing fine. Grandma Simmons asked him to bring her by sometimes. Ernestine gave her a funny look as though to say, *Really?* By the time they made it home, Nadeen was back from church. Patsy's spirit dropped. They walked in and put the food down on the table. Kenny told everyone to go and wash up.

The next thing they heard coming from the back was Nadeen yelling at Kenny. They had all just gotten home from church what was wrong? What could have gotten her mad so fast?

They tip toed up front to see what was going on. "I want you out of my house right now! Do you hear me? I want you out right now! I'm so tired of this! She said.

"I don't need you here! I can take care of this house and my children by myself. I don't need you! Get out!"

"Nadeen. I was going to call and get an extension. I didn't get as many hours as I usually do this last pay period. Be patient. God will take care of us. Just calm down. The lights are still on so why are you so upset? The lights didn't get cut off. What's wrong with you?" Kenny asked. "There is nothing wrong with me! I mean what I said. Get out now! Go stay with your unsaved friends!"

"I'm not going anywhere." Kenny said in a tone that surprised even Patsy. "This is my house too!"

Good for Kenny, Patsy thought to herself. *Stand up to that devil. Stop letting him kick you around.*

"You better leave or you will regret it." Nadeen threatened as she began taking off her white gloves. They were slightly stained with grape juice, probably from communion. Nadeen had caused hurt and pain many times with those very hands she served Communion with on First Sunday. Patsy didn't like taking Communion because she associated her hands with *hurting instead of healing.* She would take the wafer and hold it in her hand while putting it up to her mouth and pretending to eat it. She really only drank the grape juice.

"Do you know how embarrassing it is to have a member of my church pull me to the side and tell me my lights are scheduled for disconnect on Monday? She just wanted to let me know as a favor since I was her church member." Kenny tried to reason with Nadeen but she didn't listen to him. After arguing back and forth with her for a while, Kenny decided to give it up. He walked out of the kitchen and left her cursing him. Patsy snuck to the back to talk to Kenny to plead with him to just go at least for a little while until she cooled off.

"I brought dinner and I wanted us to sit down as a family and have a good day. She comes back here talking crazy to me and telling me to get out of my own house! I'm not going to do it!"

"Daddy, please. You know how crazy she acts."

"Baby, I shouldn't have to leave my own home."

Just as he finished his sentence, Patsy turned to see Nadeen walk into the room with a pot of boiling water. Patsy felt her feet move but wasn't sure if the rest of her body did. She was trying to cover Kenny and he was rolling to the left to get out of the chair. She saw the water come out of the pot and in the air. The next thing she knew she was on fire! The water hit her back and she screamed in agony! She heard Nadeen's screams mixed with hers.

"Why did you get in the way? I've told you about getting in grown folks business!"

Kenny pushed Patsy off of him on to the floor to look at her injury. He was yelling at Nadeen.

"Nadeen! What have you done? You better call an ambulance right now! You have gone too far! This is our child!"

He cried and held Patsy telling her how sorry he was that this happened. Patsy didn't hear him 'cause she was blacking in and out from the fire on her back.

Nadeen didn't have to call an ambulance. Ann had been standing in the door when it happened and as soon as Nadeen threw the water Ann ran to the phone to call for help. The police and the ambulance seemed to take forever but they finally made it. Patsy didn't remember much after they got there. They said she went into shock. When she came to, she was in a burn unit at the hospital. She was laying on her stomach.

She was worried about Kenny. *What happened to Kenny?* She looked across the room and saw a police officer and a woman who later identified herself as Ms. Ava, a social worker. Patsy knew who she was because they wore these dark blue jackets with the name of the agency on the front. She heard them talking to Kenny and Nadeen. Nadeen did most of the talking and Kenny just agreed with her. She told them that she was on her way to the back porch with the pot of boiling water to clean off the steps.

She came through the back to ask one of them to open the door for her, when she walked up to the chair she tripped over something and the pot fell out of her hands. She said she tried to catch it but it happened so fast. Patsy heard her sweetly say, "I would never hurt my babies. This was just an accident, wasn't it, Kenny?"

Kenny responded dryly, "Yes, officer, it was an accident."

Ms. Ava, the social worker, spoke up then, "It seems you been having quite a few accidents with your children. Just a few weeks ago your baby daughter was in the hospital for poisoning and that was supposedly an accident, too. Now we have the oldest daughter. I think this may need to be investigated a little further. I'm going to want to talk to her when she's awake." She got up at that point and walked out along with the police officer.

As she passed Patsy's bed, she touched her on the head. "This child has been badly hurt and I want to know why. I want the truth."

When they left out of the room, Nadeen came over to Patsy's bed. She called her name. Patsy didn't open her eyes. She didn't want to see her or speak to her. "Patsy, baby, now you know this was an accident. You know I would never do something like this to you. You just got in the way of an argument between me and your daddy."

"If you don't say it was an accident we could lose our family. You hear me, baby? We could lose our family and your momma could go to jail and I know you don't want that."

Patsy never opened her eyes. She just wanted to get as far away as possible from Nadeen. She wanted her to go away and never come back. *Why couldn't it just be them and Kenny?* She slept for several hours. When she woke up again it was around midnight. Kenny was in the chair beside her. She moved a little bit and he heard her.

"Hey, Patsy. It's me. You need some water or something?" She nodded her head yes. He put the cup of water with a straw close to her mouth so she could swallow.

"I know you in pain right now baby girl but I want you to know I've decided it would be best if I moved out for a while. I don't want anyone else getting hurt in that house."

Patsy wanted to tell him not to leave but she couldn't speak. She could only scream it in her head.

"I'll be here with you until they say you can go home but afterwards I'll be leaving. I'm not going back home. I'll be in touch with you all but I need to get away right now and think about whether or not Nadeen and I need to stay married."

Patsy wasn't sure about what she felt at that moment other than uncomfortable. She just went back to sleep and rolled his words around in her mind.

17

Patsy had to stay in the burn unit for two weeks. The doctor said she had third degree burns to her back. Her pain had been excruciating and she'd had to be sedated most of the time she was there. The skin would take some time to heal. She would have to get steroid shots to help the blisters heal, but thankfully, she didn't have to have skin grafts.

To take her mind off of her pain, she thought about Dustin. He'd gotten the news from Sandra the Monday morning after it happened. He'd called while he was between classes. He sounded like he was crying. Patsy told him she was gonna be okay. He asked if he could come see her but she told him that would probably not be a good idea right now, plus she was flat on her stomach and wouldn't really be able to talk to him. She knew he was going to be worried about her until he saw her. Patsy had Ann to take a picture of her smiling and send it to his phone. She hoped that would put him at ease.

The doctor said he was going to release her, but not until Ms. Ava, the social worker had a chance to talk with her. Patsy thought she was gone away. She didn't want to be split up living apart from her sisters. Her sisters were very close to her and Josie was still healing from her accident. They needed to be together. Patsy just wanted things to change for the better, she wanted Nadeen to change. She wished she could talk to her and tell her how she felt but she knew that wasn't going to happen.

The Women's Prayer Circle of Greater Trials came by to visit Patsy and they just fussed over Nadeen. They hugged her and pampered her and prayed with her. They just wanted her to know she was in their prayers with all the trials the enemy had been bringing her way. They said he was trying to break a good saint down but they were gonna pray her strength. She just cried on their shoulders and said she had been through so much she just didn't know how much more she could take. She said she must be getting close to that job promotion because the enemy was throwing so much at her, Losing First Lady Craig, Josie getting into that Drano and almost dying and now her oldest baby accidentally burned. She asked them to pray for her strength. Patsy wanted to bust out laughing but was afraid she might bust the blisters on her back.

Ms. Ava, finally came by. It was a visit Patsy hadn't been looking forward to. She asked Nadeen to leave the room while she interviewed Patsy. She also asked where Kenny was. Nadeen told her he was no longer with the family. It was best due to his problems if he left the home environment. She said it was important that her children grow up with the right example and he wasn't it. Patsy put her head down at that. She knew this wasn't the truth, but to defend Kenny now might get her cussed out later once Ms. Ava left.

Nadeen touched Patsy on the hand and told her she would be right outside the door listening in case she needed her or this was too much for her. Patsy knew what that meant. She was to only say what she told her to say. She wasn't to tell this social worker what really happened.

Ms. Ava pulled up a chair and Patsy waited for her to begin drilling her about how she got burned with that hot water.

She looked Patsy in the eye and said to her, "Now you and I both know that you being in this hospital so badly burned wasn't really an accident don't we? I sense that there is something else going on here. You may not have been the intended victim but you somehow got the punishment. Who were you protecting?"

"I wasn't protecting anybody," Patsy lied. "My mom told you what happened. She was going to clean the back porch steps. She likes to use hot water to do that with. She was coming to ask one of us to open the door and she tripped over something, maybe a toy or something I'm not sure right now and so here I am." Patsy said. "Your mother still had on her usher's uniform from church when this happen from what I was told. That's not something a person would normally wear when she's about to clean the back steps now is it?" Patsy was trapped. She had to think fast.

"Sometimes she comes in and puts on an apron and some house shoes and she starts to clean without even thinking about what she's wearing."

That was good, she thought to herself.

"I interviewed several people in your neighborhood, at your parent's churches and on your mother's job. They all said she is just the salt of the earth. But I got a feeling that there's more to her than she's showing. She's involved in too many accidents at home. Just to be on the safe side, I'm going to recommend that you stay at the home of a family member, preferably your Grandmother, for a term of ninety days."

This was exactly what Patsy was afraid of, Ms. Ava splitting her and her sisters up.

"Ms. Ava, I really need to be at home in my own bed. My Grandmother is way too busy to have me to look after. Our neighbor, Mrs. Wilson, can come over while my mom is at work or church. She already looks after my baby sister."

"Your home is prone to terrible accidents lately. It's best that we find out why. I'll be making unannounced visits to your mother's home during that time. If everything seems stable then you can return. If you decide there is anything else you would like to tell me you have my business card on your table, you can call me anytime. Also, if you hear from your father, I would like to talk with him too."

She got up from the chair and closed the tablet she'd been making notes on. "I'm going outside to talk with your mother right now and let her know my decision."

She put the chair back in place and walked out the door to talk to Nadeen. Nadeen came back in and looked a little worried.

"She said you have to stay with your Grandmother for three months. What did you tell her? Did she say anything about getting the police involved?

"If you had just gotten out of the way, this never would have happened. This is your fault not mine! You got in my business and you got yourself hurt! You never should have even been back there, Patsy."

Patsy just looked at her. She would never get it. It would never be because of her that she lay in this bed with her back swollen with red blisters and a gash on her back. It would never be her fault that Kenny was gone

Patsy closed her eyes and began to pray silently, she needed the Lord so much. *God, please come and fix this. Come and get the evil spirits out of our house. Get them off of my daddy and get them out of Nadeen. Help me most of all Lord to forgive. In the name of Jesus. Amen.*

She felt a little bit better after that prayer. She was getting so tired of waiting on God to do something. She was afraid she might stop believing if he didn't do something soon to fix what was wrong. When Grandma Ruth came to the hospital to pick her up, everyone was there to help carry out her gifts and flowers. The doctor gave Grandma Ruth the instructions for taking care of Patsy's burns and when she needed to come back to see him. Nadeen told her she would be coming over to help her with Patsy. Grandma Ruth told her it would be better if she called first and she would let her know if she felt like letting Patsy have company that day.

Patsy knew that made Nadeen steaming mad but she also knew Nadeen had better sense than to say anything back to Grandma Ruth. She stayed quiet during the conversation and just let them roll her out of that hospital.

When she got outside, some of her classmates were waiting for her, Dustin was in the front of the crowd with a big teddy bear, he walked up to her and right in front of Nadeen he planted a big kiss on her cheek. Patsy smiled. Dustin must have planned this. He was good at getting people to follow him. She thought Nadeen might say something about him kissing her but she didn't. "Patsy we just wanted to let you know we missed you and hope to see you back at school soon." Dustin said. The crowd behind him clapped and cheered. Patsy just blushed. She couldn't find the words.

Ann came up to her and hugged her then her eyes filled with water. She barely got the words out of her mouth.

"Patsy. I want to come with you. I don't want to be at home by myself. Me and Josie are gonna miss you." She said. Patsy felt so bad, what was she supposed to do?

"Grandma Ruth is supposed to come and get y'all to spend some time with me. I'll only be gone for a little while." Ann looked so pitiful standing there. Patsy was really hoping that she didn't go home and start cutting herself. " Ann you stay strong. Don't you do anything." She told her as she looked her in the face. She knew Ann understood what she really meant. Ann shook her head that she understood.

"Now, girls." Grandma Ruth said as she patted Ann on the back. "You act like she's going away across the seas. She' s just going to my house. You can spend the night on the weekends. She kissed Ann on the forehead. "I'm gonna take good care of your big sister. I promise."

Patsy hugged Ann and whispered in her ear. "No cutting please Ann." Ann nodded her head okay again and let her go. Patsy had to make sure Ann was going to keep her promise to her. Once she felt like Ann would she let her go. Grandma Ruth put her in the front seat of the car and they drove away. Patsy looked back at everyone, Dustin winked his eye at her. Ann and Josie looked so sad. Josie was reaching her hand out towards the car. Patsy knew she had to get back home to take care of them.

As they drove down the hospital driveway, Patsy begin to relax for the first time in a long time. She must have slept all the way because when she woke up, she was being carried in the house by a pair of strong arms. She knew that smell, that cologne, it was Kenny. She hugged his neck and kissed his rough beard,

"Daddy! I thought you weren't going to come. I wondered where you were." She said.

"You my first baby girl! You think I'm not gonna be there for you? You know me better than that." He said as he laid her down on the bed. Grandma Ruth put her in the pretty blue room with the kitten wall paper. She loved this room! The pictures of so many faces that looked like her.

"I moved all my stuff out of the house last night while your sisters were sleep. Nadeen was gone to work I guess. I didn't want a scene about it after so much that has already happened. I called her this morning and told her I was gone. Told her I needed time to think about what was going on with us."

"You gonna stay here with me and Grandma?" Patsy asked. She was hoping he would say yes. They would have so much fun.

"No, baby. I'm a man. I take care of myself. I'll be coming by every day to check on you but I got me a nice one bedroom apartment about twenty minutes away from the house. That way, if you all need me I can get to you quick. I'm not going to be far. Nadeen is still my wife. She's going to need help with you all and I'm still going to take care of my girls. I also gotta work on me and I can't do that at home."

"Ann's not going to do well with this. It seems like we both left her at the same time." Patsy said.

"I'm gonna call her tonight and have a talk with her and I'm still going to be picking her and Josie up for church on Sunday if they want to go with me."

"Kenny!" yelled Grandma Ruth. "I'm about to cook dinner you're welcome to stay. I don't get in you and Nadeen's business. You my son in law and I love you. You welcome here anytime."

Kenny laughed. "I know Ms. Ruth. I appreciate that. I'm gonna visit a little while longer with my baby girl here and then we can all sit down to a good home cooked meal" Kenny stayed for dinner and they had a great time.

He kept Grandma Ruth and Patsy laughing. Grandma Ruth fixed him up a plate to carry home with him and he gave her a hug as he left out the door. He told her he would be back to see Patsy on tomorrow and if he could make arrangements he would bring Ann and Josie. Grandma said that would be fine with her.

"By the way, Ms. Ruth," Kenny said. "There's a nice young man by the name of Dustin, kind of sweet on Patsy, he might want to come by and sit on the porch with her sometimes if that's okay with you. You know his momma, Ms. Jessie, the lady that helps out at the food pantry downtown.

"Yes. I know her. Sweet lady." Grandma Ruth said. "I reckon he can come by if he calls first and stays on my porch, any further and he might get run off and never be allowed back." She laughed.

"Sounds fair to me Ms. Ruth." Kenny said. "I'll give him the message. Patsy you call me if you need me. I left my phone number with your Grandmother. "

"Okay, Daddy."

She hated to see him leave. Grandma Ruth helped her back in the house and gave her a bath with cool water and baby oil. It was so relaxing. She put the burn ointment on her back, gave her pain pills and dressed her gently like a doll. Patsy was a little uncomfortable because she wasn't use to being touched in a loving and gentle manner. It felt odd to her. She enjoyed it in a way but on the other hand she wanted her grandmother to hurry up and get it over with. She wasn't quite comfortable being rubbed. Grandma Ruth must have felt the slight tension in her body because she stopped rubbing her back.

"You want to call Ann?"

"Yes, ma'am. If that's okay?"

"That's your sister. I know you girls are close. It's fine with me. I'll go get the phone."

She brought the phone to Patsy and she dialed the house number. It rang only once and Ann answered it. She was glad to hear from Patsy. They talked a long time. So long that Patsy's medicine kicked in and she fell asleep holding the phone hearing Ann's voice as she went under to swim with the dolphins.

When she woke up it was to the smell of salmon, rice, and biscuits. Her stomach growled with anticipation. Grandma Ruth knocked on the door, "Good morning, Darlin'. You must have slept pretty good. When I came back for the phone forty-five minutes later, you were out! Ann was still talking. I had to tell her to call back tomorrow because you'd fallen asleep. Come on and let me help you get cleaned up for breakfast. You gotta get started on that homework today. You've missed a lot of days out of school and it's gonna be time for your exams soon. We want you to do well."

Patsy ate a good breakfast and sat up in the big cozy recliner in Grandma's sun room. This was the perfect place to study. Sandra was a great friend; she took good notes, wrote down all the assignments that Patsy missed while in the hospital, and drooped off Patsy's class and homework. Patsy was able to get almost everything done that day. She would break for a snack or lunch and then go back to it. It was so peaceful out on the sunroom deck. No screaming. Cussing, yelling or fighting like at her house. Sandra came by after school and picked up Patsy's homework assignments and gave her any new information they were working on in each class. Dustin stopped by every day and sat on the porch with her. They talked for ours about their upcoming graduation and going to college together. Funny enough though, way down inside, Patsy kind of missed Nadeen. *That was really crazy.* She thought. *Why would she miss all of that drama? She didn't understand it herself.*

After Dustin left Patsy asked if Nadeen had called. Grandma Ruth looked at her and said, "Yeah. She called today but I told her you weren't up to talking with her right now. I love my child but she got some ways I just don't understand for the life of me."

Later that night, as Patsy lay in bed about to doze off she thought about what Kenny told her about Grandma Ruth, maybe she had forgotten the way she used to treat Nadeen and Grandpa but Nadeen hadn't. Perhaps Nadeen remembered it because it was all she knew. She didn't know any other way to deal with her problems. Whatever it was, Patsy wanted it to be cut off with her, Ann, and Josie. It needed to be cut from the root!

18

Nadeen finally came to see Patsy. She asked how she was doing and if she needed anything. Patsy told her no. She told her Grandma had been taking good care of her. Nadeen told Patsy the social worker had been coming by faithfully. She told Patsy she would be back home in no time and things would be back to normal. Nadeen's idea of normal was not what Patsy wanted. She missed her sisters but she didn't miss that house. It was something bad living in that house!

"I hear your daddy been coming by to check on you."

"Yes, ma'am."

"Well that's good. He been sober when he come right?"

"Yes, ma'am."

"Well that's good. I wouldn't want him coming over here embarrassing you."

Since when did Nadeen ever care about her being embarrassed?

"Well, I better get on home. I got to get over to the church office to print out Pastor's sermon for Sunday. Ann been doing real good getting Josie ready for me in the mornings."

"I'll check on you tomorrow." She got up and walked out of the room. No hug, no kiss, she just got up and walked out.

That was fine with Patsy though. If she had it would have been too awkward. Patsy wouldn't know how to respond back to her so that was best. Patsy settled into her favorite spot on Grandma Ruth's couch. She was sleeping pretty comfortably until she had a strange dream that woke her up in a sweat. She kept seeing blood all over a pair of white gloves. Someone pulled the gloves off and tried to squeeze the blood out of them and the more they would squeeze the more blood would come out it just wouldn't stop. Just before she woke up from the dream, Patsy heard Kenny calling her name. He sounded like he was in trouble. It shook her so bad she woke up sweating and tired.

It took her an hour to go back to sleep and even then she couldn't get back to the relaxed state she was in when she first laid down to sleep. Patsy wondered what that dream meant. Whatever it was she hoped it didn't manifest.

A few days after the dream, Ann called. Patsy was sitting near the heater studying her final exam notes, when the phone rang. She answered it since Grandma Ruth put it next to her while she went to take a shower. It was Ann.

"Hey, Ann. What's going on?"

"Brother Ryan is what's going on over here?"

"What? What do you mean?"

"Just what I said. He been coming over here a lot since Kenny left Patsy. At first, I thought he was coming just to see how things were going at our house but then one day I walked up on him kissing Nadeen. When he saw me he jumped back. Nadeen turned around and act like I didn't see what I know I saw. Told me to go to my room and stay there."

"Ann, if you don't stop telling that lie the devil is gonna open up the pit and snatch you in."

Ann sounded vexed. "I'm not lying and if anybody gonna get snatched by Satan it's gonna be your momma and her bootleg preacher boyfriend. Today he had the nerve to ask what me and Josie wanted for Christmas. I wanted to tell him for you to go to hell with gasoline drawers on but I know that ain't holy so I just bit my tongue."

They both laughed at that.

"Kenny should have put a whipping on him the first time he caught him with Nadeen."

"Ann, this ain't gonna end good. You know that don't you? If Kenny find him over there somebody gone get some charges."

"I know. I think he spending the night over here too, Patsy. Late at night I hear her opening that front door. She think I be sleep but I don't. I can't sleep no more like I use to since you been gone Patsy. I'll be glad when you come back home. I miss Daddy, too. I can hear voices in her room at night and then later on you hear these strange noises like moaning and grunting. It sounds real nasty. One Sunday morning, I heard the front door close, it was about six in the morning. When I got up a hour later, I went in her room to get some lotion so I could get ready to go to Sunday School with daddy and I looked on his old side of the bed and I swear I saw what looks like a man's hair on the pillow where Kenny use to sleep."

"You about to make me pass out, Ann. What did it look like? Was it course short hair?"

"Yeah. I put it in a plastic bag and put it in my drawer." Even through Anne's whisper, Patsy could tell she was terrified and hot as a firecracker at the same time.

"She been lying about her and Brother Ryan. She done hurt our family with what they been doing and I'm gonna tell Daddy!"

"Don't do that, Ann. It would cause more problems. God is going to show this thing. They are members of the same church. He's not going to let this go on too long in his house. You would only hurt Kenny more if you told him that Brother Ryan was in his bed. Just keep it a secret for right now. It'll come out at the right time."

"When you coming back home, Patsy?"

"The social worker is coming by today. I'll ask her."

"You need to come soon. I don't know how much longer I can deal with this. I'm on edge."

Patsy knew what that meant. Ann was getting near the point of cutting herself again to release the tension building inside of her. She'd promised she wouldn't do it but she didn't say for how long.

"You promised me you would hold on, Ann. You gotta keep your word. I'm gonna keep mine. I'll be home soon. I promise you that. Don't lose control. I love you and you know that."

Ann was quiet for a few minutes then she responded, "I know. I love you too. I gotta go. Talk to you later."

Ann hung up the phone. Patsy was worried. She couldn't believe Nadeen had gotten so bold with her affair. *Was this really going on inside their home?* She thought, *God is really going to have to do something! Surely he saw this adultery. Reverend Craig never preached about that at Greater Trials, the way he was always looking at the legs of that lady in the front pew he was probably lusting in his own heart or doing the dirty deed hisself.*

When Ms. Ava came later that week, Patsy talked to her about letting her go early. She was reluctant to do it but after a whole hour of Patsy begging her and telling her how much she missed being at home with her sisters, Ms. Ava said she would consider it but wouldn't give her a definite answer yet. She said there were a few more things she needed to check out for instance, who this man was that she had run into twice at Nadeen's house when she made her observation visits. It seemed odd to her that he was there so much when she came by.

She said Nadeen told her he was a co-worker and a concerned church member. Patsy hated that Ann was having to live in such a bad situation. The last thing Patsy wanted was for Ann to start cutting herself again. She hoped this wouldn't effect Ann's grades. If she brought home bad grades that was going to be a whole other bad scene. Nadeen really went off the deep end when a 'C' came home. After you brought one home the first time when she got done with you it was safe to assume you'd never bring another one. The thought of a 'C' would break you out in sweat thinking about that punishment. Kenny usually left the house if a C came in on the report card. Patsy knew Ann was starting to slip further and further away from her. A few weeks before the Christmas Holiday, the grades did come out. Patsy finished her six weeks exams with all As. Grandma Ruth and Aunt Eva were so proud of her they threw her a small party!

Ann, however, failed to make the Honor Roll due to having two Cs. Fortunately, Ms. Ava was on a routine visit the day Ann brought her report card home. Nadeen promised Ann she would see her about those grades as soon as this social worker mess was over. Patsy knew it was the Grace of God that had saved Ann's skin that semester.

At the party, there was a cake and ginger ale in champagne glasses with strawberries. Grandma Ruth and Eva toasted to her doing so well in spite of all that had happened. Kenny, Ann, Josie and Nadeen were all there.

Everybody had a good time at the party but Kenny and Nadeen didn't say much to each other.

Nadeen decided to leave early so when she got ready to go, she asked Grandma Ruth if Ms. Ava had said anything to her about Patsy coming home soon. Well, Grandma Ruth must have had a little bit more than ginger ale in her glass. She shot a mean look at Nadeen and said, "You don't need her back home! You ain't got yourself together yet! You need to get yourself straight and then maybe she can come home! If it wasn't for you she wouldn't even have to be here!"

Nadeen tightened her jaw and her eyes. She just stood there and looked at her mother for a minute then she grabbed her coat and headed for the door. Patsy knew that whatever thought she had in her mind right then she knew better than to act on it.

"Come on, Ann and bring Josie. I don't have to listen to this." Nadeen headed towards the front door."

"That's right you don't! You got a hut, go to it! If you took care of your own home as well as you do pastor's maybe your house wouldn't be the devil's playpen. From what I been hearing, Pastor got somebody to take care of him and she been doing it for a while!"

Grandma Ruth yelled at Nadeen and threw her glass at the back of Nadeen's head. Nadeen ducked out of the way and the glass hit the wall and burst leaving a trail running down the wall that stunk like alcohol. Nadeen just kept walking. Kenny looked down at the floor.

Eva came over to Patsy and in a low voice she whispered, "Come on, baby. Let me help you get ready for bed. Your grandmother is having a flash back and it's best to get out of her way."

Her voice was a warning. She took Patsy to the back and got her undressed. Kenny knocked on the door.

"Patsy, you decent?"

Eva laughed, "She better be. Come on in."

Kenny came in the room and kissed Patsy on the forehead. "You want to be home for Christmas, baby girl?"

"Yeah. I miss my sisters. They need me."

"I understand. I'll stop by and talk to the social worker tomorrow," Kenny told her on his way out.

That's all I can ask for. Patsy thought. Eva stood up off the bed.

"Guess I better check on momma and head out myself. Sleep tight, beautiful." Eva said as she kissed her goodnight. Patsy heard her go out the front door and lock it. She guessed Grandma Ruth put herself to bed.

Grandma Ruth might be sleeping in late tomorrow, Patsy thought. There had been a lot of excitement going on tonight.

A few days before Christmas Eve, Grandma Ruth came and sat by Patsy. She seemed a little sad, "Patsy, Ms. Ava called me this morning and said you can go home for Christmas through New Year's Day if you want to."

Patsy could feel the smile stretching across her face. She also saw the sadness in her Grandmother's eyes.

"Well, Grandma. I hate to leave you but me and my sisters have never done Christmas apart."

"I understand a sister's love for each other, baby. I got some of my own remember?"

"You coming over for Christmas?"

"No. I'm gonna go down to Las Vegas with a couple of ladies from the Seasoned Single's Ministry. We been planning this all year and at our age if God let us make it to a vacation we need to take it."

"Eva said she would come over later and help you pack."

"That would be great. You gonna let my daddy know where I am?"

"Baby, he knows where you gonna be. He's the reason you're going. He talked with that social worker, Ms. Ava, a few days ago. You know his girls is the most important thing to him on this earth."

Patsy put her head down and smiled. "That's what he always says." Grandma Ruth patted her on the lap and got up from the chair.

"He means it. I know he got to love all of you all to stay with that crazy acting daughter of mine. She say she Holy Ghost filled but I say she mentally ill. Lord Forgive me. She mine though." Grandma shook her head and walked out the door.

Kenny came by before Eva was about to take Patsy home. Patsy couldn't imagine the holiday without her dad. "You're not gonna be with us for Christmas?"

"I don't know. I might check with Nadeen and see if she minds if I stop by. If you like I can pick you all up later after you open gifts and bring you over to my place." He said.

"That sounds good. That'll be fun and we can spend the holiday together."

She walked out with Kenny and saw Grandma Ruth standing by the door with a cup in her hand. She was sipping slowly. The smell coming from the cup told Patsy she must be feeling pretty good.

"All right now, young lady. You have fun." Patsy gave her a hug and walked out not sure of what was waiting for her at home.

When they pulled up to the house, Eva blew the horn. Ann and Josie burst out the front door. They almost knocked each other down getting out the car. Nadeen was standing in the door looking at her. Patsy got out the car and ran to her sisters. They both grabbed her bags and rushed her in the house. As she walked by Nadeen she pushed out a hello with all she had.

Nadeen responded in a nonchalant tone of voice, "Hey, Patsy."

Patsy went to the room with her sisters. Eva took advantage of this time to talk to Nadeen.

"Lil sister, please don't spoil that girl's holiday by acting like your momma." She said in a low tone. Nadeen looked at her as she stood in her front door.

"Please mind your own business and get out of my house." She tried to shut the door but Eva stopped her and smirked at her.

"That's the whole problem right there. It's your house instead of God's." Eva pushed away from the door and turned to walk away.

Nadeen came up behind her and yelled out the door, "All I have ever did was to try and live my life to give God glory and if that means keeping my home in order that's just what I'm gonna do. Now, you have a blessed holiday!"

Nadeen went into the kitchen talking out loud to herself. "I must be doing something right. I'm surrounded by people who seem to hate that Jesus is working in me."

Patsy spent the rest of the evening catching up with Ann and playing with Josie. Nadeen didn't say much to her other than to tell her to make sure the doors were locked when she left. She said she was going to sit with an elderly church member since her regular sitter was gone for the Holidays. Reverend Craig had called and asked if she would mind, it would only be until morning when her children would make it to town. Nadeen said since it was for the Kingdom she didn't mind at all. Once she left Patsy called Dustin and asked him to come over for a few hours. She missed him.

When he got there she had cups of hot cocoa waiting. He kissed her on her nose.

"You glad to be back?"

"I'm glad to be with my sisters. Kenny is really missing but hopefully he'll be around tomorrow."

Dustin took the cup of cocoa from her. "It feels good outside. You wanna go out for just a few minutes?"

"That sounds good. I love the smell of fireplaces in the winter time and all the pretty Christmas lights."

They sat outside and talked for about an hour when all of a sudden Patsy noticed a truck driving by the house slowly. She strained to see the color of it, It looked like Brother Ryan's Range Rover. She remembered it from the day Kenny almost busted his face when he caught him at the house. She panicked.

"Dustin! That was Brother Ryan's truck!"

"You sure?" Dustin asked her he hated to see her in such a panic.

"Yes! I know he saw us sitting out here. He's going to tell her. I just know he is!"

"It's okay. Maybe he didn't see us. It's kind of dark. He may have just been driving through the neighborhood."

Patsy really wasn't hearing Dustin anymore. The blisters on her back were starting to itch. She just needed him to leave.

"I don't know but you better leave now. I don't want my Christmas or yours spoiled"

"She's not going to do anything to me, Patsy. I wouldn't let her. I hate to see you so upset, though, so I'll leave. Merry Christmas and I hope you have a better New Year."

He kissed her on the lips but she was so upset she couldn't even kiss him back. She just ran in the house and locked the door.

"Ann!" Patsy yelled as she ran down the hall. "Brother Ryan just drove by here."

Ann's eyes got big, "Did he see you on the porch with Dustin?"

"I hope not. The lights were dim I'm not sure. I was so scared I told Dustin to leave."

"I hope he didn't see you two cause the temperature would change real quick in here from winter wonderland to hot as a Fourth of July Firecracker!" Ann said. She laughed at that but Patsy didn't find it very funny.

"Don't act brand new Ann. You already know this is no laughing matter."

Ann yawned real loud and said, "Come on and go to bed. He didn't see you. He need to be worried about us seeing him."

Patsy didn't sleep at all that night. When the morning came, she was up way before Nadeen came home. She was anxious and afraid. Nadeen came in laughing and talking on her phone. Patsy was on edge until she went to sleep.

Kenny called the next morning and asked if they wanted to go shopping for Christmas gifts. The hard part was getting Nadeen to say yes to him taking them. Ann took the phone to Nadeen who was sitting in the back reading her Bible.

"Momma," she said. "Kenny wants to talk to you" She looked at Ann and rolled her eyes, then she grabbed the phone. "

"Yes?" She sounded like he was bothering her. "I don't know about that, Kenny. You're not the most reliable person in the world and if something happens to my children—you already know."

She paused to listen.

"You need to have them back here before it gets dark. I mean that."

She handed the phone back to Ann, "Here. Your daddy says he's coming over in about thirty minutes to pick you all up and take you shopping. You need to take Josie with you."

Ann ran back into the bedroom and told Patsy. Kenny was coming in about thirty minutes. *Thirty minutes?* That didn't give her long. She had to have time to get cute.

She took the phone from Ann and called Dustin to find out if he could meet her at the mall. Any opportunity she could get to spend time with him she would take it. When Kenny arrived, he blew his horn; he didn't even come in the house. Patsy picked up Josie and headed for the door. "You don't walk out of my house and not tell me you're gone!" Nadeen yelled down the hall.

Ann and Patsy quickly yelled back. "Momma! We're gone!" They said. They ran out the door in case she changed her mind.

19

They jumped in the back seat of the truck, all except Patsy, she was the oldest so she sat up front with Kenny.

"Hey, Daddy," she slid in and kissed him on the cheek. She was so glad to see him. Ann leaned up and grabbed him by the back of his neck and hugged him.

He laughed. "I see somebody missed me."

"Yes, we missed you! We don't like Christmas without you, Daddy," Ann pouted.

"Christmas is about Jesus, Ann. It's not about just us. We celebrate his love for us no matter where we are. If he lets me be living to see it though, I'm going to spend the holidays with you all some way."

"Dustin's going to meet us at the mall." Patsy smiled. When they got to the mall, Kenny took Josie with him. He told Ann and Patsy to meet him back in the center court in about two hours. He asked them if he should get Nadeen a gift.

"Well, If you do, she still might not like it, but if you don't she won't like that either," Patsy said.

"I say buy her a nice church hat and a dress to match. You know she likes to look good when she walks up in Greater Trials." Ann said.

"You right about that, little girl. Wonder who she looking that good for? It ain't me. I hope it ain't the preacher and let her tell it, it ain't Brother Ryan either." They all laughed. Just then, Dustin walked up.

He spoke to Kenny and Ann then kissed Patsy. "I'll window shop with you but you can't be with me when I buy your gift."

"Why not? I want to know. I can't wait."

"No. Ann you want to go with me when I go to pick out her present?"

Ann liked hanging out with Dustin, so she immediately responded yes.

Kenny waved goodbye to them and headed off towards the toy store with Josie. They were having a great time window shopping and picking out gifts. As they passed the Family Treasurers photo shop, Ann pointed inside.

"Look Patsy. There's Brother Ryan and his wife. They with the kids taking pictures."

Dustin and Patsy both stopped and looked in the store. Sure enough, it was them. She was surprised to see them together. It had been several months since she'd heard they divorced and Mrs. Ryan had moved to another small town a few miles away.

"Now that's a miracle from God. Maybe those rumors you heard about him and your mom were just that."

Patsy looked at the picture in front of her face for a minute. *He must be trying to get his family back together while tearing ours apart.*

"Let's go. I seen enough of him," Patsy said.

"Me too," Ann said.

They shopped until their feet hurt from walking and the bags begin to wear Patsy down. Ann and Dustin snuck off and when they came back, Patsy didn't even see a bag in Dustin's hand but Ann was smiling like she had a big secret. They met Kenny back at the front of the mall center court. Josie was running around having a good time. "Come on, ladies. I'm broke now. It's time to go home," Kenny laughed and was in a better mood than Patsy had seen in a long time.

Dustin walked to the car with them, holding Patsy's hand. When they got to the car, he kissed her and told her he would give her a call later, he had some gifts he had to wrap. He walked back towards the mall.

"He's going back to get your present," Ann giggled. "He said he didn't want you guessing what it was so he left it at the store until we leave."

"You not gonna tell me what it is?" Patsy asked Ann.

"No. Dustin made me promise, plus he bought me some strawberry grape lip gloss." Ann said. She slid it out of her pocket and showed it to Patsy.

"You better not let your momma see that," Kenny said. "You know how she is about you girls wearing anything that even looks like make up."

"I'll be careful."

They strapped Josie into her car seat and headed home. They turned on the radio and sang Christmas songs all the way there. *It might be a wonderful holiday after all,* Patsy thought.

When they made it home Nadeen was gone. The house was completely dark except for the porch light.

"You kids need me to come in?"

"No, we got it. We don't want Nadeen mad at us."

Ann told Patsy the day she came home for the holidays that Nadeen didn't want Kenny in the house if she wasn't there. She said he might go snooping around and find something he didn't have any business finding. She threatened to beat the color off of Ann if she let him in.

They loaded all the bags out of the car. Kenny reached into a pretty red bag and pulled out a lovely crème colored hat with diamonds all around the edge of it. The hat was breath taking! Kenny smiled.

"You girls like this hat? I got it for your momma along with the shoes to match."

Patsy looked at it with awe. It was the most beautiful hat she'd ever seen. It had to cost Kenny a lot of money.

"It's beautiful, Daddy." Ann said. Josie reached up to touch it.

"No, baby girl. Can't touch this. We got to keep it clean to give to the woman of the house, though she thinks she the man too. But God is gonna straighten that out."

He put it back in the bag and slid the hat and shoes under the seat. He told them he was going home and work on his gift-wrapping skills or get his church member, Sister Sara, to wrap it for him. He told them he'd bring it by on Christmas. He sat in the car with the Christmas music blasting until they'd gotten in the house. Josie went to bed early because they told her they'd have a big surprise for her in the morning if she did. By the time Nadeen made it back home they'd wrapped all the gifts.

A few minutes after Nadeen got in, she was on the phone. It sounded like she was really upset with the person on the other end.

She's probably yelling at Kenny about something.

"You got nerve," she heard Nadeen yell.

He'd brought them back on time. What could possibly be wrong?

"Why is she down here with your kids and staying at your house?" She heard Nadeen ask.

Patsy put her ear to her bedroom door.

"You told me you were going to take them their gifts tonight and then would spend the rest of the evening with me! You obviously don't know who you're playing with do you?" Nadeen asked the person on the other end of the phone.

"Don't take my love for Jesus as a weakness. I ain't quite delivered when it comes to turning the other cheek. I try real hard but if you push the right button you get what you asked for. You better ask my husband!"

"I have risked everything for you and you gonna let her come to your house and stay the night? She better be sleeping in the garage!"

Just then a voice in Patsy's head whispered, *She must know about Sister Ryan and the kids being in town.* Patsy already knew what this conversation meant for them. Nadeen was gonna be in a nasty mood the rest of the night. Even if her bladder filled to the rim, Patsy would let it overflow like the Jordan River before she cracked that bedroom door open and she'd advise Ann to do the same.

She heard Nadeen slam the phone down. She was throwing things in her room and cussing out all men. Patsy fell off to sleep to the sound of Nadeen's saying something about somebody being a "mother."

Ann was the first one up on Christmas morning. She woke up Josie and Patsy and went running into the living room! Ann was so excited she just started tossing boxes looking for gifts with her name on it. Nadeen came into the room and sat down looking as though she was in deep and very dangerous thought.

Patsy helped Josie open her presents. She was trying to eat the peppermint wrapping paper. She didn't seem to have an interest in the cute little doll that Eva had bought for her or the small piano from Nadeen. Just as they were finishing unwrapping the gifts, the doorbell rang, "Who is it?" Nadeen asked through the door.

"It's me…Kenny."

Patsy and Ann both stopped. They were wondering if she was going to let him in. After all, it was Christmas day and he belonged with them. Nadeen got up and went to the door. She opened it and let him in without saying a word. He smiled as he came thru the door with an arm full of gifts.

"Merry Christmas!" He said, with a big grin on his face. Nadeen acted as though she hadn't heard a word and closed the door behind him. Josie ran up to him and grabbed him around his knees,

"Merry Christmas." She said. He almost dropped the gifts. Patsy and Ann caught them on both sides and Kenny landed on the couch with Josie. She was laughing.

"I got here just in time didn't I?"

"I know you all get up before dawn and start tearing into things."

He looked at Nadeen, "How you been, Nadeen?"

"I been great, Kenny. I been just great. You don't need to be worried about me. Just worry about your children." She snapped at him every time she spoke and Christmas Day was no exception.

Kenny sat on the couch and handed out gifts. When all the gifts were open except one big box, he reached over and gave it to Nadeen. He'd wrapped it in White paper with red hearts.

Where did he find that?

Nadeen looked a little surprised but tried to act like it was no big deal that he'd thought about her. When she opened the box, she pulled out the beautiful crème colored hat trimmed in diamonds with the shoes to match.

"Where is the dress to go with it?"

"I got the hat and the shoes; the dress is up to you." He laughed. "I hope you like it."

She looked at the hat and shoes again. "It's nice. Thank you."

Kenny looked at Ann and Patsy and smiled. "You're welcome." Patsy and Ann gave Kenny their gifts next. They included Nadeen's name too but Kenny knew better than that. He was just glad she allowed him to come and spend Christmas with them. He wasn't expecting a miracle quite yet but he was still expecting one.

He helped them clean up the rest of the mess in the living room then he asked Nadeen if he could take them over to his new apartment for the day. He even asked her if she wanted to come. She told him she had some things at the church she had to catch up on.

"You can take them with you right now if you like. I don't care to go though."

"It's Christmas Day, Nadeen. All that other stuff can wait. You're welcome to come. You haven't even been to my apartment since I moved in." Kenny said.

"You are pressuring me. Back off." She glared at him.

Kenny didn't want an argument on Christmas day so he stopped bothering her. Ann jumped up. She didn't want to do anything to set Nadeen off today! Patsy was excited they would spend the day with Kenny. Everybody raced to get changed. Kenny sat in the living room and waited.

Nadeen walked off and started making coffee. A few minutes later, they were all walking out the door with Kenny.

"Your momma seems a little distant this morning for it to be Christmas Day. What's got her vexed?"

"You know she don't tell us nothing," Patsy replied, and put Nadeen out of her mind.

20

When they got to Kenny's new apartment Patsy was surprised that everything looked so nice and neat. "Daddy, your place looks really good."

"I know how to fix up a place. Plus it didn't hurt that one of the ladies from Deliverance Rock, Sister Sara, came over and helped. Sister Sara is a natural interior decorator the way she matched all this stuff together. Her and some of the other ladies at the church were so busy in this place—I just kind of moved the rugs around," he laughed and shrugged. Patsy didn't want to hear anything about rugs today.

"She usually comes by twice a week to check on me and brings me a good home cooked meal. Heck, she even washes my clothes once or twice when I'm too busy to do it. That Helps Ministry at the church sure comes in handy." Kenny said.

Better not let Nadeen hear about that, Patsy thought to herself. Josie ran and jumped on the couch. She dug her face in the pillows. Her chin was still scarred from the Drano liquid she'd accidentally drunk a few months ago when Kenny tried to kill himself but she was so cute you looked right past that, especially with her winter hat on tied around her face. The little white ball was shaking left to right and barely hanging on as she shook her head and giggled into the couch pillows. Kenny went into the kitchen to prepare breakfast.

"Daddy, you want me to help you?"

"No. Ann can help. I need to teach her how to cook anyway."

"Can Dustin come over and hang out with us?"

"Sure. Tell my future son-in-law to come on over." Kenny yelled from the kitchen. Patsy called Dustin and he answered immediately.

"Hey, I'm at my dad's house can you come over?" She could hear lots of laughter in the background.

"I guess I can get out for about an hour or so. My sisters are in town and they got the kitchen smelling really good. Anyway, I got you a little gift and I want you to have it today." Patsy felt a small flutter in her stomach.

"Okay. Come on over I can't wait to see you." While she sat on the couch playing with Josie and waiting for Dustin to arrive, she could hear Kenny instructing Ann on how to cook and how much to measure out.

It seemed to take Dustin forever to get there but when he finally arrived he didn't waste much time giving Patsy her gift. He reached over into his black jacket pocket and pulled out a beautiful box. It was wrapped in royal blue and white paper. Patsy looked at how pretty the box was. She was sure it was jewelry. Dustin handed the box to her. She began to unwrap it. When she got all the paper off, she opened the box, her mouth fell open and her eyes had to focus twice. It was a ring! A beautiful pear shaped diamond. Several of the girls at her school were wearing them. It was what they called a promise ring.

She had never even dared to mention to Dustin how much she wanted one because she knew in Nadeen's house it was out of the question. She heard her own voice saying out loud "Oh my God! It is so beautiful!" Tears spilled over her lashes.

Dustin took the ring out of the box and put it on her finger. It fit perfectly. Ann and Kenny came out of the kitchen to get a look at it. Josie was playing with the paper that fell on the floor from the box.

"You like it Patsy?" Ann asked with a gleam in her eyes. She was smiling wider than Dustin.

"Yes I do!" Patsy said and reached over and kissed him firmly on the lips.

"Guess I better start saving up now. In a few more years we might be having a wedding." Kenny said.

Dustin blushed. "Yes, sir."

Patsy was on cloud nine all day. She told Dustin she was sorry she'd been in such a hurry she walked out of the house and forgot his gift. She told him he could come over in a few days and pick it up. They had a great breakfast courtesy of Ann and Kenny. Josie tried to feed some of it to her baby doll it was so good. When they were finished eating Kenny put the dishes in the sink.

"You all want to go over to the church with me? We have a short service this morning." "Sure." Patsy answered for everybody.

When they made it to Christmas service at Deliverance Rock. First Lady Mack was bringing the message. She called everyone up to the altar that wanted prayer. Kenny went up and took the whole family. First Lady Mack came up to Kenny, she put her hand on his forehead and anointed it with oil. She anointed the head of Josie, Ann, Dustin and Patsy. She went back to Kenny and put her hand on his head and began to moan. She had her eyes closed as she began to speak to him.

"Son of God. Seed of Adam. The Lord has not forgotten you. He sees the burdens you are carrying. He sees your possession's that the enemy has taken captive.

You must identify the spirit of the enemy and command it
to go back to the pit of hell! I command Satan in the name
of Jesus to release this man! Release his mind, release his
flesh, release his children and release his wife!" She
yelled.

Kenny dropped to the floor on his knees when she
said that, he began crying out loud. First Lady walked
around him and stood in front of him. She lifted up his
head and looked him in the eye, "Brother Kenny where is
your wife?" Kenny just shook his head. She asked him
again. "Brother Kenny where is your wife?"

He looked up at her with tears in his eyes. "I don't
know First Lady! I don't know where she is!" She
grabbed him tightly under his chin and got directly in his
face.

"And she doesn't know either ! She doesn't know
that she is in a trap set by the spirit of Jezebel! I see her
Brother Kenny! I see her! She's been taken over and
bound up. She has blinders over her eyes. She's a puppet
for Satan! He's using her to destroy you! He's deceiving
her. "You must pray for her deliverance," First Lady
Mack screamed.

Patsy felt something growing and stretching out inside
her belly. She knew it was a matter of time before it came
up through her throat. She was squeezing Dustin's hand
so hard she felt the bones of his fingers rub against hers
but he never moved. Ann dropped to her knees and began
clawing at the cut marks on her arms. First Lady Mack
moved to Patsy and put her hand on Patsy and Ann's
head.

"I break this generational curse right now in the name
of Jesus! It stops right now today in the both of you! I
send it back to the pits of hell from which it came!" The
fire spread through Patsy's belly and up into her throat.
She opened her mouth and screamed. Her mind went to a

place she couldn't describe. She saw lights then darkness. She felt something moving on the inside of her and she had to bend over it hurt so bad.

She could hear herself screaming. The last thing she was conscious of was falling to her side and she was gone. She was gone to a distant place. She heard a voice say to her "*It's almost finished. It's almost done. Stay the course. Pray. Prepare yourself for the storm that cometh for even in the storm I will be there.*"

When she came to, she was laying under a white cover. It smelled like a soft summer rain. First Lady Mack was holding Ann as she cried and rocking her back and forth. Patsy heard her softly speaking to Ann. "Stop it. Stop it, baby. Don't let that spirit destroy you."

The Ladies from the Mother Board were fanning Patsy and her head was in the lap of one of them. She just laid there for a while. It felt so good. First Lady Mack finally released Ann and stretched out her hand to help Patsy to her feet. Reverend Mack said the benediction and dismissed service. It was a quiet ride back home.

When they arrived back at Kenny's apartment everyone just took a few minutes to rest. Kenny went to the back and closed his door. Patsy could hear him praying. Josie had fallen asleep so they laid her on the couch. Ann went into the bathroom. She always ran to small quiet places for solitude. Dustin held Patsy until they both fell asleep on the couch next to Josie. An hour later, there was a knock at the door. Patsy opened and saw a young woman that looked to be in her late twenties standing in front of her with sandy blond colored hair, hazel brown eyes, and a ponytail that reached mid-way down her back. Her dress was tight through the middle and she had enough lip gloss on to fry a whole chicken.

"Oh, hi!" She said full of energy. "I'm Sara. You must be Kenny's oldest daughter, Patsy. He's told me so much about you."

She slightly pushed her way in the door. She headed towards the kitchen with what looked like a dinner plate in her hand.

"It's so good to finally meet you all. Is Kenny here?"

Patsy looked at Dustin with a look on her face that said "Who is this?" and he sat on the couch about to bust from trying to contain his laughter. Patsy was slow with her response because the woman caught her so off guard.

"He's sleep I think." She said not really sure if he was sleep or not.

"Well that's fine. I know how hard he works and all those long hours. I just wanted to bring him a little Christmas Dinner over from me and momma. I know how much he loves my red velvet cake and my fried pork chops smothered in biscuit gravy."

Really? Patsy thought. *She talking like she been knowing my daddy for a long time.*

"Honey, I'm so sorry to wake y'all up. I know y'all resting after that glorious time we had in service today. I wanted to come over and speak to you at the church but y'all was so wrapped up in the spirit I didn't dare disturb you." Patsy tried to gain her composure and not show the confusion on her face.

"Would you like to sit down?" She asked her though she acted so at home that she probably would have if she wanted. Kenny was coming out of his bedroom just as Sister Sara was putting the plate in the refrigerator.

"Sister Sara, how are you?" He gave her a hug. Patsy noticed how she looked into Kenny's eyes like a girl with a crush. Patsy knew that look. She saw it too many times when Sandra was trying to get Lavon's attention.

"I'm doing fine, sugah. I just wanted to bring something over for you to eat since it's Christmas and all. Momma and I figured you might want a good home cooked meal. I didn't know if you were going to be over here alone and hungry or have family over. It was nice to have you all at church this morning. Didn't the Lord move on today Brother Kenny?

"Yes, Sister Sara, he sure did. We enjoyed the service. I needed that break through."

"Well, I'm gonna go. I put you some food in the refrigerator. If you like I can bring more over for you and the kids."

Kenny put his arm in the small of her back and Patsy saw her face light up.

"No need to trouble yourself Sister Sara. My daughters and I are working on a little something in the kitchen right now. We'll be just fine. Tell your mother I said Thank you." He said as he slowly began walking her to the door.

"Well you all have a Merry Christmas you hear?" She said on her way out the door.

"You too, Sister. God bless you." She turned back around and looked at Kenny.

"Brother Kenny, if you need anything you call me."

Kenny smiled at her, "I'll be sure to do it, Sister Sara."

Sara walked slowly out the door as though she was waiting for Kenny to stop her. Patsy knew what was up with her. She was thirsty for her daddy! How hilarious was that? A woman young enough to be Kenny's daughter was trying to ease her way in. Patsy wondered if Nadeen would even care if she knew.

"That was nice of her to think of me. She and her mother are some good Christian women. I'm about to put both my feet in this gumbo who wants to help me?"

The next thing they heard was Ann bailing out of the bathroom. "Me! I wanna help you." She bounced into the kitchen. Patsy was glad to see her happy.

"Babe, I gotta go," Dustin said grabbing her by her hand that she wore the ring on. "I hope you like your Christmas present. It's a hint of bigger and better things to come." Patsy felt her face get warm all over as she took his hand and walked him to the door.

"I love it as much as I love you."

She walked him to the door and kissed him goodbye she hated to see him leave but she knew he had his own family to spend time with today. She decided to lay down on the couch next to Josie and finish her nap. She was still tired from whatever laid her out on the floor in Deliverance Rock that morning.

21

New Year's Eve. The world was on the brink of turning over a new year. People were shopping for party supplies and the television was full of all the late night celebrations that would be aired later that evening. Nadeen always fixed egg nog on New Year's Eve. She would drink two large cups when she got back from New Year's Eve Service and ask the Lord for a better year than the one they just got out of.

They always went to service with her at Greater Trials, this year wouldn't be much different except Kenny wouldn't be with them. He was going to be singing with the Men's Choir at Deliverance Rock He was hoping Nadeen might change her mind and join him at his church this year. He asked her but she told him she wasn't interested. She had obligations at her own church.

Aunt Eva came over wearing her party hat. She was going out to the club and Nadeen wasn't happy about that. As soon as she came through the door she was singing and dancing. She had already gotten some spirits from the liquor store. David was behind her trying to keep her standing straight.

"Hey, sister. Why don't you come out and celebrate with us tonight? We'll have you back before the church benediction."

Nadeen gave her a look like she must be crazy!

"You know I don't do that! I'm a woman of God, Eva. I don't hang out in clubs like some loose and desperate woman .You ought to do better yourself." Nadeen chided.

Eva threw her head back and laughed. "I'm as much a lady as you are and I'm also a Woman of God. I go to church but every now and then I like to get 'turnt up' with my sweetie." She said. "Momma use to go out with poppa on New Year's Eve. They would go to church, come back home, tuck us in and walk down the road to Ms. Emma Jean's house. When they came back they was laughing and singing and falling all over each other. They had been down their dancing and drinking.

"You need to come go to church with us tonight. You and David both. You a member of the choir and you out at the club instead of in the House of the Lord."

David sure enough needed to go. He needs to be dipped under the blood sicko! Patsy still hated to see the sight of him. She wanted so bad to tell her Aunt what he'd done but she didn't want to be responsible for his Home going Service because if she told Eva he was surely going to die.

"I go all through the year. Tonight I'm gonna be with my man. We gonna bring in the New Year together in each other's arms slow dancing. You gonna be by yourself with no one to hold you cause you mean as a rattlesnake"! Eva said. She turned and walked out the door with David. She must have sensed she'd gone too far.

"You won't take my joy today, Eva. Get out my house you and your so-called man so I can get ready for church."

Nadeen raised her chin and squared her shoulders at Eva."If you change your mind, there'll be room for you at the altar." Nadeen slammed the door behind them and told

Ann and Patsy to get her usher uniform together. Neither one of them wanted to do it. They knew the tension and the drama that came with being responsible for making sure each crease and collar was sharp.

"You gotta iron the heavenly garment. I can't do it. I gotta comb Josie hair," Patsy said to Ann.

"Come on, Patsy. You know I have trouble getting it right." Ann said.

"Girl, iron that transformation suit. I'll look over it before you take it back there," Patsy laughed and said.

Patsy called Josie into the den and began to comb her hair. By the time she'd gotten Josie's hair combed and gotten her dressed, Ann came back with Nadeen's usher uniform.

"Look at it Patsy. Anything wrong with it?"

Patsy took it from Ann and looked over the dress from top to bottom it was starched so hard she didn't see how Nadeen was gonna sit down in it. It was perfect.

"Ann you did good. It looks great. Them creases and that collar sharp enough to cut Reverend Craig tonight." Ann chuckled a little at that.

"Okay. I'm gonna take it in there. You iron those gloves for me real quick while I get dressed." Ann said as she walked out the room. Patsy agreed to do it. She knew Ann had been beyond stressed about that usher uniform. A few minutes later Nadeen yelled.

"Come on, girls. Let's go. I don't want to be late." They all stepped out of the room together. Instead of wearing her usher uniform, Nadeen had changed her mind and decided to wear the hat and shoes Kenny had given her for Christmas along with a gold and crème colored dress. The colors made her skin tone look a rich gold bronze. She was breathtaking. She told them the other ladies could handle the door. She was gonna rest one Sunday out of the year.

"Ooh, mommy. You look good in that hat." Ann said. Nadeen smiled real big.

"Of course. I am a Woman of God. He takes good care of me. Come on, let's go. You know every devil in town will be at that service tonight repenting for a year's worth of sinning just to go back out and do it all over again. Taking up seats saved for the Saints to give to the *Ain'ts*."

She gave them a good look over and headed to the door with her coat. Patsy whispered to Ann, "Kenny would be tickled to know she was wearing that hat and them shoes tonight."

When they arrived at Greater Trials, Nadeen noticed Brother Ryan's car. She parked next to it and quickly got out of the car to straighten out her clothes before going in. Her makeup was impeccable. She was the most beautiful woman in Greater Trials surely!

Everyone was coming up to her telling her how nice she looked and how neat her children were. She was grinning, hugging, and kissing every sister that came near her. After the opening prayer Reverend Craig came into the pulpit. He thanked the congregation for all of their prayers over the last few months since he'd lost his wife. He said he knew his life would be different now but he also knew that God would provide what he needed to get through. He reminded them God was a comforter. The congregation clapped and shouted Hallelujah. Everyone that was, except one young lady sitting on the front row, she had long light brown hair midway down the middle of her back and she wore high heeled red shoes with a two piece red and black skirt set. The split in the skirt was way up her thigh. She was sitting on the bench chewing gum and looking at Reverend Craig like she wanted to crawl under his robe right then.

Patsy wondered who she was, she had seen her at church before but didn't know her name. She looked like the same lady that had been at First Lady Craig's funeral. Once the congregation settled down, Reverend Craig said he had a surprise for the church. The person that would bring the New Year's Message was going to be one of their very own members who was recently called into the ministry. He stretched out his hand to the left and motioned for the man to come forth.

Patsy looked and felt her mouth fall open. It was Brother Ryan! Ann hit her in her side. The real shocker came when they saw who he was bringing with him as he approached the pulpit, Mrs. Ryan and his children! Patsy and Ann both looked at Nadeen out the corner of their eye. They could see her right temple throbbing, her jaw was grinding and her foot was shaking real fast! Good thing they were in church when Nadeen heard the news about Brother Ryan asking his wife to come back to him.

He apologized to the church for not being the man he needed to be for his wife and children before. He told the church the Lord spoke clearly to him at midnight a few days before Christmas. He knew he had to give up all the things holding him back and he had to get back in line with the Word of God. He told them God told him to go get his wife and children. Hearing this, the entire congregation shouted, "Amen Bro!" He kissed his wife and walked up into the pulpit to bring the New Year's Eve message.

Nadeen sat on that bench the whole service and shook that foot! She balled the handkerchief in her hand so tight Patsy was looking for blood to wring out of it. She was in another place. Josie played with Nadeen's purse strings all night and Nadeen never even told her to stop. It was gonna be a real cold ride home.

When service was over, Nadeen stood up, pressed out her dress, put on her smile and hugged her way out of that church as fast as she could. When they got to the car she went to open the door on the driver's side, as she opened it she took her car key and ran it across the passenger door of Brother Ryan's Range Rover. It left a long deep scratch.

Patsy stood there and watched her do it but she never said a word. The arrow had been shot and the weapon had been formed. The enemy was about to release his strongest attack within Nadeen! They got in the car and no one said a word. Nadeen didn't even turn on the radio.

She waved at the elders of the church and smiled as she drove by but once she got out of the parking lot she drove over the speed limit all the way home. When they got to the house, Nadeen got out of the car, slammed the door and went in the house. They all kept their distance from her. They say the darkest hour is the calm before the storm! Patsy woke up before the sun came up and went to the bathroom. When she came out of the bathroom Nadeen was walking down the hall shaking her keys. "I'm going out to the store to pick up some things. I'll be back in a little while." she said. Patsy didn't believe she was going to the store. Not the way she slammed that door. There was rage walking with her and it was looking for a fight. Josie got up a few hours later and she went to the back looking for Kenny. Patsy picked her up and told her daddy was at his new house. She could call him and talk to him if she wanted to. She shook her head 'Yes'. Patsy went to the phone and called Kenny. He answered on the first ring. "Happy New Year Little girl!" He said

"You too Kenny." Patsy said. "Josie was going through the house looking for you a few minutes ago. I think she wants to talk to you."

"She loves her daddy. Put her on the phone. She know her daddy gonna come back home. God gonna work it out and she's going to have me there with her." He said. Patsy put the phone up to Josie's ear. She just held it and smiled. She wouldn't let Patsy take it. When she tried to get it, Josie would cry and snatch the phone back. She held that phone for about ten minutes before she put it down. Patsy got back on the phone. "Where Nadeen, She still sleep?" Kenny asked.

"No, sir. She went to the store to get some stuff for the house I guess. She said she would be back in a little while."

"Really? Okay then. Tell her I said Happy New Year. Did she wear that hat yet that I got?" Patsy gladly told him yes and how good she looked in it with her new dress and matching shoes.

"That's my Nadeen." Patsy heard the back door lock twisting.

"Well sounds like she's back, Kenny. I better go."

"All right, baby girl. Call me back later."

Nadeen came in talking to herself. She was cussing up a storm. Patsy could make out some of the words. She heard them so often. She heard the phone ring and heard Nadeen pick up the phone in the kitchen and then she knew where Nadeen had been. "I don't care if I did show out in front of those people!" She yelled at the person on the phone. "You didn't care about other people when you stood up in that church last night and told the entire congregation you took your wife back! You never even thought enough of me to call me or tell me that this was what you wanted!" She said. "Now go home to your sweet little family and your old raggedy looking wife and explain to them how your face got all scratched up! Don't you ever dial my number or ring my door bell again!" She screamed.

"You don't use me like a common prostitute! Sneaking through my window laying up in my bed telling me how much you love me and how happy we are gonna be then all of a sudden you get a conscious! The Lord done spoke to you! Well, the Lord saw you, too. He saw all those times you snuck in this house too! Don't you ever come near me again because if you do I will bust your head wide open in front of your wife, Reverend Craig and the whole congregation!" She slammed the phone down.

She was coming down the hall and all of a sudden, Patsy heard her heave! It sounded like she was pulling up her guts. Patsy opened the door in time to see Nadeen holding the wall and throwing up everywhere! She was lurching forward like her whole body was possessed. Patsy jumped back

"Ann! Ann come here. Momma throwing up I need your help!" Ann came out the door and turned up her nose.

"Go get her a wet towel and help her," Patsy directed. She tried to keep Josie in the room. She was trying to get out of the door and see what was going on. Ann wet the towel and took it to Nadeen. She leaned against the wall and put the towel on her head. She was moaning and groaning like she was gonna die.

"I need someone to clean this up for me. I gotta go lay down. I don't feel too good." she said. One thing Patsy knew, it was not gonna be her! Not this! She couldn't do this. She would take a beating butt naked and wet with an extension cord before she could stomach cleaning up this mess! "Ann you gotta do it. I can't!"

"What? I don't want to do it. That's nasty." Ann said.

"Ann you better clean that up or I'll tell Nadeen about that lip gloss Dustin bought you for Christmas!" Patsy threatened. She didn't want to really tell it on her but she was desperate to get out of this duty.

"Patsy! You wouldn't do that!" Ann said pitifully. "You are so wrong for that. You a dirty trick." She said as she went to get a bowl of warm water and some Lysol to clean the mess up.

A few minutes later, they heard Nadeen again in her bathroom throwing up.

What was wrong with her? Patsy wondered.

"Patsy. Come here!" Nadeen yelled from her room. Patsy didn't want to go in the room while Nadeen was throwing up. She waited just a few minutes until she heard her stop then she went in her room.

"Patsy, I need you. I'm not feeling good. I gotta lay down. Bring me some ginger ale please. You may have to cook for your sisters." She said.

She looked so helpless laying on that pillow. It must be pretty bad if it put Nadeen down like that! Patsy stepped over Ann in the hallway and went up front to get the ginger ale for Nadeen. She knew sick or not if she didn't move with a quickness she would be the one needing some help.

When she made it back, Josie was sitting up on the bed next to Nadeen rubbing her hair. Patsy couldn't remember a time when she could sit that close to her mother and not be nervous. Josie was highly favored.

"Girl bring that ginger ale on. I feel like I been hit with a truck." Nadeen said. Patsy handed her the glass of ginger ale and waited until she told her she could leave her side. She left Josie on the bed drinking out of the same glass. Whatever Nadeen had she hoped Josie didn't catch it. "Girl what's wrong with your momma?" Ann asked. Patsy shrugged her shoulders,

"Other than needing Jesus in a real way, I don't know." They both laughed at that. Patsy sat down next to

Ann. "Ann I gotta go back to Grandma's house tomorrow." Patsy could see the sadness in Ann's eyes as she looked at her. " It won't be much longer. Don't panic just pray. Just pray that I come back real soon."

Ann started scratching her arms. "Don't leave me. Don't leave me again. I'm not gonna make it if you leave." Patsy grabbed her hand and stopped her from scratching. She knew she had to get her calm or she was going to resort to doing that 'evil thing' Patsy couldn't tell anyone about. Patsy spoke as soft as she could to comfort Ann. She knew it had to be hard for her little sister with her and Kenny both being gone.

"I'll be back in no time Ann. Would I lie to you? Didn't I promise you that when I left the hospital? I wouldn't say it if I didn't mean it. " Ann just sat on the bed and cried. Patsy pulled her little sister close to her and just held her while her warm tears melted into her shirt. *God please keep my sister strong until you bring me back home.* She prayed quietly in her mind. When Ann finally pulled herself together Patsy released her and started to get her bags to pack. Ann got up and left out of the room. Patsy's felt sicker than Nadeen. She hated to leave.

"Patsy!" She heard Nadeen yell. She put down her bags and went to see what her mother wanted. "What are you all doing in there? Josie has wasted half of my ginger ale all over her dress. Come get her and clean her up."

Patsy reached for Josie but she pushed back and rolled over to the opposite side of the bed. Patsy tried to grab her and fell on the bed on top of Nadeen.

"I know you not gonna let a two-year-old out chase you. See you done got slow living over there with your Grandma. She doin' everything for you. It's more than she did for me, I bet you that.

"But if you hadn't stuck your nose in me and Kenny's business you wouldn't be over there. Speaking of, that social worker from hell called me while I was on the phone with Eva. Said she's coming by in the morning to get you. That woman makes me sicker than I already am. She needs to stay out of my business."

Patsy knew not to respond. She chased Josie down and took her out. She decided to bake Ann a chocolate cake. That might put a smile back on her face and show her how much her big sister loved her. The cake was three layers and Josie ate it up! Ann ate a small piece. They tried to get Nadeen to eat but she said the very smell made her queasy.

22

Patsy didn't sleep at all that night. The morning came too fast. Before she realized it, Ms. Ava was pulling up in the driveway. Nadeen got up and went to the door. She was real short with her. Ms. Ava didn't even come in. She just waited at the front door. Patsy woke up Ann and kissed her on the forehead. She looked her in the eye, "Ann. I need you to be strong for me. This is hard for me but if I know you'll be strong and not cry I can do this much easier okay?" She told her. Ann's eyes started tearing up.

"Okay. Are you gonna ask Ms. Ava when you can come back home?"

"I'll talk to her when I get in the car. I promise." Patsy said. She went over to the other side of the bed and kissed Josie then she walked out of the room. She didn't get to say goodbye to Nadeen because she was in the bathroom throwing up.

"Did you enjoy your time at home Patsy?" Ms. Ava asked her.

"Yes, ma'am. I did. I was glad to see everybody. Everything went good." Patsy said.

"Did you get a chance to talk to your mother about her accidentally pouring that scalding pot of water on you?"

Patsy knew Ms. Ava didn't really believe the story she had been told.

"No."

"We didn't talk about any bad stuff. We just enjoyed the holidays." Patsy wanted to leave this subject alone. She was dealing with the scars on her back much better and they were healing. "Well. I'm glad you did. Your Grandmother has missed you."

"Ms. Ava. You been thinking about whether or not you're going to let me go back home for good?" Patsy asked.

Ms. Ava was quiet for a few moments then she answered, "I want to make the right decision, Patsy. I want you to be safe and in a good home environment. I'll think about it but most of all I'll pray about it."

They pulled up to Grandma Ruth's house. She was outside taking her lights off of the bushes in her front yard. She waved as they pulled up. Patsy got out the car and went to hug her. She missed the smell of Grandma Ruth. She always smelled like biscuits. "Glad to see you back and in one piece Patsy. I got your room all warm for you and fresh linen on the bed." She said. "Go on in and get unpacked. There's some breakfast on the oven for you."

Patsy waved goodbye to Ms. Ava and went back to her room to unpack. She looked out the window and saw Ms. Ava and Grandma Ruth talking. They seem to be having a very important conversation the way Grandma was looking in Ms. Ava's face. They were out there for a while. Patsy unpacked. Afterwards, she went up front and sat down to a wonderful breakfast. She noticed how quiet it was here. She missed Josie sitting on her lap with the bow from her ponytail hitting her in the face because it stuck up. Patsy always had to push it out of the way.

Lord Please fix it soon.

Kenny called as she was finishing up her breakfast. He told her Nadeen had called him and was asking how he was doing. He said he was so caught off guard he slept with his bedroom door locked and the dresser drawer in front of it. He didn't know what to make of that. Patsy didn't know either. She wondered if Nadeen was still throwing up.

A week after school started back Ms. Ava came to see Patsy. She told her that this would be her last week with her Grandmother if she wanted to go back home. She told her it would be under the supervision of a new case manager.

"Did you tell Grandma?"

"Yes, I spoke with her before I came to tell you. She's in between about it I can tell but I told her we'd be monitoring the family closely." Patsy hugged her and went to call Ann and give her the good news.

The week seemed to take forever to come to an end but when it finally came, Patsy was ready. Grandma Ruth drove her home and told her whenever she wanted to come over and spend the night or a few days she was welcome. All she had to do was pick up the phone. Ann and Josie were at the door when she got there. They ran out and grabbed her.

She hugged them tight. No matter what happened they would fight this battle together as one. Kenny called to see how everything went when they got back home. Nadeen asked to speak to him, Patsy was shocked but she gave the phone to him. When she finished talking she gave the phone back to Patsy and told her to go fix something nice for dinner because Kenny was coming over. Patsy couldn't believe what she heard! Just a few months ago she didn't even want him in the house and now she was inviting him over for dinner?

Something was brewing Patsy just knew it. Nadeen told her to fix him a pot roast, some collard greens, cornbread, and rice because that was one of his favorite meal. She got up later and made him a huge vanilla pudding. When Kenny arrived Nadeen had set the table and put on a real nice low cut dress. Patsy had never even seen the dress before and Nadeen never showed that much cleavage. She and Ann both wondered what was going on. The dinner went well. Kenny and Nadeen talked as though they were a happily married couple. Kenny even mentioned Sister Sara coming over to help him out.

Nadeen didn't even flinch she just smiled at him and said, "Well I will have to thank her one day for taking care of my husband. Just make sure she knows her boundaries." Patsy and Ann both almost spit their sweet tea out across the table and into Josie's mashed potatoes.

Patsy wasn't sure yet what was going on but she was watching and listening real closely. After dinner, Kenny cleaned up the kitchen. Nadeen asked him if he wanted to get a cup of coffee and come sit in her bedroom and talk. Kenny looked at Ann and Patsy with a puzzled look on his face.

"Sure, Nadeen, if you'd like. We can drink some coffee and talk. You sure you want to talk in your bedroom? We can sit in the back in front of that nice warm fire you got back there instead." He said. He must have been a little nervous himself.

"No. I got a real nice comfortable chair in there. We can talk in private. I know you been wanting to talk with me. I been so busy I haven't had time."

Patsy made the coffee and took it to them. Kenny was sitting in the chair and he seemed a little uneasy. Nadeen was sitting on the bed with a pillow behind her head and she was talking to him about work. Josie came in and sat on Kenny's lap. Patsy and Ann both decided they weren't going to sleep until Kenny left and they were going to stay close by in case something happened. They both must have dozed off because when they woke up the sun was just coming up. Patsy jumped up off the couch. *Where was Josie?* She never slept without them. Patsy looked around and then something told her to go to the window.

She went to the window and looked out. She saw Kenny's truck. He was leaning against the front car door laughing and talking with Nadeen. She was holding Josie. When he got ready to get in the car, Nadeen leaned over and kissed him on the jaw. Patsy almost fell over the chair behind her. *This has got to be a dream!* She did not just see Nadeen Simmons kiss Kenny Simmons on the jaw. That would never happen!

She ran over and shook Ann, "Ann! Ann, get up. Come look out the window."

Ann slowly got up and went to the window. She got there in time to see Kenny pulling off.

She turned and looked at Patsy with her eyes big. "Did he spend the night last night?" Ann asked Patsy.

"It looks like he did. What's going on?"

"I don't know girl. I'm really scared now. Maybe all that praying and crying is finally paying off."

"Either that or Jesus is on his way back today."

Nadeen came in the house and put Josie on the couch. Ann and Patsy both came up front to look and see who this person was in Nadeen's skin.

"You all need to go ahead and clean up. Kenny is gonna come back later and take us to the movies and then out to dinner. I need to find me something nice to wear. I probably need to get a salad for dinner my waist has gotten a little bit bigger it seems."

When Kenny came back to pick them up, he looked real nice. Nadeen had put on a beautiful rust colored sweater that made her skin look a beautiful bronze color. Kenny had picked the sweater out for her about two Christmas's ago. She hadn't worn it before because she said she didn't like the color and really didn't want anything he picked out anyway but she had it on today with some high heel boots to match and some black jeans. Kenny always liked her to wear her hair pinned up with the curls falling down on the sides of her face and neck. She wore her hair just that way today and was smelling really nice. Ann and Patsy were shocked. Kenny just stood in the doorway and looked at her.

"You must like what you see, Kenny Simmons!"

He laughed and said, "I certainly do, Nadeen Simmons. Come on girls. Let's get in the car and go over to Denise's Diner. She has a real good buffet today."

Patsy wasn't quite sure what was going on. She was holding her breath and watching Nadeen real carefully. You just never know with her. Something real strange was going on and Patsy wanted to keep her eyes open for it. When they got to the restaurant, Kenny went around to the passenger side and opened the door for Nadeen. They walked in the restaurant together as though they'd never had a fight or an argument. Ann and Patsy just kind of walked behind them and watched. Nadeen ate like an army. She had three servings of ice cream and a big bowl of nothing but whip crème but Kenny didn't say a word. She usually didn't eat that much.

Reverend Craig was there too. He was sitting with the young lady that had been coming to the church sitting on the front row every Sunday. He didn't look like he was grieving to Patsy. He seemed to be really enjoying himself. Patsy looked at the young lady—something about her face looked familiar to her but she couldn't really put her finger on it. When they got up to leave, he saw Kenny and Nadeen so he came over to speak. He thanked her for attending the services for First Lady and told her how he was going to try and go on like she would want him to.

He never did introduce the young lady with him. She just stood by and smiled at them. Patsy noticed Nadeen squeezing her napkin in her hand with a forced smile.

"Well, Pastor, it's real good to see you out fellowshipping. I think I've seen you at the church a few times," Nadeen said to the young woman. She took her hand and moved her hair off of her shoulder while squeezing Reverend Craig's arm real tight.

"Yes. I've been visiting for quite some time. Trying to get used to everything."

Patsy caught the last part of the sentence and she was confused. Nadeen told her if she needed anything to let the Usher Board know and they would be glad to help her. Reverend Craig thanked her for being such an ambassador for Greater Trials and walked out the door with the woman cleaving to him. Kenny wanted to ask about her Ann and Patsy could see it in his eyes but he kept eating on his ox tails not wanting to spoil the moment. *Something strange was going on here.*

Nadeen was eating slower and looked like she was in deep thought.

After dinner, Kenny took them to a movie. When the movie was over, on the way home, Kenny told everyone how much fun he had. Nadeen asked him if he wanted to come in.

"No, I better not. I got to meet with the men at the church tonight. We're planning something special for the women in the church on Valentine's Day and you know we're gonna need a lot of help so we have to start early. Sister Sara supposed to come over and give us some ideas."

Nadeen leaned over and put her hand on his leg, "Sister Sara seems to be getting a little too helpful with my husband. You need to let her know you can get all the advice you need right here. That is if you care too. You may have already found someone to replace me."

Kenny smiled. "She just helping out. I ain't looking for nobody Nadeen. I'm a married man."

"That's right and you remember that." Nadeen said. "Call me and let me know you made it home."

"I will." He nodded and gave her a sweet smile. "Girls, I'll be in touch with you soon. Maybe you can come over this weekend and hang out with me." He winked as he backed the truck out of the driveway.

As soon as she got in the door good, Nadeen ran to the bathroom. She threw up everything she had eaten. Patsy begin to wonder, the last time Nadeen did all this throwing up that she could remember was when she was pregnant with Josie. Surely that couldn't be it—Kenny wasn't living with her and they definitely hadn't been that close in months. A terrible thought crossed her mind *What if she was pregnant?* It would have to be Brother Ryan's cause she was sneaking around with him and he'd been sneaking in the house late at night when he thought Ann and Josie were asleep. Brother Ryan was a married man and Nadeen was a married woman they didn't have no business sneaking around anyway.

If Nadeen was pregnant that would be so shameful she could never go back to Greater Trials. Patsy would have to drop out of school due to the gossip and Kenny, Kenny would probably be in jail for assault or murder cause God was still working on him and Patsy didn't think he'd gotten to the part of "turning the other cheek" yet as far as Brother Ryan was concerned. *Please Lord. Don't let it be that!*

23

Ann and Patsy talked about the weekend on the way to the bus stop. Nadeen stayed home from work because she wasn't feeling well. "Ann you notice how sick Nadeen been lately?" Patsy asked.

"Yeah. She must have something real bad. I hope I don't catch it." Ann said. Patsy started to tell her what she thought might be the problem but decided she better wait. She did however share her view point with Dustin when she got to school. He looked at her and didn't say a word for a long time. Finally, he spoke to her "Patsy. You must be out of your mind. That can't be true. You really think your mother is pregnant by a married man in her own church?"

"Yes, I do. Ann told me he was sneaking in the house and coming over there while I was staying at my grandma's house."

"Patsy, don't tell anyone else this especially your dad, if you're wrong you could cause a lot of damage and if you're right you could cause someone to get killed."

"I ain't the one that laid down with a man that's not my husband and got a baby by him. What do I have to be scared of?"

"Just keep that to yourself for a minute. She might really have a serious illness. Look at First Lady Craig at

Greater Trials. She was sick for a long time before they really knew what was wrong with her and the next thing you know she's singing in the heavenly choir," Dustin joked.

"I'm just wondering that's all. She been so nice to Kenny all of a sudden. He just been falling for it too. I hope he doesn't get his feelings hurt." Patsy said.

"He won't." Dustin replied. "He's been praying to get his family back so maybe God is doing it."

As they were walking down the sidewalk to their class, a nice cream colored Lexus pulled up by the curb, the lady driving looked like the one that Patsy saw with Reverend Craig yesterday.

Why would she be up here? Patsy thought. When the passenger door opened, out stepped Daphne Porter. Patsy wondered why she was with Daphne. She looked at the lady again and then back at Daphne. Her mind began to work it pieced the features together of Daphne and then the lady. While she was working on the puzzle in her mind, she heard Daphne lean over and say, "Thanks for the ride, Sister. You gonna pick me up this afternoon?"

The girl was on the phone so she hollered at her again "Champagne! You hear me? Are you picking me up from school?" She asked again.

Champagne? Champagne Porter? Daphne's older sister. Oh My God! She was the woman at the church and at the restaurant? She had a reputation that would shame a stripper! *What in the world was Reverend Craig doing with her?*

"Nice ride," Dustin said.

Patsy jumped back to the picture in front of her. Daphne walked by them and rolled her eyes at Patsy. Patsy wondered if she was losing her mind, because there were too many strange things with strange answers in her head. Kenny was at the house when Ann and Patsy got home. He was fixing some things around the house that he'd been meaning to get to before Nadeen made him leave.

Nadeen was sitting in the kitchen watching him work. "Hey, girls. How was school?"

"It was all right," Ann said.

"It was good," Patsy said. "Though I saw a real interesting site this morning when I first got to school."

"Really? What was that?"

"I saw the lady that Reverend. Craig was at the restaurant with at the school this morning.
She was dropping off her younger sister."

"How is that interesting?"

"The sister is Daphne Porter. The girl who doesn't like me because I had a fight with her cousin, Eddie Porter. The girl is her older sister Champagne Porter. She has a real bad reputation around town from what I've heard."

"People can change, Patsy. She may not be that way anymore. Maybe Reverend Craig has been ministering to her."

Nadeen didn't say a word. She just rocked Josie and watched Kenny. Patsy decided she would go and do her homework. Kenny stayed around until they all went to bed. The next morning Patsy got up for school and she heard him starting up his truck. He had stayed another night. Patsy really didn't know yet what to make of this change of heart in Nadeen. She was still piecing it together, afraid of what the final picture might be.

Later that day after school, Patsy wondered why Ann wasn't on the bus, she asked one of her friends if she'd seen her.

"She said she was gonna stay and try out for basketball this year," the girl said.

Ann hadn't told Patsy anything about that. *Who did Ann think was going to pick her up from school? She knew good and well that Nadeen wasn't going to come and get her.* Patsy thought. When she got in the house, Nadeen yelled down the hall, "Ann is that you and Patsy?"

Patsy went to the back room, "No, ma'am, it's just me. Ann's friend said she was staying after school for basketball try outs." Patsy said.

"She called me. I told her I wasn't coming to get her all the way over there to that school. I'm not feeling well today. I told her she better have a way home and she better not better not be too much longer getting here!" Nadeen said.

Patsy already knew basketball tryouts might take more than an hour. She hoped Ann could find a ride home because if not it would take her another hour and a half to walk home. Things had been going pretty good at the house but if Ann didn't make it home when Nadeen thought she should be there that was about to change.

Ann called about two hours later. She asked Nadeen again if she could come and get her because she couldn't get Kenny on the phone. Nadeen told her she wasn't coming and she'd better be home in thirty minutes! *Here we go with the impossible crap again,* Patsy screamed in her head.

Nadeen knew that wasn't possible. She'd been looking for a reason to release her anger for weeks about the social worker getting in her business but she was too scared to touch Patsy right now so she would take it out on Ann. By the time Ann made it home, it was dark and the street lights were on. It had taken her about two hours to get home. She had walked home with another girl who lived a few blocks up. They both were glad for the company. Ann came in and she looked tired. She dropped her books on the front table and tried to sneak down the hall.

"You come right in here young lady! Bring my branches with you! I told you not to come in my house when it was dark. You probably been somewhere with some boy instead of where you said you were! You let me find out I'm gonna stomp a mud hole in your back!" Nadeen yelled.

Ann turned around and went back up the hall. She was so tired she just disconnected from what was about to happen. Patsy looked at her but she didn't even look back. She just took the long twisted branches to Nadeen and closed the door. Patsy got knots in her stomach. She hadn't felt this feeling in a while. It kind of caught her by surprise. She had to walk outside because she couldn't stand to hear Ann screaming from the pain.

She walked out the door with Josie and sat on the porch and cried as the wind blew across her face and dried up her tears before they could reach her bottom eyelashes. *When is it going to get better for us Lord? When?* Patsy looked up to heaven and asked. She sat on the porch for about twenty minutes, thinking. *This is why Ann keeps cutting herself. She keeps hurting herself on the outside cause she's so tore up on the inside and her own momma who suppose to have discernment can't see it.*

When she went back in the house, Ann was in the bedroom sitting on the bed crying with a razor in her hand cutting her pillow to shreds. She was ripping it the way she probably wanted to rip her own flesh. Patsy ran and grabbed her by the wrist. "Stop it! Ann, stop it before you accidentally cut yourself," Patsy begged.

"Patsy I never should have asked you to come back into this! You should have stayed with Grandma. Nothing has changed. Nothing!" Ann cried out. Patsy didn't know what to say, she knew Ann was right and she knew it was just a matter of time before Nadeen got a chance to take her anger out on who it was really for, her, Nadeen never forgot. Ann cried almost all night. Patsy helped her to get dress the next morning so she wouldn't hurt herself putting clothes on the open cuts all over her body from the branches. It was a good thing it was cold. Ann could wear long sleeves and cover up until the cuts healed. Ann gathered up her books, put on her coat and walked out the door without saying a word. She didn't talk all the way to the bus stop. She barely told Patsy goodbye when it came time for her to get off the bus and of course she didn't tell her about the shiny new, sharp razorblade in her pocket.

At school, Patsy saw Champagne Porter pull up in the crème colored Lexus. Daphne got out and her girls met her at the curb. They were telling her how much they liked the new car she was riding in. Patsy heard Daphne smirk and say, "Girl, my sister got that Pastor wrapped around her finger. He smelling her dirty drawers he so sprung! That ain't all she gonna get from him. The car is just the beginning." She walked off laughing with her friends.

Patsy tried not to look over at them and stare. She couldn't believe what she heard. Reverend Craig wife hadn't been dead even a good six months yet and he was already dating again? *He must have been seeing her before but surely he wouldn't do that? Not the good Reverend?*

Sandra came up to her while she was trying to revive herself from what she just heard. "You see Champagne driving that new Lexus? I heard my momma on the phone just the other night talking to one of the ladies at that church. They was talking about how shameful it was for her to be so bold as to come to that church every Sunday and sit up there on the front row like she was the First Lady. First Lady Craig at home sick and she out with her husband. They said he bought her that new car a few days after First Lady passed."

Patsy looked at Sandra with disbelief, "You mean he was cheating on First Lady while she was laying in her bed dying?"

Sandra put her hands on her hips. "Yes. girl. My momma said he been seen a lot of places with her. Some of his congregation my momma say, has left the church they were so disappointed in him. You hadn't noticed those spaces in them pews? Sandra asked. Patsy wondered if Nadeen had heard about this. Even though it wasn't her business, it stayed on Patsy's mind. *How could someone that is supposed to be called by God to preach the Word and save souls, bring his girlfriend into the church in front of God and the whole congregation? The Lord was gonna strike him down right in the pulpit for that!*

When Patsy got back on the bus that afternoon she was still thinking about it, Ann sat next to her. "I made the basketball team." She smiled and said. "I asked coach to call and tell Nadeen. You know he goes to the church. She ain't gonna let him know how crazy she is. She might just change her mind to save face in front of her church members."

When they got home, Nadeen was sitting at the kitchen table drinking her tea. She looked at Ann and stared at her for a few minutes.

"I got a call from your coach today." She said. "He told me you made the basketball team. Ask me if you could play because you got a natural talent. I told him that come from me! He said he remembered me when he use to come to the basketball games with his older brother. You know I use to burn up that basketball court. It was the only thing your Grandmother let me do. Daddy and Kenny was at every game. He said your basketball skills might get you a scholarship to a top school. He say he's related to Reverend Craig on his mother's side of the family says he's always hearing Reverend Craig say good things about me.

Ann you think you smart but you ain't. I'm gonna let you play but one wrong move and you are off that team and I mean it. You hear me?" Nadeen was stern.

Ann humbly replied, "Yes, ma'am." Ann knew what she was doing. She was smart. She was glad she changed her mind about going into the girl's bathroom and finishing what she'd started with the razorblade. Something told her *just wait until you get home.* One thing Ann knew was that Nadeen's image at church meant more to her than anything other than getting her crown in Glory.

24

The first Saturday in February, Patsy went to get the mail. She noticed a beautiful envelope in lace and red addressed to Mr. and Mrs. Simmons. It had no name at the top. She took the envelope in and gave it to Nadeen. She was on the phone when she handed it to her. She opened it and shouted.

"Oh, my Lord! Reverend Craig is engaged! First Lady ain't yet cold in her grave!" She said. "Eva I got to call you back. I need to talk to my prayer circle sisters!" As she dialed the number she kept saying, "Champagne? What kind of Christian name is Champagne?"

Greater Trials MB Church was packed on Sunday morning to get a look at their new future First Lady. Ms. Gladys, Sandra's mother, was even there sitting on the front row in the middle aisle. She hadn't been in so long one of the usher unknowingly gave her a visitor's gift. The future First Lady was on the front row in her tight pink dress and her big hat. Her lipstick was hot pink with a heavy coat of what looked like petroleum jelly on her lips. The pastor called her up and introduced her to the congregation. He said he was lonely and he needed some companionship. He told his members that Sister Porter had been there with him through First Lady's illness and she had been a comfort to the both of them. He told them he knew it would be all right with First Lady because she wouldn't want him growing old all alone. The congregation was silent.

The angel Gabriel could have appeared at that moment in the pulpit of Greater Trials, but no one would have noticed, all eyes were on Ms. Champagne Porter! When service ended there was a lot of whispering going on. People weren't standing around as usual hugging and smiling. They were walking out slowly shaking their heads. Nadeen made it to the parking lot and threw up outside. Patsy was handing her a napkin when she noticed Brother Ryan walk by and look at her. Mrs. Ryan came over to Nadeen and bent down next to her with her hand on her back, "Sister Nadeen you all right?"

Nadeen looked up at her and said, "I'm just fine. Thanks for asking. I just need to get home. Been feeling ill for some time now." She said and glanced over at Brother Ryan

"Come on, sweetie. She all right. Her girls will take good care of her won't you girls?" Brother Ryan asked as he almost did a relay run getting away from Nadeen.

A few days later Nadeen and Kenny went to the Valentine Day Dance at Deliverance Rock and they were such a beautiful couple. Kenny had gone shopping and bought Nadeen a beautiful strapless red dress. He bought a white suit for himself with a shirt and tie to match her dress. She wore her hair up the way he liked and even though she had to put on a girdle to get in the dress, she manage to get it on and looked beautiful. Patsy took a picture of them before they left.

It looked like they were going to a prom. When he stepped into the dance with her all heads turned, especially Sara's. She knew Kenny was married but since they lived apart she wasn't expecting him to show up with his wife at the dance. She hadn't been bringing all those

Sunday home cooked meals over just to converse. Sara also hated the fact that Nadeen was beautiful. Her long black hair curled up on her head and her caramel skin made her dress look gorgeous. Her eyes gave her an exotic and alluring attraction.

"Hey, Sister Sara," Kenny came up to her smiling and said. "This is my wife, Nadeen."

Sara reached out her hand to Nadeen but she ignored it.

"Nice party you put together here. Kenny told me how helpful you were with getting it together. We appreciate that," she said to Sara. Before Sara could bite her tongue in half, Nadeen gave her a sarcastic smile and walked away with her arm in Kenny's.

Sara couldn't believe Nadeen had just tried to belittle her. Nadeen didn't seem to want Kenny, but she didn't want anyone else to have him either. She had a strong desire to dump the whole bowl of punch she was stirring down the front of her dress.

Nadeen clung to Kenny all night. Even he was surprised. He wondered if by some small chance she was putting on an act for Sara.

They stayed out late so of course Kenny had no choice but to stay with them that night. Nadeen said she would be worried about him driving such a distance so late at night. When they got up the next morning, Kenny was in the kitchen cooking breakfast. They all sat down to eat and Kenny said he had an announcement to make. He looked over at Nadeen and she looked at us. "Your mother and I have talked about it and we are going to try and work things out. I'm moving back home at the end of the month." He said with a big smile on his face.

Patsy and Ann told Kenny how happy they were that he was coming back home. Nadeen was eating a piece of toast and smiling. Over the next few weeks Kenny slowly begin moving things back into the house. Sometimes he stayed over and other nights he stayed at the apartment.

Patsy wondered if he was sure he had really done the right thing. Whatever he thought, he put the rest of his furniture in storage and at the end of February Kenny was back at home. He would go to work, home, and church. He was at Nadeen's every beck and call. She was acting more and more helpless each day with him being back. Patsy and Ann didn't know what to make of her.

One night at dinner, Nadeen got sick, she jumped up and ran to the back, Kenny went behind her. When they came out of the bathroom Kenny was smiling real big. He asked Ann to bring her a cup of ice and a cool towel.

"Girls, you gonna have a new baby brother or sister. Me and Nadeen got us a baby coming! I tell you. I thought we were through making babies and here we are going to be blessed with one more. I love you girls but it sure would be nice to have a boy. Too many women think they wear the pants around here! I need a son to help me keep the pants away from you women."

Patsy and Ann looked at each other. Nadeen been throwing up since December and it was now the first of March. Kenny had just started back coming over and staying the night about a month or two ago. Patsy knew now what this was all about. Nadeen was setting Kenny up.

Patsy didn't believe that this was Kenny's baby. She was trying to save her reputation and image by making Kenny believe he was the father. Kenny was so excited he never even considered he couldn't be the father. He was on the phone immediately calling Grandma Ruth, his sister, Ernestine and Eva to tell them the good news. Grandma Ruth and Eva seemed very surprised. Ernestine he said was funny acting as usual, he said she just held the phone for a few minutes then said, "You will never learn," and hung up the phone.

When Eva came over a few days later to check on Nadeen, she told Patsy, "I didn't even know she was performing her wifely duties with your daddy the way she was talking so bad about him right before Christmas. But, Honey, you never know about married people. That's why I just nod my head and keep my opinion to myself."

Grandma Ruth came over and brought Nadeen some Jell-O. She sat at the table just staring at Nadeen.

Finally, Nadeen looked at her and said, "What, momma? Why you keep looking at me so funny?"

"Why you just now telling Kenny you pregnant?" Nadeen put her head down and started playing with the Jell-O in her bowl.

"I didn't know for sure before, momma. I had been sick but I thought it was a stomach virus or something."

Grandma Ruth held Nadeen's head up. "I been around a long time and I can pretty much read in a woman's face when she pregnant and how far along. Your face don't look like a woman who is three or four weeks pregnant, Nadeen." She narrowed her eyes at her daughter and made her squirm.

"What? Well I am. I know my body. Kenny and I just started back getting along a few weeks ago. It must have happened the very first night he stayed over."

"*Hpmh.* Look to me like he must have been staying over about four or five months back by the look of your throat. Kenny told me about catching you at Brother Ryan's house right before he moved out of here. You wouldn't be trying to pass off another man's baby on Kenny would you? Even you wouldn't stoop that low, would you?"

"Momma, how could you say such a thing to me? I would never do that. Brother Ryan is just a church member and a coworker nothing else. He was someone to console me when me and Kenny were having problems. He's married momma!'"

"So are you. Marriage has never stopped Satan from convincing husbands and wives to drop their drawers for someone else other than their own." Grandma said in a matter of a fact tone of voice.

Grandma got up from the table and put the remaining of the Jell-O in the refrigerator. She got her coat and headed for the door. She turned back around and looked at Nadeen.

"Daughter. I hope you know what you doing. I know what I see and I know what it means. Playing with witchcraft never ends well." She walked out the door.

"You would know," Nadeen whispered under her breath.

They didn't know Patsy had been in the living room reading and heard every word. Her worst fear about this pregnancy was now confirmed. It probably wasn't Kenny's baby. It was Brother Ryan's. The arrow of the enemy was aiming for the final destruction of this family. Patsy knew she was going to have to pray harder now. Poor Kenny, if he found out it would send him over the edge. He had been trying so hard to stay on the straight path. He had never hit Nadeen, but something like this might make him. What was she going to do? Patsy had to get to a phone.

She needed to talk to Dustin—this was bothering her spirit. She went to call Dustin. It seemed to take him forever to answer the phone.

"Hey, Patsy. What's going on, baby?" He was cheerful.

"Dustin, I got some bad news. I need to talk to you about it."

"What is it? Has something happened?"

"Something has happened all right. I found out today Nadeen is pregnant with another man's baby."

Dustin was silent for a few minutes then he spoke very cautiously.

"We talked about this before remember? You might not believe that your parents are getting along but they are. If you tell your dad you think this baby is not his it would destroy your family especially if it's not true. Maybe you're just a little jealous of a new baby coming."

"I wish that was all, being jealous. After hearing my Grandma Ruth talk to her today I really believe she is pregnant by Brother Ryan," Patsy whispered.

"Patsy! You shouldn't say stuff like that! This is your mother you're talking about! She's the Head Usher and the President of her Prayer Circle Society. She got her faults but she would never do something so disrespectful to your dad or to God." He said.

"She would do it and she has done it! I just know it," Patsy said. "I overheard my Grandmother talking to her today and my Grandmother pretty much told her she didn't believe the baby was my dad's. She said she looked farther along than just two or three weeks. She said she can tell." Patsy said.

"I pray that it's not true. Brother Ryan and his wife just got back from celebrating their renewal of wedding vows. They been on a honeymoon and everything I heard," Dustin said.

"This would destroy everything for them. Just pray that it's not true. What are you going to do? You know you can't tell your dad something like this. If you don't know for sure, you shouldn't say anything."

Patsy just held the phone. She wasn't sure what she should do.

"I need to ask God what to do. Do I say something or do I just let him do it his way, maybe he allowed me to be there to hear it so that I would do the right thing. It wouldn't be right to know someone is being deceived and not tell them.

Dustin pleaded with Patsy.

"Baby. Please leave this alone. Let God do it his way. He'll reveal it. If it's the truth he'll show it when he's ready. You don't even know for sure and if you put that out, whether the truth or a lie, Nadeen will hurt you for it."

His voice was weak and pained at the thought of Nadeen doing anything to her.

Patsy thought about the consequences. She would destroy her family and her father if she told him what she suspected. If she was right it would be devastating for Brother Ryan and his family too but sin has consequences and it's never good. *Surely Brother Ryan suspected something when he saw Nadeen vomit in the church parking lot?* Patsy thought. He was just trying to avoid the trouble he knew was coming from what he'd done. Kenny might beat him down right in that church or worse, kill him!

"I gotta go Dustin. I need some time to think about this and pray. I'll see you at school tomorrow."

"Call me back if you need to talk."

Patsy hung up the phone and went to sit in her closet. She felt safe there. She felt close to God. The enemy was just mad because Kenny was trying to get his self and his family back together again. They were happy for a change. A little peace had come into their lives and the enemy couldn't stand it. Patsy got on her knees and as she began to pray to God, the tears begin to fall down her face.

Lord. I need you right now. Lord I don't know what to do. I know you see this situation. I know in my gut Lord that this baby is not Kenny's. I know she's deceiving him. What do you want me to do? Please speak to me. Lord I need to hear from you. Lord if you could just make it not true, that would fix everything. Make it not true Lord.

She prayed as the tears ran warm down her face. She could feel the temples of her head starting to throb. Patsy sat in that closet for about thirty minutes but she didn't get an answer.

25

For the next several weeks, Patsy tried to avoid looking at her mother. Every time she looked at her, she thought about what she'd heard. She kept thinking that surely even Nadeen wouldn't pull something so disrespectful on Kenny. He didn't deserve to be hurt that way. When they went to church with her, she would see Brother Ryan and his wife sitting up front. They seem so happy. Nadeen would look at them with her jaw tensed. Patsy could tell something was bothering her. Greater Trials didn't need this scandal. It was going through enough with Reverend Craig going off and marrying Champagne Porter about a month after they got engaged.

The gossip about Greater Trials and their new First Lady was thick around town. Some of the pews were empty since he married her. The members of the Mother Board would shake their heads whenever they saw her. She would come in with short dresses, high heels and blazing red lipstick. She wore loud blonde hair mid-way down her back with spiraled curls at the end. She was well built and knew it. Her legs had just the right thickness and her waist was small enough that she didn't need a corset or girdle. She was the color of melted peanut butter and had a walk so nasty it would make a deacon sin in his mind. The Pastor seemed to be a brand new man with her. He was dressing in the latest fashions, showing off his gold watches and his name brand suits.

He looked like a peacock strutting into the pulpit these days. He stopped wearing his robe because it covered up his "blessings" he told the congregation. He said he didn't have no reason to be ashamed of the new look and the new bride God had given him.

Patsy decided it was best she stick to going to Deliverance Rock with Kenny until God told her what she needed to do about this deception that was growing bigger day by day, week by week and month by month. Kenny was working two jobs to get ready for the new baby. He wanted to add on a new room to the house for the nursery. He said he felt it was a boy this time and he would need his own bathroom. He was so happy. He was pampering Nadeen and she seem to be loving it! She even fussed less. Grandma Ruth would call the house and check on them but she hadn't been back over since she'd had that talk with Nadeen about the baby.

Patsy hadn't spoken to her Aunt Eva in a while. She wondered how things were going with her. One night she decided to call her. Patsy usually didn't get on the phone when Nadeen was home but tonight she had a real strong urge to talk to Eva. She went to the back and called her. When Aunt Eva answered the phone she heard loud music in the background and a lot of laughing.

"Aunt Eva? What you doing?" Patsy asked. She was talking to someone in the background and trying to talk to Patsy too.

"Hey baby. Me and your Uncle David just playing some cards here at the house. We got a real good card party going on and some hot fish frying!"

Patsy thought to herself, *that wolf eyed pervert ain't my uncle. Aunt Eva he touched me! He put his hands in my panties and he touched me.*

"What's going on? Everything okay over there?" Eva asked.

"Yeah. I guess so." Patsy sighed

"What you mean 'you guess so'? Nadeen been flying off the handle today? She pregnant and I'm sure she is ten times worse than ever now!"

Patsy paused for a minute, then she said, "She's been okay. I'm not too excited about the baby though." It got quiet for a minute; Aunt Eva must have gone to another room.

"Why you not happy? You not looking forward to the new addition to the family?"

Patsy felt that she could trust Aunt Eva, after all, she knew about Dustin and never said a word. Patsy decided it was safe to tell her what she suspected and what her Grandmother said to Nadeen.

"Aunt Eva. I know this may seem like a bad thing to say, but you remember when the rumor was going around about Nadeen and Brother Ryan fooling around?"

"Yeah. I heard your daddy caught her somewhere with him. She was mad about that said he shouldn't have been snooping around following her."

"Well Aunt Eva, I got a feeling that the baby she's carrying isn't Kenny's. I think it's Brother Ryan's. I mean she was getting sick weeks before Kenny came back home."

Aunt Eva got real quiet. Patsy was just about to ask her if she was still on the line when she answered her in a calm, steady voice, full of concern.

"Patsy. You know your momma has a lot of issues. She got some things inside of her that only God can fix. I know you're a smart girl, and can make good decisions.

So, I'm going to ask you to keep those feelings to yourself. Let God deal with your thoughts and your feelings. He'll work it out. Sometimes you have to hide things in your heart."

Patsy noticed Aunt Eva didn't seem surprised by what she said; that caught her off guard a little bit.

"You're not surprised that I think that?" she asked Aunt Eva.

"No. I know you've been through a lot of things that could give you that impression but I'm asking you for me, not to breathe a word of this to anyone. It would cause more strife and pain. You know your momma wouldn't like to know you were saying things like that to people. You know she proud of her reputation up at that church and she don't want no one to mess that up." Patsy just had to know so she asked.

"Aunt Eva. You know something don't you?"

"I know it's best not to let this kind of talk get out. Just let it die. Let it die, Patsy, and let God fix this thing. Look. I gotta get back to that fish before it burn. You call me another time and we'll talk. I love you."

When she hung up, Patsy thought she heard the click of another phone receiver hanging up. *Was someone listening on the other end at Aunt Eva's house or at her house?* She hoped not, it would be bad either way it went. She decided to go to bed and try and get some rest. This thing would drive her crazy if she let it.

She was turning over in a deep early morning sleep, when she heard loud voices. She hadn't heard such loud voices in months, and she recognized Kenny's voice. He was asking Nadeen something and she sounded like she was crying. Patsy got up and cracked her bedroom door so she could hear what was going on.

"Nadeen, I want you to tell me the truth right now! I want to know if you carrying another man's baby or not?"

Patsy's heart raced. *Oh. God! Oh God! Kenny must have picked up the phone last night and heard her talking to Aunt Eva!* She was feeling sick in her stomach. Nadeen was going to kill her. Maybe she could explain the conversation some other way since Aunt Eva never really said that it was true.

"Kenny why would you let someone fill your head with such evil thoughts? We've been getting along so good and now you're going to let some filthy mouth liar destroy everything!" Nadeen yelled.

"This ain't no filthy mouth liar Nadeen. This is someone I trust!"

"You don't need to trust nobody but God Kenny Simmons! I thought you knew better than that!" She yelled back at him. "I haven't even talked to Brother. Ryan except to congratulate him and his wife on renewing their vows. I was glad to know they worked things out. I tried to tell you before there was nothing sexual going on with us. We just happen to go to the same church and work at the same job. The night you walked up on us in the park I was just talking to him about everything going on between us. I needed a shoulder to cry on."

Kenny let out a loud sigh. "I better not find out you lying to me Nadeen. I know what I heard and it was suggestive of you and Brother Ryan fooling around and now here come a baby! I won't be your fool and take care of another man's baby! Do you hear me Nadeen? That is one thing I won't do!"

Patsy heard Nadeen start talking real sweet and low to Kenny. She was able to calm him and before you knew it, he was sounding like he was sorry for what he asked her, said maybe he was mistaken. Then Patsy heard her say, "Come on and lay with me for a little bit. Tell me who would have filled your head with such lies. They just upset because we been getting along Kenny. You know I can't be disturbed with all this drama! It's not good for our baby. You want Kenny Jr. to come here all fussy and jumpy cause you fussing at his momma?"

What was she going to do now? Patsy thought. Kenny was going to tell Nadeen what he heard on the phone and Patsy knew it. Nadeen had already been waiting to get her for the whole thing with the social worker invading her privacy, even though it was her fault. Patsy told Ann what happened when she woke up. Ann's eyes got real big.

"Oooh Patsy! She is gonna kill you girl! Why did you ask Aunt Eva something like that?" Anne was panicked. "Kenny heard you. He's not gonna let it go that easy. He's gonna be listening and looking now cause he's not sure."

"I didn't know he was on the phone. I didn't hear him pick it up." Patsy said. "I don't want anyone hurt. I was just saying what I felt."

"You better keep that to yourself. We all could have a real hard time now because you know he's going to tell her he heard you tell Aunt Eva."

"I know. I don't know what to do now. I better stay close to my room the next few days." Patsy slipped back into bed and under her covers to try to shut out the world.

It was several hours before she heard Nadeen's bedroom door open again. She heard her go up in the kitchen and the phone rang, she heard her talking to Mother Otis, a member of the Mother Board.

"Hello, Momma Otis. How are you on this beautiful day that God has made?"

"Yes, ma'am. He is sho nuff Good! I thank him every day for all his blessings. He been so good to me I gotta serve him!"

"Yes. You all are more than welcome to meet here on next Thursday night for your prayer meeting. I would love to have you all. It would be a blessing to my home. See you then and stay prayed up, Momma Otis. You know we fighting for the Kingdom."

When she hung up the phone she called Patsy up front. Patsy was hesitant but she knew she had to go, "Hand me that pot under this cabinet. I need it to put these sweet potatoes in."

She said real soft and slow as she rested her hand under the bottom of her stomach. She was standing near the cabinet when Patsy bent down to get the pot. Patsy could hear Nadeen's toes pop as she stepped back.

When Patsy got the pot, she stood up and turned around to hand it to her. Nadeen grabbed her by her throat. The pot hit the floor with a loud bang. She got up in Patsy's face and spoke to her through clenched teeth with the spit coming out of her mouth.

"You rebellious witch from the pit of hell! How dare you start some confusion in my household! How dare you try and break up my marriage with your poison! You got nerve calling my sister talking about what you think about this baby in my stomach. This is none of your business you hear me! You keep on trying to split up my family. You gonna get your daddy put out of here and you going with him." With every word Nadeen seemed to grind her teeth harder and squeeze her hand more around Patsy's throat.

"I'm still hot with you about that social worker. If you hadn't been in my business then you wouldn't have had to be in the hospital!" She said.

Patsy couldn't breathe she was crying and trying to move Nadeen's piercing nails out of her neck, which felt like it was on fire.

Nadeen pushed her back harder against the bar and let her nails slide even deeper into Patsy's neck before she released her. She left a scratch that burned like a match but Patsy never said a word. She just stood there and cried.

Nadeen turned her back to her. Patsy bent to pick the pot up off the floor and placed it on the stove.

Nadeen spoke between her teeth, "Get out of my face before I bust you in the face with this pot! I'm not through with this. I'm going to handle you for this and a few other things just wait. I won't forget!"

"Nadeen? Baby, you okay up there?" Patsy heard Kenny ask as he came rushing down the hall. Nadeen gave her a look.

"You better suck it up right now!" Nadeen scowled at her and Patsy knew then that whatever was coming was going to be worse than anything she'd ever gotten before.

Patsy turned her back to Nadeen and pretended she was looking for something in the top cabinet.

Nadeen smiled at Kenny as he came into the kitchen. "I'm fine. Patsy was just getting some things out of the cabinet for me. I was gonna make that sweet potato pie for you tomorrow. I was just checking to see if I had a pie pan."

"Don't worry about that right now." Kenny brushed her efforts aside and put one hand on the small of Nadeen's back and gently held her left hand in his.

"You just come and rest Kenny Jr. right now." He led her gently to the back. Patsy walked slowly back to the bedroom with her eyes full of tears. When she got to the room Ann was looking at her.

"I saw Nadeen with her hand around your neck. I got scared and came back here to make sure me and Josie didn't get in the way of that whirlwind." Ann whispered to her. "I have to stay out of her way so she won't make me quit basketball because she's mad about something you did." Ann said as she scratched her arm nervously.

"She was just on the phone talking about how good God is to Momma Otis and the next thing you know she about to peel the skin off of my neck!" Patsy said. "It's not my fault she's lying to Kenny and carrying another man's baby. God is going to take care of her for that though. I just better stay out of her way and don't make any mistakes."

Ann shook her head in approval, "Yeah. That might be a good idea right now. Nadeen is dangerous. Now more than ever. She might snap at any minute now that she knows you said that."

Patsy waited until Nadeen had gone to take her nap then she snuck and called her Grandmother.

"Grandma Ruth. I need to come over there for this week. Nadeen's mad at me about something and I don't want to stay here. She tried to choke me to death."

Grandma Ruth gasped, "What? She tried to choke you? Why?"

Patsy said it as low as possible. "She found out I was talking to Aunt Eva about whether or not the baby she was carrying was Kenny's."

"Girl, you lucky you ain't somewhere getting stitches for that! She know what that social worker Mrs. Ava told her: she better not hurt you or even breathe on you hard and let her find out. She could be in a world of trouble. Children can get themselves hurt getting in grown folks business.

"I guess you know that now. I would think you learned before to stay out of the way of your crazy actin momma. You know she got some real crazy ways."

"Please don't forget, Grandma. I'm scared staying here. I didn't mean for her to find out what I was thinking. Kenny just happen to pick up the phone."

"It's gonna be okay after a while, baby. God takes care of everything."

26

Grandma Ruth stopped by the house the next day to make sure Nadeen hadn't hurt anybody.

"Nadeen where you at?" Grandma Ruth called. "You feeling all right today?" She asked as she headed down the hall to Nadeen's room. Nadeen was laying on the bed when she opened the door.

"I'm feeling just a little bit dizzy today, momma. Glad you brought the girls home. I need them to help me around here when Kenny goes to Bible study. I'm gonna go to the doctor tomorrow and let him check me out."

Grandma Ruth sat on the bed next to Nadeen. Patsy could see her through the door as she passed by.

"You getting big now, Nadeen. That stomach is coming on out there." Grandma Ruth patted Nadeen's belly. "Ooh! I can't wait to see who this baby looks like." She chuckled to herself.

"Me or Kenny that's who he's gonna look like." Nadeen snapped the blanket off of her and moved to get out of bed. She shuffled to the bathroom and slammed the door behind her. Grandma Ruth got up and walked out of the room.

"Girls, I'm gonna go now. Take care of your momma and call me if you need me. Cause I know how your momma can get. Sometimes I wonder about her." She seemed to be talking more to herself than Ann and Patsy. "She got those ways just like my momma use to have. I wonder sometimes if our family been cursed. Patsy, you stay here for now. I'll be back tomorrow to check on you."

They all walked her to the door and gave her a kiss as she left. When they walked back in the house Nadeen begin to bark orders at them from her bed.

"Y'all need to go ahead and get your clothes ready for school tomorrow. Make sure you give Josie a bath and pack her bag for tomorrow. I'm not feeling well."

"Yes, ma'am," Ann yelled down the hall. Patsy decided to take two sleeping pills and went to bed. She left Ann and Josie up playing with one of Josie's toys. When Patsy woke up, Kenny was beating on the door for them to wake up. She could smell pancakes and bacon.

"Get up, sleeping beauty. You got school this morning."

Patsy didn't want to get up but the smell of breakfast made her turn the pillow loose.

Ann and Josie were already up and sitting at the table eating. Ann was even dressed. Kenny must have let Patsy sleep a little later than usual. "Kenny why you not at work?"

"I'm gonna go with your momma to the doctor today. She's not doing so good with the baby. I need to go just in case he decides she needs to go in the hospital and rest for a few days." He seemed nervous and distracted as he washed the dirty dishes from breakfast. As Kenny was drying off the plates they all heard a loud bump and Nadeen screamed out. Kenny dropped the plate in the sink so hard it broke. He ran down the hall and they all went behind him.

"Nadeen! Nadeen what happened?" He burst through the door and ran to the bathroom. Nadeen was sitting down in the shower leaning to the side. She was moaning and crying.

"I slipped! I slipped getting in the shower! I don't know how I did it. I hurt myself real bad. I think you better take me to the ER right now." She said as her face grimaced with pain. Patsy and Ann watched as Kenny lifted Nadeen's naked body out of the tub. She put her arms around his neck. Josie begin to cry. Patsy picked her up.

"Patsy take her out of here. This is scaring her."

Patsy went out with Josie and took her to the back. She put her in her lap and rocked her as she cried.

"It's gonna be okay, Josie," she crooned to her softly. She rocked her for about ten minutes before she stopped crying. Ann was on the couch turned towards the hallway waiting to see what was going on. Kenny came out with a wet but clothed Nadeen who was holding the bottom of her stomach leaning on him to help her walk.

"I'm gonna take her to the ER now. Patsy, I need you to get everybody ready for school and take Josie to Mrs. Wilson. I'll pick her up when we get back "

"Yes, sir." They all watched as he took Nadeen down the hall and out the door to the truck. Ann opened the blinds and they watched as he gently put her in and they drove off. They both looked at each other.

Patsy wasn't sure what Ann was thinking, but she was wondering if something had happened to the baby. Nadeen might lose it and then Kenny wouldn't have to be made a fool of. Part of Patsy felt bad for the thought but another part of her hoped God would spare Kenny the hurt and take the baby back to heaven for someone else one day. She gathered up Josie's things as she thought about the possibility of Nadeen not having the baby. Josie was plenty. She was Kenny's and that was all they needed in that house. They didn't need a lie growing in their house just waiting to destroy Kenny emotionally, mentally, and spiritually.

"Come on, Ann. Let's go. I gotta get Josie next door and we gotta make the bus."

Ann helped get things together and they locked up the house. They made it to the bus stop just as the bus came to a stop. Patsy dreaded this ride. She didn't know what to expect.

"I want to say I hope the baby is okay, but the truth is I hope it's not. I hope God takes it back to heaven so the enemy can't use it to hurt Kenny," Patsy said.

Ann gave her a look like she couldn't believe what her big sister had just said. "How can you say that? It's our brother or sister. They didn't ask to be born. You shouldn't feel like that. A baby is a blessing, Pat."

Patsy fumbled with her book bag, "This baby isn't a blessing. This baby is a bastard. It was conceived out of wedlock, as far as I'm concerned, and I don't think I could ever love it and I know it's not the baby's fault."

"You wrong, Patsy. You wrong to feel that way about a little baby. We don't know for sure if that is Brother Ryan baby or not. You thinking momma gotta repent for something and you just might be the one having to repent for how you feeling. It's wrong."

The bus came to a stop in front of her school. Ann grabbed her backpack and headed off the bus. "See you later."

Patsy didn't say anything. She felt bad about the way she felt but she couldn't hide the truth inside of her. She watched Ann disappear into a circle full of her friends on the basketball team she was surprised Ann didn't feel the same way. Maybe she was becoming cold. Cold like her own mother.

When they made it back home from school later that day, Patsy saw her Grandmother's car. She went in the house looking for her. Ann had gone next door to pick up Josie.

"Grandma," she yelled. "Grandma where you at?"

Grandma Ruth came out of the bathroom smiling.

"Here I am, baby. I wasn't expecting to see you so soon. Your momma is gonna have to stay in the hospital. I'm afraid it's not good. Kenny is up there with her. She gonna lose the baby. She ain't strong enough to hold it. God knows best." She said as she put her head down and wiped her hands on her apron. Patsy knew what she meant. The weapon had formed but it would not prosper. God was not going to allow the enemy to use Nadeen and that baby to destroy Kenny.

"Yes, ma'am he does," Patsy replied.

"She probably gonna be in the hospital for about three or four days so Kenny called me and ask me if I would look out for you all." Grandma Ruth said. "You go on back there and change your clothes. I'll get started fixing things up around here."

Patsy went to the back and was changing her clothes when Josie bust through the door ahead of Ann. Ann closed the door and looked at Patsy. "Grandma said Nadeen gonna lose that baby. I'm so sad. Patsy, you spoke this on our baby brother or sister. You know words are spirit. You spoke death on that baby."

Patsy couldn't believe Ann was saying such a cruel thing to her.

"Ann, I have no control over what God decides is best. Deep inside your heart you know this baby would have brought nothing but hurt and trouble into our house and we got enough of that already."

"We don't really know that to be true. Maybe you got something wrong. I just hate to know a little baby is going to die. It's just a baby like Josie. We shouldn't hate it. That's wrong."

"I don't hate the baby, Ann. I hate what Nadeen did to get the baby and I hate to think what it would do to Kenny. Please understand. I love you and I love Josie. But I am telling you on a stack of white Bibles descending out of the heavens that the baby Nadeen is carrying is not Kenny's. Please let's not fight about this. We have to stick together and just pray that God works all this out."

"I just feel bad because you are saying such mean things about a little baby." Ann said. Patsy walked over to her younger sister and hugged her. " I know it hurts to hear it, Ann, but sometimes the truth is painful. Let's just pray for the baby and let God have the final say so."

"Girls, come on up here and get this good hot meal. I haven't cooked a meal this big since your granddaddy passed bless his heart. I guess I'm in my feelings and all today since this thing going on with this baby, but like I told you before, God knows. He knows better than we do." Grandma Ruth touched each of them on the shoulder.

After eating dinner, Grandma Ruth told them to get some cleaning supplies together and help clean up in Nadeen's bathroom.

Patsy and Ann helped their Grandma clean up the blood in the bathroom. In the frenzy and chaos from earlier, Patsy hadn't noticed all the blood. She felt strange cleaning up the bloody spots off of the floor. It felt to her that she was bleaching away parts of her little brother. It was a baby that wasn't going to be allowed to come into their lives. She wiped the floor as though wiping it would remove the very existence of what Nadeen had done. If she scrubbed hard enough they would forget all about the baby. It was conceived in sin and though it was innocent, it would have to pay with its life for the mistakes of a church usher and her secret pastor lover.

Wonder how the good folks at Greater Trials MB Church would feel about that? Patsy thought. *God knew about this baby from the very beginning. Nadeen could fool Kenny and the sisters in the prayer circle, but she couldn't fool Jesus. He saw everything she did even when she thought she was getting away with it in the dark.* As Patsy was getting up off the floor, the telephone rang, she usually didn't answer it because it was never for her, but this time Grandma Ruth told her to.

When she picked it up, she heard Reverend Craig's voice on the other end of the phone. "Hello. Is this Patsy or Ann?"

"This is Patsy."

"Good. How you doing, baby? I hear Sister Nadeen is in the hospital. She having complications with the baby. The sisters from the Mother Board and the Prayer Circle getting some food together for you. Me and First Lady gone go up to the hospital tomorrow to check on her. Is your Father up at the hospital with her?"

"Yes, sir. He took her this morning while we were at school."

"Your Grandma Ruth there with you children?"

"Yes, sir."

"Good. Good. I'm gonna tell Sister Alexis to get everybody together and bring that food on over there tonight. You call First Lady if you need anything."

"Yes, sir. We will." Patsy lied. She wasn't going to call Daphne Porter's sister over to her house for nothing. There were enough bad spirits floating around.

"All right then. Me and the First Lady going to the movies tonight but we gonna check on your momma first thing tomorrow morning. She keeps my church running smooth and in order I got to make sure she's all right. Me and First Lady will be praying for the family. Bye now."

He need to be careful about them movies. He might mess around and see Champagne in one of them from what I heard. Patsy thought. *Lord forgive me. I know better than listening and repeating gossip, even if it is to my own self but guys do talk!*

She laughed at her own self and went back to tell her Grandma that Reverend Craig was sending some of his church members over to the house tonight. Kenny came home about an hour later. He looked like he had been crying and he looked tired. Grandma Ruth tried to get him to eat dinner but he said he didn't have the appetite right now. He gathered up some of Nadeen's things and said he was going to go back up to the hospital to spend the night with her. It looked like his hands were shaking a little bit.

He was upset and that wasn't good. He might backslide under the pressure of losing a baby he wasn't sure was his. Patsy knew she was going to have to go into her prayer closet tonight and get down on her belly for him to be strong.

Before he left, she went up to him and gave him a big hug, Ann and Josie went right behind her and did the same thing.

She saw him give a weak smile, "I love you girls." He said. "You are our blessings from God. When your momma comes back home she's gonna need you all to take real good care of her."

Before they could answer, he was pushing the door open and headed to the truck. He was hurt, and when he was hurt Patsy was hurt. She had to go to her prayer closet now, she couldn't wait. She turned and ran down the hall, she told Ann not to bother her and not to let Josie bother her.

She ran to the room, locked the door and climbed into her prayer closet. She must have been there for a while and fell asleep because the next thing she knew, she was hearing a knock at the door. It was Ann. Patsy jumped up, wiped her face and went to open the door. Ann looked concerned.

"You okay, Patsy?"

"Yes. I just had to spend some time in prayer. What do you want?" She asked Ann.

"Those ladies from momma church is up front with Grandma Ruth. They asking to see you."

Patsy cleaned her face and went up front with a smile on her face. Her head was throbbing from crying so much.

The Sisters of the Praying Circle brought enough food to feed hundreds of people. Patsy looked at it and wondered just how long Nadeen was going to be in the hospital. They visited with Grandma Ruth for several hours and by the time they left, Josie had fallen asleep on the kitchen floor with a piece of caramel cake in her hands.

"Patsy." Grandma called just as she was getting the last pieces of cake from between Josie's fingers.

"Yes, ma'am?" Patsy whispered.

"That nice little boyfriend of yours called while you were back there laying down earlier. I told him to call you back later because you were taking a nap."

Patsy didn't have to hear that twice. She rushed and got Josie into her pajamas and went to call him.

"Hey, babe. My grandma said you called me," she said sweetly.

"Yea. How are you?" Dustin asked.

"I'm doing fine. My mom is in the hospital though, she lost the baby."

"Oh man! I'm sorry to hear that. I know she's hurt about that and your dad, too."

Patsy decided not to answer since her last comments on the phone cost her the pretty brown skin on her neck. She thought it best to try to change the subject.

"You see my girl Sandra today?" She asked instead.

"Yeah. That's a whole other subject, Patsy. She looking like she is due any day now and she is still running behind Lavon and hanging out at the clubs from what I heard. She at the Teen Center every Friday night. You need to talk to your friend. When this baby comes she got to be ready to settle down. I would say Lavon too but I'm not banking on that. Then again, he might surprise me."

"Sandra can handle herself and that baby in her belly. She's gonna be just fine. She's due in a few more weeks. She probably gonna have that baby shower any day now."

"What is she having?"

"She's having a boy. She is so excited. She told me her Grandmother made her go before the church and ask them to forgive her for what she'd done." Patsy told Dustin.

"Go before the church? For what? The only person she needs to ask forgiveness from is Jesus. The other people don't matter." He said raising his voice. "They ain't holy and perfect in that church. They sin too. Just because you can't see it doesn't make it any less terrible than what she did."

"You're right, but Sandra Grandma said her Pastor wouldn't let Sandra even come visit the church sitting in there with her belly swollen and not married unless she confessed her sins and repented."

Dustin took a deep breath thru the phone then slowly said. "Why is her grandmother's pastor so concerned about Sandra when her momma need deliverance too? She ain't in them clubs every weekend passing out Holy Ghost pamphlets" Patsy laughed.

"I probably better not swim out any further in these waters." She said to him.

"Yeah. You right" Dustin said. "I guess I better let you go get some sleep. I gotta finish my homework."

"I'll look for you tomorrow." She hung up the phone and thought about what Dustin had said. *How was it that the Pastor focused more on the people forgiving Sandra than Jesus? As long as she knew Jesus would give her another chance it shouldn't matter about church folks.*

27

Nadeen came home at the end of the week. She was sitting up in bed reading her Bible when they came in from school. Josie saw her and ran and jumped in the bed to kiss her. Nadeen laughed, this was a rare sound to Patsy and Ann. She kissed Josie and asked her did she miss her. Patsy knew she wasn't going to ask her or Ann. She didn't have any love for them.

Patsy decided to excuse herself from the room by saying she had to go to the bathroom. Ann was stuck there with her now. When she came out of the bathroom, Kenny was coming through the door with a bag.

He smiled at her and said, "I had to go pick up some chocolate for Nadeen. She been wanting it for days."

Patsy watched him take it in to her like a good little puppy waiting to be patted on the head for a job well done. She didn't even look up at him when he gave her the bag, she just said thank you in a low voice.

Not long after that, the phone began ringing and people started calling to check on Nadeen. After about the fifth phone call. She got tired and irritated. She slammed down the phone.

"I wish they would just leave me alone. Just calling to be nosy! They need to let me get my rest. The next time one of them calls tell them I'm sleep." She snapped.

She obviously was feeling better now. Patsy could tell by the edge in her voice when she said it. The Ferris wheel of strife was about to be cranked back up!

Grandma Ruth stayed a few extra days and then she packed up to go home. She instructed Patsy and Ann to try and be quiet in the house the next few days and keep Josie quiet too. Nadeen was still in a nasty mood after losing the baby and she didn't need to have her buttons pushed. Patsy tried to heed that warning. Ann however, must have been staring at the ceiling when Grandma Ruth gave it.

Ann came in from school one day and she was acting a little cranky herself. She said one of the girls in her gym class had been spreading gossip about Nadeen, Brother Ryan and the baby. She slammed her books down and slammed the bedroom door. Nadeen heard all the noise and got up out of her bed.

"Who slamming doors around here?" Nadeen was annoyed. "Only person around here that gets to slam doors is me! I pay the cost to be the boss around here!"

"It wasn't me." Patsy said.

"Ann? Come here!" Ann opened her bedroom door with a mad look on her face. She went to the door of Nadeen's room.

"What makes you think you can slam doors around here? I don't know what your problem is but you better solve it in the next sixty seconds or else you gonna have a bigger problem than that! You hear me?"

"Yeah. I hear you!" Ann said in a sarcastic tone, as soon as Patsy heard it, she knew it was about to be a bigger problem. She stepped back just in time. Nadeen moved like a panther. She crossed the room with a large paddle brush. She slammed it across Ann's head several times. When it hit it made a loud thumping noise. Patsy was afraid she was going to crack her skull. Ann backed up and tried to grab Nadeen's wrist. Patsy couldn't believe what she saw. Nadeen slammed Ann against the closet door and put her hand around her throat. She got right up in her face.

"You must have lost your mind since I been in the hospital, but if you don't find it I'm gonna break your back in half! Don't you ever think you can come in my house and raise up at me!" Nadeen's voice was a low growl.

"I'm not crippled. I will beat you till you pass over the river Jordan! When you get too grown for my house it's time for you to pack your bags and get out! You better ask Patsy! I still owe her something I ain't forgot! You girls been acting really crazy lately but I'm gonna get all of that back in order real soon. You hear me?"

She slammed Ann's head one more time against the closet door. Finally, she released her grip around Ann's neck and told her she better clean that mess up in the next five minutes or get stripped naked! Ann was crying as she started trying to pick up the brush bristles. She must have been pretty upset to get an attitude like that with Nadeen of all people. Ann was just leaving out of the bedroom when Kenny came home from work. He saw the hair on Ann's head sticking up wildly

"What you been doing?" He asked as he laughed at her. Ann looked up at him with tears in her eyes and his laughter stopped in mid-air. He knew that look. Nothing else needed to be said. She went into the room and closed the door. Patsy picked up Josie and took her in the room behind Ann. She knew it didn't take much for her to pull out a razorblade and start cutting on herself. Patsy wished she could tell Nadeen what her little sister was doing but she wasn't sure how she would handle it. Would she pray for her or persecute her?

A few minutes after Kenny went in the bedroom, Patsy heard Nadeen yelling at the top of her lungs, "Those are my children! You don't tell me what to do with them! She's not going to talk to me any kind of way in my house! She's not going to walk over me! I'm the mother not her and she will treat me with respect or get out and the same goes for you Kenny Simmons!"

The next sound Patsy heard was Kenny opening the bedroom door and slamming it behind him. He hit the wall as he headed to the back. Patsy wondered why God didn't let happiness stay long in their house. Why was strife always a constant in their lives? It was the one thing that never seemed to go away. What was wrong with Nadeen? Why was she always so difficult with them yet so obliging with the folks at church? Anything they said or asked she would agree to it with a smile but at home she would shake the walls if she didn't agree with something or didn't want to do something.

After Nadeen almost beat her head in with the brush, Ann made sure she took heed to Grandma Ruth's warning along with everybody else in the house. Kenny had begun going to counseling with Pastor Mack and his wife, Nadeen reluctantly agreed to go with him but never seemed to feel up to it.

After being at home on leave for six weeks giving orders from her bedroom, she decided it was time for her to go back to work. Patsy heard her tell Eva that this miscarriage drama might have cost her the permanent supervisor position she wanted so bad. Eva must have asked her if she regretted losing the baby because Nadeen's next comment made Patsy's head spin a little bit "The only thing I regret is letting Kenny move back in here and missing days off my job."

Wow! She is cold as ice. Patsy went to bed that night playing those comments over and over again in her head.

She was shocked even though she knew she really shouldn't be.

When Patsy got to school the next day, Dustin was waiting for her at the front of the school. As usual, she smiled when she saw him. He had a flyer in his hand and he showed it to her.

"Look, Patsy. See this flyer? It's time for the Zeta Debutante Presentation. You been talking about how much you wanted to be in it since I met you. This is going to be your year!"

Patsy looked at the flyer and smiled for just a minute and then her mind flashed to her mother.

"I wish I could. Nadeen probably gonna say I can't do it for some stupid reason. The girls look so lovely with their escorts."

"You should take the flyer home and have Mrs. Mason call her. She might be able to talk your mom into it and plus, I think she's a member of the group that does the Zeta Debutante. She could help you."

Dustin seemed excited. "I'll even go out and buy a tuxedo so I can be your escort."

As they walked to class, Patsy held his hand and whispered, *Lord, I need you to touch Nadeen's heart to let me be in this debutante pageant.* Patsy thought the whole day at school how, when and where she was going to ask Nadeen about her being in the debutante presentation. She didn't even notice that Sandra wasn't in class that evening before the last period. Someone came to the door of her last period class and ask the teacher if she could see her it was urgent. Patsy went out in the hall, she'd seen the girl talking with Sandra sometimes but she didn't know her.

"Patsy, they took Sandra to the hospital. She's about to have the baby. She told me to come and find you to let you know. She was in the bathroom and water came gushing down her leg. I ran and got the secretary. The ambulance came and got her. Lavon gone up to the hospital."

The girl was talking so fast Patsy was still trying to get the picture in her head. The baby wasn't due for about three more weeks. She hoped Sandra wasn't scared. She told Patsy once that it was okay putting the baby in there but she sure hated to have to get it out.

"Thanks for letting me know." Patsy told the girl. "I'll call the hospital later tonight to see if she's had the baby." As soon as she stepped back into the classroom, the bell rang to end last period. She grabbed her backpack and ran down the hall to catch the bus. She couldn't wait to tell Ann the baby was coming. This time she was excited and hopeful.

28

Patsy ran to call up to the hospital to check on Sandra and the baby. Sandra's mother answered the phone. "Hello, Ms. Gladys. This is Patsy Simmons. I was calling to check on Sandra and the baby."

"She's doing fine, Patsy." Sandra's mother said. She had that baby so fast it almost fell out on the floor when they got her on the table." She laughed.

"She got herself a beautiful little baby boy. He's eight pounds, three ounces, and he got reddish blond hair! I don't know where that come from. Lavon claim his granddaddy got hair like that but I don't know. You want to talk to her? Hold on one minute."

Sandra got on the phone, she sounded kind of weak. "Hey Patsy. How you doing? I was hoping you got my message."

"I did! Wow, Sandra! You got a baby. Your mom says he is beautiful."

"He is. Got a big head like his daddy but he cute. I named him Solomon. He's going to be a great man. Hey. Did you see that flyer up at school about the Zeta Debutante Presentation?"

"Yeah. I saw it. Dustin thinks I should ask Nadeen about me being in it."

"You should! Girl, you been talking about that Zeta Debutante since I have known you in the ninth grade. You're going to be a pretty debutante. It's time to go for it! Pray about it first, God will touch her heart you watch and see."

"I'll think about it. You take care. I'll see you when you get home. When you bringing the baby home?"

"My little sunshine and I are coming home in two more days. Maybe you can get your daddy to bring you by to see him?"

"I'll do that." Patsy smiled at the thought of the promise of a new baby as she hung up the phone.

The next day at school, Patsy went and talked to Mrs. Mason, her counselor, about the Zeta Debutante presentation. She was thrilled about Patsy wanting to participate.

"Patsy Simmons. Are you going to be a Zeta Deb this year? I would love to have you participate. You more than meet the criteria. I know you had that one incident with that Porter boy but he's always getting in some trouble so I'm sure that was provoked. You'll have a wonderful time. It's a great way to earn a scholarship for college. You have plans of going off to college don't you?"

"I sure do, and I don't want anything to stand in my way. That would be a great point to make to my mom."

"You'll meet so many other young ladies from different schools and learn so many things to help you grow into a beautiful and sophisticated young lady."

Patsy took a deep breath and asked her, "Mrs. Mason? You think you could call my mom and talk to her about letting me be in the debutante presentation? I'm going to need someone to help me convince her."

Mrs. Mason looked at Patsy and smiled. "Sure. I'll be glad to give her a call and give it my best shot for you

Patsy. "Leave me your phone number. I'll give her a call after lunch today."

Patsy thanked her and left out of the office. She was hoping God would show her some favor with this special request.

When they got on the bus that afternoon to head home, Patsy told Ann about the Zeta Debutante presentation. Ann said she would be praying along with her that God would use Mrs. Mason to convince Nadeen to let her participate. When the bus pulled up to their stop, Patsy noticed a familiar truck pulling out of the neighborhood right as the bus stopped. It was Brother Ryan's Range Rover. What was he doing coming around? Kenny had already warned him about coming to their house when he wasn't at home. He was back with his wife—he didn't have any business coming back around. He must have heard about Nadeen losing the baby.

"Ann, did you see that truck?"

"Yeah I did. I wonder why is he risking getting shot in the butt by Kenny to come crawling around here?"

This wasn't a good sign, Patsy thought. *Nothing but trouble was going to come from this.* This might not be a good time to ask Nadeen about the Debutante Presentation after all. Patsy and Ann both walked home wondering what spirit was going to meet them at the door. When they entered the front hall, they could hear the radio in the kitchen playing and Nadeen singing. They both looked at each other with hesitation but went into the kitchen anyway. Nadeen was singing and praising the Lord. She had her hands in the air and was dancing from side to side as she cooked dinner.

She hardly ever cooked. She turned around and saw them watching her. She looked at them and said, "I don't know why you both looking at me like that! You know God been good to us. I give him all the praise!"

"Patsy I got a call from your counselor today." She said. Patsy just stood still with her heart beating waiting for her to tell her some stupid reason why she couldn't be in the Debutante Presentation.

"She talked about how much she wanted you to be in that Zeta Debutante presentation they do every year because you were so smart and so special to her. She talked to me for a long time about what a good job me and Kenny was doing raising you. She don't know it's all me. If I left it up to Kenny you both would be pregnant and high school drop outs somewhere living in a shack with tattoos all over your body parts."

Patsy still didn't move. She couldn't speak. Her heart was beating so fast that was really all she could hear other than the sound of Nadeen's voice.

"I told her since she thought so much of you, I would allow you to be in the debutante presentation but you would have to prove to me you are deserving of it. You got to do better in this house. You mess up one time and I will not let you be in it do you hear me?"

Patsy wanted to jump up and down and scream "Thank You Jesus!" but she held herself together. She could holler in her pillow when she got to the back.

"Yes, ma'am. I hear you. I won't mess up." She tried to sound as respectful as possible. She knew the clock started ticking right then.

"Ann put that fruit basket in the laundry room. I don't want Kenny to see it. A friend of the church brought it by a few minutes ago." Nadeen cocked a half smile and paused a little too long on the word "friend" but Patsy didn't care. She wanted Ann to hurry up and take that fruit basket to the back so they could both go to the room and jump up and down.

"Yes, ma'am," Ann said. She got the basket and took it to the back. Patsy followed her almost stepping on the heel of Ann's shoe.

When they got in the room they shouted quietly and jumped up and down holding each other. Patsy couldn't believe it.

"Lord. I thank you. I thank you for this moment in my life. Only you could have done this miracle and touched her heart!"

"You gotta call Dustin and tell him. Kenny got to get a tuxedo. He'll probably have to take you to practice."

"I know. He won't mind." Patsy said. "I hope Nadeen knows I have to have an escort. I want Dustin. I don't want her picking out some nerdy church boy for me. I gotta be careful with that one. Maybe Kenny can mention it to her."

Patsy couldn't wait to tell Dustin the good news. She managed to sneak upstairs and call him while Nadeen took a nap. He was ecstatic for her.

"See Patsy? God can move mountains!"

"I want you to be my escort. I have to find a way to bring that up." Patsy said.

"Well maybe I better start coming around Greater Trials on the Sundays I know you're going to be there with her." Dustin said.

"Once she realizes what a nice young man I am she'll recommend me herself." They both laughed.

"Let's just keep praying. We got about three weeks before the practices start. Just pray that I don't do anything unknowingly to push her buttons!"

"I'll be fasting and praying." He laughed and said, "She got a hair trigger when it comes to what will or will not set her off."

"Well I better go. I took a chance calling you while she's at home but I just couldn't wait."

"I understand. Love you talk to you later." Dustin said. Patsy hung up the phone with her heart beating fast and a smile she couldn't wipe off of her face. She would ask Grandma Ruth to sew her a white gown for the debutante cotillion. She was a wonderful seamstress. Just wait until Aunt Eva found out! She would do Patsy's make up for her. *That would be one night Nadeen would have to fight with her sister because Eva was going to hook her up!*

Kenny came in right after she hung up the phone. She ran up the hall to tell him the good news. She gave him a big hug first. He sat in the chair and smiled at her.

"Kenny I got a surprise for you."

"You do? What could that be?"

"Nadeen said I could be in the Zeta Debutante Presentation at school this year!"

"What?" Kenny said as he raised half way up out of the chair and looked at Patsy like he didn't quite hear her right. "That thing you been talking about since you were in the ninth grade where those girls get all dressed up?"

"Yes! My counselor called her today and talked to her. She convinced her to let me participate in the presentation. You know I was praying hard, don't you?"

Kenny laughed, "I know it! I can't believe it. That's as big as the Lord parting the Red Sea. Guess I better start looking for a tuxedo then. Who's gonna escort you or do I need to ask?"

"Daddy you know who's gonna escort me. Dustin of course, who else?"

"Now who is going to talk to Nadeen about that?"

Patsy looked at him with her little girl smile and put on her sweetness voice.

"You, Daddy," she said sweetly.

Kenny smiled as he looked into her eyes. "Ha. So now you want to be daddy's baby girl, huh?"

Patsy laughed a little bit. "I have always been your baby girl."

"I'll have to think on how to bring this up to her. Has she ever met him?"

"He was at the hospital when I got ready to come home after she *accidentally* burnt me with that water." She didn't like to think about that. Kenny looked at her with an apologetic look on his face, he spoke quietly to her, "I'm still so sorry for that baby girl. She was mad with me not you. Don't you ever put your life on the line for me like that again .You hear me?"

Patsy looked at him and put her face on his knee. "Yes, sir. But I couldn't just stand there and let anything happen to you. I love you."

"I love you too baby but don't you do that. God is going to protect me. Nadeen thinks she's the only one gonna enter into heaven's pearly gates but she ain't! I'll talk to her about Dustin escorting you."

Patsy jumped up and hugged his neck. "Thank you, Daddy."

The next day Dustin walked with her to Mrs. Mason's office.

"Guess you got the good news, huh?" Mrs. Mason asked her. Patsy grinned.

"Yes! I got it! Thank you so much Mrs. Mason. I couldn't have done this without you. I thank God for you." Patsy went over and hugged her neck.

"You make me proud, Patsy Simmons. You hear me?"

"I will, Mrs. Mason. I promise I will."

"Here is your Zeta Debutante Packet. Make sure you get it filled out and bring it with you when you come to the first meeting next week. We want to meet with you all before we start the practices to make sure you understand what is expected of you."

"I'll have it ready. Thanks again, Mrs. Mason." She walked out of the office holding Dustin's hand. She walked Dustin to his classroom and finished the rest of the walk by herself with joy leaping inside of her belly for the first time.

Things were going real good for Patsy. Kenny paid the deposit for her debutante presentation so that Nadeen couldn't use that as a reason for her not to participate. Nadeen tried to convince Kenny that it was way too much money to spend for a one-time event. Kenny wouldn't listen to her. He told her that Patsy had been doing well in school and she deserved to have this for all of her hard work. He went with Patsy to all of the Debutante meetings and workshops. Patsy felt like she was walking in a fantasy. It was getting closer and closer and she was holding her breath every day. She was looking, listening and watching for the enemy. Nadeen wasn't too happy about having to come to some of the practices for the parents. She said she had a lot of work at the church that she had to get done for Reverend Craig and she didn't like to look unorganized when it came to her work for the Lord. Mrs. Mason worked that out too.

She set the practices for only twice a week and no more than an hour. She always let Nadeen and Kenny go first so that they could finish up a few minutes earlier than the other parents.

Patsy really appreciated all of her help. The last three weeks of practice they were going to need their escorts. During practice one night she pulled Kenny over to the side, "Kenny. It's time for you to talk to Nadeen about Dustin being my escort." She said.

"I been talking to her for a week now Patsy. I told her that Mrs. Mason recommended a nice young man to

escort you and Mrs. Mason talked to her about Dustin."
He said. Patsy was tickled. They'd been working behind
the scenes already. She was so grateful.

"So what did she say? Is she going to let him be my
escort?"

"I think she just might." Kenny said. "Mrs. Mason put
in such a good word for Dustin she couldn't help but to
tell her she would seriously consider it. Mrs. Mason told
her it is a requirement for the presentation and she would
never recommend someone she didn't know very well."

Mrs. Mason was surely an angel, Patsy thought. She
had a way with words. The next day at school Patsy asked
Dustin if he could come by one night that week so
Nadeen could at least see who he was. Dustin informed
her that he had already worked it out with Mrs. Mason to
ride with her to practice tomorrow night. Patsy pushed
him a little.

"You didn't even tell me! How could you keep that a
secret?"

Dustin laughed, "Mrs. Mason is handling this. I'm
following her lead. I didn't want you freaking out with
worry about it! I'm gonna be such a gentleman your
momma might want to dance with me."

Patsy called her Grandma when she got home from
school that day and asked her if she had come by and
picked up the picture for the dress she wanted to wear.

"I got that picture and I've already cut out the pattern
from my last Sunday's paper. I don't waste no time. I will
have this dress finished in a week. Kenny gave me more
than enough money to buy the materials to make the dress
and gave me a little extra for my gas."

"Really, Grandma? You think you can have it
finished that fast?"

"What? You must not know about your Grandma? I can sew and I can cook. Those two things God gave me as natural gifts and talents."

"Thank you so much, Grandma. I love you."

"I know, baby. I love you too. I can't wait to see you in this dress. Is your Aunt Eva going to do your make up for you?"

"I'm sure she will. I just haven't called her yet. I guess I better do that today or tomorrow, Grandma?"

"Yes?"

"Did you know Dustin is going to be my escort? He's coming to the practice this week to meet Nadeen."

"I know. Kenny told me. Me and your Aunt Eva been betting on what Nadeen was going to do. I said she was going to wait until she met him then tell you no and get one of those flood pants, white sock wearing boys from her church to escort you. But Eva says she thinks Dustin is going to be such a gentleman Nadeen will say yes."

"I hope Eva wins the bet. Even though I will have to make her a home-made caramel cake if I lose." Grandma Ruth said.

"I hope she wins too. It would mess up a perfect evening if I had to have someone else to escort me."

"You asked God to work it out for you?"

"I sure did. I been praying to him and asking him to let me have this."

"Then don't worry about it. Everything is going to work out."

Patsy told Grandma Ruth she loved her and then hung up the phone.

Dustin called Patsy after Nadeen left. Patsy felt a little sick in her stomach. "Please don't tell Nadeen you're my boyfriend. If she finds that out she will never let me be in this debutante presentation." Patsy said nervously. "It means so much to me!"

"I'm not going to ruin things for you, Patsy. I'm going to introduce myself as one of your classmates. I'm also going to let her know I attend church. That's important."

"Okay. I feel a little nervous I think I better go now. I'll see you tomorrow."

"All right. Don't worry. I'm going to make you proud and I'm going to walk out of there as your escort. Watch and see. I'm a smooth operator Patsy. I thought you knew. I got your attention didn't I?"

"I hope so. We'll see how you operate tomorrow night. See you." Patsy said and hung up the phone. She laid down but didn't sleep a wink that night. She was so occupied with what could go wrong tomorrow night she forgot to call Eva about her make up. That would have to wait until she knew whether or not she would have Dustin to look beautiful for. School went by way too fast the next day. Before she knew it, Kenny was picking Patsy up to take her to practice. Nadeen came in her own car so she could leave when she was ready.

When they pulled up to the building, she saw Dustin walking in with Mrs. Mason. Her heart was beating fast at the sight of him. She loved him so much. She hoped it wouldn't show when Nadeen looked at her.

"There's your boy, Patsy." Kenny nodded to Dustin. Patsy just smiled. She hurried up and got out of the car.

As she was walking up the sidewalk with Kenny, Nadeen pulled up. They waited on the sidewalk for her. "Hey, Nadeen." Kenny said.

"I guess I gotta meet this boy Mrs. Mason says is supposed to escort Patsy in this debutante. I hope he knows it won't be no calling my house before or after this presentation if I decide to let him escort her. I don't trust any of them. They just want to ease their way into your pants and then leave you with a belly full of baby. Well not my girls. I won't have it!" She said.

"Nadeen it's just a walk onto a stage. Nothing is gonna be touching but hands and toes."

That didn't sound right. Patsy thought.

"I'll make sure of that! Come on in here!" She was walking and talking so fast she beat them to the door but she stood there until Kenny opened it for her. She went in first and Patsy after her. Patsy walked real slow. She saw Dustin standing next to Mrs. Mason. She motioned Nadeen over to her. Patsy and Kenny went to the other side of the room to watch Nadeen's body language and facial expression. That would tell them all they needed to know about her decision. Dustin shook her hand. Nadeen seem to be talking to him. He would nod his head yes or no and say yes ma'am or no ma'am to her. Patsy watched Nadeen looking at him real close and doing a lot of smiling. Mrs. Mason would occasionally laugh. It looked good so far. After what seemed like forever. Patsy watched as Nadeen shook Dustin's hand and Mrs. Mason walked her out the door.

Before Nadeen walked out she looked over at Patsy and gave her a look like "all right now." A few minutes later Mrs. Mason came over to her and motioned Dustin over.

She looked at Patsy with a very serious face.

"Patsy. I had a talk with your mother as I walked her to her car. No room for playing games with her and she is serious about what she says. She has told me under no terms is anyone else allowed to escort you in this debutante but Dustin." Before Patsy knew it she jumped up and shouted.

"Yes! Thank you Lord!" She could hear Kenny laughing at her. Dustin was smiling. She was so happy she kissed him right there in front of Mrs. Mason and Kenny.

"I told you I was going to be a gentleman."

"Come on let's go. Practice is about to start and we only have a few weeks. Patsy grabbed his hand and walked away with him. She didn't even tell Kenny goodbye. She knew he understood. When Patsy got home with Kenny that night she called Aunt Eva. She told her the good news about Nadeen letting Dustin escort her in the debutante presentation. She asked her if she could do her make up on the night of the presentation.

"Of course I'll do your make up. You're my favorite and dearest niece. I love all of my nieces but you are dear to me. You are my first baby girl and you are growing up into a fine young lady. Even if you got a Holy Ghost crazy lady for your momma. We'll keep it simple but elegant. I know Nadeen don't like you to wear makeup. Probably scared of seeing her own past."

"Thanks, Aunt Eva." Patsy said. She would entertain that last comment at another time.

"I'll bring some nice light colors over tomorrow. We can practice with them and get Nadeen to approve them so I don't have to knock her out on the night of the presentation for acting ridiculous about some eyeshadow." Aunt Eva said.

"Right. Okay. I'll see you tomorrow." She hung up the phone. Everything was going great. She was a Zeta Debutante and Dustin was her escort. What could possibly go wrong?

29

Grandma Ruth had been warned by Eva many times before. *Keep a night light on in the hallway so that you won't run into a door one night*, but of course she never listened to Eva. Until the night she almost broke her face on her nice clean cement steps. She'd been having bad episodes lately of sleepwalking and Eva had even told her she was going to move her into a nursing home if she couldn't be more careful in the house.

One night, Grandma Ruth ended up walking out of her front door onto the porch and as she headed towards the street she fell down four flights of cement stairs and landed with one leg to the right and another one twisted to the left with a bone sticking out. She'd screamed so loud that she woke up all her neighbors.

Eva had been called and rushed her to the ER where they informed Eva that she'd broken her leg and would need care 24/7 until it healed. Eva told the doctors she would take care of her in her home. Patsy was glad she was going to be able to stay home, but Grandma Ruth didn't want to stay at Eva's house; she let that be known in no uncertain terms.

The Sunday after the accident, Kenny decided he would go to church service with Nadeen since the girls begged him.

When they arrived, members of the Usher Board were just getting out of their cars. They ran over to their Head Usher and smothered her with hugs and questions about her mother.

Kenny put on his jacket and took Josie by the hand, "Come on girls. The sisters of Greater Trials have taken your mother away leaving the rest of us to lick our own wounds." Ann giggled.

They walked in the church and sat down. Nadeen assumed her post at the back door and watched the congregation and the other ushers. Patsy looked around the church but didn't see Reverend Craig or First Lady Champagne. She wondered who was going to bring the message.

She didn't have to wait long to find out. After the choir sang their hearts out, the choir director, Brother Eugene, stood up in his pink shirt, grey suit with matching pink socks, pink lemonade colored shoes, and a fresh roller set. He asked the congregation to please stand for the Man of God. Out walked Brother Ryan. He was looking solemn like he'd been in deep thought. He had on a beautiful purple robe with a gold cross on the front. He looked almost like the pope. Patsy wasn't sure she wanted to sit through this sermon. It was going to be hard for her to focus on what was being said because of who was saying it. He asked his family to stand and he poured out beautiful words of praise about his wife and his children.

The congregation ate it up. Patsy just sat there looking at Brother Eugene who was chewing gum and cleaning his fingernails while rocking his foot. Patsy suspected he wasn't quite right but she couldn't say for sure because that would be gossip and that was a sin!

She looked over at Kenny and he seemed to be watching the congregation instead of Brother Ryan. He was probably thinking about how he ran him out of his house a few months earlier.

Brother Ryan gave a powerful word from what Patsy could tell. The church was rocking and rolling. Folks were shouting, running, dancing, and fainting all in the aisles. The choir members were falling out and Mrs. Ryan danced so hard her ponytail came loose. It was hanging from her head and you could see the stub of her real hair struggling to stay wrapped around a rubber band. Kenny, Patsy, and Ann clapped occasionally.

Nadeen was standing at the back door with one hand behind her back. She seemed to be staring right through him. She probably didn't notice she wasn't wearing her church smile at that moment. When service was over everyone talked about how Brother Ryan was growing in the word and getting more anointed every time he came before the congregation.

Patsy and Ann just walked past everyone and tried to get to the car as soon as possible. Kenny and Nadeen got stopped by other church members wanting to ask about Grandma Ruth.

As Nadeen was about to open the car door, Mrs. Ryan came up to the car, "Nadeen? My husband told me about all the hard work you do around here in the church office to get us ready for Sunday Service and I just wanted to thank you and I hope your mother gets well soon. Let us know if we can do anything for her."

Nadeen stepped back from her and looked at her like she had an antenna on her head. She must have caught her off guard.

"Uh. Thank you, Sister Ryan." She said and got in the car. Kenny started the car and drove off. Sister Ryan just stood their waving goodbye with a smile on her face.

"Her husband need to tell her about a bag of peppermints." Nadeen sneered. "She don't care nothing about my momma and I don't care nothing about her!"

"Now, Nadeen. You just came out of church service full of the Holy Ghost. Don't let the enemy use you like that. She was just trying to be nice and show some concern."

Nadeen looked at him and said, "You don't know women! She wasn't being sincere. She was putting on an act for those other women out there because she got to play First Lady today!"

Patsy couldn't believe she said that. *Who could put on an act for the church folks better than you, momma,* Patsy thought to herself.

30

"Eva. Eva where you at?" Nadeen yelled around the house. They heard her call from the back.

"Nadeen! Girl come here and see what your momma did to me!" She yelled back. She sounded like she was about to cry.

They all walked to the back bathroom, when they peeped in, Aunt Eva was covered in what looked like spaghetti sauce and pasta. Nadeen and Kenny both laughed. "Eva what happened to you?" Kenny asked.

She looked at them like she wanted to spit nails. "Nadeen's crazy mammie dumped her bowl of canned spaghetti on my head and then threw the bowl at me. Bein' in that wheelchair, she meaner than ever and got more strength in that right arm than a man hauling wood."

"I know she didn't stand up on her own and do that so how did it happen?" Nadeen asked.

"I took the bowl to her and was trying to get her to eat it; she kept turning her head so I told her she would sit there and rot before I tried to feed her. I put the bowl in her lap and she dropped the fork on the floor. I reached down to pick it up and the next thing I know, she was bashing me in the head with the bowl and spaghetti sauce was everywhere!"

Ann and Patsy tried not to laugh out loud. They knew they couldn't hold it much longer, so they took Josie and went to find Grandma Ruth. They laughed all the way, Grandma was sitting in front of the window looking out at the children playing.

She didn't see them come up.

"Hey, Grandma," Ann said. "We heard you been throwing spaghetti rings at Aunt Eva."

Grandma Ruth looked at her and smiled, she tilted her head back like she wanted to laugh out loud. Patsy put Josie in her lap, as she stroked Josie's sandy brown hair.

"She know better than giving me some canned mess! That ain't nothing but dog food in that can. They pretending it's meatballs but it ain't. I'm not gonna eat that!"

Ann and Patsy both laughed. She had spaghetti sauce specks on her dress.

"Well, Grandma Ruth what are you going to eat?" Patsy asked her.

"Get me a honey bun," she whispered. Patsy listened real hard and focused on her lips she understood her real good. "Go on girl! Sneak in that kitchen and look in my cookie jar and bring your Grandma one of those honey buns. Go on before I get you for moving too slow. Don't let this wheel chair fool you! I still got some fight in me. You hear me?" Patsy didn't want to find out how much fight she had in her.

"Yes, ma'am. I know where they are I'll go get them." Patsy went to get the honey bun, as she was headed to the kitchen, Nadeen and Kenny were coming into the room.

When she brought the honey bun back, Nadeen looked at her, "What are you doing with that honey bun?"

"I know you ain't gonna give that to her. She's not supposed to eat that. She should have eaten her dinner Eva made for her."

Grandma Ruth turned to Patsy and rolled her wheelchair toward her. In the process, she made sure to roll over Nadeen's open toe shoes. Nadeen screamed. Grandma Ruth motioned for Patsy to open the honey bun and put it in her mouth.

"You did that on purpose momma!" Nadeen said. She sounded like she wanted to cry. Kenny smiled a little bit and touched Grandma Ruth on her hand.

"How you been doing, Momma Ruth?"

She bobbed her head up and down as she slowly chewed small pieces of the honey bun. She just kept eating and bobbing her head. When she finally finished the honey bun, she motioned for Patsy to come nearer to her, Patsy was a little scared. She didn't know what she might do. Patsy leaned down to her face and Grandma Ruth kissed her on the jaw and rubbed her face with her right hand. Patsy smiled.

By that time, Eva came to the back. "Patsy, watch her. She quicker than a rattlesnake. She might strike at any minute. Honey, Sister Ruth is something! When them good sisters from the church come over here she just as humble but as soon as they leave, she peel off that costume and get back into her own flesh and it ain't pretty."

Grandma Ruth looked at her like she wanted to knock her wig off of her head.

"Momma don't look at me like that. You know I'm telling the truth!"

"How is the physical therapy going, Eva?" Nadeen asked.

"She making good progress. The doctor says she'll be able to get around pretty good in a few more weeks. He says she's tough as leather."

"Well, we better go," Nadeen said.

Everyone but Nadeen hugged Grandma Ruth on the way out.

"Bye, Momma. See you later and please keep them nasty ways to yourself."

When Grandma Ruth get better she gonna get her for that smart remark, Patsy thought.

"Nadeen you ain't got no word yet on who they gonna choose as a permanent supervisor at your job?" Eva asked her as she got ready to leave. "You better stop letting them folks use you like that. They gonna get all they can out of you and then hire somebody with less experience and for less pay. Then they gonna make you train her because you know too much." Nadeen rolled her eyes at her.

"Eva you have no idea what it means to wait on the Lord do you? As hard as I been working in the Kingdom of God I know that job is mine. It's just a matter of time before it manifests."

"We gone see, but I say they are gonna use you up, dump you out and leave you standing their holding a bed pan wondering what happened."

Nadeen headed out the door and yelled back to her sister, "Love Jesus instead of being in my business and you'll be fine," and slammed the door behind her.

Nadeen talked about Eva all the way home. She criticized her for not having faith and for shacking up with a man that wasn't her husband. Patsy had to listen to Nadeen complain all the way home but this time it didn't bother her because she had a Debutante Cotillion to prepare for and she was trying to focus on learning how to waltz with Dustin.

The next few weeks were exhausting for Patsy. She had to stay at practice a little longer to work with Dustin on the waltz. Kenny caught on real fast and she could run through practice with him but Dustin pretended he had two left feet so he could hold her close a little longer when they practiced

A week before the debutante presentation Mrs. Mason announced they were going to start having earlier practices so they could get the final kinks ironed out of the cotillion.

Patsy had to call Kenny at work to let him know to pick her and Ann up from school and take her straight to the practice that night. They were going to start an hour and a half earlier than usual.

They made it to practice before anyone else so Kenny decided to go around the corner and get sandwiches. By the time they all finished eating, Mrs. Mason was pulling up and all the other girls started arriving. Nadeen called the center and told Mrs. Mason to let Kenny know she wasn't feeling well tonight and wouldn't be coming but she promised to be there the next night. Mrs. Mason had to stand in for her when it came to the parent's waltz. It was funny to see Kenny with someone else even if it was just a practice.

They finished practice with an hour and a half to spare. Kenny took Dustin home and Patsy got out to walk him up the stairs to his house. She kissed him goodnight and walked back down the stairs. Kenny and Anne were grinning when she got back to the car.

"What are you grinning about?" Patsy asked them. She already knew.

"Nothing, little love bird," Kenny joked. Patsy just blushed and got in. She wasn't going to let Kenny worry her. They drove home with the windows down and the radio blasting. Life was so good at this moment!

"Hey, Kenny? You think Nadeen will let me go on that International Church Ministry trip with your church this summer?"

Patsy had heard it was a great opportunity to minister to kids in different countries and might even get her some scholarship money for school from the church.

"It would be a great way to spend part of your summer. Maybe if we pitch the idea from the standpoint of scholarship money and church recognition she might. I'll have to start fasting about that now cause it's gonna take Jesus for sure to make her say yes."

Patsy and Ann both laughed because they knew he was right.

As they got near the house, Kenny started to slow his truck down. He was staring out of his front window, easing up to it as though something was keeping him from seeing what was directly in front of him. He put his face as close as he could to the window.

"Is that Brother Ryan's Range Rover parked in front of my house?"

Patsy didn't quite recognize her father's voice. She looked and her heart started racing. Her stomach started churning and her mouth got dry. Her thoughts screamed.

Why was his truck here? Kenny told him once before that he was never to come back to their house. He made it clear if he caught him here again it wasn't going to be good! Surely he hadn't been foolish enough to try Kenny.

She froze in the seat. Kenny stopped the truck about six feet behind Brother Ryan's. He was looking straight ahead and not saying a word. He cut off the truck and got out. He was walking fast and focusing on the front door of the house. Patsy jumped out of the truck. Nothing was moving fast enough for Patsy right now! She wanted to call Kenny but the words wouldn't come out of her mouth. She was running to keep up with him.

When he opened the door they didn't see anybody, Patsy's mind immediately went to the worse scene possible.

Lord. Please don't let her be in the bed with Brother Ryan! Kenny is going to lose it and he is going to kill somebody up in here tonight! She could see the scene in her head, Kenny opening that bedroom door and Nadeen and Brother Ryan laying naked under the covers speaking in unholy tongues! As Kenny turned to go down the hall towards the bedroom, they heard voices. Nadeen was talking loud, Kenny stopped in his tracks and made a motion with his hands for her to stop. Patsy *wondered* where Josie was. *Nadeen must have put her to bed so she could visit with this shady church member,* Patsy thought. They heard Nadeen talking as though she was crying.

"Why did you even come here? I'm moving on with my life just like you did! I gave you my heart and you walked all over it! You told me you were separated from your wife and that there was no chance you would get back together with her. Then I come to church and get a bomb dropped on me! How do you think that made me feel?" She shouted the words and Patsy didn't even have to strain to hear.

"Nadeen, I was trying to do what was right in the eye sight of God!" Brother Ryan yelled. "He was whipping me bad for what I was doing with you and for what I'd done to my wife and children!" When he heard this, Kenny braced his hand on the wall.

"I almost lost my husband because I believed you were the man for me! I risked my reputation at church for us and you do something like that to me? You didn't even have the decency to tell me!" Nadeen shouted

"I just didn't know how to tell you Nadeen. I wanted to but I didn't know how!" Brother Ryan sounded like he was crying. "I been wanting to apologize to you for a long time. I wanted to talk to you that day at church that you got sick but I couldn't it was too many people around."

"Sick, huh? You know it was more than me being sick! You saw me and you knew I was pregnant and better than that you piece of scum. You knew that baby was yours!"

Kenny's head raised all the way up as he almost fell backwards. He seemed to be moaning. Patsy heard him and her heart began to break as he spoke.

"Please Lord! Please tell me it's not true! She wouldn't do that to me!" He moaned. Ann walked in just as Kenny started moving down the hall holding his balance with his hands on the wall. Before Patsy could grab him to stop him he flung open the door to Nadeen's bedroom. Brother Ryan turned around just in time to see Kenny come down on him fist first. Nadeen jumped back in shock and started screaming.

Kenny landed on him and started beating him in his face. They were tearing Nadeen's bedroom apart.

"I told you if I ever caught you here again I was going to kill you and I meant it!" Kenny roared. "How the hell you gonna come into my house and talk to my wife about loving her and how much she means to you? You supposed to be a Man of God yet you been screwing a married woman! You should have been loving your own wife more than mine cause your wife is gonna be a widow after tonight I promise you that!"

Nadeen was trying to pull him off of Brother Ryan but she couldn't. Kenny was gone! He was dangerously out of control. He was hitting Brother Ryan so hard Patsy could hear the punches as the blood and spittle flew out of his mouth. He looked like a rag doll tossed in the wind. She could only stand and watch him get what she thought he had coming to him. She wasn't going to get Kenny off of him.

Nadeen looked at her with panic in her eyes.

"Why are you just standing there? Go and get some help! He's going to kill him if we don't help him!"

"Oh my God, Patsy! Do something!" Ann screamed. Patsy wasn't going to move. Nadeen was pulling on Kenny's shirt but couldn't budge him. Brother Ryan was bleeding pretty bad and he was trying to crawl away from Kenny but he couldn't get far. Every time he tried to go forward Kenny would slam him back down and keep pounding on him.

By the time Nadeen ran out of the room, he somehow managed to crawl into the hallway. Kenny was still picking him up and pounding him down. Ann stood with her hand over her mouth in shock. Patsy wanted to cheer Kenny on! She wanted him to bash Brother Ryan's face in! The thrill of it was a bit scary to Patsy; it had to be evil to be enjoying this so much.

Nadeen came back down the hall running. Patsy looked at her and then she saw it. It was large and silver. She froze. Nadeen was holding a gun and yelling at Kenny to stop before she shot him! Kenny didn't hear her but Patsy did. Ann began to yell

"Stop, Daddy! Stop! She has a gun! She has a gun!" Ann yelled. The words registered with the picture in front of her face and Patsy sprang into motion. She went towards Nadeen to grab the gun, Ann ran out the back door to go and get help. As Patsy got close to her, Nadeen called Kenny one more time and he looked up, as he looked at her with an animal crazed look in his eyes, he saw the gun, she pulled the trigger and Patsy heard the gun go off three times.

She looked back at Kenny and saw his body jerk backwards from the first shot. When Nadeen fired the next two shots, he fell over to the side of Brother Ryan. Patsy saw it and she heard the shots but everything began to move in slow motion. She heard a scream come from her belly so loud she must have pulled it from years of being abused emotionally, mentally, and spiritually. She ran to Kenny and blood was flowing everywhere. *This couldn't be happening!*

"God, no! Not now. Please Lord! Please don't let him be dead! Please Lord! I can't live without my daddy!" She screamed so loud she drowned out the rest of the world. She put Kenny's head in her lap and started shaking him to wake up but he wouldn't open his eyes! She looked towards the door and saw Eva rushing in. Grandma Ruth was in her wheel chair at the hallway entrance, she was looking in at Kenny on the floor and she was crying as she mumbled under her breath. "Nadeen! Oh my God! Nadeen what have you done?" Eva rushed over to Kenny and knelt down

"I think he's dead, Nadeen! I can't get a pulse! I think he's dead!" Patsy heard her say the words he's dead, heard her own voice scream "No, God! Please No!" and then the darkness opened up and Patsy fell into it— without Kenny she didn't want to live!

As she went under, she heard her aunt say, "Nadeen! I knew one day your fake sanctified ways were gonna catch up with you!"

31

Ann's heart was pounding and the tears were blocking her vision. She was fighting the urge to go in the bathroom and slice her wrist wide open. This was way too much for her, but she knew she had to help Kenny. He was on the floor dead or dying in front of her. She saw Mrs. Wilson's house but it seemed so far away. She had a million potted plants on her porch. Ann and Patsy were usually really careful not to knock one over but tonight Ann didn't care. She ran out the door and across the street to her house. She jumped up on the porch and heard the ceramic pots crash to the porch as she started banging on the door.

"Mrs. Wilson open the door! My daddy's been shot! Open the door!"

Mrs. Wilson came to the door looking startled, "Ann? Child what is wrong with you?" She asked as she opened up her screen door.

"Mrs. Wilson! Please let me in. I need you to call the police. I need the police or an ambulance!" Ann cried. She was breathing heavy and it was so hard to talk.

"She shot my daddy! Please Mrs. Wilson! Please hurry up and call the police!" Ann begged.

"Oh, Father above!" Mrs. Wilson said. "Sit down. I'm gonna call right now! Jeffrey! Jeffrey get up and go across the street and check on Kenny!" She yelled as she went to the kitchen to call the police. Ann was sitting on the couch crying. She could hear Mrs. Wilson on the phone screaming at the police.

"I said it was my neighbor's house! She lives across the street. Can you just get the police here quick? Yes. Peace View Avenue. It's a red brick colored house with dark wood shutters. Hurry please!"

Mrs. Wilson hung up the phone and came back in the living room. "Ann. Give me just a minute to change out of this robe and I'll head over there with you. Jeffrey! Get across the street!"

Mr. Wilson came out of the back.

"I'm on the way now!"

"It's okay, Ann. I'm headed over there now. It's gonna be okay married people get into it sometimes. We just have to stay in prayer."

He pushed the front door open and ran down the stairs. Ann could see him running across the street. She could see the light on in the doorway of their house. Grandma Ruth was on the porch keeping the door open.

"Okay, baby." Mrs. Wilson said, "Let's get across the street. I pray we don't need the coroner instead of an ambulance. What got all this started anyway?" She asked as they headed out the door.

"Brother Ryan."

Mrs. Wilson stopped for a moment and gave Ann a funny look.

"Brother Ryan? The new minister at the church?"

"Yes, ma'am." Ann was quiet when she responded.

"Lord Jesus. I don't think I want to know. Come on."

She grabbed Ann by the arm and ran across the street. They saw the police and ambulance coming down the street as they got halfway there. They picked up the pace to get out of the way.

Ann made it to the front door first. Her mind was trying to register the scene in front of her. Why was Patsy on the floor? She wasn't moving. Had Nadeen shot her too? Was Patsy dead? Ann's mind raced.

She looked a few feet away and saw Kenny laying still on the floor blood pouring out from beneath him. He wasn't moving. She couldn't put this together it was too much. She heard her Aunt Eva calling on Jesus and asking, "Nadeen what have you done?" Eva collapsed and rocked back and forth on the floor.

Nadeen was just standing there wide-eyed with the gun at her side. Mr. Wilson took the gun from Nadeen and sat her down. Ann could hear Mrs. Wilson behind her as she put her hand on her back.

"Lord, God. We need you right now Father! We need you in this place!" she prayed with everything she had to give.

"Ann, let the police in, baby. They got the ambulance folks with them. They gonna take care of your daddy, baby. He gonna be all right."

Ann couldn't move. She was numb. She felt detached from her body. Her father and her sister were both lying motionless on the floor. She felt the strength of Mrs. Wilson's hands moving her out of the way because she couldn't do it herself.

She watched as the paramedics ran in the house with the stretcher. Grandma Ruth came over to her in the wheelchair.

"Come here, baby. Come here." She held out her hand but Ann could only cry. Then her mind snapped into place.

"Where's Josie?" she asked out loud. "Where is Josie? She felt a new rush of fear run through her belly.

"I didn't see her, baby," Grandma Ruth said through trembling lips.

Ann got up and went to the door. She saw the police in the kitchen talking to Nadeen. One of them was putting the gun in a plastic bag and the other one had his notepad out asking her questions. Brother Ryan was in the chair behind her talking with another officer, his eye was swollen and he had blood coming from his mouth.

Kenny was bleeding pretty bad. The paramedics were putting something over his mouth and calling his name.

Ann prayed quietly, *Please Lord! Don't let him be dead.*

She walked up to the stretcher, "Daddy? Daddy wake up." She begged him. She felt the tears rolling down her face. She touched his arm. "Daddy, please wake up. Please don't leave us. You just came back."

Eva came up behind her and put her hands on her arms to pull her back.

"Ann, let them get him to the hospital, baby. They gotta get him to the hospital to try and save him."

Ann watched them roll her daddy out the front door past her Grandma. Grandma Ruth reached out her hand to touch him and with the other hand she muffled her cries with her handkerchief. Mrs. Wilson walked over to her and wheeled her into the house. Just as she got her in, the other paramedic brought Patsy back around.

As soon as she came to she began asking them about Kenny.

"Where's my daddy? Where's my daddy? Is he dead? Somebody tell me! Did she kill him?" She was frantic. Eva went over to her and spoke softly in her ear.

"Patsy, baby. They took him to the hospital. We need to get to the hospital to see about him."

"Your crazy sister did this! She was up in here with her boyfriend, the good Reverend-So-Fake and Kenny walked in and caught him. He told him never to come back to this house! He told him what was going to happen if he came back!"

Patsy was so angry she didn't care if Nadeen heard her or not. Eva helped her up from the floor.

"Come on, baby. Let's get to the hospital and see about your daddy. Where's your baby sister?" Patsy looked at Ann. "Ann where is Josie? I hope she didn't get hit by a stray bullet. Oh God! We have to find her! Let me check in the back."

Patsy held on to the wall still a little shaky. Ann went behind her.

"I was coming back in here to look for her," Ann said.

They saw her baby doll on the couch and her juice cup. "Josie! Josie where are you? Come to Patti! Come on, baby!" She could barely speak around the lump in her throat.

Patsy walked up the stairs and stood near the toy chest by the glass door. She heard a whimper. It was faint but she heard it. She went towards it.

"Josie? Josie you in there?" She asked softly. Patsy pulled back the toy chest and there was her little sister. She was laying on the floor under Patsy's blue blanket, sucking her thumb and crying. Patsy's heart almost broke. Poor baby Josie. She was so little to be going through so much. Patsy bent down and picked her up. She grabbed onto Patsy's shirt and started crying louder. Patsy rocked her and rubbed her hair.

"I got you, sweetie. It's okay. Big sister got you. Don't be scared." Ann came back in the room.

"You found her. Where was she?"

"She was hiding behind the toy chest. Come on. Let's get to the hospital to see about Kenny."

"If he dies, Patsy I'm leaving this house." Ann warned. "I'm gonna run away. I can't do this anymore. Nadeen probably gonna go to jail. I hope she rots in there. She won't be so tough with a cell full of murderers and sodomites."

Patsy had never heard Ann speak with such venom, but she understood where it was coming from. They walked down the stairs and into the hallway like they had done so many times before, but there was something different about this walk now, Patsy could feel it, she felt like something was changing inside of her, inside of this house.

The police were handcuffing Nadeen as they came up front. She had her head down as they walked her past them. Patsy felt a sadness pass all over her. She didn't understand it. Why would she feel sad for Nadeen? She had put them through so much hell for so long and now she may have killed the one person in the house who helped them to hold on to their sanity. The police told Brother Ryan he was free to go but they would be in touch with him real soon. He walked out with the officer shaking his head and wringing his hands.

"How am I gonna explain this to my wife? How am I gonna go back to my church with this scandal?"

"Sir. You are gonna have to work that out. It seems to me you need to do some soul searching. If this man dies you and his wife both could lose everything you have."

No one spoke to Brother Ryan as he walked out. Grandma Ruth was glaring at him like she wanted to finish what Kenny started. Mrs. Wilson offered to keep Josie for them, but Patsy thought they should all stay together.

"Mrs. Wilson could you make sure the house is locked up for us. We need to get to the hospital to check on Kenny." Eva asked.

"I sure will. I'll help you all in any way I can. Call me if you need me to bring something for y'all. I'm gonna be praying for the whole family."

"Thank you, Mrs. Wilson. You have always been such a good neighbor."

As they walked out the door, Reverend and First Lady Mack were getting out of their car. They had two other cars pull up behind them. Patsy recognized them as members of Deliverance Rock. Reverend Mack ran over to them.

"Sister Patsy, what's going on over here?"

"I got a disturbing phone call from one of the members of my congregation who said someone who lives in this neighborhood called and told them there was an ambulance and policeman at your house."

Patsy looked at the pastor, his wife and the members of the congregation and thought to herself, *This is what it means to be a family.*

"My daddy has been shot, Reverend Mack. Nadeen shot him."

He looked at her with disbelief on his face. First Lady Mack stepped up.

"Baby, what you mean? Your momma shot him! Why would she do something like that She's the Head Usher at her church," First Lady said.

"Ask the good Reverend Ryan also known as Reverend So Fake from Greater Trials why he got my daddy shot. He was here. He knows what happened and why."

Eva walked behind her and opened the car door for them to get in.

"Pastor and First Lady Mack, we appreciate you all coming over to check on Kenny. He's at the hospital probably getting ready for surgery. We have to get there right now. If you like you can follow us."

Pastor Mack nodded his head, trying to take in what Patsy had said.

"Yes. We'd like to go with you to the hospital to pray for our brother. He's a good man. Come on, First Lady. Let's follow them."

He looked at the other congregational members and motioned for them to follow him. They all got back in their cars and followed Eva to the hospital.

The ride was quiet. Patsy could hear Ann in the front seat sniffling. She must have been scratching at her arms because Patsy heard Eva talking to her.

"Ann. Baby I see you digging at your wrist. I seen that before. I know what that means. You gotta stop. This has to stop. I know what you doing. I know real well what you doin." Ann started crying harder and louder.

"Momma?" Eva said to her mother in the back seat. "Momma, Ann been cutting on herself."

Grandma Ruth began to moan. She started whispering down low.

"You won't get her. You won't get her. Not then. Not now. You won't!" She hissed

"Patsy did you know your sister been cutting on herself?" Eva asked Patsy.

This just wasn't the time. This was too much.

"Yes," she said pitifully.

Eva looked at her through the rear view mirror. "You tell your momma about this? She know?"

Patsy shook her head and said, "No, ma'am. I was too scared to tell her. Ann hides it most of the time. She cut under her leg most of the time. I just see the blood that's how I know when she been doing it."

She felt the tears fill up in her eyes.

"Lord Jesus. Please stop it." Eva said. "We gonna leave this in this car for right now but after this storm settles I'm gonna have a talk with my sister. She done passed this mess along to my niece."

Patsy frowned at that statement. She didn't know what her Aunt meant by that and right now she was too worried about Kenny to figure it out. She just sat in the back seat next to Josie to keep her calm. Josie was holding on to her finger and wouldn't let go.

When they arrived at the hospital, Kenny's baby sister, Ernestine, was there. She was mad. She'd gotten a call from one of her friends at Deliverance Rock who worked at the hospital and she came immediately. It was no secret she didn't like Nadeen so she hardly ever called or came by. She always told Kenny that two nuts couldn't stay in the same room together. She never wanted Kenny to marry Nadeen in the first place and when she did get into a fight with Nadeen she never failed to let her know it. But, she loved her nieces, or pretended she did when everyone was watching. When she saw Patsy, Ann, and Josie, she ran to them.

"Oh my poor nieces. My poor babies. Why didn't somebody call me? I would have come and got you all. I told my brother not to marry that Jezebel! She can fool the folks at Greater Trials with her white gloves and her hallelujahs but she don't fool me! She a hell cat and now everybody know it!"

Any other time Eva would have stepped in and handled her for talking about her sister but right now she was focused on whether or not her brother in law was going to live or die.

"Ernestine, I know you're upset right now but we need to be looking out for Kenny and praying that he make it instead of pointing fingers and calling names."

"You can say that! It ain't your brother in there fighting for his life. It's mine and I'll call her any name I want to call her crazy bat straight out of hell!" She yelled at Eva. Grandma Ruth pushed herself to the front and wheeled right up to Ernestine.

"I know that's your brother and that you love him." She frowned. "He's like a son to me and I love him too, but if you don't sit down somewhere, shut up, and pray,

I'm gonna bust you in your face and put you in a bed beside him! You hear me? I have had enough fighting tonight."

Just as Ernestine was about to say something back to her, Pastor and First Lady Mack came through the door. Ernestine quickly ran over to Pastor Mack.

She ain't so different from Nadeen after all, Patsy thought.

The doctor came out and said that they would need a family member to sign the papers to operate on Kenny. If they didn't do it soon they may lose him. Ernestine said it should be her since she was his sister. No one argued with her. She signed the papers and the doctor said he would prepare Kenny for surgery and come back to let everyone know how it went in a few hours. The church members took Josie and got her something to eat.

It took the doctors four hours to operate on Kenny. Patsy seem to hold her breath the whole time. When the doctor finally came back to talk to them. He told them Kenny managed to pull through the surgery. He had been hit twice. The first bullet went straight through his shoulder but the second one was inches from his spine and that was what took so long, they had to be very careful not to damage any nerves in his back and paralyze him for life. He would be in ICU for a while.

"Can I go and see him now?" Ernestine asked. It seemed to Patsy that she was disregarding them. They were his children. He was their daddy.

The doctor looked at her and smiled, "Give him a few minutes. I'll come back and let you know. They'll only let you in two at a time so decide who will go in first."

He glanced at Patsy and Ann.

"Patsy, I think you and Ann should go first. He needs to see his girls," Eva said.

Ernestine turned and looked at her.

"I'm his sister. I was here first. I should get to see him first. Your sister is the reason he's in here with tubes in his nose!" She yelled at Eva. Pastor Mack stepped up and whispered something in her ear and walked her to the back of the waiting room.

"I'm gonna get my day with that sister!" Eva said under her breath. "You girls going in first and that's all it is to it!"

32

"**M**r. Simmons is ready for visitors now," the doctor said. "He's heavily sedated but you can see him. You can talk to him. I'm sure he can hear you."

Eva stepped up to him, "His daughters will go in first then the others." The doctor nodded his head.

"Come this way, young ladies."

Patsy and Ann walked behind the doctor. When they got to the room he opened the door for them and stood back so they could go in. Patsy saw Kenny and she began to cry again. He was hooked up to so many different tubes and the machines were beeping. It looked like he couldn't breathe and the machines had to pump his chest to get him to. They walked up to his bed and just looked at him. After a few minutes Ann reached out and touched his arm. "Daddy. It's me and Patsy."

Kenny didn't move. Patsy didn't know what to say to him. She was still trying to believe he was laying in this hospital bed because of Nadeen. He almost died because of her. *Who told her she had the power of life and death in her hands?*

After a few minutes, she kissed him on the jaw and prayed over him. When she finished she squeezed his hand and she noticed the machines got a little louder. She saw a tear come from the corner of his eye.

She looked at Ann, "He can hear us, Ann. He can hear us and he's gonna fight so he can come back to us."

The nurse came in and told them visitation was over for right now. They would have another visitation time in about an hour. Ann and Patsy didn't want to leave him. It seemed someone was always in the hospital when Nadeen got mad!

"Kenny. We'll be back in a few hours." Patsy squeezed his hand and her and Ann walked out. She put her arms around Ann and tried to be the strong big sister she needed. Ann could lean on her; she was gonna lean on God. He was always there to carry them both.

When she got back to the waiting room, Dustin was there. Patsy ran to him and hugged him.

"Thank you for coming. Everything happened so fast I didn't have time to call you. How did you find out?"

Dustin turned and pointed in the corner, there was Sandra. She was sitting there rocking Solomon to sleep and Lavon was with her sleeping in the chair next to her.

"She got a phone call from one of the girls at the school. She called me and asked me if I'd talked to you. She went by your house first and saw Mrs. Wilson leaving. She told Sandra what happened so they came and got me."

Patsy went over to Sandra and Lavon. Sandra looked up at her. "How is your dad doing?" Sandra asked. "You know he's like a dad to me to. If something happens to him I'm going to be tore up, girl!" Patsy rubbed the baby's head as she talked to Sandra.

"He just came out of surgery a little while ago. They have him in ICU. We just came out of the room with him. He can hear us but he can't talk. He's on a lot of drugs."

Patsy said. She reached over and gave Lavon a friendly tap on his head. He woke up and smiled at her.

"Girl, how you doing? Your dad all right? I'm praying he makes it."

"Thank you for bringing everybody." Patsy said. Lavon smiled.

"You know your girl wasn't going to let me rest until I got her up here to see about you and she made sure I went by and picked up Dustin."

"You know I can't do the debutante now right?" Patsy asked Dustin.

"I understand that, Patsy. I know you couldn't enjoy it with your dad here. Anyway you wouldn't want anyone else to waltz with you."

Patsy half-smiled. "I'm glad you understand."

"Where is Nadeen, Patsy? I heard someone say that the police took her to jail." Sandra asked.

Patsy just nodded slowly.

"You know you gotta pray for her too. She's still your mother no matter how messed up she is." Sandra said.

"I don't know if I can do that right now. She almost killed my dad." Patsy said.

Sandra looked into her eyes sincerely and said to her.

"If you don't pray for her Patsy. Who will?"

"I don't know, Sandra, but right now it can't be me."

She kissed Sandra and the baby and told Lavon to take them home to get some sleep. She'd call her later that day with an update.

Eva was wrapping Grandma Ruth up to take her home. "Patsy you all want to go home for a little while and get some rest? I gotta get momma home so she can do her physical therapy."

Patsy didn't want to leave. "I'm gonna stay here for a little while longer. Take Ann and Josie home with you and let them get some rest. I'm not going to leave Kenny."

Eva walked over and kissed her on the forehead.

"You such a strong girl, Patsy. Kenny got his self a trooper! I knew you would say that. I'll bring you some lunch and a change of clothes when we come back. If you need me before then just call the house." Eva turned to Ann.

"Ann, you and I gotta have a serious talk about this little problem that seems to have been passed down to you." Grandma Ruth swatted Eva on the hand.

"Now ain't the time to bring that up. You know Nadeen is real sensitive about that you best to keep it quiet."

"That's the problem now. Everybody so busy trying to make her out a Saint don't nobody want to remind her she ain't. This baby is gonna end up in a mental hospital just like–"

Grandma Ruth popped Eva real hard on her wrist before she could finish talking.

"Enough I said! Enough!" Eva rolled her eyes at her mother then started out the door.

Patsy kissed Josie and Ann then watched them walk out behind her Aunt Eva. Just as Patsy was about to settle down in a chair next to Dustin, Ernestine came into the waiting room.

"Your daddy better pull through this. I'm going to do my best to convince him to get out this time. If he doesn't leave her she's going to kill him! She couldn't take her own self out so she wants to try to take out my brother!"

Patsy didn't feel like talking to her Aunt Ernestine right now. She obviously was talking out of hurt so she wasn't making a whole lot of sense with some of the stuff she was saying. She just wanted some quiet time. Her whole life had almost been turned upside down when she saw Kenny lying on that floor in his own blood.

"You hear me girl?" Ernestine said. "You probably just as crazy as your momma! You should have tried to protect my brother from that nut. What were you doing? On the phone with your little boyfriend over there?" Patsy tried to get out of the chair to confront her but she felt Dustin squeeze her hand tight. She could feel a wave building in her stomach and she knew once it reached her throat she would show her just how much a fool she could act right about now.

Dustin stood up and approached Ernestine, "Ma'am. My name is Dustin. Patsy loves her dad so I know she did all she could to try and protect him. We all need to just pray for Mr. Kenny and the whole family."

Ernestine looked at Dustin as though she wanted to spit out nails.

"Son. I don't know you and you sure enough don't know me because if you did you wouldn't be up in my face talking to me right now!" She spat the words between her teeth. She put her finger up to his face and was about to tear into him when a nurse came in.

"Are you all with the family of Kenny Simmons?"

Patsy's heart begin racing, "Yes," she managed to get out. Her throat was real dry. The nurse smiled at her.

"Well. He opened his eyes a few minutes ago. He is still very weak but he opened his eyes."

Ernestine put her finger down and begin dancing in the waiting room.

"Thank you Lord! Thank you for hearing my prayers! You saved my brother and I Thank You Jesus!"

She seemed so much like Nadeen. Patsy now better understood why they didn't like each other. Two bad spirits together in the same room there ain't no way there could be peace! Patsy took Dustin by the hand and walked around Ernestine dancing in the waiting room.

"Come on. Let's go call Aunt Eva first and then Pastor Mack and give them the good news."

The nurse let them go in and visit Kenny a few minutes early before visitation actually started. Patsy walked in the room and could still hear the machines slamming against each other. The tubes were still in him. He was sleeping. She held on to Dustin's hand as they approached the bed. She called his name softly and touched his stomach. He opened his eye and turned his head to her.

She smiled at him. "Hey Kenny." She still didn't know exactly what to say to him. He looked past her at Dustin. Dustin lifted up his hand at him and smiled. Patsy saw a slight smile come from the corner of his mouth.

"Everybody been here praying for you, Mr. Kenny. We been botherin' God all night about you. I guess he got tired of us sitting at the Throne of Grace beggin' him to save you."

Kenny smiled as he kept going in and out. The medicine kept him drowsy. Patsy would make small conversation with him in between. The nurse came in and told her it was time for the next visitor.

It was Ernestine; she came in running up to the bed crying.

"Oh, lil brother! I thought you were gone from me! I thought you'd left me!"

She rolled her eyes at Patsy as she came close to the bed. Patsy felt sorry for her. She was acting. *Wonder if she knew God sees the heart.* She couldn't call on the name of the Lord and roll her eyes at her brother's daughter because of her hate for her mother and expect God to be pleased with her.

The doctor moved Kenny to a regular room on Monday. Patsy and Ann didn't go to school that day. Patsy stayed at the hospital and looked after Kenny. Dustin came by to see her. When he walked in she was feeding Kenny. He didn't really need her to, she just wanted to take care of him.

"Look at Nurse Patsy." Dustin joked. She laughed.

"I'm just helping him out. He doesn't mind."

Just as she finished feeding him the phone rang. Patsy answered it, there was silence then just as she was about to hang up she heard her voice.

"Patsy? Patsy this you?" It was Nadeen. Patsy hung the phone up. *Why was she calling here and when did she get out of jail?*

The phone rang again. Patsy wouldn't answer it, Dustin looked at her.

"Are you going to answer the phone or not?"

"It's Nadeen!"

"She's calling from the jail?" Dustin seemed just as alarmed as she was.

"I don't know. I didn't ask her. I just hung up!" She thought she was whispering but Kenny heard her.

"Patsy was that your momma on the phone?" He asked in a weak voice. Patsy wanted to lie to him but she couldn't.

"Yes, sir."

Kenny had a strange look on his face. He looked down at his hands and played with his wedding band. He looked back up at the television again and then said to her,

"I didn't raise you to be disrespectful. If she calls back, you talk to her. No matter what is going on with us, she is still your mother and you are supposed to honor her. You hear me?" Patsy didn't understand this. He should have been glad that she hung up on her.

"Yes, sir," she said reluctantly.

When Aunt Eva came Patsy told her and Grandma Ruth what happened. Aunt Eva told her that someone had paid her bail and she was out. She was at home asking if she could come and talk to Kenny. That was probably why she called up to the hospital. "I don't want her up here. She might upset him." Patsy said.

"Baby, that's not for you to decide. They got to handle this themselves. It has nothing to do with us." Aunt Eva said. Grandma Ruth wandered over to Patsy.

"Grandbaby, we can't get between husband and wife. God put them together and we are not to come between that. They have to work this out. When your granddaddy was alive we had our disagreements but he didn't allow no one to get between us. We worked it out our way and Nadeen and Kenny will do the same."

Patsy didn't care to hear that.

The door opened to Kenny's room and two police officers walked in. One of them was the officer that brought Kenny home once after he had been out for several days doing God knows what! Patsy wondered why they were here. They both tipped their hats as they came in, "Good afternoon, ladies."

They said. Everyone spoke but looked around at each other trying to figure out why they were there. Officer Butler, the officer that brought Kenny home when he had been missing for three days went up to his bed.

"Mr. Simmons how you feeling?"

Kenny nodded his head at the officer.

"Mr. Simmons. We came by to let you know your wife was released on bail this morning. We need to know if you plan on pressing charges against her. She could have killed you and if you didn't have an angel on your side, she would have. That bullet almost paralyzed you from what the doctor told us."

Patsy looked at Kenny. She waited to hear what he would say. Kenny looked at both of the officers. "No, sir. I will not be pressing charges against my wife. We'll work this out our way. Thank you for your concern though."

The other officer spoke to him next. "Mr. Simmons. Your wife did try to kill you. You realize that don't you? She shot you multiple times to protect her boyfriend, some so-called minister at her church. Why would you want her to get away with that?"

Kenny's voice got real deliberate and firm when he spoke this time. "My wife and I along with God's guidance will work this out. Whatever we decide will be based on God's Will for our marriage. She is the mother of my children. I will not have her sitting in prison. I thank you again for your concern, now. Goodbye!"

The officers looked at him and turned to walk away. One of them turned back as they headed out the door and said, "If you change your mind Mr. Simmons. Give us a call. We're here to serve and protect you know."

Kenny just pushed the volume button up on the television remote. As soon as they left, Kenny turned it back down and the phone rang. He looked at Patsy. "I'll get it."

He spoke in a low tone on the phone. He was on the phone for quite a while. When he hung up, he called Eva and Grandma Ruth over to his bed and talked to them. When he finished he called Patsy over.

"Baby I thank you for all you done for me. You know I love you. I want you to go on home tonight and get you some rest. Take Ann with you."

"I don't want to leave! I want to stay here and help you. I don't want to see her." Patsy begin to cry and she put her head down on his chest. He rubbed his hands through her hair.

"Baby girl. I need you to do this for me. I appreciate all you have done but I need you to go home and take care of things. Believe it or not, your momma needs you too. You go on home." Patsy just cried more. She didn't want to leave him.

Grandma Ruth grabbed her by her arm. "Come on, Patsy. Come help me get Ann and Josie out the waiting room. They need to come say good night to your daddy. Come on now."

Patsy lifted up her head from Kenny's chest. He smiled at her.

Ann and Josie came back to the room and said goodnight to Kenny. Patsy walked out the door with Dustin even though she didn't want to go. She didn't want to go back home and walk through those doors that her father was rolled out of. She was tired of having to be strong. She wanted to just give up sometimes but she knew deep down inside too many people needed her strength but she, she needed the strength of God. As they walked out of the doors to the parking lot, Josie yelled, "Momma!" and she pointed across the parking lot. Patsy looked and she saw Nadeen walking up the sidewalk towards them. Her stomach tightened inside and she turned to look at Ann. Ann put her head down.

"I'm gonna cut out now. I'll call you later or see you tomorrow at school." He knew this was going to be a tense and private moment.

"Okay. Thanks for coming."

Nadeen walked up to them with a faint smile. Josie reached out for her. She took her and gave her a big kiss on her face.

"How is momma's baby girl? I sure did miss you. Give me a hug." She said as she hugged her tighter. She looked at Patsy and Ann but didn't say anything to them.

"Hey Nadeen." Eva said. "Kenny waiting for you." Nadeen gave Josie back to Patsy. "I know. We talked on the phone. We just need some time to talk this thing through. It's best it's just me and him. I brought my bag so I can look after him tonight."

"That's the least you could do." Grandma Ruth mumbled. Nadeen looked at her.

"What you say, momma?"

"You need to get on in there and fix things with your husband and see what he has to say instead of worrying about what I'm saying!" Grandma Ruth said.

"Patsy, I need you to fix the children something to eat and make sure they get to bed on time." Nadeen ordered.

Patsy answered dryly, "Yes, ma'am."

"I'll be back in the morning," she told Eva.

"That's fine and when all this settles down I need to talk to you about something real important dealing with my niece. Some things gotta be pulled up by the root in this family."

Nadeen looked into Eva's eyes and gave her a slight frown then she turned and walked through the hospital doors towards the elevator.

"Come on, girls! Let's go. Momma that includes you!" Eva said. When they got home Patsy noticed that the house had been cleaned spic and span. The spot where Kenny fell had been cleaned up and the rug that use to be there was gone. The house smelled like cinnamon and pumpkin pie. Nadeen must have cleaned it as soon as she got home to erase what happened. The physical can be erased but the spiritual and mental trauma take a special kind of balm that only God can apply. He would have to use a couple of bottles on their family. Patsy went to bed early. She was exhausted. She knew she had to go back to school tomorrow. She was going to need all of her rest to deal with the stares and gossip that would be waiting for her.

Morning came fast. Patsy moved with dread. She finished breakfast and had so much time on her hands she decided to take her time and walk slowly to the bus stop. She and Ann both knew this was where it would begin.

"Ann don't let anybody get to you today okay?"

"I'll try, Patsy, but I can't promise. I might just blow up if the wrong thing is said to me today. I'm tired. My daddy almost died and my momma is the one that almost killed him all over some fake preacher!"

"I know," Patsy soothed. "But Kenny doesn't need us to bring him any more stress than he already has so let's try to do it for him"

Ann frowned at her big sister, "Patsy, I go to school with one of Brother Ryan's son's. Do you know how uncomfortable that's going to be? It's all around town what happened!"

"You got to put on the whole armor of God now Ann. It's not going to be easy but we can do this. We're almost at this bus stop. We gotta be covered. Don't let them break us. We will not cry in front of them or bust them in the face no matter how much we want to!"

They both laughed. That helped. The bus pulled up as soon as they got to the stop. They could feel all eyes on them as they went to the back and sat down. They rode silently to the next stop, which was Ann's school. As Ann got up, Patsy grabbed her by the wrist.

She whispered to her, "Think about Kenny."

Ann nodded her head. Her usual circle of friends surrounded her and made a circle around her when she got off the bus.

That's good. She'll be all right with them.

Now she had to prepare herself. She was gonna need all of God's Angels to go with her. The demons in high school were far more evil than junior high school. When the bus pulled up she saw the smile of the first angel in her life, Dustin, he was looking into the bus trying to find her. She stayed focus on his face as she stepped off the bus. He came up to her and wrapped his arms around her waist. She felt better already.

"Good morning, beautiful," he said. They held hands as they walked down the sidewalk through the crowd of stares and whispers. Sandra met them and hugged her.

"I'm glad you're back."

They all walked to class together. This first period was going to be preparation for her. The next class she wouldn't have Dustin there to block out the gossipers and the stares. The next class would have Daphne Porter, and she always seem to be in the mood for a good fight or argument. Patsy walked out of her first period class prepared for whatever would come her way.

Sandra walked with her telling her all about Solomon and all the cute things he was learning to do. This was one time Patsy was glad she talked too much. As they neared the stairs to go up to her next class, she spotted Daphne Porter. She was standing next to the stairs with her crew. They saw her coming. Patsy took a deep breath. "You don't need that crap today. Just say the word and I will wipe this hall with her. I don't mind going home for a few days. I need to be with my baby anyway." Sandra said. Patsy laughed.

"You ain't going home to spoil that baby. We're going to walk by her like she ain't even there. No matter what she says."

As she got closer to Daphne, she saw her staring at her. She walked to the stairs and started walking up. As she put her foot on the second step, she heard Daphne's wicked voice.

"Watch your back! You might get a bullet" She said. The girls with her started laughing. Patsy kept walking. Sandra stopped and turned around to face Daphne.

"You need to be watching for my fist in your face! You stupid skank!" Sandra yelled at her as she headed up the stairs toward Daphne. Patsy grabbed her and yelled.

"No Sandra! Don't you give her the satisfaction! She got issues of her own. Picking with me is the only way she can deal with her own demons." Patsy held Sandra's shirt tight as they passed Daphne.

"My daddy always told me to pick your battles. It's all about timing. I'll get my chance with Daphne Porter and when I do, I'll come out victorious. Believe that girlfriend. Patsy said.

"When is Kenny coming back home or is he coming back home?" Sandra asked. Patsy gave Sandra a confused look.

"What do you mean or is he coming back home?" She had never thought that he wouldn't come back. He wouldn't leave them, not his girls.

"Patsy, I don't mean any harm. I'm just saying. This one right here almost took him out. He might be done this time." Sandra said.

"Sandra, my daddy would never leave us. You see when he moved out that one time he was right down the street and even then he wasn't gone long. He can't leave Nadeen alone no matter what she does. She got a root on him my Grandma Ruth says."

"Well, if he comes back this time I'll believe it."

Patsy watched out for Daphne the rest of the day. She knew this wasn't over. Daphne wanted a reaction out of her and she wasn't going to be satisfied until she got one. It seemed like she was determined to be a thorn in her side.

Things at home with Nadeen were tense. Patsy and Ann stayed in their rooms a lot when they got home. Nadeen was out on leave from work. The people at the Gardens of Peace Nursing Home thought it would be best to give things time to die down at work. Everyone was talking about what happened. Nadeen was worried that she may not get the night supervisor position because of what happened with Kenny. Nadeen saw this all as a trick of the enemy to get her eyes off of the prize. Kenny was always letting the enemy use him and in return he was always getting in the way of her plans. As usual none of it was her fault.

When Kenny was finally released from the hospital. He slept on the pull out couch upstairs. Nadeen catered to his every need. Maybe she was grateful that she wasn't sitting in the city jail waiting to go to trial. Kenny had the upper hand this time but he didn't use it. He was just waiting, waiting on an answer from God. He believed it was gonna come soon.

33

Reverend Craig and the new First Lady Craig came by about a month after Kenny came home. Kenny didn't have much to say to him but Nadeen hung on his every word. He told her he was so sorry he couldn't get by sooner but trying to keep up with his new wife was keeping him pretty busy. This made Champagne laugh. She crossed her legs and tried to pull down the mini skirt that was just about showing the sunshine between them. Maybe she really had used a bag of magic potion on him, the way she had his nose so wide open. Patsy never saw his first wife wear anything so short and revealing to church or anywhere else.

Patsy made it her business to dust the furniture near the living room so she could hear Reverend Craig talking to Nadeen. Kenny excused himself after he arrived, said he wasn't feeling well and needed to lay down.

"Sister Nadeen, I was real sorry to hear about the little problem you had with your husband but I see that you all are working it out. That's good."

Nadeen sounded so pitiful, "Well Pastor we're trying. Don't want to give the enemy no room in here to destroy our marriage. You know I been trying to be a good wife for a long time. I been with Kenny through all of his bad habits and drama. I been just praying and keeping quiet."

"Yes, Sister Simmons. Prayer is always the best answer to any problem. I'm curious though. Why was Brother Ryan over here? I heard that's why things got a little out of hand. I never figured your husband had a jealous bone in his body."

"Well, Pastor. He was checking on me to see how I was doing that's all. He was being a good church member and friend. My husband just got the wrong idea when he came in and he scared me so bad I thought he was going to kill me or kill Brother Ryan." She sniffled, trying to make herself cry.

"Brother Ryan was just holding my hands praying with me. When he finished he hugged me but Kenny—he came in, saw him hugging me and got the wrong idea. The next thing I know he was jumping on Brother Ryan and beating him something awful! I just meant to scare him Pastor. I never meant to pull the trigger. You know I'm not a violent person. I am just a humble servant of the Lord."

"I know it, Sister Simmons. I tried to explain that to your sisters in the Prayer Circle Society. They come to me with some concerns as to whether or not you should remain the president or not because of the rumors they heard. One of them said she was told you was having an affair with Brother Ryan and your husband warned him before about what would happen if he caught him over here again but I told them those kinda things might go on at Deliverance Rock but they don't go on in ours. They believe you shot him on purpose. I told them you was a good and faithful church member. You're a praying woman. I told them not to give in to the enemy's lies trying to destroy your good character."

Nadeen grinned through crocodile tears, "Pastor, I appreciate you so. Thank you for speaking up for me. You know I'm at that door dressed in my white every Sunday and I pay my tithes. I try to help anybody that's in need.

Brother Ryan is just a good friend of mine. He was my prayer partner."

Patsy wanted to run in the room and scream at Nadeen, *"You know you need to stop that lie! You ought to be ashamed lying to the Pastor!"*

"Well, don't you worry none Sister Simmons. I see your household is in order and you and your husband are doing fine. I'm not going to let them remove you from any positions you hold at the church. You been too faithful for that!"

He patted her hand and moved to get up. "Well, I better get along now. First Lady wants to go down to the Casino for the seafood buffet. I gotta keep her happy you know." He chuckled. Champagne pitched in then.

"I'm still learning to cook Sister Nadeen. Sometimes I just hate putting him through my cooking so I take him to the Casino for a good meal. We even got blessed down there a couple of times. We hit the jackpot! Pastor took some of that money and bought some new robes for the choir. I tell you God is blessing all around."

Patsy thought to herself, *She's as bad as her sister in the head. They both screwed up.* Patsy heard them getting up coming towards the doorway so she headed to the back.

"Kenny, you okay back here?"

"Yes, baby. Ann and Josie been taking good care of me. They beat me up then give me some water to re-group before the next fight." He laughed. It was good to see him laugh again.

"Is that man gone yet?"

"Yep. Him and his Wanta be First Lady just left to go to the Casino for dinner." She said. They both laughed. Nadeen came into the room.

"Kenny. I'm going to go to the store and pick up some things. You need anything?" This surprised Patsy.

"No. I don't need anything." He said. His voice sounded different now when he talked. Patsy noticed it sounded empty. He sounded tired. He was tired of trying to win her love, tired of dealing with her temper, tired of walking on his tip toes around her, He was tired of trying to make up for his past mistakes. Patsy was thinking, *'what's coming Lord?'* Eva showed up at the house just as Nadeen pulled off. She came in the house a little out of breath.

"Hey baby. Your daddy up?"

Patsy directed her to the back room where Kenny was resting in a chair. "Hey, brother-in-law how you feel?"

Kenny gave her a slight smile.

"I'm still here, sister-in-law. I can't complain. How you doing?"

Eva was amazed. He had just taken multiple bullets from her sister and he sits here saying he can't complain. She tried to hide the amazement from her face.

"I'm good trying to keep momma and David from driving me crazy. I see I just missed Nadeen."

Kenny sat up in the chair. "Yeah, she had to run to the store. I'll tell her you came by."

Eva sat down and turned to Kenny. "Well, I really wanted to talk to you first."

"About what? If it's about what happened with me and Nadeen, I don't want to talk about that. We trying to move past that."

"No. It's about Ann." Eva said.

Kenny looked confused. "About Ann? What about her? I know this has been rough on all my girls." He said and put his head slightly down.

"Kenny Ann is cutting herself. She is and has been doing so for some time."

Kenny felt his heart skip a beat in his chest. He couldn't seem to catch his breath. He sat all the way up and looked at his sister-in-law.

"She doing what Eva? What you mean she cutting herself? She can't be. She wouldn't hurt herself like that. That spirit can't be in my girls."

Eva felt a sadness spread from her chest all the way through her legs. She couldn't look him in the eye, so she focused on her fingers in her lap.

"Kenny she is. She is cutting herself and Patsy knows about it. I wanted to tell Nadeen but I don't want her to persecute the girl. I was hoping you would talk to her. She needs you. All your girls need you. You know where this thing is coming from." She finally looked up to meet his eyes.

Neither one of them wanted to say the name. Kenny just looked at her knowingly without a word. Eva stood up despite the weakness in her legs.

"I just thought you needed to know brother-in-law." She patted him on the shoulder and walked out. Kenny sat there in a daze for quite some time. He needed God to give him the words to say to his little girl. He needed the words to save her from this thing that had decided to show its ugly face again.

He sat in the chair for what seemed like hours praying for the right words and the right way to reach his daughter. He finally gained enough courage to call her into the room.

"Ann? Ann, come back here for a minute I want to talk to you."

Ann came into the room smiling.

"Come sit on my lap." He patted his lap and motioned for her to sit down. Ann grinned and sat down on his lap.

"What's up, Daddy?"

"You know I love you don't you?"

The grin left Ann's face and she suddenly had a sick feeling in her stomach. She felt instantly something was wrong.

"Yes, Daddy. I know you love me. Why you ask me that?"

Kenny grabbed both her hands and placed them in his. "I want you to stop." He looked directly in her eyes. He saw the sadness there.

"I want you to stop cutting yourself. I know about it. I even know why you are doing it but I need you to stop it. If something happened to you, I don't think I would be strong enough to live, baby girl. It would break my heart. Do you hear me?"

The tears ran down her face. She couldn't speak. She was ashamed and she was relieved. Relieved that her daddy knew. Her daddy who was supposed to be big and strong and fight the demons in her head for her. He knew and now that he knew maybe the thoughts would go away. Kenny hugged her close to him.

"I know. I know why you do it, baby girl. It's not your fault. It's not. It's a curse baby. It's something I should have stood up to a long time ago and it never would have gotten in this house. I should have been the watchman on the wall at all times but I wasn't, I got distracted while on my post and this thing has snuck in and tried to take my babies but I won't let it. Do you hear your daddy? I won't let it take you."

They sat in the chair and cried together. He rocked Ann for a long time that night. He rocked her until she finally told him the truth. She showed him the truth, even the cuts on the back of her thighs. It hurt Kenny to see it but he needed to. He needed to see what his disobedience had caused in his girls. He knew what God had told him a long time ago but he kept trying to work it out his way, thinking God must have gotten it mixed up or that maybe it really wasn't God talking to him after all about what it was gonna take to get his household back in line, but in his gut he knew it was. Patsy stood at the end of the hallway listening to Ann purge her tears into her daddy's chest and she felt a burden lift off of her too. She was so glad that Ann could finally let it out. Maybe now she would heal.

When Nadeen finally came back home, Kenny told her he was going to take the girls to church with him when he got better. She just sighed and went to her room.

A few weeks after that brief conversation, Kenny did just that. He took them all to Deliverance Rock with him. He'd asked Nadeen to go since they were having a special recognition for ushers at the church that Sunday. She agreed to go only as support for her other sisters in the Kingdom that stand as the doorkeepers in the House of the Lord. Reverend Grady Mack preached with a fervor Kenny had never seen or felt before. The anointing was so high no one could sit down. Reverend Mack came out of the pulpit and began to walk the aisles. He preached as he walked.

"Don't leave here today carrying that same burden within your heart! God has too many good things in store for you! Let it go! Let it go today and be healed! I know you're tired. God has shown me your weariness. I can walk down the aisle and feel it!"

All of a sudden, a woman stood up and screamed from the top of her lungs for God to help her.

Patsy turned around along with everyone else on her pew and looked at the woman on the right side of the church. She had on a big floppy hat. Patsy thought she looked familiar but she couldn't really say where she had seen her face. She began to move out of the pew and come forward. She had her hands raised and Patsy noticed she was wearing a beautiful ladybug bracelet.

Patsy had seen that bracelet somewhere before. She kept thinking about where she'd seen it. She heard the lady's voice again and then the picture flashed before her face. It was Sister Ryan, Brother Ryan's wife! Patsy was surprised. She had never seen her at Deliverance Rock. She was usually at Greater Trials supporting him. Patsy watched her come down the aisle towards the altar; she saw the hurt she was carrying. She was bent over as though she was in extreme pain and she was calling out to God to help her to forgive. The other people that came to the altar were walking slowly and quiet tears rolled down their faces but Sister Ryan was struggling to make it.

First Lady Mack went up the aisle and met her. She wrapped her arms around her waist and helped her to make it to the altar. She fell down at the altar. Kenny stood up and looked at her. He began to move out of the pew towards the aisle past Nadeen, He kept looking at her until he got to the aisle and stood directly behind her. He lifted up his hands and began to cry. He never said a word. Patsy felt Ann squeeze her hand. They looked at each other but didn't say a word. They both were amazed at what they were seeing.

Patsy glanced at Nadeen. She was sitting there shaking her leg and fanning. Her eyes were closed and she was rocking back and forth humming to herself. Pastor Mack prayed a powerful prayer over the people and then he asked all of them to rise up and go back to their seats, but he asked Kenny and Sister Ryan to stay. He called his wife to the front and asked for the anointing oil. He lifted Sister Ryan to her feet. He spoke to her first.

"Sister, I don't know your name. I've never seen you here before but God is telling me that you've been deeply violated. Someone has taken your trust. Someone has hurt you deeply and you've carried that inside of you for a long time but today, God is going to heal your heart.

"Your household is out of order. But God will restore! He will restore in seven days. In seven days, he will do a new thing! Do you believe that my sister?"

Sister Ryan cried out "Yes!" and lifted her hands toward heaven with her eyes closed.

"Thank you, Jesus!"

Next, he stepped over to Kenny. Pastor Mack stood in front of him and just looked for a few minutes, then he gently spoke to him.

"Brother Simmons! Brother Simmons, I know you're tired. I know you're weary. You been fighting one battle or another in your life for sometimes. It seems that every time you get set free from one thing, the enemy forms another weapon stronger than the first. He keeps trying to destroy you because he knows. He knows that God has great things in store for you. You have to do what he has been telling you to do. It's not for you. You hear me? You gotta give it up today!"

Kenny dropped down to his knees with his hands in the air. His cries began to get louder and louder. Sister Ryan reached over and grabbed his hand.

"You're going to have to release and do what the Lord has told you to do. It'll only be for a season until he has opened blinded eyes.

"You have to move my brother. You think that you're the captive that needs to be set free but it's not you. He's trying to get to the one that doesn't know they're being held captive. You hear me, Brother Simmons?"

Kenny nodded his head.

"You want victory, Brother Simmons?"

"Yes! Yes, Lord! Help me to do the hard thing, God! Help me Jesus!" Pastor Mack anointed Kenny and walked back into the pulpit. He motioned for the benediction and church was dismissed.

34

Kenny and Sister Ryan both stayed at the altar that day way after everyone left. Patsy didn't know what to say. When he finally rose to his feet, he came back to the pew and hugged her. He motioned for Ann and Nadeen to go.

Nadeen started murmuring when she got up, "I came to hear the Word of God. He just said an altar prayer and dismissed church. Is this what you all get over here? You need to come back to Greater Trials, honey. We get our praise on over there! We praise him in the aisles and we get our dance on!" She motioned her arms as though she was dancing.

She missed what just happened here, Patsy thought. *She was sitting right there and she missed God.*

Kenny didn't say much on the drive to Denise's Diner. Nadeen did most of the talking and he just kind of nodded. Patsy could tell he was deep in thought. When they got to the restaurant, he didn't laugh and talk when he ordered like he usually did.

Ann even noticed it, "Patsy what's wrong with Kenny?"

"I think service was really deep for him today, Ann. Pastor Mack spoke some serious words over him."

Half-way through the dinner Kenny must have decided he needed to go ahead and ask what everyone else must have been wondering in the back of their minds.

"Nadeen. Nadeen did you know that was Sister Ryan up there at the altar next to me?"

Nadeen looked a little disturbed by his question. "Was that her? I wasn't sure. She looked a little familiar. She should have been at Greater Trials with her husband. He being a pastor and all she's supposed to be there with him. How did you know it was her?"

"I've seen her at Greater Trials the few times I been there with you. She seemed like she got a much needed release today. God is going to do something in her life in seven days. I can't wait to hear that testimony!"

Nadeen kind of shrugged her shoulders, "I guess. I don't talk to her much."

Nadeen never would have guessed that seven days later Brother Ryan and his wife would be moving to Kappaville, Texas, to head up one of the largest churches in their denomination and receive a six figure salary all because she finally laid her burden down.

When they finally made it home, Patsy could hear Kenny's voice in the room talking to Nadeen. Nadeen came out of the door.

"You do what you want to do. You can listen to him if you want to and lose everything!"

Patsy went to bed that night wondering what was going on. Maybe the morning would shed some light on it. Everything seemed fine the next morning. Nadeen didn't say much to Kenny, but he kept smiling and made breakfast for everybody. He left a few minutes late and gave Patsy and Ann a ride to the bus stop.

When they got out of the car he looked at them and smiled, "I love you girls no matter what. I'm always gonna be here for you. Remember that, okay?"

Ann and Patsy both looked at each other. "Okay." They said. Again Pasty had that feeling in her stomach. She felt like she was sitting on a landmine waiting for it to explode.

Who is about to end up in the hospital now?

35

"**N**adeen, that's it?" Kenny asked. "You got nothing else to say to our daughter about the way she acted at school?"

Ann had gotten into a fight in the school cafeteria and hit a boy in the face with her tray. Kenny had to go and get her from school. He was upset that Nadeen wasn't upset about her actions.

"She needs to know that's not the way to settle things. She got to set a better example. This madness has got to stop."

Nadeen looked at him like she wanted to spit in his face. She closed her Bible over her hand.

"I guess you want me to raise up some submissive little girls that will let any man walk all over them or beat them to a pulp in their own home, huh?" She asked Kenny as she stood up. "Well I'm not. The women in my family are fighters. We are survivors and most of all we love the Lord. We're not pushovers. My great-grandmother was a fighter till the end and that same fierceness runs through my veins so no—I'm not going to try to change my girls. They are gonna be fine just like their momma, grandmomma, and great-grandmother."

Kenny just stared at her.

"Is it fine or fierce for your daughter to be cutting herself?" He yelled at Nadeen. Kenny saw the color drain from her face.

"What? What lie are you spitting out Kenny? You shut up telling that lie right now! Don't you release that in my house!" Nadeen yelled at him.

Kenny could see she had been shaken by his words. His heart ached a little for her even now but he knew he had to stand up to her for the sake of his girls.

"I wouldn't lie about something like this, Nadeen. You know better. You so busy running behind Reverend Craig and the other folks at Greater Trials you don't even know what the enemy is doing in your own house. Your daughter is cutting herself, Nadeen! Ann is cutting herself just like you did!" He saw Nadeen look at him like a wounded animal.

"You're a dirty liar, Kenny. You are a mean and dirty liar. Why would you lie on your own child like that? And how dare you bring that up in front of my children!"

Ann and Pasty both looked at each other with their mouths open. They couldn't believe what they'd just heard.

Nadeen had done the same thing?

"Get out! Get out of my house telling those lies in front of my children!"

Kenny was too tired to fight anymore.

"You know what? I should have gone a long time ago but I couldn't. I wouldn't. I kept trying to work it out myself but I have accepted that I can't and for the sake of my babies, our family and our marriage I have to go!"

He walked away from Nadeen and headed towards the back room.

"You been letting momma put things in your head Kenny! I know that's who it was. It was either momma or Eva. You don't know. You don't really know!"

A few minutes later, they heard the front door open and Kenny's truck start up. They ran to the front door to see what was going on. Kenny was putting a suitcase in the front seat of his truck. Ann and Patsy both opened the front door and stepped out. Patsy felt her breathing start to get faster and her feet were walking faster yet Ann seemed to be keeping up with her. When they got to the front yard, they both ran around to the driver side door of the truck.

"Kenny where you going?" Ann asked. Patsy held her breath; she wanted to make sure she didn't miss this explanation.

"I got a call about a job in Miami and your mom and I decided it would be a good idea for me to take it. It's fifteen dollars an hour more than I make right now and it'll give me and Nadeen some time apart to think and to pray."

Kenny stared at them for a minute and then gave them both the tightest hug they ever felt in his arms.

"Remember that I love you girls. I'm going so I can make things better for us. Everything has a season and now is the beginning of a new one for me. God has been dealing with me about being disobedient to what he's been telling me to do and I can't ignore him any longer."

Patsy felt the tears come to her eyes and run down her face. She looked at Kenny and wanted to grab him by his pants leg to stop him from leaving.

"Why are you leaving us?" She asked between snot and tears. "You can't leave us here with her like this! We won't make it!" Kenny held her close to him.

"Patsy, you're the strongest one of all. You and your sisters are going to be just fine. I won't be gone long. I'm coming back I promise. By the way, Nadeen agreed to let you go on that International Ministry trip with my church this summer. Isn't that good news?"

Patsy didn't care about that right now. She was sick to her stomach. She wondered why she could never have happiness in her life. Ann spoke in a soft, weak voice.

"If you leave she's gonna take it out on us! Is it because of me, you're leaving? You upset about me cutting myself? I promise I won't ever do it again! I'm sorry. I promise I'll never act like that again if you stay. I promise!" Kenny wiped the tears from her face.

"Baby, I'm leaving because I love you, not because I'm mad at you. I been in the way too long. God gotta do things his way and then I can come back. He already told me I was coming back. This is only for a short season." He said. "This is all part of God's purpose. It'll work out for the good of us all.

"The Lord opened this door for me at the right time. I'm gonna walk thru it before he closes it. This is only for a little while. I'm going to be sending money home to you all and calling you all every night I promise."

"Please don't go, Daddy!" Ann cried. She was sinking into a low place; Patsy could hear it in her voice. It was a place call hopelessness. Patsy knew it because before she made her prayer closet she was in that place herself. Kenny held the both of them and kissed them on the forehead. Then he picked up Josie.

"I'm doing this for you too little girl. You gonna be free of this thing. Daddy gonna make sure. I promise the Lord will bring me back. I promise that to you because God promised it to me." He handed Josie to Ann and turned to Patsy.

"Patsy you stay in touch with me about your Church Ministry trip. I already paid Reverend Mack your registration fee." He got behind the wheel with three sets of teary eyes watching him.

He drove out of the driveway throwing kisses at them and waving. Ann and Patsy just stood there with their minds reeling in disbelief.

God why are you doing this? Why are you letting this happen to our family? We been through so much already! Why are you doing this? The thoughts screamed in Patsy's mind.

Ann turned to her and Patsy held her while she cried into her shirt. She kept saying, "I won't do it again! Daddy please come back! I won't do it again!" Patsy had to be strong for her and Josie.

How could she go out of the country now? Ann couldn't take another person she loved leaving her life.

"Patsy! Ann! Get in here. You girls gotta learn that men are weak! When things get a little rough they run! They abandon their families and use all kind of excuses to make it seem like it's all right. You see what your daddy just did? They all do the same thing! He try to tell me God told him to go but I don't believe that! The Lord would never tell a man to leave his loving wife and his children!"

Patsy didn't want to hear this crap right now! She was trying to figure out what just happened and why.

She walked past Nadeen and could hear her cussing Kenny for leaving. As she walked into the kitchen, she heard the evangelist on the radio speaking, "If you want God to fix that wife or that husband, sometimes you gotta move out of the way so he can get to them. You gotta move out of the way and stop blocking them from God's way of dealing with them. Let them fall so the Lord can come and pick them up! He gotta deliver them when they don't know they need deliverance!" The voice shouted through the radio.

The phone rang. Startled, Patsy answered it. It was the hiring manager at the nursing home. Patsy was so stunned that she just yelled down the hall.

"Momma. It's the hiring manager from your job!" She put the phone down on the countertop. She stared at the front door.

At that moment, it seemed to Patsy as though there was a voice speaking to her. The voice was explaining it to her so clearly there was no question.

That's why Kenny is leaving. Patsy heard the voice tell her. *He has to move out of God's way. God is gonna have to break her to fix her! He has to get at the root of this evil spirit to save us all from this curse that runs in our veins! He has to show Nadeen herself. She will never see if Kenny stays because she is too busy looking at him. Kenny has to move so God can deliver Nadeen and stop the spirit of Jezebel in her bloodline!*

Patsy felt a peace and an understanding come all over her. This was not the storm she and Ann thought it was, but it was the beginning of the latter rain and God's word had promised that the latter would be greater.

About the Author

 Felicia Kelly Brookins is a member of Christ Covenant Church International in Clinton, Mississippi. She is married to Minister Jason H. Brookins and they have one amazing son, Phillip J. Brookins. She is the Founder of both Write The Vision: Writers Conference and also Inspired Resources Writers Club of Clinton, Mississippi, which hosts local authors every month in the Clinton-Jackson community.

She is a 1989 graduate of the University of Southern Mississippi where she earned a Bachelor of Science Degree in Broadcast Journalism.

CPSIA information can be obtained
at www.ICGtesting.com
Printed in the USA
FFOW02n1657070817
38588FF